PRAISE FOR *THE BLOOD TREE* – BOOK ONE IN THE GREATER GOOD DARK FANTASY TRILOGY

'Great Book! It didn't take me long to read as I couldn't put it down. The best book I have read in a long time. The only bad thing is now I cannot wait for the next book.' Verified Amazon Customer

'Stuck in isolation with a pile of books to choose from, I'm so glad I started with The Blood Tree! Lyndell took me to a world I just didn't want to leave. In a world where we are craving connection, Fallon makes you fall in love with the good she sees in the world and the fight she has despite her demons. Her everlasting love for her family, the environment and animals only make you want her to win more. The ending of the book literally had me devastated because it meant that I would be waiting for more. The only cure is that I know this is only the beginning of what is sure to be an epic trilogy. Loved it. Words so beautifully written and a heroin who makes you fall in love with her heart, it's a book worthy of the time it will steal from you.' Verified Amazon Customer

'This book is impossible to put down! Lyndell takes you on a phenomenal journey as she captures the ancient story of good versus evil and brings out some of the real issues of our times. The main character, Fallon, also reminds us of what is important in this world: our environment and our humanity. The descriptions of the Silver City and the existence of the supernatural were expertly detailed, and you can't help but fall in love with the characters that are fighting for the greater good. I can't wait for the next book in this trilogy to see Fallon unlock all the secrets of her otherworldly past and The Blood Tree. I just didn't want this first book to end, it's that good!' Marcia Fry

'Lyndell Casella takes you on a gripping, hang-by-the-seat-of-your-pants story. This book is a high-throttle journey through the realms of light and dark. It gives readers a glimpse into the angels that both safeguard and exploit humanity, as well as a front-row view of the thin veil between multiple dimensions. This novel has left my heart rate elevated with intrigue. The

Blood Tree *is going to be the next big read. It will leave you eagerly antici-pating the second book of* The Greater Good Trilogy*.'* Tairiau Bridgart

I feel such empathy for Fallon and her struggle with fighting the evil permeat-ing mankind. Her journey is a long and arduous one with many twists and turns throughout her story. Once started, it is hard to put this book down, and the excitement of what is coming next, good or bad, keeps you rapidly turning the next page. I can't wait to see where Fallon/Gabrielle's story takes her in the rest of the 'Greater Good Trilogy'! Nola Thorburn

THE GREATER GOOD TRILOGY

BLOOD
FOR GLORY

LYNDELL CASELLA

Queensland, Australia

Cover design by Judith San Nicolas
Typeset in Devangari 18/36 pt and Goudy Old Style 9/12pt
Printed and bound in Australia by IngramSpark
Prepared for publication by Dr Juliette Lachemeier @ The Erudite Pen: theeruditepen.com

A catalogue record for this book is available from the National Library of Australia

Blood For Glory: The Greater Good Trilogy - Book Two – 1st ed.
ISBN 9780645280425
E-ISBN 9780645280432

Dedication

To Fred. For always believing in me.

Book Two

Book Two

Prologue

The light flickered as a candle flame fluttered in an imaginary breeze, casting shadows around the darkened room. Dominic Caridis moved his eyes over the vision before him. His first sensation was that he could see clearly once again, and taking a deep breath of appreciation, he savoured this unexpected new reality.

His gaze moved to the bed, and he smiled with anticipation. Before him was the young woman who had mutilated his sight, the one person he desired more than anyone else. Not with the craving of lust, but with the urge to hurt her as she had him. But this night, he would take more than her sight.

He didn't flinch as he drove the nails through the woman's wrists and into the bedhead behind. Instead, he saw the brutality as insurance for his plan. Gabrielle Harrison had no way to escape, nowhere to run from his rage.

The flash of pain in her wide green eyes did nothing to stifle his longing to see her suffer, and he would take out those eyes as revenge for plunging him into darkness. Meeting his ruthless gaze, she tossed her head and screamed into the unholy silence, but there was no one to hear the cries. No one was coming to her rescue.

His attention was distracted by the drip of blood as it trickled from her slender wrists to pool red on his pristine white sheets.

Fascinated by the stark contrast of colours, he dipped his fingers into its warmth and gently traced a line down her nose and across her parted lips, then rubbed it over his own face and through his hair. Embracing his victory, he pressed his bloodied hands against his face to inhale the scent and marvel at its composition. Strangely, the re-born angel had absorbed all the elements of this world, but it was not the usual, bland, salty bouquet of human blood. Instead, her blood still embodied the now and the forever, and he appreciated that this was no ordinary citizen he held captive but a living, breathing mira-cle.

Nostrils flaring at the heady aroma, Dominic sucked it deep into his lungs, even holding his breath for a moment before letting it slip softly out between his teeth. Sensory membranes triggered a powerful arousal that rushed through his blood like a line of cocaine. Simulta-neously, he dipped the palms of his hands into her blood then rubbed it over her perfect naked body, painting her in this exotic concoction until she lay there in all her magenta glory.

Stripping off his own clothes, he climbed naked onto the bed and let his body press against her, pushing her deeper into the mattress. He smiled as his provocation caused the distress in her that his tor-tured soul sought. He wanted her to know pain, to feel its opus, to be saturated in agony. This night she would know all about his physical, sexual and emotional torment.

He stared into those green eyes, a colour that had haunted his dreams. As he was so close, he fell deeper and deeper into their in-tense hue. Under this mesmerising spell, his body pressed down harder on her soft, yielding flesh to take her as his own.

'Wake up.' A raspy voice invaded his sanctum of retribution. 'Wake up, Dominic.'

The stranger's voice drew him back to the bleak truth he was seek-ing to escape. His empty eye sockets knew only darkness as his consciousness plunged him back into a world that he despised. 'Who are you,' he asked, turning over on the bed to seek out the intruder. His face was bandaged to contain the fluid that seeped out of his oozing eye sockets at night.

'A friend who knows what your heart is dreaming about,' the visitor hinted mysteriously.

Dominic reached out to touch the trespasser who had broken his dream. Feeling across the sheets, he found a hand. It was large, with skin as rough as sandpaper. The nails were long and sharp, and as his fingers traced the claws that could tear through flesh with ease, he knew who had disturbed his fantasy of revenge. 'What do you want of me, demon?'

'Are you not afraid?' the spirit probed.

'No. Should I be?' He rolled onto his back to stare at a ceiling, one that was beyond the veil of blindness.

'Not at all. I only want to show you something,' the stranger responded.

'I'm blind, so what's the point?' he grumbled.

'Come, give me your hands,' the demon entreated.

'Why?'

'Trust me,' was the only answer he received.

Dominic sighed deeply and sat up to hold out his hands. Jinn took them and placed them over his own eyes. He felt the moisture under his palms as the demon pressed his face against them.

'Now, place your hands over your own eyes,' the raspy voice instructed.

When Dominic took his hands away for Jinn's face and covered his own hollow cavities, he gasped in surprise as his sight wondrously returned.

'What have you done?' His breath caught in throat.

'It's only temporary. But, if you are obedient and do as I say, it could be a permanent gift.' Jinn spoke the promise of reward, and it hung between them.

'What do I need to do?' Dominic stared around the room, revelling in this unexpected offering.

'Take my hand and come away with me,' Jinn invited him.

He didn't hesitate to grip the calloused hand tightly as gravity released its hold and they were swept away.

Within a slip of time, the subject of his fantasy lay asleep before them, completely unaware of their presence in her room. Dominic gazed in wonder at the vision before him.

Her long blonde hair was swept across the pillow. He watched mesmerised as her chest rose and fell with each deep breath, and her lashes lay like shutters, hiding the glory of green behind.

Dominic's heart began to pound, and with his stomach churning, he turned to his guide. 'I can't believe we're here, and so close that I could almost touch her,' he whispered wetly with anticipation.

'Stay still, we don't want to wake her. Not here and certainly not now.' The demon caught the hand that was already outstretched.

'I don't understand. Do you bring me here only to taunt me with what cannot be done?' Dominic pulled his hand away from the demon's firm grip.

'This is not the time or the place. Besides, there is no need to rush, not when we can take our time to assemble her chaos and destruction.' He calmly drew Dominic back from the bed.

'We must leave her, but only for now.' Jinn took his hand again and swept him away to another place.

This time they sat on the very top of the Sydney Harbour Bridge and rested on the ironwork with their legs dangling over the side. Far below, the hum and lights of traffic crossing the bridge lit up the night.

'Who are you?' Dominic broke the silence.

'I am Jinn, and I serve the Morning Star.'

'Why am I here, Jinn?'

'Because your hate sends ripples through our world, and it seems that destroying Gabrielle Harrison is a shared ambition.'

'Yes, I would do anything to make her suffer.'

'Anything?'

'Yes, ask and it shall be done.'

'Good, now that we have cleared that up, we are going to plan my quest for vengeance,' Jinn spat.

'You mean our vengeance?' Dominic raised his brows at the demon. He truly was a demon now. In his time away from the light he had progressed way past being a fallen angel.

'Yes, our vengeance. She has taken something of great worth from you. Your sight. And as for me, this demon hunter has pursued me across the ages, disrupting my entertainment and returning me to the dirt beneath the earth. Now she is within my grasp, and I am going to extract as much pleasure this opportunity affords me.' His claws raked across the metal rails, while his contorted face attempted to smile with maleficent glee.

Dominic studied Jinn's expression as he spoke. He saw none of the former angelic glory left in his features; instead, the once-noble face was twisted with hate.

'What revenge do you have in mind and how long do I have to wait?'

'You won't have to wait too long before we take everything from her, make her regret ever becoming human. Until we destroy what she most loves, rip it out of her heart until she curses the day she took the place of that dead infant.'

'What will be my part in this diabolical plan?'

'You, son of man, are the key. It will be your hand that plunges the knife into her beating heart.'

'It will be my pleasure,' he whispered menacingly.

And just like that, Dominic was deftly woven into Jinn's evil design. 'Your lord of darkness will reward you when you deliver the angel's blood to him.' Jinn dangled the prize tantalisingly.

'My reward?'

'He can give you power and wealth.' Jinn smiled as he knew the weaknesses of men.

'I don't need either. What I want is my sight back,' Dominic bargained.

'If that is your wish, it can be done.'

'Can it?' he asked with scepticism.

'Of course it can. Lucifer will steal the eyes from another.'

The promise was so enticing that Dominic could almost feel those new eyes filling the vacant holes in his face. 'How will you reach me?' he asked.

'When you dream, Dominic, I will be there waiting for you,' Jinn promised.

Before he grasped the coarse hand again, Dominic asked Jinn his own question. 'If you were once all angels, why do you now hate them so much?'

Jinn stared at Dominic for a moment of reflection before his fervent retort. 'We rebelled in the City of Angels to take control, but we failed, and after all this time we're tired of being exiled from our true home. For too long we have suffered their scorn and undying pious judgement. Now in this millennia, it's time we took back what is rightfully ours and make them our slaves for all eternity. Now is our time for glory.'

Dominic just raised his brows at the former fallen angel's expressive explanation. Good luck with that, he thought sardonically, before another swift tumble through time took Dominic back to his bed. This time, he drifted off to sleep with the hint of a smile upon his warped, burned face.

One

Gabrielle Harrison woke with a start and automatically reached for the blood tree pendant she kept under her pillow. She lay very still and listened to the dogs whining as they paced around her bed. 'What is it, boys? Is someone in the house?'

Holding the amulet in one hand, she reached out to stroke Goliath's big head when he lay it upon the side of the bed, at the same time sending Sampson a message with her mind to stay calm.

Gabby inhaled deeply, sniffing the air to detect the presence of danger, and noticed the teeniest hint of decay that exposed the presence of demons. Leaping out of bed, she walked straight through the wall into Joe's bedroom, with the Titans racing through the house to find her. Taking a breath to steady herself, Gabby exhaled in relief when she saw Joe still deep in slumber, snoring ever so softly.

After heading downstairs, she let the dogs outside to check the outer perimeter. Then as quietly as possible, Gabby opened every door in the cottage to check for the intruders. But after a thorough search, she'd found no trespassers, demon or otherwise.

Eventually Gabby went back to bed with a Titan on each side for additional protection. In this heightened state, she couldn't sleep, so instead she moved under the covers and let her mind explore the memories that lay beyond the shroud of time.

Yes, she had been a messenger, a fierce warrior serving the light. Closing her eyes, she recalled the swirling power of the Eye of God, the sacred portal between the realms. She reminisced about the history between the angels and their exiled fallen brothers. How long ago they had been united as one, but now a great rift divided their kind. After the rebellion, the immortals were now pitted against each other, caught in an undying war.

Gabby was thankful to have the supernatural protection of her blood tree pendant and hoped it could shelter them from the tsunami of malevolence she feared was speeding towards them.

She hadn't told anyone about the pendant, not even Old Joe. It represented a truth she held close to her heart. The knowledge that she had sacrificed her immortality to save Frank and Kathleen's baby all those years ago should have made her feel like an imposter, but instead she treasured this life and the mortal family she called her own. The most difficult loss to bear was not being able to see her angelic sister Josiel, the one ally she had depended on throughout the ages. *I miss you, Josiel.*

In this new life, she had to protect her family and friends from the demons who hunted her. Gabby would do anything to keep them safe. Father Gerry had contacted his friend, Father Ignacio in Rome, and together they were working to better understand their enemy. 'Remember, they are zealots and will stop at nothing to achieve their objectives,' was Father Ignacio's solemn warning.

The underlying menace could have paralysed Gabby's close circle of friends with fear, but all of them refused to sacrifice their freedom to the shadow stalkers.

Trying to settle, Gabby closed her eyes and concentrated on her beloved Blood Tree. She remembered the vibrations of its heartbeat and how the thrumming of blood flowing through the fine network of veins in each leaf had always calmed her greatest fears: the constant dread that the angels were not doing enough to protect the innocents.

As the meditation began to take effect, she felt slightly less anxious. Huddling deeper into the soft covers, Gabby closed her eyes and sent a message to the Titans to stay alert while their enemies were circling in the darkness.

It was only as the sun peeked over the horizon that she fell into a light sleep.

The twilight sky in the Silver City was crackling with a brewing storm as Gadriel marched through the grand gates. The council was on high alert, especially after Josiel couldn't be found, no matter how far and wide their legion of scouts scoured the earthly realm.

Knowing he didn't have much time before he would be brought before the council for flouting their order, Gadriel rushed to find Puriel. He wanted him to understand his motive before this misunderstanding caused any more discord between them.

He found him in the conservatory of wisdom, with its high, graceful ivory arches reflecting the purple sky. The floor shimmered with a sparkle of blue, and it appeared as vast as an ocean to cross over. Before taking a step, Gadriel tucked his fiery-tipped wings a little closer to shield himself from the anticipated hostility.

The soft light cast a shadow over Puriel's face, but even so, his features seemed etched in stone as he stared out of the window.

'Puriel, my brother, can we talk for a moment?' Gadriel called softly when he stood a little closer.

Puriel turned around to glare with disappointment at Gadriel. 'The time for talking is over. Now is the time to act. Gadriel, I hope you agree to end this fiasco. Surely now, you admit that leaving one of our own in this sham was not only foolhardy, but dangerous.'

'You may be overreacting, Puriel. It's not as disastrous as everyone fears.' Gadriel reached out his hands towards him in supplication.

Refusing to consider Gadriel's rationale, he stepped closer to him in anger. 'Gadriel, how can you possibly say such a thing? Fallon has used her powers, an action sure to destabilise the already frail accord between us and the fallen.' Puriel glared into his brother's eyes.

'Why do we tiptoe around the rebels? it was Lucifer's lust for power that started this war!' Gadriel dropped his imploring arms and instead argued his growing sentiment just as fiercely.

'Maybe because we signed a treaty with the exiled angels long ago, and maybe because we should honour our pledge. Have you considered that this unlawful action may now compromise our access to minister to the sons of men? Can you not see why I am so angry about your involvement in this revolt?' His dark brows drew together in wrathful dismay. 'Does any of this worry you, Gadriel?' Puriel urged him to understand the importance of his concerns.

'Of course it does, my brother, but supporting our angelic friends can hardly be considered a revolt.' Gadriel dropped his voice lower, trying once more to reason with him.

'So, we must agree to disagree once again. But what now? Josiel has been missing since that day, and we still don't know if she is in the clutches of our enemies or hiding from the consequence of her actions.' Puriel shook his head in exasperation and turned his gaze back to the twilight sky. It seemed he was looking for answers where they didn't exist.

'Josiel is safe, for now at least. She is exactly where she needs to be,' Gadriel reassured him.

Puriel spun around to look at his brother. 'So it's true. You are involved with their schemes. And instead of intervening in a situation that can only cause us more pain, you want our leaders to turn a blind eye,' Puriel hissed.

'Puriel, I just want you to wait a moment in time to see what transpires. What seems like a catastrophe may yet be part of a greater plan,' Gadriel implored him once again, craving for Puriel's mind to be as vast as his wings.

'Gadriel, I cannot agree with your theory, and you will have even more trouble convincing the council of this "greater plan".' Puriel suspended the dialogue by marching stiffly out of the vast chamber.

Gadriel went to the same window to watch him leave. Puriel's whole posture was tight with ire, his wings drawn close against his back. Looking down at the deep blue floor, he searched for his own answers. *How did I get caught up in this intrigue? What started as support for a friend now seems more like a war against my own kind.*

His next visit was to the Blood Tree. Coming to the same branch where he and Josiel had sat together not so long ago, Gadriel closed his eyes and let the thrum of the mighty tree wash over him. Only here did he feel that Fallon was somehow fulfilling her destiny.

Soon after, Gadriel was summoned before the council. Reluctantly leaving the refuge of the tree, he trudged up the stone stairs, each step feeling more difficult than the last. Finally, he stood before the wise ones and bowed his head with respect.

Saraquel was the first to speak. 'Gadriel, you are a leader, and your scouts look to you for guidance and wisdom. Now you have not only disobeyed our commands, but you have assisted those involved in the beginnings of another rebellion.'

He tried to argue but Saraquel raised his hand for him to be silent.

Remiel spoke next. 'After what has transpired, there is great temptation to agree with Saraquel. My only question is: Why do you and Josiel disobey our edicts to aid Fallon? The now-angel/human seems to wield a hold so strong over you both that it overpowers your duty to the Silver City.' Remiel tipped his head to one side in interest.

'It is only the bonds of love, Remiel, and a sense that this is all part of a greater plan.'

'What greater plan do you speak of?'

'Remiel, I have only this deeper feeling that Fallon becoming human is not the disaster that some believe, that it is actually her destiny, and that we must help her.'

'You speak of such nonsense, of rebellion, in front of the council.' Zinnia spoke for the first time. 'Do you know what I see? I see unrest and contempt for the law, and it is imperative we stop this before we have another uprising. My brothers, you must show strength and rebuke Gadriel for disdainfully ignoring our order to remain in the Silver City.'

'What do you propose, Zinnia?' Saraquel asked.

'Clamp his wings, then he has no opportunity to again rush to their aid.'

Gadriel gasped at this proposal. The pain and insult of not being able to spread his enormous wings made him cringe with horror.

'Surely such a harsh action is not called for?' Remiel argued.

Gadriel could stay silent no longer and his outburst sealed his fate. 'You treat one of your own with such contempt and yet tiptoe around our enemies. Lucifer and his hosts are where you need to show your strength and might! You must act to halt his violation of the treaty,' he argued with a jut of his jaw.

'Enough,' commanded Saraquel. 'My mind is with Zinnia.' Saraquel nodded his acquiescence.

'Then it shall be done.' Zinnia looked at each of her brothers. Saraquel held her gaze while Remiel kept his eyes on Gadriel and silently shook his head in dismay. He had been outvoted.

It seemed no sooner had Zinnia made her proclamation that several angels came forward to seize and drag Gadriel out of the council chambers, marching him down the stone steps to a fate he dreaded above all else.

He was hauled into a room without windows, with no view of the twilight sky and no witnesses to the shame about to be forced upon him. In this small chamber, he was held down by the strength of many as they pushed a sharp silver bolt through sinew and bone, holding his wings tightly together. Gadriel roared his outrage of pain and anguish as they mutilated him.

When the ordeal was over, he stayed slumped in the corner of the small room long after the other angels had departed. His brothers too felt the shame of what had been done but had obediently followed the orders of the elders. Gabriel ached from the injury, and the great warrior now sobbed with humiliation. How could those who loved him act so dishonourably?

Eventually he stumbled along the streets of his beloved city to seek the comfort of the Blood Tree. In isolation, he dwelled beneath its vast branches while all those who passed by turned their faces away from him, mortified by his penalty.

He'd become a symbol of shame, and over time, his fiery glory faded to a dull rust red.

Two

University was over. Gabby, along with her close friends, were getting ready for their graduation ceremony.

Eddie Saila, her dearest childhood friend, had called earlier, which had been a difficult exchange for them both. 'I'm so happy for you, Gabby. You've followed your dreams and now you're a scientist. I can't wait to see the difference you will make to this planet.' His voice sounded tight and choked with emotion. It was so unfair that he had missed the milestones they had planned all those years ago. Now he was getting left behind in prison, paying a high price for a moment of youthful rage.

'Thanks, Eddie. I just wish you could be here today to celebrate with us.' Her voice sounded flat in her constricted throat.

'Me too,' he whispered softly.

Gabby couldn't hold back the tears when she put down the phone.

Wiping them away with the back of her hand, she went outside to sit for a moment of quiet in the rose garden. The Titans came to sit on either side, sensing her mood as she sighed deeply with regret. It was hard to fully enjoy this achievement knowing that her best friend wouldn't be there to share the occasion. But the Harrison family had all come to hear Gabby give the valedictory speech.

Joe had tears trembling on his pale lashes when he shared a glance with Kathleen at the university auditorium. Gabby was on the stage in her graduation gown and cap, challenging her fellow students and urging them make their lives count for good, to save their planet, to love their families, to work for their communities and to accept the diversity of their fellow man. 'Don't waste a moment,' were her final words as the applause exploded around the auditorium.

Her family all stood to their feet, clapping so hard that their hands stung red, all the while laughing with joy as tears poured down their cheeks. That night, it was toast after toast when they feasted at their favourite Italian restaurant. This night was the reward for years of study, the stress of exams and the completion of their respective degrees. A rowdy crowd that included all the extended families of Gabby, Elisabeth Wright and Paul Montgomery. Only Michael Tisch and Ben Giles had no loved ones at the happy gathering. Sadly, Michael's father still held a grudge over his choice of career and refused to have any contact with his son.

Once their graduation was over, they opened the Greater Good Environmental Society. Office space was rented, furniture purchased and accounts were opened, and only then could their work begin. It was slow at first, until their reputation and efforts began to be recognised by other environmental organisations.

True to her word, Miranda started at 'the society', which became the casual name for their non-profit company. Initially, she worked as a volunteer until her studies in IT became indispensable to the daily running of their office.

They soon understood that she loved plans. Miranda had plans for everything, a plan for the plan, they liked to joke, but they all admitted life was a lot easier with her plans. It was liberating to know that nothing would ever be forgotten, and soon Ben found himself relying on her administration skills to manage his speaking commitments.

'Honestly, I don't how we would manage if Miranda hadn't adopted us,' Ben commented to Gabby over a morning coffee. 'Even Paul and Elisabeth are getting along, well, mostly anyway.' He smiled with mischief.

'That's a very big win.' Gabby shared a laugh with him.

Paul Montgomery and Elisabeth Wright were the most highly strung in the group as they were both so passionate that their opinions sometimes collided. When this happened, it was a tempestuous clash. With Elisabeth's fiery tenacity and Paul's ardent pursuit of perfection, they were either fiercely disagreeing or laughing as best friends.

'Do you know what really makes me happy? It's to see Miranda smiling, laughing and enjoying life again,' Gabby almost purred with contentment.

'Yes, it's like a weight has been lifted off her shoulders,' Ben agreed wholeheartedly.

It was a diverse team at the society. A team with different personalities and a good balance of outgoing and reflective people – extravert versus introvert.

Gabby loved that each associate was responsible for their area of expertise. Ben looked after the media, press releases and public speaking. Gabby and Joe were the scientists, working with university laboratories and government bureaus to facilitate environmental strategies and impact studies.

Elisabeth looked after the legal side of the business, making sure they were complying with government standards and abiding by the full requirements of the law.

Paul was responsible for cultural research and seeking opportunities to engage with communities around the world.

Michael was the accountant; he looked after the society's finances. Each associate drew a small salary, just enough to pay for their living expenses. The remaining resources were funnelled towards the environment and helping those in need.

Over the next two years, it all began to work as dreamed. Gabby was humbled to be given this opportunity to work for something she believed in: The greater good of humanity.

Ben was an advocate of the anti-whaling movement, and in the 2000, he was working with Greenpeace to draft a formal letter of protest to the Japanese government.

'Gabby, I can't believe that such barbaric practices are still operating in the twenty-first century. They claim to only hunt a small number of whales for scientific research! Harvesting Right Whales, Humpback Whales, Minke and Grey Whales, surely this makes too many species susceptible? 'Did you know that no one tracks the number of whales they kill, and their ships react aggressively if anyone tries to report on their activities?' Ben rubbed his hands over his face and neck that were burning with resentment as he considered the lack of will to stop something so despicable.

A couple of months later, Ben was particularly quiet and distracted.

'What's wrong, Ben?' Gabby asked as she sat on the side of his desk.

'I can't stop thinking about the Minke whales in Japan. It's almost that time of the year for the barbaric cultural practice of slaughtering them. Fishermen use a wall of noise in the water to herd whales into this Forgotten Bay and literally slash them to pieces with knives attached to long poles. The water becomes a sea of red, and after this terrifying, painful death, their meat is sold for human consumption.'

'It breaks my heart too, Ben, that people still treat whales with such disrespect, especially when they are such sentient creatures.' Gabby pressed her hand on her heart as it clenched in pain.

Ben drew her hand away and held it tightly as he tried to explain the background of cruelty with this cultural custom. 'Well, with depleting fish stocks, whales and dolphins are blamed for this reduction in supply. Instead of acknowledging that human beings are responsible for overfishing, they choose to destroy these peaceful giants of the sea.'

'What can we do to help?' Gabby pressed.

'There's a mission coming up shortly, and I want to go there and hinder the slaughter. I've been in touch with some guys from Greenpeace, and they want me to fly from here to Osaka and then drive with them to Forgotten Bay. We're hoping to interest the media to broadcast this to the world, and then maybe public pressure can make it stop.'

'How do you plan to hamper the attack?' Gabby asked curiously.

'Well, I have half a plan that hinges on you, Gabby. We just might be able to avoid the slaughter if you come along. I haven't said anything yet to John or Cameron from Greenpeace, just in case you can't come, or it doesn't work.'

'When would we need to leave?' Gabby asked without hesitation.

'Next Tuesday afternoon.'

'Let's go and save those whales.' Gabby smiled for the first time during this conversation.

'Excellent. I'll ask Miranda to book our flights.' Ben felt the tension ease in his shoulders as a smile teased the corners of his mouth.

That night, Gabby locked up the office on her own. Normally there was at least one other colleague finishing late with her, but on this occasion, life had called each friend in a different direction. She could have called Joe, but as it was already after nine o'clock, she didn't want to disturb him so late at night.

Walking along the darkened streets, she kept glancing over her shoulder. It felt like someone was following her, but when she looked back, the street was empty. She sighed a breath of relief when she arrived at the railway station and hurried to check her train departure.

Suddenly, Gabby's stomach cramped viscously, and she quickly looked around for a bathroom, slamming the cubicle door shut as she made it just it in time. When she had finished, she crossed to the sink to wash her hands, only to stare at the tired face looking back at her.

Inexplicably, her image began to blur in the mirror as it was replaced by a familiar, twisted visage. Gabby stared at a demon she had known only too well in her former existence.

'Do you remember me, Fallon?' the tight lips spoke the words from within.

'Jinn, I would never forget all the horrible things you've done,' she whispered fiercely back at the face of her enemy.

'You are a mere mortal now and no longer have the power of the light.' Jinn smiled maliciously.

'Immortal or mortal, I'll still do my best to stop you.' Gabby surreptitiously took the blood pendant out of her jacket pocket and gently placed the braided cord over her head. The warmth spread over her heart, pulsing with power.

Using the force within the pendant, she pushed her hand through the glass mirror to take hold of Jinn's throat and drag him out of his hiding place.

Jinn hissed at her aggressive move and now stood before her in his magnificent decay. Towering over her human form, he made a lunge to attack Gabby, but instead she ducked under his outstretched arms and grabbed him around his knees, bringing him crashing down. Here they grappled with each other, rolling over the dirty floor and smashing into the cubicle doors. Until Jinn gained the upper hand to sit perched upon her as he wrapped his scaly hands around Gabby's throat, squeezing the air out of her windpipe. Gabby thrashed beneath him until she was able bring her hand up to plunge her pendant deep into his evil eye.

The burst of energy that surged from the pendant threw Jinn off her and across the room. Quickly taking this moment of reprieve, Gabby moved through the tiled walls of the amenities and rushed out on to the station platform. Hoping that the few people waiting along the platform were not paying too much attention, she ran on to the train waiting at the station, not caring where it was going.

Finding a seat in the least-populated carriage, she sat at the very back and took deep breaths to calm her wildly beating heart. She brushed the dirt off her legs and tidied her dishevelled hair as the train began to move out of the station.

Speeding through the night, all seemed to be routine until the lights went out. Those travelling in the carriage with Gabby startled with fright as they were plunged into darkness. 'Stay calm and remain in your seats while we restore the lighting as quickly as possible,' the guard announced over the PA system.

Gabby pressed into her corner when she felt someone take a seat beside her and turn to her with glowing red eyes. 'You can't get away from me, Fallon. Surely you remember how we move so easily through man-made barriers?'

She glared at him. 'What I remember is how many times I sent you back to the dirt beneath.'

'Not this time. I'm going to be your shadow in this human life and torment you with misery. You will know no happiness, only fear.' Jinn glowered triumphantly.

'Love always triumphs over fear, and that is something Lucifer and his followers never seem to learn. No matter how many times you are defeated.' Gabby felt a deep-seated wave of resentment, and in the rush of fury, she reached over, lifted Jinn off the seat and pushed him out through the exterior of the train. She watched the glowing eyes until an approaching train whizzed past and took the demon with it.

Not long after this, the lights flickered back on and all the passengers sighed with relief that they were no longer travelling in the dark with imagined monsters.

It was very late when Gabby stepped inside the cottage to meet Joe's worried frown. 'Gabby, are you alright? The Titans have been rushing around the house and... why do you look like you've just seen a ghost?'

'Worse, Joe. I've just had an altercation with a demon.'

Joe and Gabby sat at the kitchen table with a hot cup of tea while she told him about the apparition at the railway station. She omitted the parts about recognising Jinn, their physical struggle and moving through walls, but shared the significance of the warning.

Joe rubbed his hands over his face as the whiskers scraped beneath. 'We can't give in to them, Gabby. No matter how powerful they appear to be, we cannot live in fear.'

'I agree, Joe.'

'What do you want to tell the others?'

'Nothing at this point. We are already aware of the danger, and I don't want to scare them with this latest threat. We keep going, and live our lives for the greater good, no matter how short or long it will be. We're not going to be defeated by dreading what they may or may not do.'

Joe squeezed her hands to show his full support of her resolve.

Within days, Gabby and Ben were in a taxi hurtling through the afternoon traffic to Tullamarine Airport.

Striding into the terminal, Ben reached down to take hold of her hand. It felt good to be together, stronger as two than one.

As the plane began its ascent, she asked Ben some questions about the rest of the Greenpeace team. 'Can you tell me more about the other activists involved in this venture, Ben?'

'Well, John Holmes and Cameron Trist have been supporting many agencies over the last decade and have worked extensively on whale conservation. It's going to be a boon having these guys on board as they're recognised around the world as the face of whale preservation.'

They talked about work and home until both slipped into a light sleep.

Gabby's head had wobbled to rest onto Ben's shoulder, and she sat up, embarrassed at cramping his personal space.

'I'm sorry, Ben. I didn't mean to take up my space and yours.'

'No need to apologise. I'm happy to be your support any time, so feel free to lean on me.' Ben had been secretly revelling in the close contact.

It was cold when they walked out of the airport in Japan, and their first impression was the sea of people. They stood out in the crowd with Gabby's blonde hair and Ben standing taller than most of the Japanese people.

Gabby was relieved that Ben had studied Japanese at university and marvelled at how fluent he was when they checked into Hotel Tokyo. They planned to have dinner with the other protesters who had flown in earlier that day. After a warm shower and change of clothes, they sat enjoying an Asahi beer in the bar, when Ben saw John and Cameron walking towards them. Standing up, he waved them over and made the introductions. 'John, Cameron. Please let me introduce my colleague and friend, Gabrielle Harrison.'

John had no reticence in staring at Gabby.

'John you're staring,' Cameron playfully poked him in the ribs.

'Sorry, Gabby,' he apologised.

'No offence taken, John.' Gabby shook his hand in friendship.

After enjoying a meal of local produce, they ordered tea and started to share ideas on how to hinder the hunt. 'We could swim out into the bay on surfboards to float around the whales. With the media presence, the hunters wouldn't dare slice us with their blades, not with the world watching.' Cameron spoke with conviction. He was the most senior of them, probably in his late forties, with sideburns of grey hinting at his age.

'Would it be possible to hire a boat?' Gabby asked them.

'Why a boat? It would be better if we were in the water with the whales. The hunters will be using boats to herd them into the bay, and we can't stop them with just one boat.' John leaned his elbows on the table while frowning in confusion.

'I was thinking that if we got there first and stopped the whales from being trapped in the bay, then there isn't any need to risk injuries to ourselves or them.' Gabby smiled into his bemused expression.

'How do you propose to stop the whales from entering the trap? Especially when we have one boat, and the locals have plenty,' Cameron snorted impatiently.

A small look passed between Gabby and Ben, then he spoke up. 'If we can get there early and go out with a boat, we'll be able to guide them out to sea and away from danger before the hunt even starts,' Ben reassured them.

'What are you going to do, hang over the back of the boat with a huge bag of tuna to lure them away to safety?' Cameron sat back in his chair and crossed his arms.

'You will just have to trust us, and anyway, we can always fall back on the surfboards idea if our attempt fails,' Ben smiled grimly at their unconvinced faces.

After the meeting, they retired for the night on traditional Japanese tatami mats and woke up to enjoy a nice, hot miso soup. It was an unusual meal for breakfast; the soup tasted salty and had small chunks of tofu floating in the clear broth. Gabby loved it as it cleared her head and left a pleasant, warm sensation in her belly.

That morning, John and Cameron took them to meet their local contacts, Mikako and Yuichi, who bowed several times over Gabby's outstretched hand. In this meeting, the men explained what they needed: transport to Forgotten Bay, a driver, some short surfboards and a boat with someone to operate it for them.

After several phone calls, Mikako confirmed he'd hired a fishing boat to take them out on the water first thing the next day, and that Yuichi would travel with them to ensure everything went as planned.

The next morning, Yuichi was punctual and had the van waiting for them outside the hotel. It was dark and cold as Gabby climbed into the back of the car, only to choke slightly from the overpowering smell of dried fish and seaweed as she buckled up.

Driving through the darkened streets, she looked out of the window to watch the buildings flash past. Illuminated by streetlights, she marvelled as one urban sprawl connected with another, and apartments, high-rises and chimneys filled the landscape. Stunning pink cherry blossoms broke the monotony of drab grey concrete walls and roads; their beauty was like sweet bursts of colour in this industrial landscape. Plum trees were throwing their white and pink blossoms into the bouquet, soft colours representing a culture that had such extreme contradictions. A culture that was so respectful of each other and yet showed very little emotional attachment to whales and dolphins.

The dawn was breaking when they finally arrived at Forgotten Bay, and Gabby was the first to stumble out of the van. She gulped in the fresh, cold air to clear her head and nauseous stomach as the others stiffly climbed out behind her.

It was a beautiful, peaceful location. Looking out across the calm ocean, it seemed difficult to believe these same waters would soon be bright red with the blood of innocent, guileless animals. Such ugliness in a place of beauty was graffiti of the worst kind, and once again the contrast was not lost on her.

Yuichi parked the van and went to the jetty to find the fisherman and his boat. Old Junichi seemed happy to rent his boat to the protesters. He explained to Ben that not all Japanese were whale killers, and that he was proud to be their boat captain. They piled into the boat and took off just as the sun was peeking over the mountains, each grabbing the side as Junichi pointed his boat in the direction that he knew the hunters would take.

To their dismay, there were already lots of boats heading out. The hunters were also getting an early start. They knew they were approaching the right spot when they could see even more boats bobbing stationary on the water.

Gabby sat at the back of the boat, getting as close to the water as she could. From this vantage, she kept reaching out her mind to make first contact, not feeling any whales for the moment. Their boat rocked back and forth on the small swell until Ben got seasick and vomited his breakfast over the side.

Junichi just smiled at his greenish-hued face.

'What the hell are we doing here?' Cameron asked John in exasperation.

John just raised his brows in disdain and replied with, 'God only knows.'

Casting her mind out repeatedly like a net fishing for the pod, Gabby tried to make the first contact. Suddenly, she felt them. She sensed their hunger and intention to feed on the schools of fish nearby. Their minds were active, and Gabby gasped at their intelligence.

She leaned out over the water and called to the oldest whales, the matriarchs of the pod, with minds of a profound sense of time and gentle wisdom. Their knowledge of fishing grounds and navigating the oceans seemed endless, and they knew all the underwater sounds to traverse the yearly migration. It would be great to spend time with these creatures and learn from them, and Gabby secretly wished she could share their wisdom and experiences with the world, but today it was more of a crusade than a sabbatical.

She gasped with pleasure when she saw their grey backs rising slightly out of the water as they swam towards the boat. Wise eyes looked up at Gabby as they took turns passing by the boat, and before long, they were surrounded by whales, their smooth skin gleaming in the blue water. With dorsal fins fanning small waves, they swam gracefully around the boat, rising to the surface to breathe with a whoosh of air. Those in the boat stared in wonder at the whales' dark grey and white markings and the long, elegantly pointed mouths. It was such an honour, a privilege, to be this close to these majestic creatures of the deep.

'What the hell is happening?' Cameron shouted out in astonishment.

Ben just grinned back at him with excitement.

Everyone except the driver was hanging over the sides of the boat, trailing their hands over the sleek backs of the milling whales.

The hunters also shouted with anticipation as they spotted their prey and tried to move in closer to chase the whales into the trap waiting for them. They started slapping the water to intimidate the whales away from Gabby and into a place where they could take control of their movement.

The whales pressed closer, and sensing the imminent threat, Gabby sent them an urgent message. *You and your young are in great danger here today, and you must follow me to safety.* She showed them her thoughts on how the seawater would turn red with their blood.

Ben asked Junichi to take them as far away from the bay as possible, out to sea and quickly. The boat's engine sputtered to life, and as they began to move away from the feeding grounds, Gabby telepathically called to her friends to follow them without delay. *Come with me, and I will take you away from this place of pain and death. You must trust me, so bring the young and follow us.*

The whales moved behind the boat and in precision they swam out with them. The escaping whales made the hunters furious. Some fishermen even fired flares into the air to startle the whales away, but Gabby's mind held them close to her.

A news helicopter hovered overhead as they filmed this unnatural phenomenon. It was an image that would captivate the world: The unforgettable footage of Gabby standing at the back of the boat with sea water spraying her blonde hair all around her face.

Gabby was hardly aware of what was going on around her. Instead, she stood with her arms flung wide, focusing all of her attention on the hundreds of Minkes that were following them out to sea. Their boat was leading a stampede of whales.

The hunters' boats tried to block their advance; they moved in front of them and created a V-shaped trap. This could be just as fatal for the whales as the bay, and in desperation, Gabby called out to the others for help. 'You have to break through their blockade,' she shouted at Junichi.

Ben saw that soon they would be moving into the top of the trap and knew they had to choose quickly. He shouted above the din of water slapping and the helicopter flying overhead. 'If we increase the speed and hit them at full throttle, we may be able to break through, but I'm not sure what will happen to us or the boat. Are we prepared to smash our way out of this, or do we surrender and let them have their way?'

Everyone was so pumped on adrenaline that they shouted without hesitation, 'We keep going!'

Yuichi and Junichi joined in. It was impossible not to be swept up in this magic, and no one wanted to see these majestic creatures slashed and killed.

'We don't care what happens now. Just do it, Ben,' John and Cameron both yelled at the top of their lungs.

Junichi looked back at his crew and with an exuberant shout increased his speed to full throttle. The engines screamed in protest as the propellers swirled a foamy whirlpool behind the boat. The whales followed as the distance narrowed between their enemies and the open sea.

Fast-moving boats at the very top of the trap got closer and closer, so close that Ben could see the determined eyes of the hunters on board. It wasn't until the last moment that they realised the whale rescue boat wasn't going to stop, and suddenly they all started screaming at the same time. Some of the hunters dived overboard to avoid the impact as Ben yelled to hold on.

The impact was shattering. Gabby's head snapped back so hard that she thought her neck must break from the sudden impact. The boat was now just drifting along in a cloud of smoke.

Gabby could hear shouting through the dim light, and even though she felt disorientated, she looked around to see if anyone was hurt. Ben was slumped over the front dash and the Japanese captain was nowhere to be seen. Yuichi and Cameron were on the floor, quiet and not moving. John staggered over to see if they were conscious.

'Yuichi. Cameron. Mates, are you okay?' he asked hoarsely in the smoke-hazed gloom.

Yuichi just groaned, and Cameron opened his eyes to see John leaning in close, his mouth was moving but he couldn't compute the words.

Grunting, he rolled onto his back to stare at the sky. 'Did we do it?'

'Come and look,' John said as he pulled his friend up to support him to the side of the boat.

They staggered to the side and saw the mass of whales beyond the wall of boats. Grasping his friend in a weak hug, Cameron tried to shout but it came out as a hoarse croak. 'We did do it.'

Gabby's hands framed Ben's face as she inspected a deep gash in his forehead. He had blood dripping off his chin and over the floor, so she quickly reached into the small cabin to get a towel, pressing it on the wound to stop the bleeding.

'Gabby,' Ben whispered, 'are you hurt? Is everybody okay?

'Yes, Ben, we're fine.' She didn't yet mention that Junichi was missing.

They got Ben to lie on the floor and placed him on his side. Yuichi regained his sensibilities enough to get to his feet and begin tinkering around with the boat to see if he could get it working again. He kept turning the ignition key until the engines caught and struggled to life. Now they all turned their attention to finding Junichi.

The whales were still all around the boat. They were leaping out of the water, and some swam close to the side of the boat, raising their heads above the water to look at Gabby.

She mentally asked the whales they could find the fisherman. 'He's a good man who came here to save you.'

Yuichi followed, driving the boat in a search pattern. Gabby felt a flash of excitement and leaned out over the back. There was Junichi! He was being pushed through the water by the snout of a whale, the whole time spluttering and choking from the waves the momentum caused as he sped towards the boat.

Gabby called out to the others to reach out to help him aboard once the whale brought him close to the side. He was laughing and choking at the same time. Ben was a little more alert now and sitting against the side of the boat with the towel held to his head. He listened intently to what the old man was saying, so that he could tell the rest of them.

He relayed the story that the fisherman had gone flying out of the boat when they had crashed and swallowed a lot of sea water. He had begun to sink beneath the waves when he felt the nudge of the whale as it came up from below and started pushing him to the surface and back to the boat. At first he had thought it was a shark and panicked, but soon realised the creature was trying to help him. As Junichi wiped his face with a towel, he declared that today was a day for miracles.

Their damaged vessel limped along to continue their journey out to sea, and this time they had no opposition from the other vessels. The whales followed them in their mass exodus, with the helicopter still hovering above capturing the moment.

When they had travelled as far as their boat and fuel supplies allowed, Gabby sent a message to her friends to never come back to these hunting grounds. She told them that if they came back here, their pod would be slaughtered by hunters and sent this warning to all the adult whales: Stay away from this place and warn your young to never come here.

The whales leaped all around the boat. They had never felt such close contact with the human species, and it was a revelation to understand Gabby's mind, as she could theirs.

Everyone hugged, laughed and cried, and even with their aches and pains they cheered as the whales disappeared out of sight.

Stocktaking their injuries, Ben had a deep gash on his head, Cameron probably had concussion, John had bruises, Yuichi's forearm was swollen and might be broken, and Gabby felt like she had whiplash in her shoulders and neck.

In exhaustion, Gabby slumped against Ben, and he held her thankfully against him, doing his best to absorb her sudden fatigue. In wonder at her unearthly abilities, he tilted her head back to look into her eyes and mouthed a silent 'thank you'.

His towel had fallen off, and he had blood matted all through his hair with a trail of red running down the side of his face. Reaching up, she gently touched his face, all the while smiling softly with happiness. It was another moment of tenderness that Ben would store in his 'Gabby' treasure trove.

They were so ecstatic and relieved at the success of their campaign. The whales were safe, there was no blood in the water and thanks to the helicopter above, they knew the whole world would witness this rescue.

When their boat was once again secured to the jetty, they saw several serious government officials striding furiously along the wharf towards them. It was explained without ceremony that they were getting deported immediately, and they were told that if they ever came back to Japan, they would be arrested.

Ben was worried about the fisherman and the driver. He spoke to the officials to see if they were going to face any repercussions. He explained that Yuichi and Junichi were only paid guides, and they did not support the campaign.

The officials assured Ben that they wouldn't punish their own people for such stupidity. Junichi kept hugging them as they said goodbye. He said his life had changed today, and it was an experience he would never forget.

Before they left, Yuichi shook Ben's hand with his good arm, while the other arm was in a sling waiting for medical attention. John and Cameron had promised Junichi they would be in touch and send funds to repair or replace his boat, whatever he needed to keep his business afloat.

Ben needed stitches in his head, but it would have to wait until they got back home. Gabby improvised with a bandage in the meantime, which only made Ben look more heroic as they boarded the flight for home.

They were met by the Australian media when they landed in Melbourne as it hadn't taken long for the footage to be beamed abroad. John and Cameron spoke to the journalists, while Gabby took Ben to get medical attention.

When they finally staggered out of the taxi after Ben had been seen to, it was welcoming to see Joe's small cottage again and find that it was overflowing with people. Everyone from the society was there, as well as a stack of other friends all excitedly celebrating the mission's success.

Old Joe hugged Gabby close to him. 'Good work, Gabby. I am so proud of both of you. It turned out far better than even my wildest dreams.'

'It's all because of you, Joe. You have made us what we are today.' Gabby wanted Joe to know how much he meant to all of them.

'You, this,' he spread his arms out to include the noisy bunch of people in his small house, 'makes an old man very happy.'

Gabby hugged him back until someone called her to the phone to speak to her family as they wanted to ask her all about the mission.

Everyone stayed up hour after hour, drinking wine and coffee and laughing and feasting all night. Revisiting each part of the adventure, retelling the details with spirit and passion. The news coverage was of nothing else. It was on all the channels: the whales, the boat collision, the driver getting escorted back to the boat by the whale, Ben's head bleeding everywhere. It all looked so much more dramatic and exciting as they watched the footage over and over again.

The next morning, they were very busy at the society, with many enquiries about their conservation programs, and volunteers hoping to assist with the environmental recovery work.

Three

Connor Faradene sat in his expansive inner-city Melbourne office, preparing for another day as CEO of Faradene Enterprises. He had arrived early and was enjoying a coffee as he scanned the meetings in his daily calendar. Like usual, the small TV screen flickered from the wall across the vast room. It was normal for the sound to be muted, and he was never sure what caught his attention on this particular day.

For some reason, he happened to look up and saw an image of a young woman standing at the back of a boat with hundreds of whales following her out to sea. It was such an extraordinary sight that he sat staring at the screen, coffee cup halfway to his mouth, transfixed on the cameras when they zoomed in on the woman with long blonde hair and sun-kissed skin.

Just then, she tilted her face and seemed to be looking right at him, her eyes making his hand tremble and breath catch in his throat. Suddenly, he felt an insane amount of interest in what was on the screen. The coffee was abandoned as he fumbled around in the desk drawer to locate the television remote.

After turning on the volume to listen to the news report, it wasn't long before his secretary, Lauren Barnes, opened the door to see what could have made him break his usual code of silence.

'It's amazing, isn't it?' she nodded towards the scene on the screen.

'What's it all about?' Connor asked.

'These environmental activists went to Japan to stop a slaughter of whales. Apparently, the story circulating is that the young woman telepathically called them away from danger, then led them safely out to sea.'

'What, you think that's possible?'

'To be honest, it all sounds a bit farfetched, but who knows. It's been all over the channels this morning, so they are getting heaps of airtime, and that woman is extremely photogenic, quite beautiful actually.' With a cheeky grin, she quietly closed the door.

Connor kept skipping through the different channels. All his other plans for the day suddenly seemed redundant. In resignation, he buzzed his secretary. 'Lauren, could you please locate the contact number of the environmental agency. I feel a moral obligation to offer a donation.'

'Yes, that's a great idea. I'll email all the details to you.'

'Thanks, Lauren.'

'On to it, boss.'

Moral obligation, my foot. She chuckled to herself as she googled the whale rescue in Japan.

For two days, the images of Gabby haunted Connor. He saw them every time he closed his eyes and lived with them in his dreams. On the third day, he walked out of the office and asked Lauren to cancel all appointments because he would not be back for the rest of the day.

She smiled and nodded almost knowingly.

He had no trouble finding the address for their downtown office in Hayes Street. After parking his Mercedes, he located the correct floor in the old-fashioned brick building. Hesitating slightly, he stood outside the glass doors of the Greater Good Environmental Protection Society, as Connor was not the type to act impulsively. But, taking a deep breath, he took the plunge to be spontaneous for a change.

Connor noted the series of rainforest and reef photographs adorning the walls as he approached the reception desk. A dark-haired girl smiled in a friendly manner when he asked if Gabrielle Harrison was available. 'I'll need to check, and who shall I say is asking?'

'My name is Connor Faradene, and I wanted to discuss a donation.' He smiled at Miranda in the most charming way.

Miranda ducked out the back and soon returned. 'Gabby won't be long, if you would like to take a seat.'

Connor sat watching her answering call after call, his nerves tightening with each shrill ring.

Before too long, Gabby breezed out from behind a dividing wall and held out her hand in introduction. With blonde hair wound in a loose knot at the back of her head, it emphasised the unblemished skin on her throat and shoulders. Wearing casual white slacks with a soft yellow shirt, the whole effect was summer freshness from the top of her head to the white sandals on her feet.

Connor's first sense to react was smell, and it was a heady scent, like nothing he had ever inhaled before. He wanted to absorb as much as he could. It was the combination of sweet grass, flowers and open forest.

The second was that now-familiar sensation of being winded; suddenly, it was hard to breathe. This woman was far more beautiful in person than on the television screen.

'Hello, I'm Gabrielle. Miranda mentioned you wanted to see me about our conservation programs?'

'Yes, for sure.' Connor felt tongue-tied at the sound of her voice.

'Would you like to come through to my pod so that I can share our different activities with you?'

'Yes, of course,' was all he could stutter from his suddenly clumsy lips.

Gabby smiled encouragingly once they were seated at her small desk.

'I happened to see your courageous actions in saving the whales and would like to offer financial support to your cause.' His voice had a slight twang, hinting at time spent in the United States.

When Gabby looked into his light blue eyes, they reminded her of ice glaciers. Eyes that could be cold and calculating; however, there was warmth sparkling in them today and he was smiling. His good looks made her stomach jump with nerves as she explained the mission statement of the society, showing him the different campaigns they had available for donations and how any donated money would be spent.

Gabby confirmed that their association was registered as a non-profit organisation and that he could claim his contribution as a business tax deduction.

He couldn't keep his eyes off her. His mind was in a spin and Connor heard himself offering a staggering amount of money. It would be their whole annual charitable subscription given in one lump sum, instead of spreading it over several good causes.

Shocked by the amount of money he was offering them, Gabby sat back in her chair and swallowed nervously. 'Maybe you should take twenty-four hours to reconsider such a generous offer,' she insisted.

'I'll hold off as you ask, but only if you will join me for lunch.' He smiled at her encouragingly.

Gabby looked down at her plain gold watch and nodded her acceptance. She took Connor to the healthy sandwich bar around the corner, where they sat outside under a brightly striped umbrella. Their conversation was intelligent and lively as Connor had also attended the University of Melbourne. After graduating with a degree in commerce, he had continued his studies in the United States at Harvard in Boston.

'Are you from Melbourne?' he asked.

'Far North Queensland. I came here to attend university and decided to stay and start up the society. I'm lucky to have a group of dedicated people working with me, and I still can't believe how far we have come in such a short time.'

Time flew so quickly, and Gabby gasped when she realised it was approaching two o'clock in the afternoon. 'I really must get back. We have been overwhelmed with calls since the whaling protest was televised.'

Connor remembered his own reaction when he saw Gabby saving the whales. Probably every red-blooded male in the country wanted to have lunch with her now. After walking back to her office, Connor took his leave. 'I'll come back tomorrow with a cheque and sign that paperwork.'

'Thank you, Connor, but please don't feel obliged to be so generous. We are appreciative of even the smallest of donations.' She held out her hand to him and he shook it.

Holding on to Gabby's hand, he didn't want to let go. *Stop making such a fool of yourself*, he silently scolded himself. All previous scorn of falling in love was suddenly being superseded by his obsessive urges.

Once she returned to her pod, Gabby kept thinking about him too. It was amazing that they had felt so comfortable from the first meeting, like old friends catching up after time apart. He was polite and attentive, not at all stuck up or full of his own importance, and she would not even be a little bit human if she wasn't attracted to his good looks and that fascinating accent. However, she reprimanded herself that romance was the last distraction she needed now, as their work was only getting more consuming.

True to his word, Connor was back again the next day to drop off the cheque and finalise the paperwork for his corporate donation. He asked if Gabby was free to join him for lunch again, but she shook her head rather regretfully.

'I'm sorry, Connor, but we're working through lunch today.'

'What about dinner tonight?' he asked without hesitation.

'Sorry again. We're just so busy now, but maybe another time.' She did want to see him again.

Just then Ben walked into the front reception and saw Connor shake Gabby's hand, and he raised his eyebrows in question.

Once she said goodbye, she handed Ben the cheque. He whistled in appreciation at the sum donated. 'Every cent will go to a good cause,' he promised.

'I know it will, Ben,' she grinned.

That evening, Gabby was waiting in the airport arrivals lounge when her eldest brother Jacob walked in. Hugging him close, she saw he looked more and more like their father Frank. Now tall and lean, he had to reach down to hold her.

Having Jacob visit Melbourne was like San Remo in Far North Queensland was once again amongst them. He brought Gabby and Joe up to date with all the local news, and the memories of beach life pierced their hearts with homesickness.

'How is Eddie going, Jake? Has the family been visiting him often?' Gabby asked.

'Of course we are, Gabbs, and he's doing okay, considering where he is. I think having his friend Barry makes prison misery a bit bearable,' Jacob reassured her.

Jake got along with everyone and most nights they all congregated for dinner at the cottage or went out at one of the many restaurants in and around the city.

The week's visit was over far too quickly and Gabby felt the tug of home as Jacob walked away to board his flight. San Remo would always be her place of dreaming, and now that the bad memories were fading, it was her refuge again.

The next morning, Connor called again to ask if she would like to have dinner with him. Hearing his voice brought a blush to her cheeks, and a smile involuntarily curved her lips. *What is so special about this man? He affects me like no other. Just the thought of him has butterflies fluttering in my stomach.*

After listening to him lay out his dinner plans, she responded with more than a hint of regret in her voice. 'I'm sorry, Connor, there still doesn't seem to be enough hours in the day for work let alone the pleasure of a night out.' Gabby tried to hold him back, more to protect herself from this unexpected attraction.

'Just one dinner, Gabrielle, and if you don't like my company, then I promise never to bother you again,' he persisted.

'It's not that I won't like your company...' Her voiced trailed away as she didn't want him to know the real reason she stopped any man getting too close.

'It's decided then. I'll pick you up at 7 p.m. from... where do you live?'

With his 'no-nonsense' tone, he'd brushed her excuses aside.

After another successful day at the office, at exactly 7 p.m. Connor knocked on the door, and Gabby invited him in to meet Old Joe.

The two men took stock of each other while the Titans sniffed Connor all over as if they were seeking a banned substance.

'That's enough now, boys,' Gabby commanded them. They both looked at him with menace and then came back to sit on either side of her.

After this curious interlude, they left in Connor's low-slung sleek black Mercedes sports car and went to a small Italian restaurant called Buccia on the Yarra riverfront. The food and wine were delicious, served by attentive, friendly staff.

During the meal, they covered a wide variety of topics, exploring their upbringings and range of experiences. Gabby smiled as Connor discreetly manoeuvred his enquiries to ascertain that she wasn't seeing anyone.

She listened with interest as he described his years spent in the United States. Gabby did the math to guess he must be in his late twenties. Then he returned the favour while she explained how their association began and what they were trying to achieve.

Connor was staring at her in a mesmerised trance.

'I'm sorry, Connor. I've been told before that I get carried away when I start talking about science and nature.'

'No way. Do I look bored? I could sit and listen to you for days on end. Tell me, did you really contact those whales telepathically?'

Gabby looked down at her hands in her lap, uncertain about how much to reveal to this new friend. Would he believe or ridicule her? 'It may be difficult to believe but yes, I did call them away from danger.' Gabby smiled a little apprehensively.

'Can you do it with people as well?' Connor cleared his throat nervously.

This time she shook her head and pulled a face at him.

'Whew, at least my thoughts are safe then, for now anyway.' He laughed. 'But what happens when you make this contact? What do you see?'

'It's more like sensations, with memories acting as pictures to tell a story,' Gabby tried to explain the unexplainable.

'I can't even imagine what that would be like. It must be a bit freaky.'

'Now you know why I choose to be a vegetarian, after knowing how these creatures feel and see the world.'

'Maybe I shouldn't have ordered meat.' He glanced down at his plate with a measure of conviction.

'Being vegetarian is my choice, not one I would impose upon you,' she reassured him.

After chatting and laughing like old friends, the night came to an end far too quickly.

When he dropped her home, Connor stopped outside the house, and she was out of the car before he could lean over for a kiss.

'Thank you for a lovely night, Connor,' Gabby said softly through the open window.

'Thank you for coming out with me, and I would really like to see you again?' He staged the reply as a question.

'Let's wait and see,' Gabby hedged.

The Titans were waiting at the gate and very excited to see her. They circled her, sniffing for any scent of danger. Once they were satisfied, she went inside to find Ben and Joe sitting around the computer and analysing data.

'Did you have a nice night, Gabbs?' Old Joe looked up over his glasses.

'Yes, Joe, we had a lovely time.'

Ben just kept looking at the screen and didn't even acknowledge her presence.

'Would either of you like a cup of tea'?

'That would be lovely.' Old Joe compassionately noted Ben's silence.

Four

Every night as Dominic settled into sleep, he wondered if he would see the fallen angel, or demon, Jinn. The visitations didn't happen very often, but he loved it when they did. Being able to see again, even if it was only during the dream, was something he looked forward to.

This night, Jinn was there waiting for him in the shadows of the slumbering, and he took Dominic's hand as soon as their eyes met. 'I have a treat for you tonight, Dominic. You are going to see firsthand one of the celestials. We captured one of our enemies as he came through the eye.' Jinn's dark persona was illuminated by his glee at their success.

'The eye? What eye do you speak of, Jinn?'

'The Eye of God is a one-way portal the messengers created to stop us leaving this dimension. We were unable to access it from the earthly realm, but that was before Lucifer's illumination. Now we have the power to break through their barriers. With this evolution, we can get to the next stratosphere, so it won't be long before we take back our city. And the best part is that the Council of Angels seem oblivious of the impending peril. I can't wait to see their faces when we march through the gates of the Silver City. But enough of history.

For now we have caught one of these unsuspecting messengers, and I'm going to take you with me tonight.'

Without any further discussion, Jinn grasped Dominic's hand as they plunged through space and time. When he opened his eyes again, they were entering a tunnel that took them deep beneath the ground where the shadows lurked and the smells were not of this world.

Dominic's other senses had developed after the ruination of his sight. His hearing and sense of smell were sharp now, and both were galvanised in this strange place. Jinn led him through a network of tunnels until he felt he became part of the dirt that surrounded him, beneath his feet, along his sides and above his head.

Eventually, they reached a cell deep beneath the living, and here Jinn ushered Dominic into its dark interior. Without ceremony, Jinn shone a fiery torch on the creature suspended by smoking chains from the ceiling.

Dominic stepped back in shock to see an angel up close, for it was an astonishing sight. Even though this messenger was covered in dirt, and had many missing feathers, it was taller than any man and powerful in muscle and bone. With black-tipped feathers matching his startling raven hair, the handsome features were twisted with pain and frustration at being held captive by his misguided former brothers.

He was straining against the bonds that held him, and Dominic saw this was no ordinary shackle. A dark shadow clung to the links, and it evoked a decaying odour. He sensed it was more than the strength of metal that held such a powerful creature enslaved, the matter eating into him like a cancer.

The angel spoke to Jinn in a tongue he didn't understand, and he watched the exchange with interest. Listening to the tone and body language, it seemed the angel was defiant, while Jinn was mocking him with their entrapment.

The exchange ended with Jinn grabbing a long, sharp piece of stone and plunging it into the angel's side. A gaping wound opened in the flesh but there was no blood, a point Dominic noted with interest. In response to the attack, the angel landed a blow with his foot that sent Jinn flying into the dirt-packed wall.

Jinn stood and tilted his disfigured face up towards the captive. With spittle spraying between them, he sneered with contempt. 'You will stay here in this place of torment, a place with no light, no joy, until you become like us. I promise you will wither and decay as the light inside you fades, and only once you accept your fate and pledge to join us will you be released.'

The angel replied with deadly resolve. 'I am Raphael, the protector and healer of souls. I make this promise to you and all those who have succumbed to evil: I will rot in this cell rather than align myself to your cause. For even if you have broken the treaty and invaded our realm, your vile schemes are doomed to fail.' His powerful voice echoed off the walls and seemed to shimmer in the air.

Jinn responded to Raphael's insolence with another slash across his chest, smiling with satisfaction when the angel grunted in pain. 'We'll see how long your insolence lasts. It won't take long before you see there is no other choice.'

After this confrontation, Jinn led Dominic back through the labyrinth and eventually swept him back to his room.

'What kind of chains bind the angel? I sensed a dark power emanating from them.'

'Dominic, humans seep a lot of matter. You only see the tears they shed, the sweat they secrete, the blood they gush when cut. But we see far more. Their joy exudes from them like flashes of light, their happiness sparkles like diamonds, their pain burns red and their suffering is a dark cloud. We've learnt to harvest this darkness and weave it into a force that can shackle even a being as powerful as you saw in that cave. It is the accumulated human suffering woven into that manacle that binds Raphael more than the strength of any chain.'

'How did you even capture something so powerful?'

'We were waiting for him on the other side of the eye, where we had the element of surprise. He wasn't expecting us to be in the restricted domain and we had the advantage of numbers. One of us could never capture an angel, especially an archangel, but as many we were able to subdue him enough to get the chains wrapped around and hold his wings in place. From there, it was only a matter of bringing the angel to our asylum of darkness and to wait.'

'Wait for what?'

'Wait for the darkness to take its toll. When ethereal creations are prohibited from the light that made us, we start to break down. Our glory fades, our strength weakens and eventually our will to serve the souls of man withers and dies. So, Dominic, over time that glorious being will become exactly what I am.'

'I'm now beginning to understand the history between you and them.'

'This is just the start of our uprising. Eventually, we will make them all servants under our rule. Now it is time for the blood of humans to wash away the rot, to cleanse us of the decay, and for the follows of the Morning Star to reclaim our glory.'

Dominic just nodded at Jinn's passionate proclamation. He was still deeply awestruck by the close-up encounter with a light bearer. It had been an extraordinary night.

Five

Several weeks later in Connor's city office, he sat at his desk and scanned the high-rises of inner-city Melbourne through the enormous glass windows. Until the flashing on-off red light on his phone interrupted his far-away thoughts, insisting on his attention.

He dragged himself back to the moment and smiled to himself at how much time he was wasting on daydreaming. 'Gabby dreaming' it should be rightly called. He picked up the annoying, insistent call and abruptly said his name.

'Connor Faradene. Darling, I have almost forgotten what your voice sounds like. Have you been overseas?'

Gina Perry. Good old Gina, a long-time friend and part-time lover.

'Gina, how have you been?' Connor chose to ignore the sarcasm.

'How have I been? I'm feeling a bit neglected. Seriously, Connor, I have left so many voicemails on your mobile that I'm practically hoarse. However, enough of my complaining. I'm calling to see if you want to team up for the Leukaemia Foundation charity ball next week.'

Conner tapped his forehead in mock despair and was about to explain to Gina that he was unavailable, when a brainwave hit him. This would be a great opportunity to introduce Gabby to his circle of friends. So far, he had only been mixing with her group of 'enviros' as he secretly called them.

'Actually, Gina, I've met someone, and I was planning to take her along as my date.'

There was a prolonged silence as Gina processed this news. Up until now, she had thought a marriage proposal would soon be forthcoming. 'Really, Connor. Do I know this someone, or is this an angle to make me jealous?'

'Gina, why would I want to make you jealous? Ours has been a long and enjoyable friendship, but nothing more. I thought you agreed to be a friend with benefits?'

'Of course, darling. It has all been in good fun with no strings attached. I will look forward to meeting, hmm, what's her name?'

'Her name is Gabrielle, and I just know you'll love her, Gina.' He began to speak about how beautiful and intelligent she was, and how he was excited that all of his friends would get to meet her at the ball.

'Well, torah, darling. Catch you next week at the ball.' Gina cut him off and hung up a little too quickly.

Connor grinned with pleasure that she had taken it so well. She didn't seem at all put out by his news of Gabby.

Now he just hoped his invitation would be accepted, as he secretly thought it would be easier to catch a moonbeam than Gabrielle Harrison. He had never worked so hard to spend time with a member of the opposite sex, as most of his admirers were ecstatic if he showed them attention. Not Gabby. She was different in every way. He had spent the last few weeks courting her, with invitations to lunch, coffee, whatever moments he could steal from her busy schedule.

Tonight, he planned to invite her to be his plus one at the ball.

When Joe met him at the door, he pointed towards the kitchen, and Connor noted with pleasure how Gabby's face lit up when she saw him. Putting the last glass away, she hesitated as he leaned in for a hug.

Connor quickly held her close before she could dart away. 'I've been thinking about you all day and it's becoming very distracting,' he murmured into her ear.

Her skin tingled wherever his touched hers, and she marvelled at her physical response to him. But when Old Joe came into the kitchen, Gabby moved away from Connor.

'Sorry, Gabby. I just wanted to get a glass of milk before I started on that wind farm assessment we were discussing earlier,' he apologised.

'No problem, Joe. We're just going to sit out with the Titans for a while.' She led Connor out to the veranda to sit and enjoy the cool night air with the dogs, who squeezed themselves between them.

'So, tell me about your day,' Gabby said as she smiled at the dog's antics.

Connor started telling her about the ball next week and how he wanted her to attend as his partner. 'I can cover all the expenses, Gabby. It doesn't need to cost you anything.'

'I would love to accompany you, Connor, and I'm sure I can rustle up something for the night,' she smiled.

'Gabby, it is formal dress, so I really don't mind paying.'

'Don't you trust me to dress appropriately?' she asked him cheekily.

'Of course I do. You could wear a hessian bag and still outshine every other girl there. I just didn't want my invitation to be a financial burden on you.'

'I'm sure we can manage to come up with something that looks right for the occasion.'

'Okay, I will leave it with you. I'll be in a black tuxedo if you need to know what to match. I can't wait to introduce you to my circle of friends as I know they're going to love you.'

'I hope so, Connor. I'm not very sophisticated and am more comfortable discussing physics than society news.'

'Just be yourself, and they will be as smitten as I am,' he reassured and hugged her awkwardly across the two guardians glaring up at him.

Soon after Connor's invitation to the ball, Gabby and Joe caught the tram to visit Francine Maurisey in Chapel Street. It was an exclusive address that was lined with dress shops, shoe shops, jewellery shops and every expensive form of retail therapy one could imagine.

Joe led Gabby into the beautiful French salon where all the furnishings were antique and the dresses had no price tags. Customers who worried about the cost didn't belong in Francene's world.

Joe asked the assistant if she could tell Francine that Joseph was here.

Gabby raised her brows at the formal name, as they had only ever called him Old Joe or Joe.

A stylish woman who must have been in her mid-seventies appeared from the back of the store, and her eyes grew round with shock when she saw Joe. It was the kind of response that was reserved for special friends, and Gabby realised she must have been a lady love of Joe's from time past.

'Oh my goodness, Joseph! All these years, I have thought you were dead. You disappeared up into that wilderness and I never heard from you again.' She stood before him with arms crossed in exasperation.

Having the decency to look shamefaced, he mumbled that he had come back to Melbourne to look after Gabby. 'Gabby, this is Francine,' he offered as solace. 'Francine, this is Gabrielle Harrison.'

Francine turned to look at Joe's companion and started making clicking noises as she ran her eyes up and down.

Gabby wasn't sure how to react and looked at Joe with wide eyes.

'This young woman is divine. Is she yours, Joseph? Where did you find her? I must have her for my next gala fashion parade. We can get a portfolio done and send it off to my friends at Grazia!'

'Heh! Slow down, Francine. One thing at a time. Gabby is a scientist who is not interested in fashion.'

'A scientist! Oh my blessed angels, what a waste of God's creation for this girl to use her brains instead of that face and body.'

'Francine, that's just how it is, but in saying that we do need your help. Gabby has been invited to partner Connor Faradene to the Leukaemia Foundation's charity ball in a few days, and we need a dress.'

'Connor Faradene! Well, you have come to the right place, and your good friend Francine will look after everything for you.'

She walked around Gabby as if she were a horse for sale, making small noises and talking to herself. *Long legs, straight posture, lovely long neck, high cheekbones, wide forehead, thick hair, and those eyes, oh my, they're out of this world.*

'Joseph, I have the most amazing dress that will work a treat,' she remarked dramatically before bustling off and calling orders as she went.

Francine told Joe and Gabby to sit on the lounge, and soon after, one of her assistants came with coffee while they waited for the exotic little French lady to come back.

Gabby mused that Francine was still a great beauty, and she had such flashing dark eyes that sparkled with intelligence. Her hair was coloured black and swept up into a twist on top of her petite head. She looked like a yoga enthusiast, because even in her advanced years, her figure was toned and lean.

The subject of her daydreams returned with a sheath of gold wrapped in clear plastic over her arm. 'Come with me, young goddess. We have some transforming to do.' She shooed her assistant ahead of her and gave Gabby a firm nod to follow them both.

'Joe, I'm scared of her.' Gabby leaned over to whisper in his ear in mock protest.

'So you should be,' he whispered back, grinning.

Timidly, Gabby followed the two ladies to the back of the store where huge dressing rooms waited for them. The mirrors were everywhere, reflecting her image from every possible angle.

They asked Gabby to take off all her clothing so that she was standing there completely naked, except for her underwear.

'No need for modesty here.' Francine clicked her tongue again.

The assistant folded her garments and put them to one side while Francine took the gown out of its packaging. Everyone gasped when its glory was exposed. The gown was like captured sunlight woven into a fabric.

Even Francine murmured with pleasure as she stroked the glimmering fabric. 'Melbourne socialites will be talking about you in this dress for many years to come,' she proudly reassured Gabby.

Gabby felt humbled to be wearing this wondrous creation. Butterflies trembled inside when it slid over her head and settled against her skin.

'Now with this gown, you don't wear any underwear. Just your skin and the dress are all you need. Your hair should have a half-up style so that the impression of sunshine is extended from the top of your head to the soles of your feet,' Francine instructed.

'I bought this dress wondering if I would ever see a figure perfect enough to wear it, and when I looked at you, it immediately came to mind.' Francine practically hummed with satisfaction.

There were no secrets with the fabric. It clung to Gabby like a seductive glove, every hollow and curve was illuminated like a ray of light. The dress was like a second skin with a gossamer cape that tied at her throat and floated behind with a touch of royalty.

Francine slipped some high-heeled strappy sandals onto her feet. 'Connor Faradene is tall enough for you to wear heels and not overshadow him,' she mused. 'Now come and show that crafty old fox Joseph how beautiful I've made you today!'

Francine and the assistant went first and then called for Gabby to come out and show Joe the dress. Goddess was exactly what popped into Joe's mind as he watched Gabby shimmering towards him. The dress was not a tacky gold but exactly the colour of sunshine illuminating a sandy beach on a beautiful fine day.

Gabby looked like she had descended from heaven and was completely out of place amongst these earthly beings. Tears came unbidden into Joe's eyes as he briefly remembered the broken young girl he had found in the dirt that horrible day many years back after Andrew Bolton had left her for dead.

'Francine, my dear, I knew you would know exactly what Gabby should wear. This gown is astonishing. I have never seen anything like it before in all my long years.'

'And you never will again, Joseph,' Francine hugged him with tears in her eyes as well.

'Gabby, you will dazzle them, absolutely dazzle them,' Joe murmured.

Gabby hugged him lovingly and then he turned to Francine. 'We haven't discussed the cost of this gown.'

'No charge for you, my old friend. I bought that dress on a whim. It was a priceless work of art and I just had to have it. Now, dear woman, it is yours, because I don't know of any other person that could wear it like you do.'

'Are you sure, Francine? Money is not a problem, you know that.'

'It is not a problem for me either, Joseph. You should know that too.'

They both laughed at their joke, and he gave her an affectionate hug, while Francine patted his back with affection.

Francine once again gave instructions on how Gabby should wear her hair and makeup and reluctantly let them leave her salon. She called after Joe that she would be in touch soon.

'I think she still has feelings for you, Joe,' Gabby teased him as they made their way home again.

'Such feelings are for the young, not an old man like me,' but he smiled at her banter anyway.

Six

The night of the ball arrived in a flurry of activity. Gabby spent the afternoon at an uptown hair salon where two stylists worked elaborate plaits and twists into her up-style until it too was an image of perfection.

Then the team applied her makeup, careful to make it light and shimmering to suit the sunlight of her dress. When she finally stepped out of her bedroom into the lounge room, there was silence as everyone just stared.

Gabby watched as Ben almost swallowed his tongue. Elisabeth and Miranda had tears brimming in their eyes, and they both wanted to hug her but were too frightened to ruin the illusion. Paul and Michael just gaped with their mouths open; they looked like goldfish until she broke the spell. 'Come on guys, it's just me all dressed up,' she embarrassingly reassured them.

'Wow,' everyone said at once, and she burst out laughing.

Just then there was a knock at the door, and Joe ushered Connor into the room. 'Wow,' he whispered, and everyone except Ben started laughing again. Connor looked around but didn't quite get the joke, so he held out his arm instead. 'Princess, your chariot awaits you.'

She had to command Samson and Goliath in her mind not to approach in case they accidently damaged the delicate fabric of the gown, but they were not happy to be separated from Gabby and whined with unease.

Once in the car, Connor started the engine, then turned and watched her for a moment. 'Gabby I can truthfully say that as long as I live, I will never see anyone as beautiful as you.'

'It's this dress, Connor.' She laughed. 'It's a Cinderella dress that would make any girl shimmer and shine.'

'No, Gabrielle Harrison! This dress was made with only you in mind,' he insisted.

'You look incredibly handsome too,' she blushed slightly as her eyes roved over his apparel.

Connor had noted the desire in her eyes, and his heart swelled with pleasure.

They arrived at the Melbourne Casino where the ball was being held, and as soon as Connor stopped the car, the hotel valet opened the door for him to come around and assist Gabby to alight.

Connor took her hand and drew her out of the vehicle into continuous camera flashes, blinding them as they stepped onto a red carpet that swept up the stairs and into the entrance.

Society reporters were going crazy taking photos, asking Gabby and Connor to pose from different angles. Smiling happily at the cameras, she felt excited to be out with such a good-looking man and couldn't resist the excitement of this glamorous occasion.

Her eyes were wide with wonder as they made their way into the grand ballroom, the light sparkling off the huge crystal chandeliers hanging from the ceiling. There were giant vases of fresh flowers everywhere, and the scent of roses overpowered the many fragrances worn by the hundreds of guests milling around the room.

The floor was polished cream marble and perfect for dancing and the whole effect was one of sophisticated elegance. Remembering the glory of the Silver City when she had traversed the realms as Fallon, she had seen some spectacular displays of grandeur, but the magic of this night ran a shiver of excitement across her skin as the enchanting scene unfolded.

Connor was stopped every few steps to greet a friend or acquaintance, and they all exclaimed with delight so see such a charming young lady on his arm.

Gabby saw the women cast their eyes over her dress while the men stood taller and straighter as they greeted her. Connor, the city's most eligible bachelor, seemed to enjoy surprising his friends, and he looked as smitten as Prince Charming with Cinderella on his arm.

Some of the guests recognised Gabby from the whale conservation campaign in Japan and asked her questions about the protest. However, it wasn't all business, and Gabby danced the night away, either with Connor or one of his many friends. She held the whisper-soft cape over her arm as she swept around the room.

Just before midnight, Connor drew Gabby aside to meet his parents, a tall, handsome couple who were surrounded by a circle of well-dressed influential people. Robert and Faye Faradene were gracious and friendly towards Gabby.

The only cloud on the horizon was the hateful glares thrown her way from a woman with deep red hair. Connor had introduced her as 'Gina', an old friend of his family. Eventually, Gabby had to ask one of Connor's friends about the woman's bizarre behaviour. 'Mark, who is that woman over there? She's been glaring at me all night.'

'Gina was Connor's previous squeeze, and now that she's seen you, all those wedding plans are coming crashing down,' he chuckled. Everyone knew Gina Perry was brittle and manipulative, everyone it seemed, except Connor. Mark was happy he'd found someone as lovely as Gabby, and swept her back onto the dance floor.

'It's very early days for us, but I didn't know he already had a girlfriend,' Gabby stammered in embarrassment.

'Sweet woman, don't worry about Gina. She was the one invested in that relationship, and certainly not because she loves Connor.' He smiled as he spun her around, close to Gina's scowling face.

'Whatever do you mean? If it's not for love, then why invest in a relationship?' Gabby asked, confused.

'Oh, there is love, but it's the love of money and prestige that fills Gina's heart.'

Gabby wasn't sure how to respond, so she didn't say anything. Sometimes silence was the best defence.

When the final waltz was announced, Connor took Gabby by the hand and led her out to dance. She was a perfect fit as her body pressed up against his, and the current of attraction had him buzzing with desire.

As they moved slowly together around the ballroom, Gabby noticed Francine on the edge of the dance floor. She looked beautiful in a vibrant turquoise floor-length gown with her black hair swept up into an elegant style. Francine saluted Gabby with her champagne flute, happily acknowledging the stir her protégé in the magical dress had caused this night.

It truly was an enchanted evening, and Gabby almost expected the car to change into a pumpkin when it stopped outside Joe's little cottage. When she turned to thank Connor, his lips softly settled upon hers.

Her first reaction was fear as her heart began to race, and the familiar prickle of sweat tickled along her spine. However, despite her initial reaction, Connor kept gently placing kisses over her face and then sampling the nectar of her soft, trembling lips.

Connor moved his mouth over Gabby's like a wine connoisseur does with a favourite bouquet. Gently savouring her taste, sampling the texture of her soft unblemished skin, he took his time, enjoying the moment that he'd fantasised about for so long.

Before Gabby knew it, she found her heart was racing, not from fear but from desire. She breathed a soft moan against his lips as she moved her body closer to his warmth.

He wished time could freeze so that this pleasure could last forever.

Moving his exploration from her face down to her throat, she arched her neck to enjoy the sensation. Gabby wanted this delicious moment to never end, but end it did with the arrival of the Titans. Their giant heads were level with Connor's in the car, and as he turned, their sharp teeth and baleful eyes were very close. Too close for comfort.

Gabby laughed at their antics, and it broke the intimate mood.

Connor sighed his surrender and smiled into her joyful, flushed face.

'Well, my lady, I think your bodyguards are telling us that our night of unsupervised freedom is over,' Connor ruefully remarked.

'Certainly, seems that way.' Gabby smiled back at him. 'Thank you, Connor, for such a magical night. I thoroughly enjoyed every moment, especially meeting your friends and some of your family.'

'It was entirely my pleasure. I was the envy of every male there.'

'I'm sure that isn't true,' she protested.

Just then, the dogs really began snarling, and Gabby quickly made her exit out of his car before they could scratch the paint work. She turned to wave to Connor and was escorted inside with one guardian on each side.

The next morning, Gina Perry sat on the white leather couch in her stark-white decor apartment high above the traffic in Collins Street. She had walked to the corner store to buy all the newspapers they had in the stand, then flicked hurriedly through the pages until she discovered the photos and articles of Connor and Gabrielle.

Screaming in frustration, she screwed up every page and threw them onto the floor in a fit of temper, punching the plush couch cushions over and over until they were covered in newsprint. Her face flushed red, and spittle gathered in the corners of her mouth as she shouted at the city sky scape, 'I hate her more than I've ever hated anyone in my life. She is a thief, stealing my future and happiness!'

Enjoyable friendship! Gina cringed as she remembered Connor's tone. It was the old don't make a scene tone that men used with women who they were already thinking of 'as the ex'. Her mind touched on the sex they had shared, and she had always believed they were much more than friends.

'Don't frown, Gina,' she told herself. 'Frowns only cause wrinkles.' She consciously smoothed fingers across her pale forehead. When her violent rage had subsided, she became very calm, almost like a serial killer once he settled on his next victim. After showering away the bitter taste of this setback, she made up her face and slipped an exquisite emerald-green silk dress over her head, letting the designer lines settle on her curves. Slipping her feet into stilettos, Gina perused the mess on the expensive couch. Her inked handprints were all over the soft, pale leather, a spectacle of wrath that she had no intention of cleaning.

That's why I hire minions.

Turning away in disdain, she locked her apartment and drove to her mother's fashion emporium, where rather than do any productive work, she spent the remainder of the day scheming how to ruin Gabrielle Harrison's life and get Connor back into hers.

Seven

This night, Dominic sought the sanctuary of sleep and hoped that Jinn was waiting for him on the other side of consciousness. He longed for the world of light and colour again.

Jinn worked on Dominic, pulling him deeper and deeper into his world of hate, building the bonds of trust and teaching him how to turn off any pangs of conscience. Not that Dominic had much in the way of conscience. But Jinn reinforced the belief that their quest was worth the sacrifice of human life. That innocent bystanders were necessary for Lucifer to regain his position of power. 'My master will reward you not only with your sight but also with fame and glory once we've created our new world in the Silver City,' Jinn reassured him.

'Only if it happens in my lifetime,' Dominic huffed with impatience.

'It will. It's getting closer now, but there is still much to do before we see his splendid return.'

'When do we start taking our revenge on Gabrielle Harrison?'

'Time moves differently in our realm, Dominic, but don't fret as I can promise you that our longing for revenge will soon be satiated.'

Jinn had brought him back to the very top of Sydney Harbour bridge, which was their preferred meeting place.

When the rendezvous was over, Jinn's scaly hand took hold of Dominic's, and he was once again plunged back in darkness with only violent thoughts and dreams to paint his world.

In the Vatican, another unearthly being inhabited the human world, and she moved through the corridors in ethereal invisibility.

Josiel's favourite place was a small, secluded chapel built at the very back of the vast estate, one that was not known to tourists. Here she liked to sit amongst the marble angelic sculptures.

Each week, Josiel would watch a young woman slip inconspicuously into the chapel, dropping to her knees at the altar after making the holy symbols across her chest.

The devoted supplicant would stay kneeling in silent prayer all morning, until the day she stood before Josiel. 'I see you, enlightened one. I see your form within the sculptured pretenders, and I have felt you watching over me.'

'You see me?' Josiel asked her, keeping her form ethereal.

'Yes, but you do not need to reveal yourself. I see your light shining brightly.' The stranger smiled as she stared up at the marble shapes.

Josiel could not resist the opportunity to make contact after so long in exile, so she took the risk of showing herself to this human saint.

'You are so beautiful,' the young woman gasped when she saw Josiel standing before her in angelic glory.

'Come, commune with me.' Josiel took her to the deserted pews. Here they sat and began to speak softly.

'Who are you and how can you see what others cannot?' Josiel asked gently.

'My name is Sister Isabelle, and since I was a child, I have had the sight. To see the spiritual world beyond the human eye, it once frightened me, but now it is a great source of comfort. Can I ask why you stay here when I know the messengers move between the realms?'

'I am in exile, Sister Isabelle; I am ex-communicated from my own kind.'

'Angel, how sad. May I ask what did you do to be exiled?'

'I helped a friend instead of following orders.' Josiel smiled in memory of her actions.

'I'll pray that you will soon be forgiven and welcomed back to heaven,' Sister Isabelle whispered reverently.

'Do you serve God here at the Vatican, Sister?'

'I serve God, but not here. I work for a sect within the holy church that stands against the dark one. We are the shield that protects the believers and non-believers from his evil. Father Ignacio is our superior and is the wisest, bravest priest I know. It is he who assigned me to work undercover in the devil's lair.'

'Where is this place?' Josiel prompted her.

They talked long into the night, and Isabelle spoke of an organisation buried deep beneath the holy city, unseen to the eyes and ears of society but not the church.

'Are you in danger there?' Josiel asked.

'I would be if they ever found out who I really am, but to them I am just a cook. It is an evil place where terrible crimes are being committed.'

Josiel was attentive. 'What crimes do you speak of?'

'In my position, I don't see it, but there is talk of many deaths. Too many,' she whispered.

'Why are people dying?'

'The rumour is that they are killed for their blood.' Isabelle shivered in revulsion.

'Who are these people being murdered for such a vile reason?'

'Young people, old people. They even breed them for their human farm. Babies are born at a secret location and then brought here for the cult's atonement.'

'What kind of atonement do you speak of, Sister Isabelle?'

'Something evil, and somewhere far below from where I am authorised to go.'

Josiel stayed quiet in consideration. The blood of an innocent soul held great power as it had not yet been tainted by sin or disease. What was Lucifer doing with this harvest of souls?

'Can you please show me this place, Isabelle?'

'Yes, but I must be careful not to cause any suspicion.'

Isabelle took Josiel through a labyrinth of twists and turns along cobblestone alleyways, until they came to steps that took them down to a deep basement. Isabelle's hands pushed against a wall that moved completely sideways. Behind the wall were several levels of old wooden stairs to traverse, and these took them deeper still, far beneath the hustle and bustle of the ancient Roman city.

When they reached the bottom, it smelled like rotting food and sewerage, and there before them was one more door. An old brown wooden door that Isabelle opened and moved through, but a dark shadow pushed Josiel back before she could enter. No matter how hard she tried, she could not move across the lintel.

The area was sealed to her kind, and access was denied no matter how she changed her form to enter. She shoved it with her power, only for it to ricochet back at her. Josiel called her back. 'Isabelle, I cannot go through. There is a force field that won't let me enter.'

Isabelle's head popped around the door. 'What do you mean? You are an angel and can go anywhere you want,' she whispered.

'Not here. There is some sinister power stopping me from following you.' Josiel couldn't understand this strange phenomenon. She had always been able to enter the secret places in the natural and supernatural realms. Was this a new trick of Lucifer's? To keep them ignorant of his actions?

'Is there nothing I can do?' Sister Isabelle's voice whimpered with disappointment.

'Go ahead, Isabelle. I'll think of something,' Josiel reassured her.

Josiel tried over and over to push through the door, but no matter how many times she tried, the force field refused her entry. Finally, she sat on an old wooden apple crate and considered her options. Turn away and go back to hiding? Wait and hope that Gadriel would find her in Rome? Support Isabelle whenever she was able to visit the chapel? Accept that Lucifer was in this realm and that it always resulted in betrayal and pain?

What would Fallon do?

Josiel stood up as she knew Fallon would never abandon someone who needed help or turn a blind eye to suffering.

There was one way – but not something angels normally sanctioned. Demons possessed humans and animals to make them succumb to their will. Josiel had no intention to move her essence into a person, but she could do it to an animal. Perhaps the force field wouldn't recognise her in another shape?

What kind of animal? A bird would be good as she already knew how to fly but it would be too conspicuous indoors and would soon get either killed or released. A bug was too small and vulnerable – what if someone stood on her? Maybe a rat? No, it was too big and would be noticed, but a mouse...

Yes, a mouse might be just the right size. She could scurry quickly out of sight and hide in corners to observe the illicit activities.

For hours she sat in the darkened space waiting for her spirit animal to appear. The small grey mouse that ever-so-delicately poked its nose out to sniff the air was the perfect candidate. Quick as a flash, Josiel swooped to pluck it up by the tail and held it squirming in front of her face. *Don't be frightened, little friend. I just need your tiny body for a moment in time.*

Focusing her whole attention on the little rodent, Josiel smelled the mouse, felt the softness of its coat, counted the beats of its frightened heart, and stared into the mouse's beady black eyes until they filled her sight. She fell into their depths until suddenly she was the mouse.

Falling onto the floor on her back, she quickly flipped over onto her tiny pink feet and scurried across to the door. Very carefully she placed one foot in front of the other as she moved under the door, expecting at any moment to be repelled by the force field, but to her amazement she moved through without any resistance.

Twitching her nose in excitement, she sniffed around for Sister Isabelle's scent so that she could locate her in the building.

Picking up the smell, Josiel took off on her mission to investigate Lucifer's hide-out. Once she was in the kitchen, she found a safe place to hide in a small hole under the timber cupboards. Here she could listen and observe the comings and goings and all the conversations, both trivial and important.

It seemed these levels were utilised for domestic purposes like sleeping, eating and bathing, but the lower levels were more 'operational'. Josiel needed to get to those lower levels to see what was so secretive, even to those who lived within these walls.

All seemed to be going to plan until she saw a cat jump up on the kitchen bench and begin to meow hungrily. This was no ordinary cat. It looked more like the size of a medium dog, with pointed ears and a ferocious expression on its face.

Suddenly her choice of host seemed far too edible.

Isabelle shooed the cat off the seat and went back to cutting vegetables. 'No dinner for you, Fisk. You need to catch more mice.' She smiled as the cat rubbed himself between her legs.

'Not now, Isabelle, not tonight,' Josiel willed.

Eventually, the intimidating ginger cat grew bored of begging and went after easier pickings, while Josiel patiently waited for the quiet of night.

Once all had settled, Josiel as the mouse left her sanctuary and began to seek a way to the lower levels, but there were no stairs going down, only solid steel doors that must be lifts. Waiting out of sight for an opportune moment when a lift should open, the tiny mouse waited several hours until the early morning staff began to move about.

Quickly she darted through the opening doors and hid trembling in a corner while the lift whizzed down several levels. She had to be just as fast to exit when the doors slid open again.

Once she was on this level of the building, the atmosphere was very different. Here, she felt misery everywhere. Josiel could almost taste it in the air.

The sterile rooms were vast and divided into small spaces with only half-walls, which provided some privacy but were not exclusive. Just as the mouse was about to go further into another vast adjoining room, she smelled Fisk the cat, and felt sure he had sniffed her too.

The frightened mouse had nowhere to hide, so she took off with Fisk racing closely behind. Spinning around a corner, she sensed the cat wasn't as nimble when he slid out across the mirrored marbled floor. However, he quickly recovered and made up the distance until Josiel could feel his hot breath and sharp teeth just beyond her own pink mouse tail.

I must do something. I have to leave this host before it's too late.

This part of the building was so new and shiny, and there were no holes in the walls or cupboards to scurry beneath, only tiles and steel. Panting from the exertion, the mouse took a flying leap to land on a chair, a plastic chair, so there was nowhere to hide. Instead, she turned and waited for the cat.

Fisk knew the hunt was over. The mouse had mistakenly provided him the perfect place for tonight's reward: the feast. So, almost nonchalantly, he stood on his hind legs and raised his face and fangs to the small creature.

As his large green eyes came up to eye level, Josiel prepared to leap from one host to another. She smelled the cat, imagined feeling the softness of its fur and stared deep into the cat's eyes, falling under their spell, until they filled her world.

Suddenly, Josiel found herself as the cat with the small mouse caught between her teeth, and it was squealing for mercy. Ever so gently, she lowered her head and released the prey within her mouth to lightly place it once again on the ground, and then she stepped back.

The mouse looked at the cat as if this was some trick, but when the feline didn't pounce, it took off across the floor, determined not to waste this second chance.

Now, Josiel could move more freely as nobody would suspect Fisk doing his rounds and hunting for vermin. Quickly leaving the first room to investigate the adjoining space, she found there were many infant cribs lined up across the room. Some were empty and others had babies either sleeping or crying. Amongst this cacophony, nurses moved around the room managing their care.

Isabelle had said these monsters were farming humans for blood. This was abhorrent. As Fisk, she continued to walk under or around the cribs until she arrived at more steel lift doors. Here, he waited with his tail twitching back and forth across the shiny floor.

Eventually one of the nurses carried an infant into the lift and pushed the green button. 'What are you doing here, cat? You should be in the upper levels catching mice.' She frowned down in repri-mand.

Knowing this moment was precarious, Josiel began to purr and rub herself against the nurse's legs, and this flattery finally won the approval for her to travel in the lift.

'What harm can a cat do, I suppose?' The nurse smiled as Fisk sat at her feet in gratitude while the lift descended.

Once the doors opened, Fisk took off in the opposite direction to the nurse to explore without supervision. This space felt like a science laboratory. Clinical and heartless, with the faint vibration and hum of an engine in the background.

Moving stealthily through the rooms, Josiel did her best to remain unnoticed unless someone decided this was off limits to the mouser. There were people in white overalls coming and going from a room where the engine hum was emanating from. Carefully, the cat slipped inside the opened doorway and hid as far back in the room as possible. Here, Josiel was blinded by a bright light emanating from the ceiling and was about to go to investigate when the nurse came into the room.

Pushing back quickly against a wall, the cat stayed frozen in place as the nurse went about her work. She stared in consternation, not understanding the purpose of these apparatuses, until suddenly Josiel saw the truth through Fisk's eyes. This was why Lucifer had placed a blockade around his activities, to conceal his theft of the light, the very essence of life itself.

Here in this place of disinfected evil, innocents were being sacrificed for their fragment of divinity. Souls were being denied their reward of the afterlife. This was a hell on earth.

Hissing in shock and disgust, Josiel cringed against the wall. This was why the demons had become so bold, so fearless about breaking the treaty, so eager to travel through the Eye of God and into the City of Angels.

Cunningly and without mercy, Lucifer was preparing to once again challenge for supremacy. How many innocent lives had been sacrificed for his evil ambition?

Josiel began to wretch, the shock making the cat's body regurgitate last night's hunt. Needing to escape this place of sorrow, she quickly padded back to the lift and impatiently waited for someone to press the doors open. Her breath was suspiciously quick, while her tail twitched in agitation.

Following her own cat scent, Josiel was eventually able to scurry back through the building until the cat reached the unused door that Isabelle had been secretly escaping through. Here Josiel met a problem. She couldn't reveal herself in the devil's lair in her true form or she would be trapped inside by the force field, yet the cat was too big to slip under the door.

Meowing loudly, Josiel scratched her cat claws into the wood, hoping the discord would bring someone to his aid. Luckily, it was Sister Isabelle who rushed into the room and stood staring at Fisk in disbelief.

'Fisk, what on earth are you doing in here? Come away now. I don't want anyone to know about this door,' she whispered as she picked up the cat to remove him from the room.

Fisk scratched his claws across her arm, making Isabelle drop him in shock. Clutching her bleeding arm in disbelief, she watched the cat rush back to scratch at the door and meow loudly for its freedom.

'You are the strangest cat, Fisk. Well, if you insist on going through there, I hope you know it's a one-way trip,' she whispered in dismay as she quietly unlocked the door.

With a look that may have said 'thank you', the cat stepped over the protected portal to the world beyond.

Josiel left her host when she got back to the side entrance, but did ensure Fisk was brought up to the cobbled laneway. Before moving off, he took a moment to look around and seemed somewhat disgruntled to be removed from his familiar territory.

It was almost a relief to reach the chapel where she could once again disguise herself and have time to consider the shocking discovery. Lucifer was going to once again challenge the light to rule, and Josiel was sure it was only a matter of time. But how did she tell the council? They would not hear her report as she was no longer considered a trustworthy source.

If only Gadriel would come to her. Where are you, brother? I need you now!

His absence had been sorely missed, and she was beginning to believe he had been unfairly treated upon his return to the City of Angels.

Josiel implored the heavens above, which remained mute to her fretful cries.

Eight

Completely oblivious to the brewing storm in both realms, Gabby was busy working for the greater good, using all networks to discuss the success of their anti-whaling campaign. At one television interview, the conversation drifted to the Leukaemia Ball and the pictures that were out in the Sunday papers.

'So, Gabrielle, expensive gowns, champagne, caviar. How does someone who fights for the poor justify the cost of such a lavish night?' the male interviewer challenged.

'Actually, Zac, the ball supports the Leukaemia Foundation and their work with sick children, so I think the money raised by this event will go to a very worthy cause. At our organisation, we acknowledge that the ability to acquire wealth is as valuable as a doctor working amongst the sick. Without wealth there would be no one to care for the less privileged, so I encourage people for their own wellbeing to share their good fortune rather than hoard it selfishly.'

'What's in it for the rich if they give away their money?' Zac countered

'There is scientific evidence that you will live longer and be happier if you share your wealth with the less fortunate.'

'So, you are saying that if I practise philanthropy, I will be happier and live longer?'

'Yes, this is a proven fact. For us to survive as a civilisation, we really must start caring for others and the planet we inhabit. We are a brotherhood of man who are sharing a planet that could be facing irreversible damage.'

'Scientists have been talking about climate change for years now, yet here we still are, no apocalypse yet,' Zac continued to play the devil's advocate.

'I agree it may sound theatrical and over-dramatic; however, talk to anyone who has experienced an earthquake, a flood, a cyclone or a tsunami, and they will tell you firsthand that it feels like an apocalyptic event. Just because it isn't happening right here and now, doesn't mean that our planet is not failing. Natural disasters are going to be a lot worse and happen more frequently, until we can no longer deny the truth.'

The presenter decided not to continue this line of questioning so instead turned his attention to the whale-saving mission.

The Titans were on patrol every night and seemed to be especially vigilant when Connor tried to spend time with Gabby. No matter how hard he tried to befriend them, they were the gatekeepers, and their growls were a warning to keep his distance.

Desperate to spend time with Gabby on neutral ground, he suggested they take a drive to his parent's country estate, near Wangaretta. She agreed, so early one Saturday morning they set off for the weekend.

Samson and Goliath were squeezed into the back of his silver BMW 4WD. Even in this car it was going to be a tight fit, but Gabby refused to leave them behind. Connor wound the windows down so that the dogs could enjoy the wind in their faces, and he couldn't resist glancing over at Gabby. He felt his heart physically clench when she turned to smile at him; her beauty was making it difficult to concentrate on driving.

She was seemingly just too perfect, and to amuse himself he imagined that she was a lost angel and half expected God to come looking for her. An angel that may have feelings for him. Connor was not one to walk away from a challenge. He wanted Gabby to desire him, to burn for him the way he did for her.

Ironically Gabby was thinking about Connor too. Desire was a new experience for her; ever since the rape, she had believed that she would remain single. But now, the wall around her had been breached, and she finally felt the need to touch and be touched, to enjoy physical contact. Connor had shown her a glimpse at how exciting lovemaking could be.

To break the monotony of the drive Connor asked about her childhood. 'What was growing up in San Remo like? I want to know everything about you.'

'Life was perfect at San Remo, and we had such freedom in our neighbourhood. Our neighbours, the Sailas, did everything with us, and we were more like family than best friends. The beach was a paradise, and still is, with sandy shores, clear blue water and acres and acres of bushland to explore. As kids, we had endurance tracks and cubby houses to sit out the heat of the day.

'We would climb up high to our wooden platform anchored in the branches and lay against an array of old household cushions while we gorged ourselves on mangoes and lychees. The only sounds were the cicadas singing in the trees – at times they were so loud we could hardly hear ourselves speaking.

'When it wasn't so hot, we'd build these monumental sand castles on the beach and have bonfires. Those nights, we would sit around the fire toasting marshmallows and telling stories, and my older brothers delighted in scaring us with ghost stories.'

'Tell me about one of their ghost stories.' He glanced across with a twinkle in his blue eyes.

'Well, my personal scariest story was the Min Min light.'

'What's the Min Min light?' Connor asked with a raised eyebrow.

'It's a story of the dead stalking the living with this alluring light that floats out of the cemetery and seeks its victims in the darkest hour of night. If you see a Min Min light, then you have no choice but to follow it. Even it leads you over a cliff, it lures you to join the dead.'

'That surely isn't real?'

'Apparently, you see them in the outback, these fast-moving balls of light. The Aborigines believe it's their dead elders looking after their country. But my brother Jacob made it all about the lights' deadly intent to kill you.'

'I wish I had siblings, even if they do terrorise you,' Connor admitted.

'When I look back, it was a pretty special childhood, not just the place, but our people as well. Your turn now. I want to know everything about you as well.'

Connor considered her childhood adventures with family and friends there every day, parents there every night when she went to sleep, and compared it to his lonely days and nights.

'Sometimes being born into wealth can bring as many pitfalls as privileges. Most of my childhood was spent away at boarding school. At first, I was desperately lonely and all I wanted to do was go home.

'My parents were often away for business, so I spent a lot of time with our horse trainer, Fred, who became a surrogate father to me in many ways. During the horse show jumping season, we would take off for six to eight weeks travelling all over the country in a truck with Solomon loaded into the back. Those days are my best memories now that Fred has passed away and Solomon is in his golden years.'

'That sounds so lonely, Connor.' Gabby reached over to place her hand on his arm.

'It was at times, but I really can't complain when you consider how some childhoods play out.'

Gabby's heart ached when she imagined how sad he would have been and wished he could have roamed the beach with their gang and been a part of all their adventures.

The car ate up the miles as their conversation roamed over different topics, and once they turned off the main road, Connor explained how his father was passionate about raising racehorses. 'The property is huge, and the paddocks are separated by tall thorn brush fencing, which is necessary to stop the stallions fighting. My father believes in raising horses in as natural a state as possible. His theory was that if the foal was raised in a herd, it makes the horse tougher and less prone to injuries.'

'Any natural environment has to be what's best for an animal, as nothing wants to be fenced off from what it loves,' Gabby mused. Then without warning, she gasped as an overwhelming sense of anxiety and pain surged through her body. Grabbing hold of Connor's arm, she squeezed it tight in fear. 'Connor, please stop the car just up ahead. There's an animal in trouble, and we need to help it.'

Pulling over on the verge, he looked around and then at Gabby in confusion. 'Where, Gabby? There's nothing here.'

Undoing her seatbelt, she impressed upon the dogs to stay at the car because they would frighten the horses. 'Connor, how do you get through the screen fencing?'

'No way, Gabby. You can't go in there. There's a wild stallion, and he will stomp us into the ground. Even if you set your dogs on him, it would still be a nasty fight.' Connor put his arm around her shoulders and tried to lead her back to the car.

'No, Connor.' She shrugged him away. 'I can't ignore the call for help, so even if you decide to stay here, you just need to tell me how I can access the paddock. Or do I have to tear this thorn brush apart with my bare hands?'

'Seriously, won't you listen and just come back to the car,' he implored her.

'No, I can't. Don't you see that I have to help, no matter how dangerous it may be.'

'Just wait here a minute.' He went back to the car where the dogs growled at him and bared their teeth. 'Don't worry, dogs, you can kill me if I survive the attack of a crazed horse.' He reached under his seat and brought out a .22 calibre rifle, checking that it was loaded.

He was frowning with frustration as he came back towards her with the gun.

Gabby shook her head. 'Connor, I want to help, not kill them.'

'This is just insurance, Gabby. I would rather it be the horse than one of us, and I promise I will only use it if I have to.'

She stepped aside for him to lead the way and heard him muttering something about insanity; however, against his better judgement, he did show her the small trapdoor concealed into the corner of each paddock. They crawled through, and she took off at a run towards a hill, Connor staying close behind her.

Just as they crested the hill, she could hear thundering hoof beats getting closer and closer. Grabbing hold of Connor, she held him steady against her. 'Stand behind me and stay absolutely still, do not move a muscle,' she murmured.

Gabby could feel terrible anger. This horse was coming to attack and destroy. He had smelled them and was now intent on protecting his herd. Urgently sending him a message, she impressed upon his mind that they were not a threat. *Your mare is in trouble, and we have come to save the foal.*

Connor cringed as the stallion suddenly appeared over the rise, charging towards them until it seemed he would run them down. But he did stop, right in front of them. When he reared up, his hooves almost struck their heads. He was a stunning grey that stood at least seventeen hands high, his huge, thick neck tight with tension, and he came at them with his teeth bared, ears flattened and ready to attack.

Moving slightly to one side, Connor crouched down and aimed the rifle at the horse's heart. His finger half-squeezed the trigger, just waiting for the right moment to place the shot.

Gabby saw Connor get ready to shoot this magnificent animal and despite her thudding heartbeat, she maintained eye contact with the angry horse and stepped forward. Repeatedly, she kept reassuring him that they were no threat, just here to help his mare.

'Don't shoot, Connor,' she whispered as the stallion took a step back and then trotted around them a few times, snorting aggressively before coming to stand before Gabby.

Still crouching with the gun, he watched as the horse dropped his head and stood eye to eye, staring at Gabby until she reached out and placed one hand lightly on its face. He watched them in astonishment. Later he told her how close he had been to dropping the big horse. One wrong move and he would have pulled the trigger.

Once Gabby got through the horse's initial anger, she imprinted upon the stallion that they would do their best to help the mare birth her foal. After this exchange, the stallion shook his head and snorted, before turning and trotting away. 'Come on, we have to follow the horse.'

Connor stumbled behind, saying, 'Gabby, what the hell just happened?'

'Not now, Connor, later. We have work to do, especially if we are going to save your father's horse.'

Puffing heavily, they ran through the tall green grass until they realised the stallion had stopped at his herd. The mares and foals looked at them with fear and quickly moved away from the mare on the ground.

The chestnut mare was lying on her side with her distended belly heaving with each contraction. No matter how much she strained, the foal was stuck fast and would not move. Gabby crouched beside the mare's head and gently stroked her ears, the whole time murmuring words of comfort and reassuring her that they were here to help.

'We need to get her up.' Gabby took off her belt and tied it around the mare's neck to pull and tug until she staggered to her feet.

'Connor, you need to hold her while I check the foal.' Gabby could see that the translucent sac was still covering the protruding delivery, so not having any other option, she went to the back of the horse to lean in close and pull on the sac with her teeth until she could get a tear going. Once the seal was broken, she was able to expose one of the foal's hooves.

The other hoof wasn't visible, so Gabby gently pushed her hand into the birth canal to feel for it. She tried to grasp the tiny, slippery hoof, but the mare's contractions kept pulling it away from her fingers. The mare groaned with exhaustion and turned her head around to look back at Gabby.

Come on, we need to work together to get your foal out. I feel your exhaustion, but don't give up now. Finally, Gabby was able to grab hold of the other hoof to re-align the two feet then she felt for the foal's head. All now seemed to be in position, so she kept a constant downwards pressure on the front legs to guide the foal through the birth canal. After a short time, Gabby could see the head emerging, then the shoulders. She waited while the mare paused to gather more strength, and when she saw the horse's sides contract for the last push, she knew they would soon have their foal.

Suddenly the tiny horse slid out and plopped onto the ground. The mare trembled with fatigue and turned to look at her offspring lying at her feet. Moving with care, Gabby kneeled beside the still form. Realising it wasn't breathing, she took off her shirt and used it to start rubbing its coat to stimulate some response, but it appeared to be stillborn.

Come on little one, you must breathe!

Connor released the belt from around the mare's neck, and she spun around to sniff at her foal, sensing it was in trouble. He crouched beside Gabby as she tried to find a spark of life in the tiny body. Gabby kept reaching out with her mind, urging the foal to breathe. Using her shirt again, she cleared the mucous from the small nostrils, not wanting to give up while there was some small chance that this beautiful little animal might survive.

After what felt like an eternity, they finally saw the filly's small chest rise with a shaky breath, and her beautiful eyes opened for a first look at the world.

'Now we wait for the blood to clear from the placenta.' Gabby smiled for the first time.

They stayed close to the weak little foal, coaxing her to keep breathing, then several minutes later the mare pushed a few more times and the afterbirth landed at their feet.

The large, bloody mass splashed against Connor's trousers, but he didn't even notice. The cord broke and now the foal was free to stand and nurse.

All the other horses stood around them in a circle, watching the proceedings, and a little further off, the stallion stood snorting and shaking his head.

Gathering up the messy afterbirth in her arms, Gabby carried it away from the birthplace and buried it. She hoped it would give the mare and foal a bit more time to gather their strength before they had to flee from the menace of wild dogs or dingoes.

They stood and watched with wonder as their little miracle took her first wobbly steps towards her mother. Connor laughed and hugged Gabby, and they felt like proud parents when the filly butted her mother's teats looking for milk. She was golden chestnut in colour, like her mother, with a perfect white star on her forehead.

Both mare and foal had a much better chance now, so they stood watching in contentment, until the stallion came up and butted Connor in the back. 'Hey, that's no way to say thank you!'

'I think he's politely telling us it's time to go.' Gabby couldn't resist laughing at Connor's offended expression.

Connor watched in amazement as she approached the huge beast and reached up to gently stroke his face. In response to her touch, he lowered his head and let her rub him around the ears.

'Goodbye, friend. May you live a long life,' she murmured and respectfully stepped away.

As they walked back towards the car, neither of them spoke about what had just happened. It felt like they had shared a spiritual experience where there was surely death, but instead they had brought life.

Samson and Goliath were happy to see Gabby safely back at the car, so they barked and wagged their enormous tails with delight, sniffing at the strange smells all over her clothes.

'What's my mother going to think when we arrive with our clothes covered in dirt and blood?' Connor laughed.

'Not such a great impression, is it?' Gabby grimaced as she glanced at her own appearance.

It was another twenty minutes of driving before they arrived at the homestead. It was an elegant home built with wide verandas to cool the interior during the hot summer months. The honey-coloured sandstone bricks blended so naturally with the surroundings and contrasted beautifully with the green grass and well-tended gardens.

Faye and Robert Faradene came out to meet them when they heard the tyres crunch on the gravel drive. Samson and Goliath bounded out of the car to stand beside Gabby, safeguarding her in this unknown place with countless unfamiliar smells.

Connor stepped forward to greet his parents, and then he turned to reintroduce Gabby. Naturally, they were a little taken aback at their appearance, but before either of them could comment, Connor put his hands up in surrender. 'Shower, coffee and then we'll give you the story of this.' He pointed to the blood smatters on his trousers.

Gabby remembered meeting Connor's mother at the ball, and she greeted her again with the same good manners of grace and sophistication.

Connor got their bags out of the car, and they wandered into the house as the dogs took up residence at each side of the front door. Gabby loved the interior decor; it was tastefully designed to portray country comfort and relaxation.

Faye showed her to a prepared room, and after a cool, refreshing shower she strolled back to the veranda to enjoy brewed coffee and some delicious pastries. Connor was already there, and once Gabby was passed her hot drink, he began to describe their adventure with the foaling mare.

Robert Faredene seemed astonished that they didn't get killed by the stallion. He questioned them in detail over the branding of the mare and the description of the filly they had helped deliver. 'Gabby, you must be one hell of a horse woman if you could whisper to that ornery old stallion and stop him smashing you both into the ground.'

'To be honest, Mr Faradene, I haven't had any previous experience with horses, but I guess I just have a certain way with animals.' She watched him shake his head in disbelief and raise his eyebrows at Connor, who just grinned back at him.

'So, if you haven't grown up around horses, Gabby, how did you know what to do?' Robert quizzed her further.

'I do have a love for animals, so anything that relates to them catches my interest, and I saw a similar situation on one of those television veterinary shows. When I saw the mare displaying similar symptoms, I hoped that we could help her and applied the same technique.'

'That's an amazing story, and I'm still in shock that you didn't get killed. In fact, I know that horse, and he can be particularly aggressive.'

'Connor, you could have put Gabby's life in danger,' Faye reprimanded her son.

'Mother, I tried to talk her out of it, but she is a force to be reckoned with,' Connor countered in his defence.

That night they sat at the long timber table where there was lively chatter, ranging from current affairs, politics and of course the environment.

'Gabrielle, it's not that simple. Surely you cannot be so naïve to think companies will abandon profits to save the world, especially when there is still a lot of ambiguity around these scientific warnings.' Robert grilled her without mercy, with Connor and Faye sidelining to see who would come out of this debate intact. They had opposing views as Robert Faradene was about enterprise and business, and Gabby was about protecting a vulnerable planet.

To get her point across, she asked them to consider her viewpoint, just for a moment. 'There is so much more to consider than short-term gain. Please, I ask each of you to try to imagine what will happen to this planet if we are right in our predictions. With climate change, floods and fires will ravage the world, ice will melt and the seas will rise, displacing island communities. There will be food and water wars until the earth is completely overwhelmed by the damage we've inflicted. No one will survive if the fallout is as great as some in the scientific community believe. There will be no place for industry and profits if the world we live in has been destroyed by greed and ambition.'

Faye smiled at Gabby with a gleam of admiration in her eye, and Connor just grinned at his father with his 'I told you so' expression.

Robert nodded thoughtfully.

After dinner, Connor found some old rugs for the dogs to sleep on, and Faye brought them some huge meaty bones to chew on. They seemed content lying there on the blankets and holding the bones steady with their feet as they gnawed at the meat, so Gabby wished them goodnight and left them in peace to enjoy.

After saying goodnight to everyone, she also retired to bed. After such an exhausting day, her eyes refused to stay open one minute longer. *Connor looks like his dad*, was the last thought that drifted through her tired mind.

Nine

The next morning after breakfast, Connor took her hand with an invitation. 'Would you like to meet Solomon?'

'Yes, I would love to, but is it okay to bring the Titans? They're happier when I'm in sight.'

'Of course. I'm sure they will want to keep you safe, most likely from me,' Connor said with a grimace.

Winking at the dogs, she said, 'At least I know you'll be on your best behaviour with my two bodyguards close by.'

Samson and Goliath whined in agreement and licked her hand.

They all walked down the slope away from the house, until a substantial stable block and training facilities appeared in the distance.

Connor showed her around the back, and next to the huge sand arena was a paddock with sparkling white palings. Under a massive rain tree stood a white gelding who tossed his head and neighed when he recognised Connor. He left his shady spot and came trotting over to the fence with his ears forward and a youthful spring in his step.

'Well, old fella, how are you enjoying retirement?' Connor spoke quietly as he climbed through the fence. The horse lowered his head and gently blew into Connor's face; it seemed a form of communication between two old friends.

Gabby sensed the contentment oozing from the horse. He was enjoying all the patting and attention.

They spent the day exploring the property and after dinner sat in a vine-covered gazebo under the stars. Gabby's heart started beating faster as Connor slowly brought his face closer to hers. She could feel his warm breath on her face, and his image blurred out of focus as his lips gently touched then settled on hers. Taking it so slowly, he moved as if he were holding a fragile butterfly. His touch was so gentle that it was hard to bear the sweet sensations running through her body.

With passion rushing through her veins, she arched her back to bring their bodies closer together as Connor's mouth moved from her face to the sensitive planes of her throat. He placed his lips over the pulse, noting the furious beating of her heart, and she placed her hand on his chest to find that his was also beating rapidly.

Connor's expression was so intense, but she could see he was trying not to frighten her. He seemed to find it hard to maintain that self-control as he moved back to kiss her mouth, but instead just stayed there staring into her eyes as if weighing up the consequences.

With great effort, he drew back and gazed at the starry night instead. She felt humbled that he didn't move to take advantage of her sudden awareness and onslaught of desire. Gabby thought of the pleasure that could be hers if she could only push through these insecurities and learn to trust again.

Little steps.

They were both thinking of this without realising their thoughts were connected, and she sensed that Connor felt a great exhilaration that she was beginning to want him too. Gabby caught a glimpse of a normal life for herself, one she had assumed would be impossible after her brutal attack.

Neither sure how long they stayed there, with just the sounds of the bush around them, Gabby felt at peace on this land, while the animal inhabitants were happily going about their night foraging. She knew it was time she explained her past. One half of her wanted to tell him and the other half was scared that he would see her through different eyes. Deep down, she didn't want to ruin this, but the honest part knew he deserved the full story before he got any closer.

It was time. It would be unfair to keep this secret any longer.

Gabby turned to place her hands on each side of Connor's face, taking a moment to stare into his blue gaze. She memorised his features in case this was the last time she was this close to him, unsure if he would lose interest once he knew the truth.

'Connor, I want to tell you why I haven't been so keen on intimate contact. It's not a good story, and I understand if your opinion of me changes after hearing it. Believe me when I say I won't blame you in any way, but it is only fair that you know my past before you become any more emotionally attached to me.'

'Gabby, what are you trying to say?'

'It's time you knew the truth.' Taking her hands away from his face, she folded them in her lap and in a very small voice told the whole story of how Andy had hurt her that day. 'I didn't suspect any trouble when I saw the boys standing across the path, as I knew them from school. It was only when Andy grabbed my arm roughly that I realised he intended me harm. I thought I could pull away until he tripped me backwards, and once I was on the ground, the other two held me down so that Andy could beat me.

'I fought as hard as I could, but he punched my face over and over with both fists, beating me senseless. After that, it was like I was watching some poor girl being attacked, until he raped me, then the pain and humiliation was so great it had to be met with body and soul.'

Her face crumpled a little bit more as she said, 'After breaking several of my ribs by kicking me repeatedly, he finally broke a bottle and cut me up down below. Andy made a horrible mess, so much that I had extensive surgery to repair the damage. It was Joe who found me that day on the dirt track. I was a mess, abused, bleeding and broken.'

She told him every gruesome detail so that he didn't have any illusions about her sexual experiences, and she could feel the tension building in his body, his muscles growing tighter and tighter as Gabby told him her truth. The tears were running down her face by the time she finished. It almost felt like she relived the whole event as she openly shared her experience in full to another person for the first time. 'Connor, until tonight, I have never told anyone my account of the rape. So you see, I'm damaged goods now, and you deserve so much more than that.'

Connor was in a state. His blood surged hot with revenge, and he wanted to smash those boys until they were only a smudge on the ground. He desperately wanting to avenge the thugs who had caused her so much suffering. At the same time, in conflict with the violence he was experiencing, he wanted to hold and cherish this broken woman until the world ended. To protect her from every bad thing out there and never see those beautiful eyes cry again.

He had never felt this strongly in his life before. Tears were running down his own face and dripped onto Gabby's blonde hair that was now pressed into his chest. Adrenaline was flooding every muscle in his body as his heart pounded with pent-up emotion.

In the silence that followed, he hugged her even tighter if that were possible, until he said in a choked voice, 'Gabby, I want to kill those bastards for hurting you. My blood is literally boiling in my veins right now. Where are they? Did they get thrown in jail for doing this?'

'Two of them are dead, and I don't know or care where the third one is,' Gabby sniffed back her tears.

They sat in silence for a while, each trying to process their feelings.

Gabby thought Connor would probably walk away from these complications.

Connor couldn't stop thinking of her being held captive, while those pieces of shit hurt her, until suddenly the dam of emotions burst, and all of his feelings rushed out. 'Gabby, I don't mean to frighten you with too much too soon, but I have fallen so deeply in love with you. What you have just told me has only reinforced the depth of my feelings and nothing can change that now.'

'Connor, are you sure? I don't want you to love me because you pity me.'

'It's not that at all. I've have been nursing these feelings for a while now, and I just want to reassure you that what we have is forever, for me at least.' He held her away from him to look deeply into her eyes.

Gabby saw love clearly stamped over his features and sobbed with relief into his warm chest until there were no more tears. Connor whispered soft words into her hair as he instinctively rocked her back and forth in comfort while the night gave them shelter.

The dogs sensed her distress and came closer until all her grief and guilt was spent.

Gabby tried to explain how the assault had affected her family. How it had hurt her parents and brothers. How Eddie had tried to avenge her and was sentenced to jail for manslaughter and at best would be there for several more years.

'You see, Connor, the tragedy is that it wasn't just me those boys hurt. They damaged my family, ruined my best friend's life and caused a great deal of pain for their own families. If they had known the consequences, they would never have stood together on that terrible day.'

'Gabby, I'm truly sorry. I had no idea anything like this could have happened to you. I thought you had been brought up on fresh air and sunshine to turn out this wonderful. I could never have imagined you carried these scars.'

'It took a long time to heal, Connor. It was Joe who brought me back from depression and despair, and as you have seen, I am still fearful of intimacy.'

'I'm so sorry, my love. From now on, we move along that path at whatever pace you're comfortable with.'

They sat there until the moon began to wane, then Connor bent to gently kiss her tear-stained face. 'I truly do love you, Gabby, and no matter what happens I always will. I have never said that to any woman before in my life, so this is all new. For me, you will be the last and the first, the last girl I'll ever want and the first girl I have ever loved.'

She smiled back at him. 'I think I love you too, but I'm not sure yet where this will lead, Connor. I don't know if I can ever truly forget my past, and only time will tell if I can love you as you deserve.'

Connor just hugged her and stroked her hair. He knew that no matter what had happened in her past, Gabby was more than he deserved, and then some.

After many weekends at the homestead, Connor saw his parents become attached to Gabby as well. Who could resist her combination of beauty and kindness, a virtual angel on this earth, this girl he loved.

Connor took great pleasure in teaching Gabby to ride. Riding alongside her over the countryside gave him such a sense of contentment, and it wasn't long before he secretly began to search for her own horse. Something special that would match Gabby's spirit and sensitive nature.

As soon as he saw Bella Noir step out of the stable, he knew this was the one. The mare was completely black, and being a Friesian, she had a luxurious mane and tail, and a high-stepping gait. He was sure it was going to be love at first sight.

The day of their first introduction, Connor made Gabby stop before they got to the stables. 'Gabby, I have a surprise for you, but you have to stay here and keep your eyes closed.'

'Okay,' she smiled.

'No cheating now,' he called out as he went to get the horse.

Gabby obediently didn't look, even as she heard the clip clop of horse shoes coming towards her.

'Gabby, let me introduce Bella Noir.'

Opening her eyes, she gasped with pleasure at the beautiful creature. With her black neck held high and flowing mane, she looked more like a gleaming marble statue than a living breathing thing.

'Bella,' Gabby softly called her name. *Beautiful girl, I see you*, she said as she linked with the horse's mind.

The mare stared at Gabby in confusion until she sensed a friend then dropped her head and pushed her face gently into Gabby's chest.

Gabby ran her hands over the silken feel of the mare's shiny black coat, and during this time, the horse made small whinnies of pleasure as she touched her body and mind. It was a connection never felt by the mare before, as humans always used force to make their intention known, never their minds.

But it wasn't long before Gabby and Bella moved and thought as one. She loved letting Bella run like the wind, with her tail flying out behind her like a banner. The joy and freedom were exhilarating, and there was nothing more exciting than flying across the land on God's chariot, an animal designed for speed and agility.

Riding out together with the dogs running alongside became a favourite pastime for all, animals and humans.

Ten

As promised while living in Melbourne, Gabby retuned to Cairns every six months with Old Joe to reconnect with her family and visit Eddie. Autumn was upon them once again when the trees disrobed to lay their amber glory on the ground, showing the world how easy it was to let go.

As she watched the leaves fall, Gabby had an unsettling feeling that Eddie was calling her home. It wasn't anything he had said in his last letter; it was more of a tug on her heart.

They wrote letters to each other every week; even now with emails and modern forms of communication, they still maintained this personal way to share their news.

There was nothing better than opening the letterbox to find this treasure. The smell of the paper and the slant of his handwriting made it seem he was in her world for that tiny particle of time, knowing this same piece of paper had been held in his hands not too long ago.

Eddie had told her many times that her letters came on angel's wings, as some days they were the only sanity he could hold on to. He was now halfway through his sentence, and she knew that he was feeling the cost of how much he had lost while dreading the sacrifices still to come.

Flying from Melbourne to Cairns and seeing the Great Barrier Reef strung out like a string of precious jewels from the plane window and landing amongst the rainforest mountains was the homecoming she always looked forward to. Then there was the joy of seeing her parents waiting in the arrivals lounge, and after hugs and baggage collection, they were off to San Remo, Gabby to her childhood home and Joe to his cottage.

Gabby also longed for the company of her loyal guardians and went straight out to the garden to find a group of curlews congregated under the mango tree. Recognising her straight away, they excitedly gathered around Gabby when she stretched out on the grass. The little flock was clucking with contentment, all happy to be close to her again, all ready to protect. Gabby's gaze touched each one lovingly, as these unusual friends had been by her side since the beginning of her human life.

During the lively family dinner, the siblings quickly settled back into their niche: Jacob the eldest, the bossy one, Thomas the sensitive peacemaker and Gabby the adored younger sister. Frank and Kathleen Harrison smiled with contentment to see their family once again gathered around the table, watching their animated interaction.

The next morning, Gabby borrowed Frank's car and drove to the prison, tapping the steering wheel in anticipation of seeing Eddie again. The wait in the visitor's room seemed to take forever, and she kept watching the door, drumming her foot in eagerness. It had only been six months, but it always felt like years since she had seen her best friend, and her pulse jumped at the prospect of the first glance.

As soon as Gabby saw Eddie, she knew something had happened. He carried himself differently, and there was a bounce in his step to match the excited gleam in his eyes. Hugging him tightly against her, she breathed in his essence and enjoyed the feel of him in her arms.

'Eddie, it's so good to see you again.' She smiled up at him.

'You're a sight for sore eyes too. Come and sit down, Gabby. I've got something to tell you.'

He began his tale and spoke softly but quickly so that he could give her all the details before the visiting time was over. 'Greg Stanton is the doctor here, and I have been working with him a lot over the last few years. He's a decent man and disgusted at the way this place is managed. It's criminal what they inflict on the prisoners, and just because these people have made mistakes, it doesn't mean we are all less than human. But finally it seems the government is going to step in to stop the abuse.

'I can't disclose all the details, but suffice to say that due to our testimonial in a recent investigation, Barry and I have been granted an early release. The only condition is that we go quietly and don't speak about our involvement in the investigation to friends, family or the media. As you can imagine, we're desperate to get out of here, and readily agreed.'

'Hold on, Eddie. What kind of abuse? I know there's a lot you haven't shared about being in prison, maybe to protect me or even more so to protect yourself. How have they hurt you?'

'That's all behind me now, Gabby, and it's not something I will ever talk about, not to anyone. Only God knows what's been going on in here, and it's best that you don't. But now I really don't care as long it stops and I'm out of here.' He was determined not to break his privacy clause.

'I'm so sorry, my friend. You've never deserved any of this.' Gabby reached up to place her hand on his cheek.

'It will soon be over, and that's all that matters.' He placed his hand over hers.

'Yes, that's all that matters, but I still can't believe it. When will you be home?'

'Gabby, you are the first person to hear my news. It was only confirmed this morning, and I haven't even told my parents yet. I'm almost afraid it's too good to be true.' His grin grew wide with anticipation.

'Oh Eddie, your family are going to be overjoyed to have you back in their lives.' Gabby's smile stretched as wide as Eddie's.

She barely noticed the tears flowing down her face as she gazed upon the relief and joy in his eyes. The shadows still lurked there, more than hinting that something horrible had happened here. 'What will you do now?'

'Apart from the thrill of freedom, what I really want to do is go out to the remote communities. To live and work alongside the local kids, hoping to make a difference, showing them purpose and leading them away from trouble.'

'Sounds like a wonderful plan, Eddie, and with all of this experience, I am sure you will make a massive difference. You won't be preaching at them but sharing your own story, which is something much more powerful.'

'I'm sorry, Gabby. I've bowled you over with my news but haven't even asked about Connor. From your letters, he seems to be more than just a friend.'

'Connor's fine, all my friends are fine, and don't you dare apologise. This is a life-changing moment for you, for me and for both of our families.'

Gabby didn't mention Eddie's news to anyone at home. She spent time with her mother talking a lot about Connor. Kathleen was intrigued and looked forward to meeting this young man who had made such a big impression upon her daughter.

When Ruth Saila called the next morning, she was delirious with excitement. Gabby joined in with everyone's blissful revelation of Eddie's early release. This was such an unexpected turn of events, and a big party was immediately planned to celebrate.

To be a part of such a momentous occasion, Gabby made sure she was still in the north, and almost everyone who lived at San Remo beach was invited. The whole community had been following Eddie's progress in prison, and they were so happy to see him home earlier than anyone had dared to hope.

Eddie's homecoming was met with great excitement.

The Sailas dug a huge hole in the sand at the beach and built a Kup Murri, where they roasted meat and vegetables wrapped in banana leaves over the hot rocks. The food was beautifully cooked, and the guests filled their plates to overflowing.

The moon above watched as children fell asleep on blankets thrown on the sand around the fire. Friends and families sat in small groups to share stories and comment on Eddie's good fortune.

Barry Vilphene was a welcome guest. Eddie watched him mingle with the young and old, hoping this mob could give him a better life than before prison.

He loved being home and savoured each small detail. His bedroom was almost exactly as he had left it seven years ago. Although everything looked the same, he knew it was forever changed after so many years behind bars. He was no longer that naïve young man with stars in his eyes who thought the world would treat him right.

Life had taught him that bad things often happened to good people, and they were all victims. Each person carried hurts buried deep inside from that fateful day. Gabby's family, his family and Old Joe. With the wisdom of hindsight, he acknowledged his life had taken a turn for the worst, but now it was up to him to take strength in what he had survived and turn it all around.

He would never say that such brutal experiences had made him a better person, but at least now he had a lot more emotional intelligence. It was more than just empathy; it was an understanding of how victims of child abuse and those living with addictions suffered. There was nothing that he had not seen or heard now, and his time in prison had opened his eyes to the horror that was a part of many daily lives.

Sexual abuse by a father or brother, children with alcohol and drug addictions, physical abuse so cruel that you could not imagine any human inflicting it upon another – nothing could shock him now.

Eddie wasn't going to waste his future dwelling on the past. Instead, everything he had learnt would be used to help those in need. Maybe his small contribution could counterbalance the thoughts of hate and killing that had almost consumed him behind bars. Now it was his second chance to make a fresh start and see his life count for something.

Although he couldn't disclose the reason to anyone else, it was still possible to recollect the facts in his mind. He remembered how it all began the day Dr Greg Stanton had sent him a message after breakfast. How he had locked the door as soon as Eddie arrived at his office.

The door had never been locked before, but Eddie trusted him so he sat in the chair and waited for some explanation. Greg had brought his chair from around the other side of the desk and sat in front of Eddie, knee to knee.

Eddie still hadn't spoken. He'd just raised his eyebrows in question and held his tongue.

Doctor Stanton had looked searchingly into this young man's face. So much had hinged on today, so much for them both. He'd said, 'Eddie, I need to ask you something of grave importance; however, before you answer me, I want you to think very carefully of the implications. As you are already aware, I have always been actively opposed to some of the unlawful practices at this establishment, and I am sure you share these sentiments.

'The reason I mention this is that, believe it or not, some people in high places have started asking questions, discreetly, but asking all the same. They approached me off-site to enquire if I would testify in a private hearing with the commissioner of corrective services. As you can imagine, I was very motivated to see change here and committed myself to the process, but they also said they would need at least two reliable witnesses from amongst the prisoners themselves.'

Eddie started to speak but the doctor held his hand up to silence him. 'Of course, I immediately thought of you. No, just wait, and don't say a word until you hear the whole story. I can hear you thinking, *Why would I make my life in here anymore torturous by informing, when it would only make the rest of my time even more unbearable?*

'I can understand all these reservations and would be feeling the same myself, so I want you to know the offer that is on the table. I must reinforce with the strongest of warnings that everything said here is strictly confidential and must not be repeated to anyone else, not ever. The commissioner is so motivated to enforce change that he has personally offered an early release for two exemplary prisoners if they testify about the actions of the current manager. But only on the condition that they sign a confidentially clause.'

Eddie's eyes had widened at this unexpected possibility. 'Doctor Stanton, I was about to say that I don't care what kind of ramifications there would be to stop this monster. I would gladly testify against him no matter the cost to myself, but if they are offering a release from this hell, then I am even more enthusiastic to put my name on any document to see him prosecuted.'

'Oh, he won't be prosecuted. They're keeping this quiet and sweeping the messy business under that giant rug that governments keep for these situations. There will be a private hearing between you and the commissioner, and from that meeting he will ascertain that you have not been scripted or coerced in your statement. Once he is satisfied with your account, there will be paperwork to sign, and you would be released under the guise of early discharge for exemplary behaviour.'

Doctor Stanton had allowed allow a small smile to play around the corners of his mouth as he spoke the word every prisoner dreamed about: freedom.

Eddie had felt like he was in a dream himself; in fact, he even rubbed his eyes and blinked firmly a few times to make sure he hadn't been sleeping and could really believe this was happening.

'The other prisoner I was considering for this meeting was Barry Vilphene. Do you think he is a good choice?'

'Definitely a good choice. He's been a good friend since I first arrived here and has always tried to alleviate some of the suffering caused by the manager and his comrades,' Eddie assured him.

When Greg Stanton had called in Barry and shared the same proposal, his reaction was immediate. 'Fuck yes, I want to see that arsehole's cover blown. I just wish he would see time behind bars and get treated the same as what he's done to us.'

After this, it all had happened quickly. Eddie and Barry had just stared expressionless when they faced the sacked prison manager. His threats no longer held any power over them.

'You bastards had better watch your back 'cause one day I am coming for you.' His face was puffy and red, and his features twisted with hatred as they led him away from the private hearing.

There had been nothing in the media about the inquiry, and a new manager had been quietly appointed while several vacancies for guards suddenly became available. Eddie and Barry had been released soon after this, and Ruth and Billy Saila were there to collect them both.

Eddie's thoughts settled back to the present, back to good times with celebration dinners, surrounded by family and friends.

Just then his father's cousin Charlie grabbed his attention and started telling him about all the good fish he had caught just at the end of San Remo beach when the tide was changing.

Gabby looked across at Eddie as he laughed and talked with his family and friends. He was a man now, thinner, more angular and covered with sinew and muscle. His beautiful mocha-coloured skin had lost none of its attraction, and he must have felt her stare as he looked up and their gaze locked in silent communication.

Eddie noted the changes in Gabby too. Physically, she was just as beautiful as ever, maybe even more so, if that were possible. The difference was that her eyes no longer looked so haunted, there was a new softness shining in them.

Eddie smiled to break this solemn moment and walked across the sand to gently place his big arm across her slender shoulder. They leaned against each other just like old times.

People drifted away with hugs and smiles, everyone happy to see the family reunited.

The next afternoon, just before the sun set, Eddie came to take Gabby for a walk along the beach. They strolled hand in hand along their childhood playground, followed once again by a trail of protective curlews.

Gabby could almost imagine she heard the echoes of laughter from a group of uninhibited children playing along the sandy shore. The ghosts from the past were haunting her today.

Stopping at the far end just near Old Joe's cottage, they dropped down on the sand to wait for the sun to disappear and the moon to make its welcome debut.

'Okay, Gabby, now we have time for you to tell me all about him.'

'Who?' she asked innocently.

'Connor, you schmuck.' He nudged her mischievously.

'We're still in very early days, Eddie, taking our time to get to know each other. But he is a good man and I know you will really like him.'

'If you like him, then of course I will. We're still family, and if he's in your life, he's going to be in mine too.'

'You always say what my heart needs to hear.'

'I know.' He smiled and hugged her close.

Gabby let her head drop against his shoulder as they sat in silence with the sun against their backs. The heavily rainforested mountains were cloaked in shadows as the moon rose to lay its golden trail across the ocean. It was a companionable sharing of the world and each other that only old friends can fully appreciate.

As Eddie stood at the airport waving goodbye to Gabby and Old Joe, he still struggled to believe he was free to go to Melbourne whenever he chose and still half expected to be locked up at night.

Eleven

After a month of preparation, Eddie was about to say goodbye to San Remo on his own terms. His mother hugged him fiercely close before reluctantly letting him go, and Billy just shook his hand and slapped him on the back with his sisters Nellie and Lizzie waiting to have their own farewell embraces.

'Remember what I told you. Don't pick up strangers and call us at the sign of any trouble. Your father and I are only a phone call away,' Ruth warned them again.

'I know, Mum. I promise we'll be careful and to call you as soon as we arrive.' Eddie smiled at her protectiveness, even though he was now a grown man.

'Don't worry, Mrs Saila, I've got his back,' Barry reassured her.

'That's all I ask.' Ruth smiled through her tears.

Eddie got into Billy's old ute and leaned out of the window for another look at the family home and his loved ones all standing outside. He would never again take any of this for granted. Prison had taught him that lesson far too well.

They had all their worldly goods packed into the back of the ute, along with the tools they had scavenged from garage sales.

Their wide grins spoke of the thrill of freedom; nobody could appreciate making decisions independently than someone recently released from incarceration. Some prisoners without support or a safety net felt vulnerable back in the community and soon re-offended to go back to the routine of prison. But Eddie, and luckily Barry by association, had significant support from the Islander community in Cairns and throughout the Gulf country. Eddie's uncle Esra had suggested the two boys travel up to the remote community to assist with his youth program, hoping they could mentor some of the local teens.

This was exactly how he thought his life on the outside would look, so Eddie jumped at the offer, and Barry was more than happy to tag along. They had AC/DC playing loud on the radio as they sang along to 'Thunderstruck', the car eating up the miles along with the assortment of food Ruth had packed for their journey.

The creek crossings were daunting but exhilarating as the water rushed up over the tyres, and the roads were jaw-jarring at times. After they crossed the South Mitchell River, the car started veering to one side so badly that Eddie had to pull over to investigate.

'We've blown the back tyre, Barry,' he shouted from outside.

Barry climbed out of the car and looked around at the dwindling light. 'Do you want to change it now or camp here for the night?'

Eddie stretched his cramped muscles and agreed they could fix it in the morning and still get to Kowanyama in good time.

They drove the car a little way off the road and into the bush alongside the river, where Eddie got a small fire going. Sharing a beer with Barry, they sat on the side of the bank to enjoy the glory of the setting sun. After a simple dinner of franks and beans, they leaned against their swags and chatted with the easiness of old friends.

The night had a cacophony of sounds, frogs croaking, insects chirping, the scrabble of small mammals foraging and the barking of crocodiles. As they slept, Eddie dreamed of Gabby, the same dream he'd often had in prison. They were walking along the beach, holding hands with the curlews trailing protectively behind, but instead of smiling at him, her mouth opened wide to start screaming. He was confused. His favourite dream had never turned into a nightmare, so what the hell was happening?

His eyes popped open when he realised the screams were real, so without hesitation he leaped out of bed to find Barry. 'Barry, where are you mate?' he shouted into the darkness.

'Eddie, a fucken croc has got me. Help, help me!' Barry's terrified voice filled the darkness.

Eddie grabbed the torch they had ready and raced to find his best friend in the hope of saving him from a horrible, violent death. Rushing along the slippery, muddy bank, he shone the torch towards where he could hear Barry screaming for help.

'Oh my God,' Eddie whispered in horror when he saw Barry being dragged towards the water. A massive crocodile had a grip around his upper leg, and no matter how much Barry thrashed or punched it, it refused to let go of its prize.

Eddie reacted instinctively, never considering his own safety. He ran towards them and jumped on the back of the huge saltwater croc. With his legs straddling its wide girth, he began to beat the top of its head with the torch. The creature didn't even react, it just kept pulling Barry towards the water with Eddie now riding on top.

'Go for the eyes, Eddie, for God's sake, or we'll both be fucken dead,' Barry shouted out in horror and pain. Eddie could only see his silhouette in the low light but felt his terror. It was so thick in the air that he could taste it all around them.

Eddie tossed the torch aside and leaned forward to find the eyes of the beast. As he sought the eyeballs, he heard the splash of water when the tail reached the river. There were only seconds left to get it to release his friend, and if this didn't work, it would be too late.

His large hands scrabbled over the tough, knobbly skin, fumbling to find the eye socket as the belly slid into the water. *Where the fuck are the eyes?* his mind screamed in frustration.

Just as it was almost over, his fingers plunged in to gouge the eyes out if he had to. Pushing his fingers in deep, the cold-blooded animal began to twist its enormous head to get away from the intrusion. Eddie was brutal with desperation, plunging his fingernails into the sticky moisture that protected the eyeballs.

Suddenly, it was over. In protest of Eddie's attack, the crocodile released Barry from its jaws and slipped backwards into the sanctuary of the muddy river. Luckily, Eddie rolled to the side to land in the shallows as it moved out of sight.

In terror, he grabbed hold of Barry and dragged him out of the water and back to the safety of the bank. They lay there for a few moments, but terrified it would return, Eddie picked Barry up and stumbled back to camp.

When he placed him back on his swag, Eddie fumbled in his backpack to find another torch, crouching down in front of Barry, puffing from adrenaline and staring in fright. Both were shivering with shock at the close call.

There were several deep puncture wounds on his thigh where the croc's teeth had taken grip to drag its prey into the water, where it would have done death rolls to drown Barry. Crocodiles often drowned their prey first and then stashed the body underwater to feed on later.

Grabbing a bundle of T-shirts, Eddie pushed against the blood oozing from the brutal wounds. 'How on earth did it get you, Barry, when we were both sleeping a safe distance from the river?'

'I got up to have a cigarette and didn't expect the bloody thing to be out of the water. I must have tripped over it in the dark and then it grabbed me by the leg, fucken hell.'

'Those filthy cigarettes nearly killed you earlier than I predicted,' Eddie growled in frustration. 'The teeth have made a mess of your leg, mate. I have to get you to town tonight. If I prop you against a tree, do you think you can hold the torch while I fix the flat tyre?'

Barry sat in the dark with his back to a tree, clenching his jaw in pain. At first the shock had alleviated any feeling, but now the burning agony was all he could think about. 'Hurry the fuck up, Eddie,' he grunted in hurt.

'Okay, the spare tyre is on. Let's get you in the car and on our way.' Eddie picked Barry up with ease and gently sat him in the passenger seat. Quickly tossing the remainder of their gear into the ute, he took off in a spurt of gravel.

Bashing on his uncle's front door in the middle of the night, Eddie apologised as Ezra opened it in dishevelment. His confusion changed to concern when he was told about Barry's accident. 'Eddie, you jump in the back of the ute, and I'll drive over to the nurse's house.'

Working in the remote community, the nurse had seen it all. With no fuss, she cleaned and dressed the wounds and radioed the Flying Doctors. The next morning as they were about to stretcher Barry onto the small plane, he grabbed hold of Eddie's arm. 'Bloody hell, Eddie, you saved my life, mate,' he muttered, obviously uncomfortable with the tears that shimmered in his eyes.

'Barry, I owe you anyway. You saved my life in jail, so now we're even.' Eddie squeezed his forearm with affection.

Barry spent two weeks in the Cairns Base Hospital being treated with antibiotics and daily dressings to ensure the puncture wounds were healing. Then he was flown back to Kowanyama, or Kowie, where Eddie and his uncle were waiting to collect him.

Eddie excitedly introduced Barry to a bunch of kids he was already building friendships with. Barry was nicknamed *Croc Man* by the locals for surviving the attack from the large saltie.

The two young men now had a second chance at life and weren't going to waste a moment of it.

Twelve

Landing lightly and stepping through the golden gate of the Silver City, Zadkiel had little time to appreciate the wall of embracing angels or the glow of light that permeated his home. Instead, he walked the pathways with purpose, determined to find his friend Anael.

He had an exciting discovery to urgently share with him. He'd found Raphael.

Raphael's last mission had been assigned by his leader Puriel, an undertaking from which Raphael had not returned to the City of Angels. The council had authorised a search party, but in the meantime Zadkiel and Anael frantically looked for him whenever they went through the Eye of God.

They had traversed the realm of man for so long, seeking any signs that he had been taken prisoner, but finding no trace of him. Until now.

As a last resort, Zadkiel had placed himself in the sentient dimension, floating along in the world of dreams. He'd found this was a cunning way to spy. In this state, he could hear all the dreams, the fervent desires of the humans longing for love, wealth or revenge – the bare truth articulated in their subconscious. He could even access the furtive whispers of the demons who moved through the dark underworld. Zadkiel had glided over this sea of dialogue, keeping his presence hidden and dismissing most of it, until he'd heard the furtive whisper of a demon.

It had been Jinn boasting to Dominic that they had captured an angel.

Unknown to them, Zadkiel had tracked their path deep beneath the dirt, into the bowels of the earth itself, and here he had stood out of sight, enduring Raphael's screams of torture. Knowing it was fruitless to show himself without support, he silently promised his brother he would come back to save him.

After searching through the streets of the City of Angels, he found Anael in the collective, where he sat with brothers and sisters telling a story in his own gregarious way. He liked to talk with his hands, and most of the time it was quite comical to watch the performance from afar.

But this time, Anael stopped mid-sentence when he saw the expression on Zadkiel's face as he approached. Standing up, he drew Zadkiel away from the other messengers and placed his arm across his shoulders to ask quietly, 'Did you find him? Tell me.'

'I did. I'm sure it's Raphael the demons have captive.' Zadkiel's eyes flashed with anger.

'Rather than wait for the scouts to act, we'll rescue him ourselves.' The outgoing angel grabbed his brother as his eyes gleamed with the need to act, to save Raphael from the fallen angels that had captured him.

'Anael, we must be careful. You saw what happened to Gadriel when he took unsanctioned action. The wise ones bolted his wings together!'

'Yes, but Gadriel didn't think it through. We need to be more strategic when we break Raphael out of his prison and bring him home. We take him straight to the ushers of the light, where they will heal him and replace his mantle. Only then do we report his capture by the rebels.'

'How do you propose to get him out of there? Especially if he's in their stronghold, surrounded by our enemies.'

'My dear Zadkiel, you know me. I'm never short of clever ideas that turn into the most brilliant plans.'

Zadkiel just raised his brows. As much as he loved his brother, Anael's exploits were not always remembered as the most *brilliant plans*. 'Let's just hope your brilliant plan works to bring Raphael home.'

'First, we must find a quiet place to make the brilliant plan'. Anael led him away to a corner where a stone bench sat between the shimmering white walls, a place out of sight from the busy corridors of power.

'How are we going to free him when there are demons all around?' Zadkiel frowned.

'We need a distraction. Maybe a flame thrower would work?'

'How are we going to manage that?' Zadkiel said, shaking his head.

'I know how.' Anael's eyes shone with a glint of determined recklessness.

Soon after this exchange, they waited for Uriel as he left the Flame of the Divine tower. 'Uriel, our dear brother, we need your help.' Anael caught his arm and led him away.

Uriel looked back at Zadkiel apprehensively as he was directed to sit on their secluded stone bench. Under the twilight sky, the two angels laid out their proposal. At first, Uriel was unwilling to get involved. 'This sounds too dangerous. There would be only three of us against a hoard of fallen angels, who are more demon now than angel after so much time away from the light,' he argued, setting his jaw.

'Yes, but their power has eroded over the years, so how much damage could they do?' Anael dismissed his concerns.

'It's a numbers game, Anael, and this is how they would have captured Raphael in the first instance. The number of them would have overwhelmed him.'

'Your concerns may be justified, Uriel, but tell me, what would Raphael do if you had been captured and tortured?'

Uriel held his gaze a moment before dropping his head with shame. 'He would do anything to rescue me.'

'Then there is your answer. Surely you will do the same for him.' Anael embraced his shoulder encouragingly.

'How do you even imagine that I can leave the Silver City with a spark from the eternal flame? It would be discovered immediately, and we'd all be arrested for treason.' Uriel still had concerns about the validity of their scheme.

'Uriel, we all know the flame protectors carry the spark within to ensure the flame can never be extinguished.'

The flame tower sat in the very heart of the Silver City, high above all the other temples. Tended by a few elects who mysteriously carried the spark within, this mighty flame cast a golden glow in the sky, a promise of light and love for the angelic citizens.

Uriel didn't argue. In this instance, he once again raised his eyebrows at Anael. Their gift was supposed to be classified information.

It took some time to convince Uriel that they had covered all contingencies and mitigated the risks. 'This is how it will play out. Uriel and I will wait for you on the other side of the Eye of God,' said Anael.

'Zadkiel, you report for duty and collect the new soul for delivery. But, instead of taking it straight to its birth mother, we make a detour to save Raphael.'

'Are you sure this will work? That the innocence within a new soul is enough to break those bonds of suffering,' Zadkiel asked hesitantly, almost afraid to hope.

'It has to. This is our one chance to set him free. We won't get the element of surprise a second time.'

'We will have to hurry. We won't have much time from the collection of the soul to its time of delivery. We don't want this new life to be collateral damage to save Raphael. It is up to us to see them both safely to where they belong,' Zadkiel exhorted his collaborators.

Each messenger nodded, understanding the gravity of this mission. Two lives depended on its outcome, one mortal and one immortal.

When the time came, Zadkiel stepped up to accept his precious cargo. As a life bearer, he held the illuminated capsule close to his chest, immediately knowing its birthplace. As planned, he found Uriel and Anael waiting for him on the other side of the Eye of God and knowing time was short, they flew off to liberate Raphael.

Zadkiel led them deep beneath the crust of the planet earth, seeking the demon's cell. Here, each one split up to undertake their own part in the rescue.

Uriel stealthily stole into the corridors. He had the most difficult part of the mission. But being able to shadow his form with smoke as well as brighten it with fire would allow him to blend into the dim corridors. He had to remain in the shadows until he could ignite a flame as a distraction to draw the demons away from the cells.

Anael had the most painful part. He would approach the guards and take a beating so that Uriel could reach the interior quickly.

Zadkiel had the most important part. He was to release his brother from the shackles of misery.

Just as Uriel disappeared, Anael boldly marched into the corridors of the prison. He had to sustain the punishment long enough for Uriel to succeed.

The fallen angels that congregated around the cells could hardly believe their eyes: a messenger that came to them, arrogant and without fear. It was their dream come true as they leaped upon Anael to tear into him. He fought back bravely, but with so many, it wasn't long before he was no longer visible. He became a lump on the ground with so many of his fallen comrades clamouring over his vast shape.

Quickly moving into the maze of hallways, Uriel hoped something would guide him to their meeting place. It was voices that called him forward, until he stepped into a vast cave with a multi-coloured stone throne shimmering in its centre.

Here he saw two rebel angels talking intently. It was Sut who sat in the sparkling seat with Jinn standing before him. Spinning in amazement, Jinn had no time to react as Uriel held out his hand to create the spark. Smiling just a little, he lifted it up high to blow the flame towards their dumbstruck faces.

The fire was so powerful it whooshed around the room like a banshee released from captivity. Sut and Jinn rushed to hide behind the bright throne, from where Sut shouted orders for his hosts to come to his aid, to strike down this intruder.

Uriel stayed hidden against the side of the cave until the room was filled with yelling hosts of the underworld. Then he cast a wall of fire across the entrance, sealing their enemies off to give the angels more time to release the tortured Raphael.

Turning away from mayhem beyond the fiery barrier, Uriel swiftly retreated back through his shadow of smoke, to return to Anael and finish their brother's liberation.

He found him sitting on the ground holding his head in his hands, with wing feathers torn and open wounds gaping across his torso.

'Anael, are you badly hurt? Can you still fly?'

Taking Uriel's hand to stand up, Anael shook the dirt off his feathers, and ruffled them back into place before gruffly answering, 'Of course I can fly.'

'Come on then, let's get this over with.'

Anael did lean a little on Uriel as they headed towards the cell where Zadkiel was waiting. Once they broke open the cell door, they all stopped to stare in horror at what hung before them.

Raphael swung from the roof like a slaughtered beast, and he had already begun to darken with being away so long from the light. His body was torn to shreds with wounds inflicted upon wounds, but the most heartrending was to see his once-magnific head hanging in defeat. Dark, smoky chains exuding despair held him securely in place.

Zadkiel entered the cell and softly called his name, 'Raphael, brother, we are here to save you,' he whispered.

Raphael raised his head, almost expecting this to be a dream.

Anael grasped the chains to break them but instead he groaned in pain from the jolt of misery that seared through his hands. He grabbed hold again as he braced himself for the rush of distress to blister his skin. 'I can't release him.' He strained until the cords in his neck became visibly rigid.

'Let me burn them off.' Uriel held open his hand and a small flame obediently hovered above his palm. Holding the flame to the chains, they began to smoulder and smoke. The angels had to turn their faces away from the stench of death that exuded from the hot manacles, while Raphael did his best to stifle the scream that rose from his chest and out of his rigid throat.

Knowing that time was running out, Zadkiel then spread his mighty wings and flew up to Raphael where he pressed the capsule of new life against his heart. Hoping the flood of light would release his brother from the chains of sorrow.

When Zadkiel's feet stepped back to the ground they saw the flush of hope begin to move across Raphael's body. It was the innocence, the promise of new life, that broke the bondage of pain and anguish. As the purest form of power sparkled across Raphael's body, the chains fell away to smoke at their feet.

Raphael fell into Uriel's waiting arms, and the three angels didn't delay in making their escape. Anael was still able to assist carrying the broken angel back to the Silver City while Zadkiel speedily delivered the new soul to its new family.

As he watched the little baby boy lovingly cradled in his mother's arms, Zadkiel sent the child a special blessing for also saving his angel brother.

It took Raphael a long time to recover. Anael and Uriel had carried him into the chamber of light where the ushers had removed his darkened and shredded mantle, laying him down with his wings spread on a shimmering marble slab as they attended to his wounds.

Their illuminated hands moved above and over his body, binding together the gaping lesions in his flesh. The most difficult treatment was to extract the decay that was already putrefying his essence. To remove these deep stains, they had to immerse his whole body, including his vast wings, into a pool of light.

Here Raphael remained submerged until the rot was forced out by the flow of energy, the source of all life in the universe. Only when the ushers were satisfied with his recovery did they place a new shimmering mantle over his shoulders, a protective shield to keep him connected to his source of power.

Raphael's first visit was to Gadriel, who sat excommunicated under the Blood Tree, and it was here that he told him of his capture and torture.

Gadriel held him as he wept.

'Gadriel, I know the council holds you responsible for Fallon and Josiel's actions, but after what I've heard and seen, I think there is a great war coming. I just hope the council can see beyond their own pride and start supporting the messengers who see this truth and want to push back against Lucifer's advances.'

'Thank you, Raphael. All that you have told me causes me great sadness but also hope that one day we can all be united again in our city.' Gadriel grasped his shoulders in appreciation of Raphael's trust.

Raphael's capture caused considerable conflict between the wisest of their kind, as they now had evidence that the demons were indeed violating the treaty. Josiel had warned them of this very infringement all that time ago, and their indecision was now causing harm to the messengers who served the sons of man.

Zinnia, Remiel and Saraquel now had determine their response to this ambush. Puriel was the most dismayed by Raphael's capture, as he now found himself questioning his judgement. He'd rejected Gadriel's supplications to understand his motives and now as much as it pained him, it seemed he'd been mistaken. Mistaken about Fallon, about Josiel and sadly about his brother Gadriel. But it was his stub-born pride that kept him from apologising to his dear brother, as much as he knew it was the right thing to do.

Thirteen

Connor invited Gabby over for dinner at his apartment in Toorak, longing to have her all to himself. Her truth had not dampened his love; in fact, it made it even more potent. He wanted to devote his life to cherishing and protecting her from any further harm, hoping with time that she could move beyond those bad memories, and that love would heal the hurt. Every time he held her in his arms, he cursed that monster again for what he'd done.

Mentally he exorcised the ghost of Andy Bolton from their lives; he had already done enough damage. Tonight was theirs, where love was a shield from the painful past.

She arrived on time. Old Joe had bought her a little yellow smart car, which was perfect for getting around the city, and it had the least detrimental effect on the environment.

Connor took off her coat and drew her close to him. Gabby trembled when she felt his body pressed against hers.

'Are you cold?' Connor stepped back so that he could look into her eyes.

'No, I'm fine.' She smiled up at him.

They laughed and talked over dinner, feeling relaxed and comfortable with each other. Connor poured them another glass of wine when they sat on the couch to listen to music. Ever so slowly, he moved closer to place soft little kisses over her face, her shoulders and along her arms right down to her fingertips.

'You know I love you, Gabby, and I would never hurt you.'

She silently nodded.

Connor moved to her long slender throat.

Gabby laid her head on the back of the sofa and felt the room slowly spinning, dizzy with desire and emotions that had been suppressed for far too long. No longer a terrified teenager, she was now in her early twenties and felt the need to accept this love being offered.

Let it happen tonight, she whispered to herself. *Let it all go.*

Connor sensed her rising desire, and slowly he undressed her, taking his time to build her excitement. Each part of her that he exposed was kissed and caressed with tenderness. He ran his fingers softly over her skin while he kissed the sensitive areas on her throat, taking his time to thoroughly explore her body before going any further.

Gabby was panting small gasps of pleasure as Connor's lips and tongue touched her lightly. Waves of sweet sensations washed over her, reminding her of what the cult master had done that day years ago, but this was much stronger and empowering. There was love expressed in every touch.

Connor shed his own clothes discreetly and moved his naked body over Gabby's, feeling her arch closer into him, unconsciously thrusting her hips and driving him crazy. Every follicle of his skin tightened, and his heart began to pound like a drum.

Despite the powerful surge of lust, he still held off. He wanted her in the throes of passion before taking her as his own. Gabby's pleasure was his priority as he gently made love all over her body, sucking her nipples until they stood like soft pink towers, kissing her legs and then moving down to her inner thighs.

When his tongue gently brushed the petals of her labia, Gabby rose up in excitement and surprise. Nothing had ever felt like this before. When his tongue slipped inside of her, she cried out with delight. His tongue slid in and out of her and she rocked against the thrilling pressure building inside her. Connor gently caressed the ridged scars inflicted by Andy Bolton and ever so softly kissed the damaged tissue where the torture had left its mark. He would spend the rest of his life undoing the damage from so much hate.

Gabby started to move and lift her hips under his skilful touch as he sucked and rolled his tongue over her clitoris. The sweet sensations rippled like a pebble dropped into a pond. They began where his tongue was pressing and spread across her in waves of pleasure, until she was crying out in ecstasy as her body exploded, convulsing with spontaneous wonder. The world had stopped and now...this was all there was.

Connor's own arousal only increased when she orgasmed, and as she grabbed hold of his shoulders in the spiral of climaxing, he couldn't wait any longer. Gently, he pushed his throbbing cock inside her, filling her with his love. For a moment she stiffened in alarm, but Connor understood her fear, and immediately he slowed his movement and whispered words of reassurance.

'Gabby, trust me. I promise I'll never hurt you. I love you with all of my heart,' he spoke softly as he placed tiny little angel kisses all over her face.

Gabby let the tension go. Finally, she put the past behind her as she felt her body sink into the sofa to take him without resistance.

Connor's heart exploded with love when he felt his body become a part of hers. It was a sensory overload, and never had he felt such emotion when making love. This was like touching the sun. Moaning out loud as the tidal wave of passion coursed through his veins, he was scaling previously unknown heights of sexual euphoria. He was drowning in her love, sinking under its power until he found it almost impossible to breathe. Connor tried to keep his thrusts slow and soft until he felt Gabby reaching for more, then he felt her open like a flower to the sun.

When he felt her hips lift towards him, asking for more, wanting all of him, he let self-control slip away and trusted his body to speak to hers. It was a whirlpool that lifted them up together, higher and higher until oxygen thinned. Then, when it felt like they might die, they climaxed together and slowly drifted back to a new world.

With their bodies wrapped around each other as the soft afterglow encased them, their breathing slowed, but they kept touching and caressing any exposed skin that their hands could still reach.

Connor had never experienced such feelings before. The wonder of making love to her felt like his world had tilted, and his whole perception of sex was forever changed. This was not just copulating, it was a joining of two souls; this night, they had married their minds and bodies. He knew he would never love another woman the way he had just loved Gabby. It was more like loving a creature of the divine.

Gabby was half awake, half asleep, wrapped up with contentment. She had never felt more like a woman than this moment. It felt like she was a goddess with a worshipper wrapped around her, and the power of sex exceeded her wildest imaginings. Smiling with exhilaration, she knew that Connor had enjoyed it just as much, as his shouts of gratification had been as loud as her own.

They fell asleep exactly the way they were, wrapped up together like a gift on the sofa.

Connor woke as the first rays of light flooded the room. He lay there cherishing the weight of her laying on top of him until she opened her sleepy green eyes. 'Come with me,' he said.

Once they had disentangled themselves off the couch, he took her hand to lead her into the shower and tenderly washed every part of her body. Exploring her beautiful sleek lines, he couldn't find one blemish on her, not one mole or freckle, just silky golden skin enclosing her exquisite frame.

Gabby did the same to him and found endearing little scars. 'Is this a scar or birthmark?' she asked as she examined an irregular mark on his butt cheek.

'The Faradene brand. Every male Faradene in the last one hundred years has been born with the same birthmark. One day, our son will bear the same.'

Gabby blushed pink at his claim to a future son.

After showering, they fell into the softness of his king-size bed and made love all over again. Gabby could not believe how much she enjoyed sharing these sensual delights with Connor. Her fear and loathing seemed ridiculous now that she could look at it all from the other side; this experience was not related in any way to Andy Bolton's violation of her body. Connor was like a devotee coming to worship at the temple, and she found she was equally besotted with his athletic male physique. As she lay in the tangled sheets, tingling and yet totally relaxed, she watched Connor get up and go into his dresser to retrieve a small box.

'This is just a small token of my devotion Gabby.' He held out the box to her.

Opening the lid, she saw a beautiful emerald ring. 'It's very beautiful, but I can't accept this, Connor.'

'Why not? I love you and want to spoil you a little.'

'I'm not the type of woman who expects to be showered in gifts. You know I value a simple life,' she explained, trying not to hurt his feelings.

'Just this once then, Gabby, to celebrate our relationship, please?'

'Just this once then,' she relented and slipped the exquisite ring onto her right hand. Green and blue shards of light sparkled in the depths.

'When I saw it, I was reminded of your eyes. It doesn't really match nor do them justice, but I don't think anything could.'

'It's stunning, Connor,' she smiled as he leaned to gently kiss her on the forehead.

They were back to work the next morning, so Gabby woke early to go back home. Connor walked her to her car and kissed her deeply through the driver's window before she pulled away into the traffic.

Both were oblivious to an interested onlooker who watched their every move with murder in her eyes.

Gina had planned to drop into Connor's apartment to see if she could interest him in having breakfast with her before work. She had been stopped in her tracks when she saw Connor walk out with that stunningly gorgeous woman and kiss her. They were now intimate, she could tell just by their body language that they had become lovers.

It had made her temper flare to see her lifelong plans being wiped out by one passionate kiss. *I could strangle her with my own bare hands,* Gina thought to herself as she turned around and strode quickly back to her car. Leaning against the gleaming black bonnet, she called a friend. 'Gavin, I need to talk to you. Can you meet me for breakfast at that café in Market Street? You can, good, see you in about half an hour.'

She sat in the car tapping the steering wheel as the cogs in her overactive brain went into motion. *I need to find a way to stop this. Think, Gina.*

But, with no inspiration forthcoming, she revved the expensive car's engine in fury and merged with the morning traffic. Arriving at the café first, Gina ordered for them both and sat sipping her expresso while she waited for Gavin to hurry in.

Good old Gavin, he was better than a girlfriend, a good-looking guy who thought like a woman, so it was the best of both worlds. Gavin was gay and had been Gina's best friend since high school.

He walked in dressed impeccably in a light grey pinstriped suit, and every woman watched him cross the room to sit with Gina. 'Hello, darling, what's up? Frowning again? If you keep this up, you'll wrinkle that beautiful face prematurely.'

'Thanks for meeting me, Gavin. I'm in a pickle and need your advice and maybe help with this one.'

Gavin raised his eyebrows in question.

Gina looked him over. Gavin was from a wealthy family, but not as rich as Connor's. Gina wanted to be married into the richest family in the country. She wanted the power that came with such prestige, and nothing else would do.

Even though he would never be enough for her, Gavin was good looking, almost six feet tall, with blonde hair, blue eyes and a nice athletic build. He was a decent catch for a man or woman.

'Well, come on then, spit it out.' Gavin had no idea the direction her thoughts had been taking her, he just thought she was procrastinating.

'Did I tell you Connor has a new girlfriend?' she began.

'No, you know I only just got back from Europe two days ago. So, who is she and how did you let that happen?'

'I didn't let it happen. Connor made it happen without even telling me. He saw her on television saving some pathetic whales, and it seems he has fallen under her spell.'

'Whales? Do you mean to say he is dating Gabrielle Harrison, the environmentalist everyone is talking about? Lucky Connor,' he raised his eyebrows again.

'Gavin! Show some loyalty to me please.' Gina punched his arm in mock protest.

'Okay, Gina. Tell me all about it.'

'I called Connor to confirm we were going to the Leukemia Ball, and he dropped this bombshell on me. For three years we have been seeing each other and instead of a proposal, I get dumped.' Gina's face suffused red at the insult.

'That must have been a shock. Do you think he was as invested in the relationship as much as you were?'

'Of course, we were heading towards matrimony until she came into the picture. Now I have to somehow get Connor to ditch her instead of me.' Gina narrowed her green eyes with a hint of menace.

Gavin moved their coffee cups aside and took both of her hands to give them a squeeze.

'It's alright, love. I'm sure Connor will see you are the woman for him.'

'Maybe you're right, but I'll do whatever it takes to remove her from his life.'

'God, you sound like the bloody exterminator: "I will do whatever it takes!"' he mimicked.

'Gavin are you going to help or make fun of me?' Her voice dripped with venom.

'Of course I'll help you, darling. We go way back, after all. Why don't you visit where she grew up and dig up some dirt to tarnish her glossy image? Then Connor might think twice about being too close to a scandal. It's worth a try,' he soothed her seething temper.

'Maybe you're right. It might be worth going back to her home town, check out her local identity.' Gina's mind had switched gears, going from murderer to investigator.

'If anyone can ruin a reputation, it's you, Gina. Now, have you told your mother about my new range? I want to get it into her store.'

'Gavin, you'll have to ask her for yourself. Anyway, I must go and pretend to be interested in the family business. You'll pay for the coffee, won't you?' Gina kissed him on the top of his head and floated out of the busy café.

It was Gavin's turn to sigh. What a high-maintenance filly Gina could be. She had always been a good friend, but he felt sorry for anyone who got in her way when she wanted something.

In his mind, he sent a message of warning to this Gabrielle Harrison. *May the angels protect you from the wrath of Gina Perry.*

He gave the money to the cute male waiter. *Oh, if only I was eighteen again,* he thought as he walked outside into the wintery morning.

The more you knew about your enemy the better prepared you were to ruin them, so Gina found herself reading every snippet of information she could find about Gabrielle Harrison. Most of it was textbook success, an honour student, passionate environmentalist. It all stacked up to 'Little Miss Perfect'.

One article written after the whale rescue mentioned she had grown up in Cairns, so Gina decided to make a trip to north Queensland to see if there was any muck to be found. Gina landed in Cairns and nearly fell backwards when she stepped out of the airport. It was like stepping into a sauna.

She dragged the bright silk scarf from around her throat, already feeling the sweat trickling down her back and gathering moisture between her breasts. *Why would anyone want to live in this godforsaken climate*, she thought as she swept royally into a cab and ordered him to take her to the Shangri-La Hotel.

The blast of air conditioning eased the panic of the cloistering heat a little. Gina checked in and once in her suite she stripped off to lay naked on the king-size bed, affording herself the pleasure of imagining life as Connor's wife.

Gina was already from a wealthy family, but it was the power that came from old money that she craved. Plus, Connor owed her. It was the time she would never get back, and it all couldn't come to nothing more than a fling.

Also, her pride had been slighted. Didn't he understand that nobody said 'no' to Gina Perry? Being an only child, she had never experienced the companionship of a sibling or learnt the skills of sharing. Everything was hers, there for the taking, and the world looked after strong, manipulative people like her. Bleeding hearts were soft, and Gina despised their compassion; humans were like animals and sometimes there had to be collateral damage.

History showed that the arrogant and strong were the ones who were written about for future generations to read.

I will literally choke the life out of her if I have to. I'll kill her with my bare hands if I can't get her out of Connor's life any other way, Gina vowed as her heart burned with revenge and contempt for Gabrielle Harrison.

After some refreshments, Gina dressed for the tropics and ventured into the oppressive tropical heat to tackle her quest. The best car available was a Ford Astra soft-top, which she wound down to let wind lift the long red hair off her perspiring neck.

The GPS navigated her to the destination, and even Gina could not fail to note the beautiful countryside. The mountains were so close she felt she could almost reach out and touch the lush green canopy, and it was so green that it hurt her eyes.

However, no matter how scenic the landscape was, it was the weather that Gina found crippling. She couldn't stop sweating, and even just thinking about it made her sweat more.

Driving into San Remo, Gina disdainfully dismissed the rudimentary housing. How could anyone be content to live so small? She could fit most of these cottages into her own living room! It was a joke that someone raised in these circumstances could ever think she was good enough to marry a Faradene.

That he could even consider this was so foreign to her. Gina had always thought Connor was the same as her, and that they were suited to each other. They spoke the same language, the words of wealth and privilege, just as their friends did.

She pulled up at the small café on the beach and was thankful for the cooling breeze blowing off the water. Ordering a juice, she smiled encouragingly at the girl serving behind the counter. Calling her over for another drink, Gina did her best to encourage the local to talk.

This potential source of information was a pretty Islander girl, about nineteen years old, with lovely white teeth and long, curly black hair. Gina leaned in, speaking softly to make a connection with this naïve unassuming local. 'What's your name, sweetheart?'

'Selina,' the girl replied.

'Selina, I'm a friend of Gabrielle Harrison's, and my family has recently donated a lot of money to her environmental work. I have a feeling that she grew up somewhere around here. Is there any chance you know her?'

'Everyone at San Remo knows Gabby. She's our local celebrity, and we're proud of the all the good things she's been doing in Melbourne. Did you see her save the whales on television? She's so beautiful, like an angel, don't you think?' Selina said.

'Oh yes, she is the most beautiful woman in the world, and we all love her in Melbourne too. It must be this place, to grow in a paradise like this, where everyone is so kind and lovely around here,' Gina innocently stated.

'Not always,' Selina murmured.

Just then the café manager called out that there were orders waiting to be served. Gina caught hold of Selina's arm before she moved away. 'Selina, I'm staying here for a few days and would love a local guide to show me around,' slowly blinking with wide-eyed innocence.

'I'm not sure if I would have time with my job and everything,' the young woman stalled.

'How about I pay you $1000 for a day of showing me some of the sights.' Gina smiled in a friendly fashion to disarm the small-town young woman.

'That's an awful lot of money. Are you sure?' she asked hopefully. Gina didn't hesitate to offer silver to this yet unwitting traitor.

'Absolutely. How about I meet you here tomorrow and you can show me all the haunts that my best friend Gabrielle enjoyed when she lived here.' So they agreed to meet at 8 a.m. the next morning.

Gina dragged herself out of bed early the next day and was waiting for Selina when she walked up to the beach café. They spent the morning visiting the places where Gabby grew up: the tiny house, the school she went to, even where Old Joe's beach cottage was situated on the beachfront. And the beach water tower where Gabby and Eddie had often hung out together.

By lunchtime, Gina felt she had won the young woman's trust, so she suggested they stop for a break. To seal the deal, Gina passed over the envelope of cash and then manipulated the conversation around to Gabby and her unblemished upbringing.

'Growing up here is beautiful, but sometimes even in paradise bad things can happen,' Selina said as she bit into her toasted sandwich.

Gina pretended she knew about Gabby. 'Especially poor Gabby,' she said with more than a hint of empathy as she smiled vindictively inside.

'So, you know, then. Yes, poor thing. It was horrible when she got attacked by Andy Bolton all those years ago.'

'Oh yes, that was tragic. How did it happen again? Gabby did tell me about the attack years ago, but I've forgotten how bad it was,' Gina cunningly tricked Selina.

'It was a long time ago when Andy Bolton raped and beat Gabby almost to death, and then her best friend Eddie got sent to jail. He kind of accidently killed one of the boys involved in Gabby's assault. There was such an outcry because those kinds of crimes just never happen here.'

'What happened to Andy Bolton?' Gina asked with just the right amount of horror and sympathy in her voice.

'Well, that's part of the mystery. They found his bones in the bush, but nobody really knows what killed him.'

Gina sat there shocked. This was far too much to absorb in a hurry. An unexpected titbit that should be mulled over, enjoyed and savoured like a sip of fine wine, a moment too glorious to rush through.

I wonder how much Connor knows? A slow, malicious smile spread across her smooth face, while her eyes twinkled with evil ambitions.

Doing her best to hide her eagerness, Gina sympathetically extracted every delicious morsel out of this triumphant surprise. Once she was satisfied there was no more, she abruptly ended their little rendezvous.

Selina was surprised there wasn't more to do for her generous fee, but Gina was in a hurry to get back to the hotel. She couldn't wait to start spinning her web. All she had to do was speak a few words to the right person to change the public perception of Ms Perfect Harrison. Selling everyone an unblemished, pure image when she was actually soiled goods with a close friend in jail for murder.

An enchanted paradise teeming with rapists and murderers, that's how she would portray 'Gabby's' homeland. With no need to linger any longer in this backwater, Gina couldn't wait to get out of the claustrophobic humidity.

The next day, she sighed with relief when her black Audi slipped back into the chaos of Melbourne traffic.

Over dinner that night, she summarised her goals and objectives. Her number one priority was to marry Connor – her number one problem was that he thought he was in love with that hillbilly, so her number one solution was to publicly humiliate her and make Connor reconsider his choice.

Gina was a firm believer that one makes their own good luck. Just like yesterday, who could have thought it would be so easy to expose such gruesome facts on Connor's lovely, fresh debutante?

Gina was proud of her disconnection to any conscience. She was ice inside and out, with no regrets for the casualties that got in her way. Love made people weak and vulnerable, and even her parents didn't evoke any sentimental feelings. *The world is mine and so is everything in it*, was her motto.

It may take a while for her plans to fall into place, but it was all about the right timing. Gina was confident the opportunity would come and when it did, she wouldn't hesitate to grab it with both hands.

The time did come, even sooner than she could have hoped, when two weeks later she was having lunch with Gavin. They were laughing and chatting when a brown hand dropped onto Gavin's broad shoulder.

'Hello, old friend. I haven't seen you for ages.'

'Marcus Walsh, you old devil. Are you still sneaking around and listening at doors?'

Marcus Walsh was the editor of the gossip column for *The Age* newspaper. He laughed at Gavin's little dig and winked at Gina in a conspiratorial fashion. 'I know you're one of my avid fans, Gavin, so why do you protest?'

Just then Gavin's phone started to buzz, and he excused himself to take the call.

'Gina, darling,' Marcus purred as he slid into Gavin's vacant seat.

'Marcus, it is providence that we should run into each other to-day. I would love to have a little chat with you. I've a very tasty morsel for your column.'

'Beautiful, Gina, the belle of Melbourne society. I always have an open-door policy for ladies with your kind of connections.'

'Then let's meet tomorrow at the Coffee Grinder on Collins Street at 10 a.m.'

'Sounds good to me, Gina. see you then. By the way, tell the old boy that I have to run along and will catch him in the not-too-distant future.' As he said this, they both glanced outside to watch Gavin speaking intently on his mobile phone.

Gina smiled at her accomplice as she sipped her coffee, heart fluttering with excitement to see her plans deliciously drop into place.

'Don't you look like a cat who has just bathed in a bowl of cream,' Gavin said quizzically when he came back to their table.

Gina just grinned in response.

The next morning the day dawned bleak, cold and raining, more like a winter day than autumn. Melbourne had such inclement weather – sunny one minute and then cold and raining the next.

At the Coffee Grinder, Gina ordered and waited for her first move in the game against Gabrielle Harrison. Marcus breezed into the café and kissed her on the cheek, saying, 'Hello, lovely lady.'

After a gratifying sip of his own brand of poison, he pressed his fingers together and waited for Gina to begin.

Savouring the moment, she had been waiting for since that afternoon at San Remo beach, Gina moved her eyes over Marcus noting his appearance. He was a man of average height with a medium build, dark hair and greyish blue eyes, and he had a network of wrinkles resurfacing from his last Botox treatment. 'Marcus, I have a little expose for you.'

Marcus nodded to encourage her to begin.

'Have you seen the environmentalist Gabrielle Harrison on TV saving the whales?'

'Of course. Hasn't everybody?'

'Well, I have a newsworthy update for you.'

As Gina spoke, Marcus leaned in closer, suddenly keen to hear all the juicy details.

.

Fourteen

The gossipy article went to print in Thursday's edition of *The Age*, and it was Elisabeth who read it first. Hurrying over to Carlton Cottage as the sun was peeking over the horizon, she pushed her key into the door to find the Titans on guard duty. Going straight to the kitchen, she put the coffee on and sat at the table to wait.

'Goodness, Lissy, you're here early.' Gabby yawned as she stumbled towards the coffee pot. Once she had a steaming mug in hand, she sat down eyeing a suspiciously quiet Elisabeth. Something was up. She knew it wasn't good when Elisabeth took her hands away from the cup and put it carefully on the table.

Holding Gabby's hands tightly in her own, she explained the reason for this dawn visit. 'Gabby, something was written in the gossip column about you, something very hurtful and untrue. I wanted to be with you when you read it and know that we will fight this for defamation of character.'

Gabby felt her heart flutter as she read through the column, looking for her name in print, and there it was at the very end, almost thrown in like an afterthought. '*BTW, one must feel sorry for the poor environmentalist Gabrielle Harrison. Did you know she was beaten and raped at just seventeen years old and that her best friend has been in jail for murder! OMG, how does she look just so perfect, especially after these dread-ful experiences? My heart goes out to her.'*

There it was, her pain and suffering exposed to the whole country in just a couple of sentences. Gabby always knew it would come out someday. Coming to Melbourne for a fresh start was not like going to the other side of the world, especially now the world was getting smaller by the day. She had never explained to her friends here why Eddie was in jail, and they were always too polite to ask. The tears welled in her eyes as she brought them up to meet Lizzy's worried frown.

'We will fight this fool, Gabby. I will have him grovelling in court for the damaging trash he writes.'

'Lissy! It's true. This did happen to me, so we have no case against Marcus Walsh or his paper.'

'No, Gabby, no. Who could do this to you? No, that's all wrong!' Elisabeth got up and began to pace the room, her hand pressed against her forehead, which she always did when she was stressed about something. 'Why didn't you ever tell us?'

'I didn't tell you because I wanted to forget that day had ever happened. It almost destroyed my life, and it ruined Eddie's. With so much historical distress, it isn't something I wanted to remember or talk about.'

Lissy came back to the table and took Gabby's numb hands in her own again. 'Oh my God, I can't believe this happened to you. Know-ing you've carried this burden, this suffering all alone, it breaks my heart. Gabby.'

'It's okay, Lissy. Yes, it was horrible, and I could never have gotten this far without Joe and the love and support of my family. But I am very thankful to have you and my friends at my side now.' Gabby tearfully squeezed Lissy's hands.

Both women moved into the lounge room to sit side by side with the dogs at their feet.

Gabby kept reading the article repeatedly in her mind, almost wishing it away by concentrating all her energy on it.

Watching her with a worried expression Elisabeth suggested, 'Maybe you should stay away from the office for a few days until the publicity settles down? We can protect you from any further humiliation, so let us be your champions.' She hugged her friend tightly as her eyes spilled tears.

'No, I won't hide. I have run away from this long enough, and I will speak on my own behalf. I just wonder how this guy discovered the story after so many years, and why now?'

There was a knock on the front door and Gabby opened it to Connor's outstretched arms. 'Gabby, I am so sorry. How did that bastard find out?'

She snuggled into his strength and mumbled against his shoulder that she had no idea.

Joe came back from his morning walk, looking quizzically at Elisabeth and Connor there so early. 'Is everything alright?'

'Joe, you need to look at this.' Elisabeth led him back into the kitchen, where Gabby's coffee sat cold on the table. Joe leaned over to read the paper, and his wrinkles intensified as he frowned in anger. He scrunched the paper into a ball of print.

'This is a violation of privacy, isn't it, Elisabeth?' he seethed.

'Not if it's true, Joe. Then there is nothing we can do, except protect Gabby,' she sorrowfully explained.

Gabby led Connor back to the couch and held tightly onto his hands.

'Gabby, you must know I didn't tell anyone,' he whispered.

'Connor, I never thought it was you. I know you would never hurt me like this. Our work does generate opposing voices, and none of us can predict where they will strike.'

Just then Ben burst into the room. 'Gabby, are you okay?' He pulled her off the couch and into his arms. 'Is this true?' Ben always felt she had suffered a great trauma. He didn't want it to be so, but he instinctively already knew she carried the burden of past pain.

'Ben, I think you already know the answer to that question.' Gabby leaned back to look into his concerned blue eyes.

'Gabby, I'm bloody murderous. I want to kill that piece of scum. Who is he and where is he now?'

'Ben, please calm down. It happened years ago, and vengeance is why Eddie has spent some of the best years of his life in prison. Let it go. It was a bad thing, but I am still alive and moving forward. I don't want anyone else to get hurt because of me.'

Connor watched the raw pain etched into Ben's face and felt sorry for him. How hard would it be to love someone this much and not have it reciprocated? Personally, he had never experienced unrequited love and now saw its raw cruelty. It must be the same agony revisited repeatedly, and he wondered why Ben just didn't run as far as he could. It must be like having a drug addiction, no matter how much it hurt you, you just couldn't let it go.

Old Joe came in with a tray of fresh coffee and suggested they all sit down and talk. 'Gabby, do you want me to at least tell everyone what happened that day?'

Gabby nodded her permission and sat with the cuff of her dressing gown pressed against her mouth.

Joe told her friends in a pragmatic way what had happened that fateful day, and he didn't embellish it or take away from the horror either. In respect to his promise to the people of the red land, he omitted the part of the Spirit Ants. He explained that Andy Bolton had been fatally attacked by a host of wild animals. Then he finished up by telling them what had happened when Jacob, Thomas and Eddie had confronted John and Mick.

There was silence in the room, and all eyes were on Gabby as she sat there with no expression on her face. It was just blank.

Gabby was far away. She could feel the scratches from the stones under her back and Andy's hot, sweaty body pressing down on her as he whispered words of hate into her ears. The panic that he was going to hurt her and the inability to push him away, she could still feel the burning pain of his sexual invasion. The tearing force of his attack and the stinging pain when he cut her savagely. Even the salty taste of blood in her mouth. It was so vivid that suddenly Gabby was there again, reliving the suffering. Until with a shudder she forced herself to came back to the present, unstuffing the fabric out of her mouth and looking up at Connor to reconnect with real love. She needed this love to combat the loathing that was spreading throughout her mind. His love had changed everything, she knew this, and sought the warmth like sunflowers turn to the sun.

When Connor wrapped his arms around her, she sobbed her relived pain against his shoulder. Then Ben came over and kneeled beside them, wrapping his body around her back to offer his love and support as well.

Their bodies looked like two hands held in prayer with Gabby in the middle, until her sobs slowly ceased. Afterwards, they sat on either side of her on the couch with the Titans close by, and Gabby was surrounded by love.

Joe cleared his throat and asked Elisabeth about the best way to tackle this problem.

It was good to hear Elisabeth's voice talking about a strategy. It cleared the air and brought them back to a sane world again.

'If Gabby wants to confront this truth, I suggest we acknowledge that this did happen years ago. There is no point in denying it, so I say we use the exposure to show how well she has coped and made her life count for something important. We show the world how she has turned something so negative into a successful positive. We can turn this spiteful hurt into helping other victims. By accepting TV and radio interviews we acknowledge the assault and turn the tide. Are you up to it, Gabby?'

Gabby just nodded. Inside, she hoped her heart could withstand the torment of so many knowing her painful past. Could she maintain her composure as the world picked through the horror of that day, examining the wounds she had locked deep within her soul? She prayed for strength to face the trials ahead.

Everyone broke up and started their day in earnest. At the society, the phones were already ringing hot with requests for comments on the Walsh exposé.

Elisabeth fielded all the calls and gave comments as agreed upon. She also set up an interview with Radio 4BC and another one on the breakfast show.

Gabby dug deep within herself, sharing her pain with strangers. She didn't deny the trauma; instead, she acknowledged how it had significantly changed everything. She spoke out about the depression and how she had wanted to end her life during this dark time, but despite the damage, it was possible to find love again.

Over the weeks and months, she became an ambassador for abused women. Those who never followed The Greater Good's environmental causes now related to Gabby as they had also suffered and felt the common need to survive and recover as she had.

Letters flooded in with heartbreaking stories of victims telling Gabby of their own experiences. Gabby took time to write to every one of the victims, telling them she understood the sadness, the feelings of shame and betrayal. She encouraged them not to give up on life, explaining that with patience and love they could move on despite the suffering inflicted on them. 'You can either stay a victim and let the assault rule your life or you can use the suffering to make you stronger, make you more empathetic, make you more human.'

Gina ground her teeth in fury when she saw that instead of humiliating her enemy, she had only made her more popular and loved by the masses. Connor only adored her more, and it was plain to see how her close friends and family rallied to protect her from any negative exposure.

How could one person have such an effect on so many? It just wasn't fair, but her Botoxed-tight face could not even frown properly. Her last treatment was still fresh and no matter how angry she felt, Gina's face remained smooth. Her glossy red hair stuck to her tears of frustration as she kicked the bathroom vanity door repeatedly.

I hate her so much, she thought to herself. *I am going to destroy her, even it kills me,* Gina promised her reflection in the mirror.

Blood For Glory

Fifteen

The Mornington Peninsular was a coastal community almost two hours' drive south of Melbourne, with rolling hills that led to the ocean, the rich soil and cold climate creating perfect conditions for wine producers.

The vines now sat barren beneath the moody winter skies, seemingly already dead, so it was hard to imagine that these twisted brown branches could produce a blood-red juice that sang a song of joy on the taste buds.

To any passer-by, The Grateful Vine looked as legitimate as any other winery in the region. No one would suspect the sinister plans being made within the sandstone brick building nestled in the lush scenery.

On this bleak day, a group of religious zealots gathered to plot Gabby's disaster. 'It's time to make our first move.' Dominic rubbed his raspy chin and gazed at the rain falling softly outside.

Those gathered belonged to a secret group spoken of as The Omega Guild, for they believed that as God was the Alpha power, the first to rule, they would be the Omega power – the last enduring force to reign over the realms. The guild was a secular order that was only known to the most devoted and zealous followers. The few who entered these 'Hallowed Gates of Hell' were a secret force in service of the dark priesthood.

The Omega Guild had stood unchallenged for many years after their powers had destroyed the most powerful priests sent by the Vatican. These priests had been oaks in the Christian faith, but they could not, however, stand against the tsunami of evil that had swept over them.

The fallen angels were preparing for battle, and they planned to seize the City of Angels for their own regime. The last time Lucifer's grab for power had failed, he'd had no choice but to sign the treaty of exclusion. Defeated and disgraced, Lucifer and his followers were exiled into the realm of men.

Now the Morning Star was transforming his decay to glory, and the treaty was weakening. When he returned victorious, the guild would share in his triumph and rewards.

Dominic was the leader of this guild branch, and he relished the task ahead. Destroying Gabrielle Harrison would quench the thirst for revenge that raged in his shrivelled heart. For months, he and Jinn had schemed to form their elaborate plan, and now they were ready to begin.

Several black-robed men sat in the warm office whispering quietly to each other. They were waiting for their master to continue. Dominic's scarred face swivelled towards those in the room, and it seemed like those melted sockets really did have eyes as the room became strangely quiet.

'Nigel, I want you to meet with Marcus Walsh, find out how he is involved and then remove him,' Dominic commanded.

'Yes, master. I will do this today,' Nigel obediently agreed.

'That will be all for today.' Dominic dismissed them.

Black robes swished across the floor as they left the room.

The sightless man turned towards the window, looking at the view from his destroyed face. He didn't see the green hills stretching down to the ocean; instead, he saw the future and savoured the reward that would one day be his.

Deliver Gabrielle Harrison to Lucifer and his eyesight would be restored.

The downtown high-rise building of *The Age* newspaper allocated a tiny corner of the vast office to Marcus Walsh and his assistant. They had a view of the notice board, but there were no windows for the gossip columnist.

His assistant grabbed Marcus's diary off his desk to check a suitable time. 'Are you there'? she asked into the silent headset sitting over her ear, yet all she could hear was rapid breathing.

'Hello, are you there?' she asked again.

'Yes, I'm here.' The cold, deadpan voice shivered across her skin.

'Marcus is free next Monday morning until 10 a.m. if you would like to make an appointment?'

'Yes, Monday morning is suitable.'

'How about nine? Do you want to come to his office in the city?'

'No, certainly not in his office. My information is much too sensitive to discuss in your presence.'

The assistant rolled her eyes at the drama. Marcus wrote a gossip column, not exactly ASIO intelligence.

'I suggest we meet at the museum right beside the Pharlap racehorse display.'

'Yes, but how will he recognise you.'

'Tell him I will carry my suit jacket over my right arm and a black umbrella under my left.'

'Okay, but before you go, can I get a phone contact, please.'

'No, certainly no phone contact, only person to person.'

There was a dull click and all communication ceased.

Well, that guy was all cloak and dagger, was her last thought before scrawling the message on the despised notice board.

As planned, the following Monday morning Marcus Walsh was waiting beside the embalmed racehorse looking for Mr Secretive. *Bet he's changed his mind and chickened out!*

A lot of people had grand ideas of spreading gossip but at the last moment they had a sudden change of heart. Just as he was turning away to head back to his car, he spotted a man striding towards him with his jacket and umbrella assigned as promised.

Marcus was a great observer of people, and he quickly noted interesting points of this person's appearance. He was a small man with a shiny bald head and something about him that looked weird. Then he realised what was different: he had no eyebrows, no eyelashes, not a single stray hair to be seen anywhere. He resembled an unfinished doll, one that the maker had forgotten to add the final touches to make it look more human.

Marcus nodded his recognition, and the man rolled his eyes to signal Marcus to follow him. He briskly walked outside the museum building and into the coffee shop to purchase two coffees. Marcus was surprised to see that the man ordered Marcus's coffee exactly the way he liked it – extra hot latte on soy with no sugar. It was interesting that he had done his homework.

Marcus tried to build some rapport and strike up a conversation while they waited but the odd little man just frowned at him and shook his head, making it clear he wasn't here to be friendly.

Once the coffee was ready, the small man turned and strode across the parkland with Marcus trailing behind him. He walked quite a distance until he found a secluded park bench under an enormous weeping willow, its branches almost screening them from public eye.

He sat and nodded for Marcus to sit beside him and passed him his coffee, and here they sat in silence with their drinks. Marcus was determined not to be the first to start talking. The sun was trying to instil some warmth into the day, but the morning chill crept through their clothing, so it certainly made the hot drink very welcome.

Several minutes passed before the man's eyes turned to him, and Marcus felt pinned as bloodshot eyes held him steady. He felt like an animal cornered with no escape, and he cleared his throat to remind himself that this was his interview. It was his privilege to toy with informants, to draw things out and make them squirm.

However, before he could take any semblance of control, his ears were assaulted by a voice so cold that it sent shivers up his spine, a coolness that had nothing to do with the outside temperature.

'Tell me what you know about Gabrielle Harrison.'

This innocuous question made his skin crawl and the coffee curdle in his stomach. The small man watched the sweat bead on his upper lip and could almost hear the gurgling.

Marcus's eyes widened in alarm as his heart began to beat faster. If he had paid attention to this intuition, it may have saved his life. He cleared his throat again to gather his racing thoughts. 'Not very much at all to be honest. Only what everyone else knows about her.'

'What was the motive for your column?'

'Listen here, mate. I don't have to explain myself to you.'

'You don't seem to understand me,' the small man whispered as his red eyes bored into Marcus's. 'Listen here, mate,' he mimicked. 'I will give you one more chance to co-operate. Why did you write an article to ruin the reputation of Gabrielle Harrison?'

Marcus shook his head in refusal then he groaned aloud in agony. An excruciating pain struck his temples. It felt like someone was sticking hot pokers through his ears directly into the sides of his brain, and he shook his head trying to dispel the agony.

'Did you do that? How?' Marcus stared at the stranger in horror.

The little man nodded once and asked his question again,

This time Marcus didn't hesitate to explain that he had no interest in the environmentalist, save having material for his column.

'Look, I'm sorry if I have pissed you off. I know she's popular with the masses due to the whaling campaign and when I was given this intelligence about her past, it was too good to pass up. I didn't mean to upset anyone this much. It's only gossip for God's sake.' But Marcus knew he was in deep trouble.

'Who gave you the intelligence?'

Marcus babbled, as he was genuinely scared. 'Gina Perry. She hates Gabrielle.'

The little man stood up and placed his hand on Marcus Walsh's chest, then looked him at him and said, 'Thank you.'

Without warning, Marcus's heart suddenly stopped beating, and like a blind being drawn down over the sun, the world he called his own became no more.

He remained there unnoticed until a gardener saw him late in the afternoon. 'Hello, mister. Are you okay? Can you hear me?'

Marcus's head was slumped back against the park bench, and the coffee cup had fallen onto the grass at his feet. When he was unresponsive, the gardener rushed back to the museum to call the ambulance. He stood by while the first responders checked for a pulse on the now-chilled body.

'Sorry, mate, he's long gone,' they told the gardener as they lifted the body onto a stretcher and placed it in the back of the ambulance. Marcus would be taken to the morgue where a post-mortem examination would conclude the cause of death was a sudden heart attack.

Sixteen

Gina pressed the remote to lock her car and walked across the car park to the lift, but by the time the elevator arrived she was nowhere in sight. She never saw the black car approaching from behind, and the abduction was over in seconds.

With her mouth covered by plastic tape and her hands held tightly by zip ties, she was roughly thrown into the back seat of a sleek black car before it sped away into the evening traffic. *Was this because of her expose on Gabrielle Harrison? Did one of those environmentalists intend to cause her harm, maybe even kill her?*

The drive seemed to go on forever with neither of the men uttering a sound, no matter how much noise she made trying to escape. Gina kicked the door over and over again in desperation to get out. *I don't want to die*, she screamed inside her head.

When the car finally stopped, she sat up to look out of the window to see they were at the Sorrento Hotel, sighing in relief that it was a public forum and not some remote slaughterhouse.

One of the men came around to drag her out of the car. They removed the tape, which stung her lips, and cut the zip ties.

'Don't make a scene or it will end badly,' one said as he showed her a gun under his robe.

Eyes wide with fear, she was silently led away, each man gently holding onto her elbow as if she were a dear friend. She was guided into a large room on the top level, which had floor- to-ceiling glass windows looking out over the troubled waters of the Pacific Ocean.

Her kidnappers let go of her arms and stepped back.

'Keep your filthy hands off me,' Gina spat at them as she quickly moved into the room, placing her hand over her sore lips and patting her hair back into place as she looked around for her abductor. In the gloomy light, the room seemed empty until she saw another man sitting at the table set for two.

'Please join me, Ms Perry. I apologise for the unchivalrous way to invite you for dinner, but I believe we have much to talk about.' His voice made the hairs on the back of her neck stand up and a chill run down her spine.

Taking tiny steps, Gina drew closer until even in the dim room she could see his face had been grotesquely burned. His eyelids had melted shut, a sight so horrible it made her gasp with shock and take a backward step. The disfigurement looked red, blistered and sore, and Gina fought not to scrunch her face in revulsion.

'Ms Perry, I understand this face is disturbing, but it is only the husk that you see, not the person inside. Please, come sit and share a meal with me.'

Instead of saying anything, she very carefully took her seat at the place set beside him as the bodyguards stepped forward to serve them dinner.

'This wine is from our vineyard. It has a delicate bouquet, which I hope you enjoy.'

'Yes, it is very nice,' she murmured as she brought the glass to her lips. 'But why am I here? Do you plan to kill me?' Gina whispered as she stared at the food placed in front of her.

'No Gina, I'm not going to hurt you. I just want to talk,' the man reassured her as he nibbled the food off his fork.

'About what?' Gina still hadn't tasted a morsel.

'About Gabrielle Harrison. I believe we may have a lot in common when it comes to her.' He almost smiled as she looked at him fully in the face for the first time.

'You know her?'

'Oh yes, very well. In fact, she is responsible for the damage done to my face.'

Gina sucked her breath in with a hiss. 'Oh my God, she did this?' Gina's cutlery fell from her hands to bounce off the table and onto the floor. She didn't bother to retrieve them but grasped the stranger's arm in shock. *Gabrielle Harrison did this? What kind of woman could inflict such debilitating wounds?*

'Sorry,' she said, releasing his arm. 'I never knew she was that dangerous.'

'Gabrielle Harrison is not what she appears to be.'

'What do you mean?'

'Well, let me tell you that she is not human as you and I are.'

Feeling suddenly dizzy, Gina held onto the side of the table as it skittered sideways. In a shaky voice she asked what he meant. 'What is she then? A fraud? Or did she try to blackmail you?'

'She is something you could never imagine, and together we can send her back to where she truly belongs.'

'Together? You want me to help you expose her.'

'I want you to help me destroy this usurper and anyone she loves.' He placed his hand over hers as he whispered his threat softly and menacingly.

'How? With your robot thugs?' Gina wanted to know just how powerful this man could be. She wasn't going to put herself at risk if he didn't have what it took to succeed.

'We have certain abilities that will guarantee our success,' the Guild master reassured her.

'Show me,' Gina pushed.

The stranger called one of his guards into the room and turned his missing eyes towards him. The man clutched at his throat as he gasped to draw a breath. His choking failed to make the stranger or Gina to come to his aid.

Gina was mesmerised that the guard was obviously choking to death and that the stranger had done this without even putting a hand on him.

The stranger turned back to Gina and allowed the guard to draw a breath. He now lay on the floor like a fish out of water, and it took several minutes before he could breathe normally again. He didn't complain or reproach his boss, he just sat up trying to regain his composure.

Gina smiled for the first time since she had been taken. 'If you can do that with your mind then I'm in, but on one condition,' she bargained.

'What condition is that?' Dominic asked.

'That you teach me to do that too. I want to be as powerful as you,' Gina demanded.

This time, he smiled.

There was a lot of discussion in the office when the news broke about Marcus Walsh's sudden death at the museum. They all agreed it wasn't a coincidence that he was dead after exposing Gabby's rape, but they couldn't settle on a motive. Why would someone punish him for the hateful words when it was obviously intended to damage her reputation. After much debate, they decided it was a mystery they may never solve.

The day began in earnest when they turned their attention to the business that was getting busier and busier. It seemed there were a lot of people prepared to embrace a simple life, small houses with minimal furnishings and shorter working hours, leaving time to invest in families, friends and their community. Many were determined to leave a lighter carbon footprint on the planet as building a sustainable future suddenly seemed a far more important aspiration.

Gabby knew there were many around the world who wanted to make a difference for the greater good.

That same afternoon, Father Gerry had asked Joe if he could meet him for coffee as he had something important to discuss.

Joe agreed to meet the priest at Lorenzo's on Little Collins Street, where he arrived first and placed the order. From his seat at the outdoor table, he had a good view of the busy city street and saw Father Gerry making his way towards him, smiling at those passing by.

The coffee arrived just as he dropped his large frame into the seat. He moved the cups to one side so that he could spread a newspaper article across the table. It was the story of the unforeseen death of one of the writers for the paper, Marcus Walsh, and his untimely demise.

'My good friend, Joe. How are you this fine afternoon? Glorious is it not.' Father Gerry often asked a question then answered it himself.

Joe smiled at this quirk and sipped his coffee.

Tapping the paper, Father Gerry asked if Joe had seen this story.

'Yes, Gerry, we've seen it.'

'Joe, this is the same person who wrote that gossip about Gabrielle, is it not?'

'Yes, it is, and I can see you are as concerned as I am. After what they did with Gabby, it wouldn't be that difficult to cause a heart attack. I just can't figure why would they eliminate him when he was intending to do Gabby an injury with his story?'

'I'm not sure about it at all, but I agree it is far too convenient. But I also wanted to see you about something else.'

'What is it, Gerry?'

'We are not alone in this battle, Joe. As you know, we have my old friend Father Ignacio in Rome working with us. He has been searching the scriptures to find a message from God, something we can use against the evil in this war. In his research, he discovered a passage in a dead sea scroll, one that hadn't made it into the holy bible. A prophecy that spoke of a final battle between the angels, which has been translated from ancient Hebrew into Latin on this long-forgotten papyrus. It was a miracle that he was able to find it in the archives, far from inquisitive eyes. But when he drew the scroll from its hiding place, he didn't hesitate to appropriate it for us.'

'What does it say? When will it get here?' Joe leaned closer towards his friend.

'I am not yet sure, but he assures me that the ancient parchment is being moved to us as we speak. He will send it through the church internal mail to keep it out of dangerous hands.'

'I would be very interested to see this, Gerry. It may give us clues on how to defeat these unearthly powers.'

'My thoughts as well, brother Joe.'

Joe stared across the street, hearing the whoosh of tyres when the cars sped by, in amongst small snippets of conversation from people walking along the street. To others they would appear as just two old men catching up for a coffee, perhaps discussing politics or retirement, but nobody would ever guess the danger they were really facing.

Seventeen

The day the scroll arrived, Father Gerry was working late in his office on the church grounds. He sighed deeply as he re-read the ancient message for the hundredth time, and getting up from his desk, he began to pace around the room.

From the first moment he unrolled the parchment, his stomach had begun to twist and turn, and it worried him that these words could cause such a physical reaction. What did it mean? Running his hands through his hair, he muttered in distress, 'Foedus deficiet cum claves qui dedecus emittit. Et tenebrae transibunt per orbem, et fluet mala intus per terras, transibunt per flumen sanguinis cum magno dolore et stridore dentium.'

Reading the Latin script again, he spoke it out loud to better understand it's meaning, 'The treaty will fail when he who is disgraced releases the keys. Then darkness will sweep across the world, and evil will flow through the lands in a river of blood causing great suffering and gnashing of teeth.'

Then there was more Latin, 'Tatum renascentis modos leviores qui ad hanc tenbras vincunt cogere possunt.' It translated as, 'Only the one who is reborn can muster the light bearers to defeat this darkness.'

The ancient scroll seemed to portent a rising of the beast from the chambers of hell... what did it mean 'he who is disgraced releases the keys?' It was a warning that a vast shadow would cover the lands, causing pain and tears for all nations.

The evil within the shadow would flow through a river of blood and cause great suffering.

But what did it mean by this? *'Only the reborn can muster the light bearers to defeat this darkness.'* Who is the reborn?

It seemed to warn of the devil and his minions wreaking havoc on the sons of man with the promise of one who could defeat him

Does this warning apply to now? Does it even mean anything after all this time?

Father Gerry fretted as he walked around, the whole time staring at the ancient document. Why did Father Ignacio believe it was relevant to Gabby and those who would do her harm? He would have to contact him urgently to discuss his translation of the prophecy, and he needed to show Joe. Maybe he would have some inkling to its meaning?

Stopping his musings, he paused to listen more carefully, turning his head towards the church when he heard a door slamming repeatedly. *Probably the wind,* he thought as he went to close it shut.

He saw the large door of the church hanging open, so he walked over to secure it, but in the night-time shadows he didn't see the intruders until it was too late.

Two large men dressed in black grabbed him from behind, and one of them put his hand over the priest's mouth to stop him raising the alarm. Once they had him within their grasp, they dragged him into the church and up to the pulpit where Dominic and Nigel were waiting.

'Retrieve the scroll,' Dominic instructed the men who had captured the priest.

'Father Gerry, I'm so glad you could join us.' Dominic smiled when he heard the priest draw air to fill his empty lungs.

The priest's eyes widened in shock when he saw the twisted scars where the man's eyes should have been. Was this the man Gabby had burnt to save Miranda?

Nigel stepped forward to restrain him with a hand on his chest. The priest could suddenly not move his arms or legs, no matter how much his brain told his limbs to run from the danger.

'Who are you and what are you doing in God's house?' he fumed.

'God's house? Where is he now? Show me your God and I will apologise for the intrusion,' Dominic taunted him.

'God does not need to show himself to you or anyone else to justify my faith,' the priest dropped his voice to a whisper.

'Faith. That is misplaced in a force who has gone to sleep, a deity who has only deaf ears to your prayers,' Dominic sneered.

'Why are you here? To insult my God in a house of prayer or are you looking for me?' Father Gerry demanded.

'Your meddling has come to our attention, and we don't want you getting any closer to the truth.'

'The truth is in the scroll, isn't it? But how did you know it was here?'

'We have powers that are not contained by walls and gates. You really have no idea, do you?' He stepped close to Father Gerry to taunt softly into his face. 'Forces like this!' Dominic turned to shout, 'Satanae servum ad me accerso.'

The wall wobbled in front of the priest, and a creature of the dark emerged with wings folded behind. It still stood taller than any man.

'Meet my shepherd, the glorious messenger of darkness, Jinn.'

The fallen angel, who was now a rotting, gnarled form, stepped forward to snarl at the priest, its sharp fangs only inches away from his face.

'Keep the scroll and remove him,' the odious creature hissed at Dominic.

'Now to stop your meddling in our affairs.' Dominic stepped back to nod at Nigel.

Nigel focused his mind to shut down the priest's heart but felt another power blocking him, no matter how hard he tried. There was a band of light shielding it from the darkness. They had him but they couldn't finish him off, and it had been a long time since The Omega Guild had faced such a powerful opposition.

'You can try to thwart us, but it will not work.' Dominic stood beside Nigel to spit the words into the priest's face.

Father Gerry stared defiantly into the twisted flesh. 'You will not win this war! Too many lives are at stake. I will let you win.' He growled deep in his throat and drew on the power of his faith.

Suddenly, in a flash of light, Nigel was thrown backwards across the room, slamming into the wooden pew and slumping motionless on the floor.

Dominic roared in frustration at the unexpected challenge.

'God is going to defeat you all. Darkness will not prevail,' Father Gerry shouted defiantly.

Dominic's nostrils flared at the sharp acidic scent of resistance, but instead of retreating, he taunted the priest with his own agenda. 'You may have this small victory, but we will win this war. Don't you see, you old fool, that your kind have been long gone, and now we hold the balance of power.' His voice echoing in the empty building was a calculated distraction as his hand very slowly reached for the short, sharp dagger inside his cloak.

But before Dominic had the opportunity to slash Father Gerry with his dagger, Jinn stepped closer to outstretch his arm and draw his talon across the priest's throat, spraying blood all over his dark, warped face.

Father Gerry's eyes widened in shock as his body collapsed to the ground, the blood flowing like a river down his robe while he gurgled his last bloody, bubbling breaths.

Dominic stood by calmly as he wiped the splatters of blood off his own face with a corner of his black robe.

Jinn caught hold of the priest's slumped body and spanning his darkened wings, he lifted him off the ground, flying high enough to drape the bloody corpse over the statue of Christ on the cross.

'You are now united with your God,' he spat into the priest's pale, lifeless face before descending once again.

Father Gerry's unseeing eyes looked out over the church he had served for so many years, and now martyred for his faith.

Jinn nodded at Dominic with satisfaction and disappeared once again through the solid stone wall.

Soon after, Nigel groaned as he slowly sat up, the room spinning around him.

'What the hell just happened?' he asked as he rubbed his hand over the back of his head to check for any blood.

'Our old friend remembered how to use his power and threw you across the room, but thanks to Jinn, it won't happen again.' Dominic's eyes looked up at the now-bloody cross.

Once Nigel was on his feet again, they walked through the red puddle on the church floor, leaving footprints along the aisle and out of the church.

The next morning, a grisly sight awaited the young priest at the parish of St John's. Opening the heavy wooden church doors, the young initiate went to prepare the morning mass. At first, he didn't notice the bloody footprints until he found the pool of blood congealing at the altar.

He was totally bewildered until he looked up and behind, where to his horror he saw his much-loved priest hanging on the cross, brutally murdered.

The unexpected gruesome site brought the young man to his knees moaning, 'No, no, this cannot be.' Screaming, he fled the church in another trail of blood-smeared footprints, calling for the gardener and nuns.

Upon arriving at the grisly scene, the nuns recoiled in shock. 'Oh God, it's our Father Gerry!' The nuns huddled before the altar in stunned dismay. 'What do we do?' They turned to the younger priest for guidance.

'Go in pairs to search the building and grounds while I call the police.' He stepped up to take charge.

When the police inspected the scene, they couldn't figure out how the priest had been raised so high. Then there was a significant delay as they had to get a hydraulic lift machine into the church to retrieve his body hanging off the cross.

The gash across Father Gerry's throat confirmed the cause of death, and in its brutal presence, the church staff whispered amongst themselves at this strange turn of events.

It didn't take long for word to spread throughout the close community that their beloved priest had met such a tragic end.

Joe arrived as soon as he heard the news. He comforted the young priest and coaxed him into telling him every detail. Had he heard any noises the night before? Had he seen anyone entering the church grounds? After realising the murder had taken place under a shroud of concealment, Joe slipped into Father Gerry's office to search for the Vatican scroll. But even after a thorough rummage, he found no trace of it.

Joe knew Father Gerry had been killed because of the scroll, and along with his sorrow, he was infuriated that evil had prevailed over good.

That night, Gabby was furious in her grief. If only she had all of her former powers, then she could punish those who had killed their dear friend. The pendant gave her extraordinary strength, but her body was still vulnerable to harm. Jinn would never have dared such a bold move if she was not weakened in her mortal state.

'Why don't you come for me?' she raged at the mirror. 'I am your enemy, not these good people around me.' Gabby almost willed Jinn or the cult to make a stand against her, even if it meant she had to end this life to save those she loved.

But no matter how much she welcomed a fight, those who wanted her dead remained silent. For now.

There was an enormous outpouring of grief at Father Gerry's funeral. His love for people had touched so many lives that the tears flowed down cheeks as they all stood before his casket. Gabby kissed each rose petal before placing them gently on his folded hands. She whispered softly into his calm, cold face, 'Dear friend, you deserve all of the rewards waiting for you.'

That night Gabby called Eddie. She needed to talk to her old friend and hear his voice again, to be reminded that life did sometimes give good news.

He happily shared his news about the building program he and Barry were working on, and how they had involved local youth to come on site to learn life skills. He shared with her the excitement of taking them fishing and how their newly forged football team was creating friends and a sense of community. It seemed he had found his purpose and was relishing his new life.

'How about you, Gabby? I've been talking so much about myself.'

'I'm a bit down just now to be honest. We lost a good friend this week, and I'm feeling very sad. But hearing about your new life has given me hope that sometimes bad situations can be turned around.'

'I'm so sorry, Gabby. Can you tell me what happened?'

Gabby told him about Father Gerry's murder without mentioning her suspicions. It was better that Eddie was kept out of all this trouble as she wanted to protect him from any danger.

'That's so gruesome, Gabby. Do you think they'll find out who killed him?'

'I'm not sure, but he was the most likeable person I think I've ever met, so I hope those responsible pay for this.'

They chatted about family and life for another thirty minutes before Gabby bid him goodnight.

The next day, Ben met her early to take the Titans for their morning walk to the park. Here they sat while the two dogs romped and sniffed their way around the familiar turf.

'Gabby, how much have you told Connor about the cult and the danger they pose?' Ben asked.

'Nothing.' She looked across at him hesitantly.

'Do you think that's fair, to him, I mean?'

'Father Gerry did warn us not to involve anyone else as that puts them at risk too.'

'Yeah, but Connor is not anyone, he's your boyfriend and should know the risks that come with us.'

'Ben, I just want something that isn't contaminated by this evil. Connor is an innocent and I really want to keep shielding him from the dark side.'

'It's up to you, Gabby, but I'm just saying, that if it were me, I would want to know everything about you. No surprises.'

'There are always surprises, Ben, even between friends as close as you and me.'

'Like what? You can tell me anything, Gabby.' He took her hand in his to squeeze it tight.

'Maybe one day, Ben. If anyone can handle the absolute truth, it's you.' She squeezed his hand back before calling the dogs to return home.

Blood Brothers

Eighteen

Connor stood staring out of the floor-to-ceiling windows of his 25th-floor office building as he just couldn't concentrate on work today. He was worried about Gabby. Ever since Father Gerry's murder she'd been unnaturally quiet, caught up in her own thoughts.

He sensed a distance in her now, like her mind was far away and her eyes seemed to looking through him, seeing more than he could comprehend.

Joe was also worried that Gabby walked late into the night, on her own in the dark. Refusing to be concerned about her own safety as she searched the streets, looking for answers or someone.

It broke his own heart a little more every day to see her so restless and unhappy. This brought home just how much she had come to mean to him. His whole world had tilted, with Gabby now being the axis he spun around.

'Connor, I need to get your decision about the Kelly contract. Are we going to accept their conditions?' Lauren called through on his phone.

'I haven't read through the conditions yet,' was his distracted response as he continued his perusal of the city skyline.

'I emailed it to you last week, Connor,' Lauren prompted.

'I'm heading out now, but I promise you I'll go through the contract tomorrow,' Connor promised as he shut down his computer. Walking out to his car, he unexpectedly bumped into Gina.

'Gina, how are you?' Connor held her at arm's length to look into her eyes.

'Well, what do you know, it's the great Connor Faradene who used to be my friend but now hardly ever bothers to call.' Gina's sarcastic reply was accompanied by arched red eyebrows.

Connor did feel a pang of guilt. He had been neglecting his old group of friends since he'd met Gabby. He wanted to spend almost all of his time within her orbit. 'You're right, Gina. I'm sorry that I've been distracted lately. How about a coffee now, have you got time?'

'Unlike you, Connor, I always make time for my good friends, so yes, a coffee would be nice.'

Connor took her to a café close by and ordered the coffees.

Watching him as he ordered, Gina took in all the little details. Ice blue eyes, tanned skin, small creases around his eyes from squinting into the sun, his beautiful, toned body that used to move over hers with such skill. *Where did it all go wrong?* she mused bitterly to herself.

'So, what have you been up to lately,' he asked as he took his seat at the small table.

'Not much really. Helping Mother in the fashion business and keeping up with social engagements seem to fill my days. So many in our group of friends are getting married. Harry and Simone are having their wedding at a resort in the Margaret River region next July.'

'Harry finally proposed? I always thought they would end up together.'

'You know, Connor, a lot of people said that about us. Yet here we are. I'm still waiting, and you have moved on with Ms Environmentalist without a backwards glance.'

'Gina, I'm sorry if you had expectations like that, truly I am. I'm not sure what would have happened if I'd never met Gabby. Maybe we would have just settled for each other, but it was never my intention to lead you on.'

Just settled for each other. Those words hurt Gina more than anything else. 'Connor, you are sounding like some misguided Mills & Boon reader. What has happened to you? Gabby's brainwashed you with all her 'let's save the world' talk. Where is that unscrupulous businessman who did whatever it took to get the deal done? He's been replaced with some super sweet Mr Nice Guy, and to be honest I find it all a bit sickening to watch such a tough, confident man become a whiney little lapdog.'

'Gina, it's not fair to take this out on Gabby.' He looked down as he stirred his coffee until some of it spilled into the saucer.

'Who else is to blame then?' Gina retaliated.

'I'm still the same person, but it's just not all about me anymore,' he bristled.

'I liked you better when it was all about you. What does your father think of all this 'money isn't everything' talk?' She tossed back in frustration.

'He probably isn't all that thrilled, but I am my own man, Gina. I don't need my father's approval to go my own way. He lived his life the way he chose, and I'm sure he will see that this is my choice. Deep down, I do want my life to count for something.'

'Oh boy, you really are becoming quite the Dalai Lama! I can't believe I'm hearing these words. Would you just listen to yourself! Wake up and come back to the real world. A world of greed, corruption, bribes and money. That is our true existence, and people like you and I are meant to rule over the masses.'

'That life no longer defines me, Gina.' He tried to make her see that people change.

'I get the picture, Connor. You don't want to listen to someone who cares about you, but just remember who your friends used to be.

I'll be here waiting when the wheels fall off the hippie camper.' Gina scraped her chair back and stalked away in disgust.

Connor watched her walk stiffly away and rubbed his hands over his eyes. The encounter had made him feel tired and jaded.

Looking at his now-cold coffee, he wondered how he had ever thought that was what he needed to be happy. Gina was exactly what he used to be, but that old version just felt wrong now. For better or worse, there was no going back.

Gina had agreed to work with Dominic after that first meeting at the Sorrento Hotel, and gradually over the months, he had drawn her into his world.

The guild had an assembly hall in downtown Melbourne, along Canterbury Road in Surrey Hills, the elite suburb with views of the city skyline. It was a cluster of old stone buildings connected by walkways: one was a meeting place while others were offices and prayer rooms. The property was sitting in prime real estate, and Gina could only guess at the value. She had probably driven past the high stone walls many times without knowing the clandestine activities happening beyond.

Dominic began by introducing her to the darker powers. Her selfish nature made her a natural at accepting the cost of such power. He had taken her as his lover to spin the web a little tighter. Sexual gratification was easy, and it was a tool to draw the prey in deeper and deeper.

He taught her how to pray and how to have daily devotions to draw on the power of evil.

The only setback was that Gina's mind got distracted by her emotions. Hatred fed her lust for revenge against Gabby, especially after her last attempt had failed with Marcus's exposé.

One stormy afternoon, Gina sat opposite Dominic and mirrored his position on the bamboo flooring of the prayer room, sitting cross-legged and resting the palms of her hands on her bare knees. She stared benignly into his ravaged face without a hint of distaste. It was a shame that he would never see her soft expression.

'The secret to transcendent meditation is to empty your mind of all distracting thoughts. It must take on a dreamy, floating sensation before you can begin to manipulate its realities,' Dominic coached.

Gina obediently closed her eyes and made a determined effort to remove all the dross from her mind. But, no matter how hard she tried, it flitted from one subject to another, almost like a skittish horse that would not stay still. After several moments, she sighed deeply and popped her eyes open again.

Dominic seemed oblivious to her fretfulness. His face looked serene even where the flesh had collapsed from his baptism in fire. Frustrated at her own lack of concentration, she leaned forward and kissed him lightly on his scarred lips.

'Gina, what are you doing?' Angrily, he jerked away. 'You must take this training seriously, especially if you want to exact your revenge.'

'I'm sorry, but you left me behind and I wanted you back.'

'It takes time and commitment to break through the first dimension, but it becomes easier once you feel it. Besides, how can you bear to kiss my face?'

'I honestly don't see the scars anymore. You don't need a pretty face to attract me. There are so many other parts of you that are superior, so stop fussing over your face,' she chided him.

'Gina, you always seem to be the exception to the rule.'

'I'm only sad that you will never see me.'

'Oh, but I do see you. With my inner eye, I see so much more. I see your fiery red hair, your green eyes that glint like a cat hunting at night and I see a heart that is full of suppressed retribution.'

'Now I am ready to try again.' She smiled with a glint of tears in her eyes.

It was later that night that Dominic and Gina silently joined a group of worshippers in the meeting hall. Gina obediently took hold of the hands on each side of her while Dominic led the chanting until the candle lit room became extremely cold.

Gina's skin prickled with the tension that filled the room until one woman in the group broke away to stand in the middle of the circle. Her eyes rolled back in her head as froth foamed from her mouth, and she began to moan like every bone was breaking in her body.

Gina watched enthralled until the woman suddenly stopped moaning. She slyly opened her eyes to stare at the group, but it wasn't her eyes that looked at them. It was a fallen angel that glared back at them and spoke these words. *'The time is almost upon you, a time where your devotion will be tested. A time when the fallen will take back the heavens to rule all the realms. Only those faithful to Lucifer will stand in blood and glory at his side. Are you faithful? Will you stand with your lord against our enemies?'*

To this challenge, the worshippers bowed low and chanted their vows of obedience. Once the possession was over, the woman collapsed on the ground, her body convulsing and shaking until she lay still.

Gina stared to see if she was dead or alive, never certain of the outcome as the cult members just left her body there when they dispersed.

After this show of strength, Gina understood this wasn't some game, it could be a matter of life and death, and she studied a lot more diligently afterward.

First, she learned the prayers of devotion, then she learned about the customs of a gathering and what role each devotee must play. She also mastered the chants that called the darkness to them.

She spent hours and hours in silent meditation, teaching her mind to separate itself from the cares of this world. Once she had mastered moving small objects with just her thoughts, Dominic started to teach her how to navigate spirit travel.

He had proven to be a thoughtful and knowledgeable mentor, and Gina found herself drawing closer and closer to her new friend, never questioning her obsessive desire to serve his dark lord. Ignited in her was now a fanatical thirst to become more than just human.

Gina was happier than she could ever remember, as she had something remarkable with Dominic: power and sex, the two most addictive cravings in the world.

On this morning, she moved closer to his side and stretched, almost purring with satisfaction. Her limbs felt loose and disconnected – never had she known such erotic pleasure. Dominic used his life force, his Eros, to bring her to orgasm over and over again without even touching her genitals. His hands pushed waves of energy across her body, causing her to arch her back and moan with arousal. When the final explosion came, she shouted her exhilaration to the heavens above.

'What are you thinking?' Gina reached up to stroke his cheek.

'I was thinking how beautiful you look in this light,' he said softly.

'What am I learning today, master?' She sighed with pleasure as he stroked her body.

'It's time for you to move from theory and start practising the knowledge you've been diligently studying.' He gathered her closer to give a demonstration.

'Gina, you must understand that the universe above loves order, whereas those who dwell in the shadows, like us, revel in chaos. You see this room now, it is tidy and everything has its place, but I prefer this.'

As he spoke, everything began to spin. The ornaments, the cushions and an after-shave bottle barely missed her face as they flew past to join the circling vortex that he'd created. He kept his attention until everything was spinning in a circle above them. Gina watched in awe until he let it fall into a disorganised pile upon the floor.

'This is what I would like to do with this world and everyone in it.' He smiled lazily as he turned his blind eyes towards her.

'I would love to turn her house upside down, Dominic. Do you think I'm ready? Just to rattle her a little.'

'We cannot compromise our plan, but once you have the skills, a little visit may be allowed. Let me consider what would be appropriate.'

Gina's eyes sparkled with malevolence, and her mouth watered at the chance to strike at Gabby and her pathetic little group of devotees. The desire to show off her new talents gave Gina the motivation to obsessively study the dark arts

Gabby woke up to an uneasy sense that someone was in her room. She had been out most of the night looking for Jinn, hoping he would show himself as before. Walking the dark streets alone with the protection of the pendant, she hoped to draw Jinn to her as she was desperate to destroy him. This night she had finally fallen into a restless slumber a few hours before dawn.

Carefully, she reached across to click the light on her bedside table. There was a shadowy shape hovering over the end of her bed. Cloaked in its own brand of darkness, it was an image that normally resided in nightmares. Gabby kicked the covers at the apparition to see if it was going to attack or retreat. In response to her violent movement, it moved a little higher but didn't disappear

Gabby felt for the blood tree pendant, which was always hidden under her pillow at night. She was not going to be caught unaware again. Holding it in her fist, its warmth and power reassured her that she was quite capable of defending herself.

Laying immobile, she watched the form begin to take a more human shape, slowly moving up the bed while she waited for it to get closer, ready to strike. When it was above her head, her hand reached up to snatch it out of the air. Catching hold of an arm, she pulled the being towards her until its face was hovering closely above hers.

The features were familiar to Gabby as she stared at the shrouded form. For a moment they each remained still, caught within each other's gaze until the being laughed and blew a puff of wind into her face

Thoughts raced through Gabby's mind. *Was this what happened to Father Gerry? Was it the same fallen brother that had stolen away his life but not his soul?*

Before she could crush the apparition into darkness, it turned to dust, tumbling over her sheets and across her startled face. The menacing laugh continued, but seemed to echo from around the house.

Joe! Was there a shadow in his room as well? It was the thought of Joe that propelled Gabby into action. She wouldn't stand by and see anything harm him. With his welfare in mind, she leaped out of bed, quickly putting the thong of the pendent over her head as she ran straight through the walls.

Her motion must have been sensed by the Titans as they began to bark and scratch at the front door, and within a moment, she was in Joe's room, shaking him awake.

'Joe, are you okay?'

His face was still crumpled with sleep when she flicked on the light switch to dispel the sense of doom.

'Gabby, what's wrong? What's happening?'

'There is something in the house.'

Joe ran out of his room to open the front door and let the dogs in. After this, they both approached her bedroom with the Titans at their side. The hackles on the dogs' backs were stiff with outrage, and their lips were drawn back, showing sharp fangs that were ready to attack. When they entered the room, the apparition was still there. As it turned towards them, a face appeared out of the shadow. Instead of disappearing when the dogs launched themselves, it began to laugh. A high-pitched laugh that tormented the dogs as they raced around the house, knocking over furniture and smashing ornaments in their attempts to catch the shadow.

Joe and Gabby were also chasing it from room to room. As it passed Gabby, she followed it through the wall and caught it in the kitchen, this time by the throat. 'Who are you,' she demanded as she held the apparition by the throat before her.

'Someone who is coming to destroy you,' it promised.

'You don't know who you're threatening,' Gabby countered the threat.

'Neither do you,' it said with menace as it once again turned to dust in Gabby's hand.

Gabby turned to see Joe's shocked expression.

'Where has it gone?' Joe said as he bent down to touch the dust covering the kitchen floor.

Gabby stood still for a moment to listen and feel for the presence of evil, but sensed it had left them – for now.

'I think it's no longer here to torment us.' Gabby drew him to his feet and held his shoulders to steady him. 'Are you alright, Joe?' Gabby asked with a worried frown.

'I think we need to talk,' was his only response. He invited her to sit at the wooden table.

'Do you want a cup of tea?' he offered, to which she just shook her head.

'Can you explain what just happened?' Old Joe shivered at the memory.

'There is much to tell you, Joe. I'm just not sure where to begin, or if I should burden you with the truth.'

'Start at the beginning and don't worry about me. After all we've been through, I don't think I can be easily shocked.'

Instead of responding, Gabby stood up and went to the kitchen wall and pushed her arm through it into the next room, all the time watching Old Joe's face as she slowly brought it back again and sat down beside him.

'What the hell was that?' he stared at her incredulously.

'Joe, you've suspected for a long time that I'm not exactly ordinary, probably since I was a child, and long before anybody else knew the truth.'

'When did you find out about this? This thing you can do.'

'It's such a long story.' Gabby looked down at her lap before raising those magnificent green eyes to stare back at Joe.

'I think it's safe to say that we're not going back to bed or getting any more sleep tonight. Why don't you begin, and we'll see where it goes from there.' He reached out to take hold of her long, slender hand in his and to give it a squeeze. 'My love and support for you will not change, no matter what you say or do, Gabby.'

From this place of love, she began to speak. Explaining her purpose as Fallon before this life, how she sacrificed immortality to save Frank and Kathleen's child, how the pendant came back into her possession, and the saga of her deep, abiding connection to the Blood Tree in the City of Angels.

Her voice didn't stop until the sun was up and the birds began their morning chorus. The whole time she sat there holding Joe's hands with a Titan placed on each side, telling the tale of her lives, immortal and mortal. Explaining that she had retained some of her angelic powers, but not all of them.

'I don't have my magnificent wings in this form,' she grieved their absence.

'Gabby, I don't know what to say. I'm trying to come to grips that you were once an angel, one that chose to live here with us. I always knew you were special, but even without wings, this is more than I ever imagined.'

'The afterlife is really something to behold, Joe. The City of Angels alone is more than you could ever imagine,' she struggled to adequately describe the glory she had witnessed.

Joe just sat there, trying to take it all in. He already knew there was more than the here and now, but to be sitting here in the presence of an immortal, one who had clothed herself as human for the greater good, blew his mind.

'I am in awe of you, Gabby, or Fallon. I'm no longer sure what name to use. This is a mind-blowing, unbelievable story, but my heart hears only the truth of your words.' He held her hands tightly.

'You really are something. A real superhero, an immortal who has sacrificed so much to save a life.'

'You are my something too, Joe. All of my good times and bad have you right in the centre, and I could never have come this far as a human without you.'

'So, what now for this mortal life?' Joe asked.

'We keep going by doing all that we can to make a difference to this world while I do everything in my power to look after our people. I love this human life that I chose, Joe, and want to live it to the fullest and not cower in the shadows, waiting for my fallen brothers and their dark entourage to strike.'

'Then how about we start with the practical stuff? I'll get us some breakfast and a hot drink before we begin the clean-up.'

'Sounds like a good idea. After all this talking, I'm famished,' the former angel smiled gratefully.

After breakfast, they kneeled on the carpet to pick up a shattered jade vase and gradually put their house back in order.

Nineteen

Gina continued to apply herself to studying the prayers and cult rituals to progress as quickly as possible. Gabrielle Harrison was strong and fast, but Gina was cunning and without mercy.

After months of training, she clandestinely planned to try out some of these new tricks, believing this could bolster the negotiations to increase her trust allowance from her father.

As she walked into the restaurant and was escorted to the table, she saw her father sipping his glass of wine. He noticed her and raised his auburn eyebrows in greeting. Gina favoured his colouring, while her face resembled her mother's.

'Hello, Father.' She leaned down to kiss him on the cheek.

He got up to pull her chair back. 'Gina, we haven't seen much of you lately.' His tone had a hint of reprimand.

'I've been busy.' She gave him a smug little smile.

'Doing what exactly?'

'Let's talk about it after dinner. I'm starving,' she chided him.

They enjoyed their meal and made small talk until the waiter served their coffee, then he again asked about her whereabouts.

'Father, I'm doing a course in human relations and negotiations. Skills once gained, will make me a very successful businesswoman.

However, it takes time to learn how to apply these unique abilities, so I need more money.'

'Gina, you should be investing your time in the family business. Your mother and I feel we are already providing you with a very generous trust allowance, for not much in return, actually.'

She stared at him to see who would drop their gaze first, and he did.

'Father,' was all she said.

'Gina, the answer is no. No more money. If it is not enough, then you will have to get a real job or to learn how to manage your money a bit better. This is the first lesson in business: live within your means.'

Gina closed her eyes, took a deep breath and then using her mind's eye she began to visualise his heart beating. Concentrating with every particle of her being on his heart, at first there was nothing, but she kept her focus until to her own amazement it was there. Each beat was so clear, so real, she could almost reach out to touch it.

Gina used her inner energy – her chi – to reach out and squeeze his heart ever so lightly.

She studied her father carefully as he rubbed his hand over his chest, and she could tell he was becoming disturbed by the small twinges radiating from his heart.

She squeezed again, harder this time. Gina took delight in seeing his eyes widen with pain and tightened her grip.

Her father bent over the table in agony, convinced he was having a heart attack. He started choking and spluttering in distress as he clasped his chest.

'Call an ambulance, please Gina,' he gasped.

As she squeezed, Gina could see in her mind's eye how his heart began quivering with stress, changing its fibrillation. Satisfied, she released the pressure and watched him sit upright with relief washing over his sweaty red cheeks.

'These are my new powers of negotiation, Father. Do I have your attention now? You will double my allowance without argument, or I will be inheriting it all a lot sooner than you think.' She smiled sweetly to soften the blow.

'You did that, Gina? This is the work of the devil!' He gazed at her with fear and disbelief.

'Father, some may say the devil, but I say opportunity. This is just the beginning of the new me, so from now on you and Mother had better do whatever I ask.'

Her father got up and left the table, and she couldn't feel sorry for him as he stumbled out of the restaurant into the street outside. She was so excited at her success with this first experiment. It was intoxicating to see her powers injure the weak and vulnerable.

Drunk with power, this was a real high, far superior to the cocaine she had flirted with.

Looking around the room, she selected her next target. There was an attractive woman with long dark hair sitting two tables over who caught her attention. She was in her early thirties and was obviously trying her best to impress the man sitting opposite. She would press her breasts together to draw attention to her cleavage as she leaned towards him to whisper secrets in the candlelight.

Gina started visualising the woman's bladder sitting just above the pubic bone. It took a little while to locate it, but when she did, she visualised it filled with urine, very, very full, so full that it was going to burst.

Gina smirked with satisfaction as she watched her victim's reaction. One minute she was flirting outrageously and the next she was writhing in pain from her bursting bladder. Her dinner companion was forgotten in a flash as she took off for the bathroom, stopping halfway across the room when urine flooded down her legs and all over the floor of the exclusive restaurant.

The woman covered her face in shame and fled to the toilets as the restaurant staff stood by in shock. The puddle of urine was spreading across the floral carpet with many eyes following its stream. Gina almost laughed into her coffee and decided that was enough for one evening. It would be a bit obvious if all their patrons suddenly began behaving this way.

Calling for the bill, she passed over her credit card and got out of there before she was tempted to try her powers on some other unsuspecting fool. There was no remorse, only a sense of entitlement to subject others to her will. Feeling like a God, she hopped into her sleek sports car.

Men thought they had the monopoly on the thirst for power and glory, but history showed that women could be even more dangerous. Women had minds that were much more manipulative and less likely to be swayed by sympathy for those weaker than themselves.

Gina loved to listen to the stories on how the guild had tortured and killed priests that tried to destroy their work. Dominic had met his match; he just hasn't realised it yet. As she settled into the car, she was shocked to see the subject of her thoughts sitting right beside her.

'How did you get in here? Gina spluttered in surprise.

'Gina, I have trained you in the dark powers so that you can serve our master, not your own gratification,' he scolded as his burned, tortured face pressed close to hers.

'Dominic, I didn't hurt anyone. I was just practising. I thought you would be proud of my progress,' she protested at his overbearing manner.

'I am disappointed in you, Gina. You cannot advance in our order until you prove yourself. The guild demands you follow orders without question.' His tone was uncompromising. Tonight, I want you to go to the meeting hall and wait for me there. If you refuse, this will be the end of your quest, the end of everything for you.'

'This is ridiculous,' she spluttered.

'Now Gina!'

His image faded out and begrudgingly she pulled into the busy city traffic with an angry frown settling on her frozen features. When she pulled up in Surrey Hills, she hunched her shoulders over the steering wheel and considered her best play. *Do I act humble and seek forgiveness or do I stand my ground?*

She didn't think Dominic would allow anything bad to happen to her. Surely, he wasn't going to actually kill her? Even so, she was bound to suffer, at least enough until he was satisfied that a lesson had been learnt.

Well, I may as well get this over and done with. Gina sighed with resignation and slid out of the low car and braced her shoulders. She stood tall and confidently strode towards the meeting hall.

A black-robed priest was waiting at the door and ushered Gina along a corridor and into the ritual room that was flickering with hundreds of candles. As she entered, she saw at least twenty other dark-robed prostrated forms on the floor with their arms outstretched over their heads.

Gina felt completely out of place in the outfit she had worn to dinner, like a tropical bird tossed amongst a flock of black crows. She kept her head down submissively and followed her guide to the back of the room and through a door into a small office.

Dominic looked up at her entrance and nodded at her to close the door, which clicked shut with a snap. He didn't speak so Gina saw no other option than to sit on the chair opposite him and wait. This was not a time to begin an argument. She'd accepted that he held the ace card and that power was the coin of this game. He sat staring at her, testing to see how long she could stay silent.

The cult master could read her aura and knew exactly how she was feeling. He was impressed that she didn't beg or justify her actions. Surely, she knew that her life was in the balance and yet there was no grovelling. Here was a human who was worthy of his training and guidance for she had all the pre-requisites for their cause: greed, selfishness and an insatiable hunger for power.

Despite all these good traits, Gina really needed to be able to submit to the higher power without question. Conceit and arrogance were weak links in the chain of command. Her lack of respect was a complication he didn't need, especially not now. This feisty beauty had to realise that he held the strings, to understand that she would only dance and sing when he commanded.

'What am I going to do with you, Gina?' he finally broke the silence with his question. 'I have shared my knowledge and trained you for our cause, not for showing off,' he admonished her.

'Power without responsibility is like putting an insane person's finger on the button of a nuclear bomb. You must learn that these abilities come with obligations. You assured me you were ready to enter our world, and these powers are not like circus tricks that you can perform in the public arena, or use them to blackmail money out of people. If people knew who and what we are capable of, it would derail decades of planning and sacrifice.'

'But, Dominic,' she spluttered until he put his hand up, freezing her tongue to the roof of her mouth.

'I am disappointed, and it is only because I believe in you that you still live.'

Gina had no option than to stay silent and wait for him to be her judge and jury, so she pretended humility and hung her head to meekly stare into her lap.

'It has been decided that we will take the chance and complete a very dangerous rite on your soul. One that has had disastrous results previously, but we are reasonably sure you are strong enough to survive and return to us. It is a transplant of souls, almost like an organ transplant, but you will be living within another life, living their experience rather than the life you had before.'

Gina's eyes went as large as she considered his words and the implications. A different life where she could not be herself? That would be like a living hell, for there was nobody as important as her.

'The soul is only precariously attached to the body, and death can swoop in to tear it away at any time. We can precipitate death as it approaches and shift the soul if enough priests can visualise the change and agree on where it is going to.'

Without thinking, she used her mind to unlock his grip on her tongue, shocking Dominic that she could do this so early in her training. 'What kind of disastrous results are you talking about?' Gina's eyes filled her face, and her voice came out choked.

'Sometimes the soul does not go to the desired entry point, and it remains forsaken somewhere in between, not living and not dead, just in limbo for eternity.'

'You can't do this to me! I thought this, you and I, meant something to you.' Gina stood up and went to the door, testing to see if it was locked, looking for a way out of this trap. After rattling the door-knob with no success, she stood with her back against it, facing her tormentor.

'Gina, nothing means more to me than obeying my vow of service, not you, not me, not anything. One day I hope you'll understand that the powers we serve are eternal and indeed worth the sacrifice of your life.'

'Dominic, please don't do this. I don't want to be anyone but me, so punish me with pain, whip me, hurt me physically, but I beg you do not send me into another person's life.'

'It has already been decided and not something I can change. Come with me, the priests have been preparing for the ceremony.'

'What if I refuse to co-operate?' she fired, a little of her former arrogance resurfacing.

'Not an option, Gina. It is either this or you die right here, right now,' he said deadpan, with no emotion.

Gina glared at him, her face burning with anger at his lack of loyalty.

Without any further discussion, Dominic rose and moved her away from the door. Opening it, he took her out of their place of solitude and back into the meeting room, where she was stripped naked and placed face up on the altar.

'You must keep your eyes closed throughout the transplant and do not move a muscle or it could end badly,' Dominic instructed her.

It was important for her not to witness what was about to happen or there could be confusion over the order of the process. It had to be their willpower commanding the soul with no interference from Gina.

The priests moved in close and each one incanted a prayer in Latin as they placed their hands on her bare chest.

Beyond their voices, Gina desperately wanted to open her eyes to see what was really happening. The priests and priestesses began chanting loudly as the sound of blood dripping into a bowl filled the air, each having donated their life force to reinforce the power of their prayers.

In her blindness, she felt people moving close to her again, and her eyes felt moist and warm as fingers stroked down across the closed lids. The same fingers were making a symbol on her forehead and rubbing something across her lips. Gina's tongue darted out the tiniest bit to taste the blood spread across her mouth. It was also rubbed over her chest and the soles of her bare feet.

'Our blood, to keep your eyes focused on your destination, to keep your mouth from speaking of this night, to keep your heart brave, to bring your feet back, and with the symbol of our lord drawn on your forehead to keep death at bay.' Dominic's voice droned in prayer as the group chanted along with him.

Gina could feel a presence drawing closer and closer until it was hovering right over her. It dropped lower and lower until she could feel it almost lying on top of her, with just a fraction of space between her body and the unholy shadow.

This must be death. I can feel the filth and smell the decaying flesh as it almost touches my skin.

Everyone could see Gina's skin bead with sweat and although she was trembling with fear, she followed their instructions and barely dared to breathe. One after the other passed over her again with their prayers until Dominic's deep voice was there at her shoulder. Gina smelled smoke and her eyes began to sting and water from the thick acrid cloud.

Dominic suddenly shouted out in Latin, 'Vibe Tibi.'

Away with you.

A flash of light appeared from somewhere above her head, and suddenly she was tumbling and spinning through a dark space. Her mouth opened to scream but there was no sound in the void, just a whirling nothingness.

Twenty

At San Remo Beach in Far North Queensland, Kathleen Harrison was doing the laundry when she took one of Frank's work shirts from the basket and held it up. *How do I get these stains out?* she wondered. Looking at the oil and sweat patches over the fabric, she knew it would take some scrubbing to get it clean again. Just then, the sound of breaking glass swung her head around in dismay, so putting the shirt into the sink, she went back into the kitchen.

Strangely, a glass that had been on the kitchen sink was now smashed all over the floor, sending splinters across the room. Looking outside, she saw a calm, sunny day, with not a breath of wind. Sighing in frustration, Kathleen turned back to the laundry, thinking this mess could wait until she had the washing machine started.

As she came around the corner into the laundry, a shadow swept across the room. Pressing her hand against her mouth to suppress a squeal of alarm, she froze in the doorway, too frightened to take another step.

After several seconds, all seemed quite normal, so she shook her head in consternation. *What a weird morning. First the glass smashing and then I think I saw a ghost in the house. Must be coffee time!*

Then to further question her sanity, she couldn't find Frank's work shirt. Searching all over the house, it never came to light, a mystery Kathleen chose not to share in case it was proof she was losing her mind.

Dominic, the guild master, held the shirt against his face, where he inhaled the sweat of a man he had never met. It was essential to get something that had Frank Harrison's essence within, and this piece would be perfect.

He had projected his body through the astral realm into the Harrison house to retrieve the incantation artefact, knocking the glass off the table as a distraction. He had anticipated the woman would clean up the glass, not interrupt his retrieval.

Now with prize in hand, he sat naked in the dark prayer room, and as the candlelight danced within the shadows, he began to sing softly. He saw Frank Harrison's features within the flame as he held the shirt and watched it turn to ash. Once the shirt had disintegrated, he picked up what remained of Frank's life and rubbed the ash over his bare chest and shouted his curse into the darkness, '*De cinere et pulvere formatus eris.*'

'From ashes and dust you were formed as once again you shall be.'

The numbing cold spread through his heart and down his arms as he waited for death to obey his command.

San Remo was the same sleepy little seaside suburb, and on this day no one suspected that death was on the march.

Frank Harrison was immersed in naïve bliss as he sat at the kitchen table. 'Have our sons left for work already?' he asked from behind the *Cairns Post* newspaper.

Kathleen brought him some fried eggs on toast and sat to finish her own cup of tea. 'Yes, they both had early starts today. Thomas is on some big job and Jacob had a breakfast meeting with his boss.'

Frank finished his breakfast and rinsed the plates and cup, then went to brush his teeth and ready himself for another day at work. As he passed through the kitchen, Kathleen reminded him not to forget his lunch, which was sitting on the bench.

'Bye darling, see you tonight.' He kissed her on the cheek and walked out to his car.

The car was about to reverse out of the driveway when on an impulse, Kathleen ran out of the house and waved him to wait. Frank stopped the car and put his head out of the window to see what the problem was.

She reached down to hold his face in her hands and kiss him firmly on the lips. 'I love you, Frank Harrison,' she spoke against his mouth.

Frank sucked on her bottom lip in appreciation of the unexpected kiss and grinned at Kathleen in surprise. 'You should say goodbye like this, every morning.'

'Be careful, darling, and have a good day.' Kathleen smiled at him as he put the car into gear and drove away.

The journey from home to work had been travelled too many times to count during his thirty-five years of employment on a channel dredging vessel. His job was to keep the channel clear for ships to dock at Cairns wharf.

On board this rusted vessel, Frank was liked and respected by his boss and fellow workers. He was known as a no-nonsense person who always treated others fairly. It was after lunch when Frank walked to the guard rail to check if his colleague Bob was clear of the steel chain before he hoisted it off the deck.

Just as Frank raised his arm to acknowledge Bob's signal to move the hoist, a crushing pain ran through the middle of his chest and across his shoulders. An overwhelming weight pressed down upon him and his lungs refused to inhale any air. As if from a distance, Frank heard himself gasping small puffs of air to keep from suffocating. Black spots danced before his eyes, and he could feel the strength draining from his arms and legs as his body brought the blood back to his major organs to maintain life.

He looked across at the beloved mountains framing the city of his birth, and time seemed to slow down. He could hear each beat of his heart, but it was strained and sluggish, and the effort of one more beat was just too hard. All coherent thought fled before the onslaught of pain, a hurt so unbearable it crumpled his legs, and the last sensation was the bang of his head as he hit the metal surface of the platform.

The phenomenon of passing from one reality to another felt similar to that moment when he slipped from consciousness into sleep. He wasn't aware of his spirit moving out of his body, but one second there was pain and then the next moment it was gone, only to be replaced with this new highly sensitive awareness. His higher spiritual self, or that's how it felt, was standing there watching the scene play out beside him. As this spiritual self, Frank saw the shocked faces when they realised he had collapsed, and the shouts of alarm as they rushed to his prone form on the ground.

Images flashed before him as he moved backwards through his life, the scenes moving quickly from adult to child to infant until he was once again a swirling force within a capsule, held safely in the arms of an angel as they flew away from this life.

'Frank, Frank, are you okay, mate?' Bob called out when he saw the big man go crashing down. He leaped over the chain then raced up the stairs to the raised platform where Frank lay unmoving on the floor.

'Help, help, somebody get help,' he shouted as he moved Frank over onto his back, trying to get a response from him.

The first-aid officer rushed over to them, checking for a pulse and breathing only to begin administering CPR. He kept inflating Frank lungs with air and compressing his chest with a regular rhythm until the ambulance arrived.

The paramedics used a defibrillation unit to shock Frank's heart back into rhythm, but it refused to co-operate. After several minutes with no response, they stopped to look up at the ring of bystanders and shook their heads to acknowledge that he was gone.

It was so quiet, only the seagulls cried their lament at the sorrowful scene playing out below. The two young ambulance officers lifted Frank's limp body onto the stretcher and laid a white sheet over him as they wheeled it back to the waiting vehicle.

When the police arrived, the ship's captain Harry Clifford offered to be the one to tell Kathleen.

This sudden tragedy was going to hit the Harrisons very hard. There was a knot in his stomach as the police car arrived at Frank's home in San Remo.

Kathleen had been feeling a sense of dread all day and was grateful as the sun settled on the rainforested mountains. She wouldn't relax until Frank and her sons came home safe.

One ear listened out for his car as she peeled and cut vegetables for dinner as they would all be here soon, tired and hungry after a long day.

Hearing the crunch of gravel, she quickly dried her hands and left the vegetables sitting on the cutting board to go and welcome Frank home. As Kathleen walked into the lounge to open the front door, she caught a glimpse of the police car sitting in the driveway. In her heart, she knew it was Frank. All day she'd had a premonition that something bad was going to happen.

Head spinning, she opened the front door and held onto its frame for support. When she saw Harry Clifford get out of the back door of the police car, Kathleen slumped to the ground. 'No Harry, don't say it. Not my Frank,' she cried out in anguish.

Harry sank down to put his arm around her shoulder as her face crumpled with grief. 'I'm so sorry, Kathleen,' was all he could mutter over and over.

After her sobs had quietened, Harry half carried Kathleen inside and sat with her on the couch. The two police officers sat awkwardly opposite them. They took off their hats and stared uncomfortably down at their laps.

Eventually Kathleen was able to raise her face to look at them with despair. 'Tell me what happened.'

Harry spoke on everyone's behalf. 'They think it was a heart attack, Kathleen, as it all happened so suddenly. He fell down onto the deck and that was it. The ambulance officers tried resuscitation, but nothing could bring him back. We are all so very sorry.'

Covering her face with her hands, Kathleen closed her eyes tightly as she tried to come to terms with the cruel truth. *How do I go on living when my soul mate has left me? We had married almost thirty-five years ago and should have had many more years together. Frank was only fifty-eight years old, far too young for his life to be over. It just isn't fair.*

Car doors slammed outside, and the policemen leaped up to speak to Jacob and Thomas. Kathleen also stood up to stumble towards her sons. She saw Jacob, so much like his father, shaking his head in denial and saying, 'No, no, no,' repeatedly.

Thomas stood rooted to the spot in shock. Nothing could have prepared him for such bad news. This morning, his father had been here alive and now without warning, he was suddenly gone.

Jacob, the eldest son, held his mother and cried hard. Kathleen reached for Thomas as well, so he moved to wrap his arms around her. Harry and the police stayed there until Ruth and Billy Saila could come over to look after them.

Thomas still hadn't shed a tear. He just took care of his mother and elder brother, then called Melbourne and broke the news to Gabby and Joe. It hurt to shatter his sister's heart as she was close to their father. Joe promised to book the next flight home, and that they would be there soon.

Human life was hard. There was so much to gain and so much to lose. Love seemed to hold it all together, but love can heal and it can hurt.

Today, Gabby's love hurt.

Her father had always been the rock she relied on. His steady love had never been taken for granted, and it was harsh to lose him suddenly like this. Joe heard her crying through the night as he lay there staring at the ceiling, trying to come to terms that Frank was no longer with them.

They flew home the next day. It was a silent flight with each lost in their own memories. Gabby lost all control of her anguish when she walked into her mother's arms, both sobbing their sorrow as they wept for all that would never be.

The next few days, they planned the funeral and supported each other for a viewing of Frank's body. Lying in the satin fabric of the coffin, he was dressed in his blue suit, the one that he dragged out for weddings, the occasional church service or to attend a funeral. Now here it was again, but this time for his own funeral.

Reaching in to hold his cold, stiff hand, Gabby's tears were flowing again. Remembering those special times, times when she had sat on his shoulders as he walked along the beach with his family. Gabby had felt so important sitting high on her perch, like a princess looking down at her brothers far below. There was no fear of falling as she'd had faith her father would always keep her safe. Now it was time to whisper her final goodbye.

'I chose this life and became your daughter, for which I have been blessed. I love you, Dad, and though your spirit lives on, I am going miss you here in this human life so very much,' Gabby wept onto his silent features.

Jacob and Thomas drew her away from his empty body. 'He's gone Gabby, this is just the shell.' Thomas pressed her face into his shoulder to hug her even closer.

Emotion welled up inside of her, choking her throat and making her heart ache. As a scientist she knew that a muscular organ like the heart shouldn't ache from emotion, but the uncanny thing was, it did. Ask anyone suffering the loss of a loved one or their best friend, they knew how much pain a heart could feel.

They would all miss him so much.

Joe and Thomas had organised everything, and the men from the harbour dredge offered to be pall bearers as they wanted to be a part of the funeral. Ben, Elisabeth, Miranda, Paul, Michael, and of course, Connor, all flew in to be there for Gabby.

There was even a television crew filming the cavalcade of cars as they arrived at the church. The whole Harrison family wore black, and many watched a pale, drawn Gabby as she walked into the church with Connor on one side and her mother on the other. The two brothers, one tall and one shorter, walked close behind, and they all seemed somehow hollow in their black suits.

It was a very touching service with many friends volunteering to tell stories of Frank's friendship and generosity. There were incidences that even his family had been unaware of, times when Frank had quietly given money or time to those in need. They say that you leave a mark on the lives of those around you, almost a brand, and for such a quiet, unassuming man, Frank had made a huge impact.

Ruth and Billy had the funeral wake at their house, where a small crowd gathered to honour Frank's memory.

Eddie had also flown home. He needed to say his own goodbye as Frank had been like a second father to him and his siblings. And he wanted to be there to support Gabby.

The afternoon was filled with stories and reminiscing of old times and precious moments shared with Frank. Kathleen retired early as the doctor had prescribed a sedative to use over these days of overwhelming grief and sadness. Something to help her to settle and get some sleep.

Connor stayed close to support Gabby as she accepted the condolences of so many friends, until Eddie grasped his forearm to draw him aside.

'Hi Connor, I'm Eddie. Gabby and I have been friends our whole life.'

'It's nice to meet you, Eddie. Gabby talks about you all the time. I'm just sorry it's under these circumstances.'

'Yeah, losing Frank so suddenly, it just doesn't make sense. This loss is going to hit Gabby really hard, so I'm counting on you to take good care of her.' The big Torres Strait Islander gripped his hand so firmly that Connor could almost hear the bones creaking.

Nodding his head to reassure Eddie, Connor saw that protective glint in those brown eyes and knew what was expected of him.

Later in the day, Eddie took Gabby's hand and drew her away from the mourners. It was only when they were alone that he brought his face close to hers.

'Gabby, I know how much you loved your dad, and I am so sorry for your loss. My heart is hurting with yours today.' His voice quavered and choked in his throat, and the tears fell past his long lashes onto his beautiful mocha cheeks.

Placing her hands on both sides of his face, she pressed her forehead against his, eye to eye as she felt his tears brush against her cheeks.

'I know, Eddie. He loved you too. We all loved him, and he knew that. Losing him like this is not fair, but we of all people know that life isn't always fair.' Gabby pulled him down to sit beside her on the grass, holding hands as they shared memories of their lives and interconnected families.

As the sun set, it was just Eddie and Gabby tidying up after the gathering. Eddie was washing the dishes while Gabby dried, and this simple domestic task was somehow comforting.

'Tell me, Eddie, how is it going up in the gulf?'

'Well, I now have a formal contract with department of communities to maintain the houses in Kowanyama. Barry and I still have a lot of work to do, but we're slowly making a difference with the locals. Seeing our commitment makes them more likely to trust us.'

'That's great. I am so proud of you. Your passion will rebuild lives as well as houses.' Gabby could muster a small smile on such a sad day.

Eddie just hugged her close to him.

That night, the curlews filled the dark sky with their melancholy cries. They felt Gabby's grief and broadcasted her sadness for all of the beach to hear.

Connor had watched them from outside as he stacked chairs, and he could see the bond they shared. It was more than friendship – it was agape love. He would have to accept that Eddie and even Ben were part of their love rectangle. Gabby came with baggage, but it was the people who refused to stop loving her that he had to share his life with.

The next day, Connor and Gabby took off their shoes to go for a walk along the beach. The sand felt good underfoot, warm from the sun's heat, and the salty spray from the ocean tantalised their senses.

For Gabby, these familiar fragrances would always speak of home. As they walked along the edge of the foamy waves, Connor heard a small hiss, and in alarm he took his arm off Gabby's shoulder to look behind.

He saw at least six sandy-coloured birds on long, thin legs following them. When he made eye contact, they raised their wings and leaned forward to snap their beaks aggressively at him, all the while making a spine-tingling cry. He felt rather than saw Gabby smile at their protective antics.

'Are they dangerous?' He stopped to look from Gabby to the curlews.

'Only if you try to hurt me.'

'Well, in that case I can relax. I'm never going to do that.' He smiled down into her green eyes.

Walking along hand and hand, a welcome peace settled upon them. It was comforting to have a special person. Someone to lean on for support during such this heartbreaking time.

'I love you Connor.'

'I not only love you, Gabby, I adore you.'

'Even my protectors?'

'Well, maybe not so much. But do I love that these vicious creatures will do anything to protect you. Very similar to me, in fact.'

A couple of weeks later, Melbourne welcomed them back with rain, a wet embrace shrouded in clouds. Kathleen had returned with Gabby as she needed to be close to her daughter during these early days of grief.

Tears pricked their eyes as they looked at the sky. Sorrow and rain, both unfailing and part of all lives.

Ben collected them from the airport, and Connor called to welcome Gabby home, promising to see her the next day. After a quiet supper, everyone retired to their rooms to seek sleep and that elusive state: peace.

Over the ensuing weeks, Gabby threw herself into work, leaving early each morning and not coming home until the skies were as dark as the shadows framing her eyes.

Twenty-one

Gabby nestled into his shoulder on the couch as Connor skipped through the channels on the television looking for something to pique his interest. Before long he looked down to see she had fallen into an exhausted sleep, so he gently picked her up to carry her into the bedroom and settle her onto the bed.

Brushing her long blonde hair off her brow, he heard her sigh as she pressed her face into the softness of the pillow. Turning off the television, he came to lay down and hold her in his arms, cherishing the way she melted into him without fear or hesitation.

The next morning over coffee, he took her hand and looked into her exquisite eyes, which were framed by shadows of fatigue.

'Gabby, I'm worried about you. Since your father passed away, you seem to be carrying the whole world on your shoulders.

'I've felt like that for a long time, Connor.' She smiled sadly into his piercing blue eyes.

'Well, how does a short holiday sound? Just a couple of weeks away from the daily grind? All work and no play can be harmful, even for a superhero like you.'

'I can't take any more time off. We're far too busy.'

'A short break will do you the world of good. I want to take you to Africa to do a conservation safari tour.'

'Maybe one day, Connor, but not right now. My mother needs me, and the society needs me.'

'They will still need you when we return. A change of scenery will help ease the pain, Gabby, and will abet the despair to pass.' He reached out to enfold her in his love.

'I know it's very human of me to be so sad, but the loss of love hurts.'

'Gabby, you don't have to apologise for being human. Loss is always painful.'

In response, she settled into his arms. He was now her refuge from the storm.

Over the next few months, Connor kept talking about Africa. Drawing on his own experiences, he painted an alluring picture of the wild landscape and marvellous animals. Determined for Gabby to take some respite from her brutal schedule, he kept dropping hints until she finally surrendered to his perseverance.

The night before they flew out, everyone enjoyed a bon voyage dinner at Joe's house, and the humble little cottage glowed with candlelight and the sounds of laughter.

Ben and Connor could be in the same room now without any obvious hostility, as a peace treaty of sorts had been agreed to since the exposé on Gabby.

Just at that moment, Gabby shared a look with her mother. Even though Kathleen smiled, Gabby saw shadows of pain in those merry eyes. Here was the truth about loss: The windows to the soul never lie.

Kathleen stared back at Gabby, and not for the first time, felt a sense of wonder. Surely an angel walked amongst them? How would she age? Would Gabby be like herself? Growing heavier over the years, while wrinkles that once only appeared during a laugh or frown now stayed like old friends? Looking at her daughter, Kathleen felt a premonition of something sinister rush over her. In alarm, she turned to Frank as she shook off the shiver of dread. Was it superstition or just the fear of the unknown that made her send a prayer off to him? *Frank wherever you are now, please look after our daughter. I could not bear to lose another. Keep them all safe, my darling.*

Connor and Gabby flew out the next morning from Melbourne to London, London to Nairobi, and their final stop was Tanzania.

It was intoxicating to land at the KLM or Kilimanjaro Airport near Arusha. The plan was to spend several days in Arusha and then Connor was hiring a fixed-wing aircraft to fly them firstly to the Serengeti Safari Lodge and then across to the Skeleton Coast National Park.

Gabby was excited about exploring the habitat of elephants, rhinoceros, giraffes, zebras, wildebeests, and of course, the big cats. *What would happen when I contact these wild animals?* she wondered.

Arusha had a pleasant climate with a cooling breeze from the Indian Ocean, a couple of hundred kilometres away to the east. It was beautifully situated at the base of Mount Meru on the eastern edge of the Great Rift Valley, with a vast vista in every direction and the snow-covered peaks of Mount Meru as a backdrop. Even the air here was different, it smelled hot and dusty. The people, the scenery, it had all the ingredients of an adventure.

After checking in at the Gran Melia Hotel, Gabby enjoyed a nice cool shower, then put on a long, flowing white cotton dress and comfortable sandals.

'Let's go exploring.' Connor held out his hand in invitation.

They stepped into the bright sunshine to discover the markets and see what delights were waiting within. The town area was modern, and they took some tourist photos standing under the Arusha Clock Tower in the main precinct.

'This was built in 1953 and the Arusha Accords was signed here on August 4th, 1993, by representatives of competing factions in the Rwandan civil war.' Connor read aloud the facts from his guidebook, while Gabby reached down to stroke a stray cat that was winding around her legs.

Once they moved on from the busy town centre, the road became dirt and the crowds increased as they moved into the market areas. Gabby stared in wonder at the women balancing such large bundles on their heads, the seductive sway of their hips as they moved gracefully along the street, their posture tall and straight.

Old Land Rover cars drove slowly amongst the people shopping at the stalls, and the locals strolled casually out of their way. Colours, smells and sounds assaulted their senses, and Gabby struggled to take it all in. The people were so happy and friendly, taking time to explain all the different fruits and vegetables.

The children followed them about like they were the Pied Piper, and Gabby couldn't resist kneeling down to their level to hug them affectionately. They shyly smiled back at her with such open happy faces. These little ones exuded a contagious exuberance.

Connor fell for their sweet demeanour and could not resist giving a little girl some Tanzanian coins to go and buy a treat. She very diligently made sure each child got a coin before the group ran giggling to their favourite stalls.

As they walked along the dirt path weaving between the stalls, Gabby suddenly stopped and tilted her head to listen. Turning away, she left Connor on the path to twist between the rowdy displays of local goods and wares while he quickly followed to see what had precipitated this bizarre reaction.

He stopped in shock when he happened upon Gabby angrily confronting a large, sweaty man. With green eyes blazing, she tipped a hessian bag upside down where several mutilated hands spilled onto the ground.

'You cut off their hands,' Gabby yelled at him.

'They're paws from dumb animals, you stupid bitch.' The man stuck out his chest and pushed towards her.

Instead of taking a step back, Gabby stepped forward to grasp him around the throat and lifted him up. 'You are the only dumb animal here, you stupid fool.' In contempt, she tossed him like a doll across the tables. The large man crashed through the market wares, spilling goods all over the ground as locals either quickly got out of the way or stood in disbelief at this sudden violent clash.

Gabby then disappeared behind a makeshift curtain to return a few minutes later with a tiny limp gorilla in her arms. 'Let's get out of here,' she said to Connor.

'Gabby, wait, what on earth just happened?'

'Not now, and not here Connor.'

The poacher was still groaning on the ground when he saw Gabby leaving with his prize. Pounding his fat fists into the ground, he shouted for someone to stop her, but the other stall owners refused to take any action. Instead, they turned away from him in scorn.

Once they arrived back at the hotel, Gabby went to speak to reception in a hushed tone before leading the way back to their room. As soon as the door was closed, she turned to Connor. 'Connor, I know you have questions, but can we just focus on this poor creature for now?'

'Alright, Gabby, but what are you going to do with it?' he asked in bewilderment.

'We are going to nurse it back to life,' Gabby stated as she hugged the small bundle closer to her chest.

They set about bathing all the urine and excrement that had matted its coat, and before long, there was a knock on the door.

The concierge had been out to purchase a milk substitute and baby's bottle, whereupon Gabby immediately made up the mixture and attempted to get their charge to take some milk.

A few drops every fifteen minutes was all they could manage at first, and slowly as the hours passed, the infant's dull eyes took on the slightest interest in life. Within a couple of days of diligent care, the baby ape was scampering around their room, creating mayhem.

A couple of days later, once the crisis was over, Connor brought up the incident at the markets. It was late in the afternoon, and Gabby was enjoying a glass of wine as she leaned against the balcony balustrade.

Where do I begin? How do I make him see that I'm not a freak? Connor deserved the truth, but the truth was just so unbelievable.

'I'm sorry, Connor, but the cruelty and barbaric actions of that despicable man just pushed me over the edge of reason.'

'I understand that part, but how did you have the strength to throw him across the bazaar? It was beyond human, Gabby?'

'I'm not sure where to start, Connor. You would have suspected by now that I am not a typical woman. A connection with animals is one of my gifts, and there are others that you haven't seen yet.'

'Is superhuman strength another one of these *gifts?*'

'Only when I'm really angry.' Gabby smiled to reassure him.

'Remind me to never get you that angry!' he murmured. 'Are there any other *gifts* I need to be aware of?'

'Connor, I promise to tell and show you everything when we get home to Melbourne. It's quite an unbelievable account, but I agree that you should know everything about me ... finally. Can I ask you to be patient just a little longer? Can we do this after the holiday?' Gabby asked.

Connor just stared back, unconvinced. 'Why not now? There is no need to keep anything from me. You know I love you and always will, no matter what you have to say.'

'This getaway is just about us, and I don't want any of the complications from home to intrude upon it. Can you contain your curiosity until then?'

'Of course I can wait. There's no rush when we have years of discovery ahead of us.'

Gabby crossed to hug him in gratefulness.

Their concierge had also become attached to the baby gorilla, sneaking up to the room to spend his breaks playing with the adorable little rascal. He had organised a wildlife rescue organisation to collect the infant. They would care for him until he could be returned to his own kind, high in the remote mountains.

Gabby hugged the lively, squirming bundle tightly before she handed him over to the gorilla wildlife carer.

'Keep him safe,' she pleaded.

The carer gently smiled and promised the infant would be returned to a band of wild gorillas when he was old enough to survive.

The next morning, a taxi took them to the small airport to pick up the charter plane. Connor introduced himself to the ground staff and went through the pre-flight check procedure.

Soon they were on their way to the safari park, and Gabby was mesmerised by the landscape they were flying across.

It was so vast, a little like Australia's outback but not yet as dusty or arid, and the grasslands were massive. Gabby could see how this country sustained the huge herds of migratory animals. Some say that Africa was the original Garden of Eden, and looking over the landscape, she could understand this notion.

Gabby squealed with delight when a herd of zebras raced across the plain, their striped legs pumping and kicking up little tufts of dirt as they sped along.

Connor kept stealing glances at her profile as she looked out of the window.

The hours droned on until they descended towards a small landing strip. Bouncing as the wheels hit the dirt, Connor expertly landed the aircraft and then parked it beside the hanger.

He got out and shook hands with the man waiting for them.

Gus was in his mid-fifties and spoke with a strong Dutch-African accent. He had a portly belly and a big white beard. He told them that he looked after the airstrip and provided mechanical maintenance to the privately owned planes that visited the Serengeti.

It didn't take long to load their bags into the waiting jeep and take the short ride to the safari camp. The camp had all the luxuries of a hotel with its clean, spacious tents and proper beds, and there was even a small ensuite built into the side. This was great for tourists as they did not have to traipse through the camp in pyjamas to use showers and toilets.

Mike was the camp manager with a team of local Swahili men who acted as guides, cleaners and cooks.

That night around the fire, Mike began to tell them stories about local folklore, sharing fascinating tales like the Baobab tree.

'African legend tells that each animal was given a tree to plant by the Great Spirit. When the hyena was assigned the Baobab tree, the careless animal planted it upside down and that is why the branches look like gnarled roots reaching for the sky instead of growing deep in the soil.'

Waking the next morning to the dawn of the Savannah, when the air was cool and crisp, it was like being present on the first morning of creation. The Serengeti has its own special smell, and the only word for it was *clean*. No contaminants in the air, it was unblemished nature.

In the early morning, their guide Uzoma called for them to start the jeep tour. Bouncing over the rough ground, he found a secluded place for them to watch the wild animals feed or gather at waterholes in the pre-dawn light.

One of these early mornings, they came across a pride of lions that disdainfully ignored them, until Gabby touched their minds. The lionesses gathered protectively around the cubs, unsure if she was a friend or foe. Gabby smiled to herself when she felt the bonds within the pride. She reassured them she was no threat as they all instead lined the road with curiosity.

Secluded in their tents at night, Connor and Gabby made love to the roar of the lions and the yips of hyenas. It was surreal to be safe in the bush while predators roamed the perimeter.

Late one afternoon, Gabby found a small glade not far from the tents and lay there in peaceful contemplation with nature, watching the setting sun tip the sea of grass to gold. A little anteater had snuffled close, not afraid to brush against her as she examined the pink membrane in his big ears, all the tiny arteries at work.

'You are a miracle of this planet, just like all the other creatures who call it home,' she whispered into those intricately designed ears.

She lay there in bliss until Connor found her.

'Here's my beautiful woman, always hanging out with the beasties.'

Gabby teased him back as the small creature scuttled away. 'Maybe that's why I chose you. Under that layer of sophistication there was a beast waiting to be set free.'

'You have set me free, Gabby. Free from all my previous assumptions about life, and I think this is a fitting setting for what I'm about to ask.'

He pulled her up to a sitting position and kneeled in front. Grasping her hand, he looked at her with those ice blue eyes and swallowed a little nervously. 'Gabrielle Harrison, will you marry me?' He held out an open velvet ring box with a sparkling diamond catching the last rays of the sun.

She just looked at him blankly and stared at the stunning solitaire. This wasn't expected at all. Of course, she knew they loved each other, but marriage? That was a big step for somewhere in the future.

His eyes were pleading with her for an answer, and her heart squeezed with tenderness to see him so vulnerable. 'Connor I would love to marry you, now and forever,' she whispered, with tears brimming in her eyes.

Connor saw those large luminous eyes fill with tears and her mouth say the words but his heart was pounding so hard that he didn't really hear the spoken words. But in spite of his compromised hearing, he could not have missed the meaning of the words or the joy mirrored in her eyes.

He took her left hand and slid the breathtaking jewel onto her slender finger, then holding her against his chest, he murmured into her hair. 'I promise to spend the rest of my life making you happy.' His lips moved down to her throat and gently kissed the soft skin while she flushed a delicate pink.

With love, she placed a hand on each side of his face and gazed into his eyes. 'Connor, you have already made me so happy. I was a prisoner of fear until you rescued me.'

She reassured him by pushing his frame down into the dry grass and rolling on top of him. His eyes widened with desire as she leaned in closer and pressed her lips against his throat.

They made love right there in the grasslands of Africa with such wild abandon, desperately dragging the clothes off each other. The landscape added to their excitement until the sudden burst of pleasure left them gasping in each other arms.

The next morning, they were driving back to camp and laughing at the monkeys' antics in the treetops when their jeep violently veered to the side. It was at a crossroads when the approaching vehicle failed to give way. Connor caught hold of Gabby as they were suddenly flung across the car. Connor's elbow got smashed against the side, and he grunted in pain but didn't loosen his grip.

Like most accidents, everything happened in a split second, and it was only the driver's fast reflexes that saved them from serious injury. With dust still clouding the air, they climbed out to look along the dirt road at the other vehicle racing away. It was a truck with canvas sides disappearing into the distance, and their African tracker guide got down on his knees and had a look at the wheel treads in the dust.

He spoke to the driver in Swahili, who then interpreted that the vehicle wasn't from around these parts. The driver was wearing camouflage army attire, which was not typical for the peaceful region of the Serengeti.

'Why would soldiers be driving around the safari park?' Connor asked.

'I have no idea, Connor, but we'll get Mike to report it to the authorities when we get back to camp.'

Everyone was a little shaken but thankful that no one was seriously hurt. Connor had a purple lump swelling on his elbow, so they hurried back to camp for an ice pack.

The next day, they had to leave the camp and begin their flight across to the Skeleton Coast. Their time here would never be forgotten, especially as it was where Connor had proposed, and everyone at the camp had shared in their excitement and joy. The cook almost cried as he hugged Gabby farewell. She waved at all the staff as the jeep sped them back to the small airstrip.

The plane was fired up and soon they were saluting Gus as they taxied toward the runway. Gabby said, 'Connor, thank you for such a fantastic time in Africa. It has been the best week of my life.'

'You are my life now.'

Gabby leaned over to kiss him passionately as they flew along.

'It's dangerous to distract the pilot,' he said affectionately

'I'll try to curb my ardour, Captain.'

'Don't try too hard.' He winked.

They relaxed to the drone of the engines as Gabby tried to absorb as much of the landscape before it disappeared. The acacia trees arched their branches over the land that gave them sustenance. This tree, the elephant and the lion have come to symbolise Africa around the world.

The land they were flying over became much more arid. They hadn't seen a river for quite a while and there wasn't as much wildlife moving about.

The air was shattered when a sharp noise shook them out of their reverie, and Connor looked about in a panic. 'That sounds like gunfire. Keep your body low, just in case.'

'Who would be shooting at us?' Gabby asked as she sank down in her seat.

Once again, they heard the same sound and then a metallic ping as something hit the fuselage.

'I'm going to go higher to move beyond their range,' Connor said.

But before he could ascend, a bullet hit the plane, and one of the engines exploded and caught fire. Connor swore when smoke began to billow out behind them. 'Gabby, one of our engines are out, so I have to bring the plane down. Hang on tight and brace yourself for a crash landing,' he yelled above the din of the howling engine.

Twenty-two

The plane was coming down fast as Connor fought the controls to level the wings. 'I'm going to get as low as I can before we hit the ground, but even then it's going to be a brutal touchdown,' he warned her of the impending impact.

Praying for a safe landing, Gabby braced her feet firmly on the floor and held tightly to the door of the aircraft. The ground came quickly towards them, and they hit hard, the plane bouncing back up into the air only to crash down again. Then it began to grind through trees, snapping branches off as they ploughed through at a tremendous speed.

Connor was trying to hold it steady with the controls, but they were still travelling far too fast. The aircraft's nose dug into the ground and the back of the plane catapulted end for end.

The windscreen smashed open, and Gabby felt her body leave the plane. After this, there was no sensation as she descended into unconsciousness.

Pacing up and down the aisle of the small chapel, Josiel felt her spirit surge with fear. She felt Fallon was in great danger with none of her guardians on duty to save her. Did she dare to intervene and rush to her aid once again?

Still living in exile, she was hidden from the council scouts who scoured this realm. Angelic scouts that would be waiting to sweep in to arrest her as soon as they sensed her aura.

Could she save Fallon and remain concealed? It was going to be a gamble; however, it was one that she couldn't refuse. Still able to move through time and space, she spread her vast wings and took off to intercept the crash before an untimely death could rob this life from Fallon.

As Fallon's human form, Gabby, flew out from the plane, smashing through the windscreen, she slipped into unconsciousness from the impact, never knowing that it was her angelic sister who broke her fall to earth.

Josiel caught her in flight and wrapped her wings around her as they tumbled across the hard ground, stirring a cloud of dust. Once they stopped rolling, she sat and cradled Gabby to check her for injuries. There was a deep gash on her forehead, so she pressed her hand against it until the bleeding stopped.

Knowing every second counted, she had to get back to her refuge, but also needed to protect Gabby in this wild land. Disappearing for a short time, Josiel then came back to the crash site. 'Fallon, there are guardians coming here soon, so trust them to keep you safe. I wish I could stay longer but I must hurry back to Rome before I'm discovered,' she whispered to the still-unconscious woman.

Josiel shook the dust out of her wings and prepared for flight, but it was too late, as suddenly she had company.

Landing lightly on the ground in front of her stood two of her brothers from the Silver City. They were fierce in face and stature, obviously anticipating she would resist their arrest.

'Josiel, sister, long have we searched the realms for you. It is now our duty to escort you to stand before the council of wisdom to answer for your actions.'

She knew there was no point in trying to escape, as she would be found now no matter how clever her hiding place was. Hanging her head in surrender, she accepted the charges made against her. Knowing her return would be marred with accusations and punishment, it was the one time she did not long to see the mighty statues surrounding the city of jewels.

Her grey eyes settled on Gabby's prone form on the ground, but at least she was still alive.

Josiel knew it had been the right choice, no matter what punishment now awaited her.

Sometime after the flames from the burned-out wreck smouldered down into a smoky pile of twisted metal, a cloud of dust heralded the arrival of a truck. A group of renegade soldiers excitedly leaped out to see what became of their target practice.

One solidly built black man called out in Swahili to his cohorts, 'There's a body over here.'

They found a young woman lying on her back with her arms crossed over her chest. Rushing up to her, they suddenly pulled up short, and one grabbed the other to draw him back from certain death. Be careful,' he hissed.

Their bulging eyes saw that her body was covered by slithering cobras, their marbled skin a symbol of death. When the snakes sensed their proximity, they began spitting fine sprays of venom into the air. This poison could be propelled up to ten feet, so the soldiers quickly moved out of range.

Muttering and cursing, they crossed their chests and made signs to ward off evil, shuddering in disbelief and fear at the snakes sliding all over the woman's body. This was bad, an evil omen.

She must have landed in a cobra nest and died a terrible death. The plane crash would have been a better passing. 'The hyenas will eat her when the snakes are finished,' one soldier remarked.

All soldiers then backed away superstitiously.

Connor groggily came back to reality and distantly heard men shouting at each other. It was as if the noise came down a funnel into his head. He could hear the sound but could not comprehend the words, so maybe it was a different language.

He slowly started moving different parts of his body to check for injuries. When he tried to move his left leg, an excruciating pain shot through him.

It must be broken.

Opening his eyes to search for Gabby, he couldn't see her anywhere. He had been flung from the cockpit when the ceiling broke open, and it was a miracle the disintegrated plane hadn't landed on him. He looked over and saw the broken, twisted wreckage but could not see his fiancé anywhere. *Where is Gabby?* his mind screamed.

'Gabby,' he croaked repeatedly as he tried to crawl towards the twisted metal.

Just then, a huge black man strode towards him and placed a large foot on his back, grabbed his hair and pulled his head up, almost snapping his neck.

'Look, Baas, this one is still alive. I think Nawvlee would like him as a hostage.'

The man they called Baas came over and pulled Connor to his feet. Connor couldn't take any weight on his broken leg and staggered backwards onto his backside. The pain from the fall shuddered through him and he cried out in agony.

'Where's my girlfriend?' he asked through clenched teeth.

'The woman is dead,' the big black man harshly told him.

'No, no she can't be,' Connor cried out. 'Gabby, Gabby, where are you?'

He tried to stand again, only to have his leg collapse. Grabbing hold of it to stop the pain, he slumped back to the dusty ground. No cry came out of his throat as his insides had turned to stone.

'Get up now,' he was told in heavily accented English.

Before he could even attempt to drag himself up, he was thrown over a shoulder and tossed into the back of their truck. It looked like the same truck that had nearly crashed into them the day before on the Serengeti.

Connor groaned in agony when he landed roughly on his shattered leg. 'I have to look for Gabby. At least let me see her to say goodbye,' he begged.

'Your friend is dead. We checked her already, so there is nothing for us here now. We're not going to load this truck down with dead bodies. There's no ransom money for dead people. Now shut up or I will put a gag on you.'

The soldier tied Connor's arms behind his back, and he lay there twisted on the dirty floor of the truck. His leg was throbbing and burning, his clothes were torn and blood oozed through in places.

He wished he was dead too. Let them shoot him. He couldn't go on without Gabby. Connor was mutilated, his other half torn from him without warning. They had been flying along with the future stretching before them and now in a split second he had nothing. Without her, it was better to die here and hopefully find her in an afterlife.

'Why, God? Why did you let me live instead of her?'

Soldiers climbed into the truck, and it took off with the engine revving loudly, bouncing across the open arid ground towards some unknown destination.

Connor drifted in and out of consciousness, and each time he woke, the pain in his leg was worse. With every bump, the sharp pain ran up his leg and made him cry out.

In response the soldiers would slam their guns into him and yell, 'Shut up or we will shoot you.'

These men had been doing target practice with their new AK47 rifles when a lucky shot had brought the plane down. To see it spiralling down with smoke billowing out of its engines caused a great deal of back patting and shouts of excitement. The men had raced to the crash site to find the plane in a terrible mess and the two occupants thrown out onto the ground, first the woman, then a man further across the grassy field.

The soldiers were self-proclaimed 'freedom fighters', and they had slipped through Rwanda undetected from the Congo. Most of their comrades had been killed by their own ranks. There was a lot of discontent as to who should be declared the leader of their new army, and rather than vote, the opposition got shot.

This small group of dissidents had taken over a mission village in the hills on the border of the Congo and now used it as their base. They had killed most of the villagers so that the soldiers could inhabit their huts, but had left the old missionary doctor and his nurse alive for their medical skills. Having their own medical team was very handy when the men kept shooting each other.

The Serengeti was the place to take rich tourists hostage, which they needed to fund the next part of their invasion. The leader, Nawvlee was taking new recruits by force from remote locations to build an army large enough to overthrow the government.

His lieutenant was another giant of a man, well over six feet tall and deep in the chest like a bull elephant. He shouted orders to his inferiors in some language that Connor couldn't follow. He noticed that they could speak English but preferred to speak to one another in their own dialect.

They drove for two days, with only a few sips of warm brown water to moisten his cottonwool mouth. He could smell his blood mixing with the other sweaty men in the back of the truck. Thankfully, he was half delirious most of the time. When he was aware of his surroundings, he measured time in pain, a dull ache when they were stationary and excruciating pain when the truck bumped over the rough roads.

It was dark and humid when they screeched to a halt, and Connor shouted when they dragged him out by the legs. Baas tossed him over his shoulder and strode to a small hut, where he unceremoniously dropped him onto a pile of hessian sacks on the floor. Connor heard him yelling to bring the doctor in the morning as he locked the door.

He was broken, body and soul. As he fell into a fitful sleep, he dreamed that Gabby was running towards him with her hair flowing out behind and calling him. When she took him in her arms, the pain disappeared, and all he felt was love.

'It's alright now, Connor. I will make you better.' She smelled so good, like a forest on a sunny day.

He pressed her tightly against him, not ever wanting to let her go again. 'I love you, Gabby. Please don't ever leave me again.'

In the pre-dawn light, the sound of his sobs woke him as he lay there remembering his vivid dream. Connor swore he could still smell her fragrance in the dirty hut. This dream had been so real, it made him forget the pain and his imprisonment, and he didn't want to wake up. Maybe her spirit was here saying goodbye? Oddly, the thought gave him some comfort to think she might still be close by. Did she know how much he loved her? Had he told her often enough?

Connor would give everything he had just to see her again.

Ben was watching television in the lounge of Carlton Cottage when the Titans rushed to the door, whimpering in distress. He got up and opened the door for the dogs to go outside. 'What's the matter, guys? There isn't anyone here. Come on inside and settle down.'

Joe also came outside to see what was happening. 'What's going on, Ben?'

'Joe, I haven't a clue. Everything seems okay.'

The dogs refused to come back inside. Instead, they ran to the front gate to bark loudly before rushing back to Ben and Joe.

Suddenly the penny dropped for Joe.

'Something is wrong with Gabby. They sense when she's in danger or hurt.'

Once again Ben called the dogs to come inside with him, but they whined and scratched at the wooden gate, so he had to go and drag one in by the collar. Once he got Goliath inside, Samson followed reluctantly. He slammed the door shut, panting from the effort of dragging the equivalent of his own weight.

The dogs lay at the front door with their heads resting on their front legs, their sad, unhappy eyes watching Joe and Ben. Their sixth sense was troubling them.

Ben watched Joe start calling Gabby's and Connor's mobile phones but neither of them had any signal. They found their itinerary to contact the hotel where they were booked into.

When reception answered at the Sossusvlei Lodge, it was the middle of the night, and it was a strong African accent that answered Joe's call. 'Hello, this is Ngambui.'

'Ngambui, my name is Joe Campbell, and I am calling from Australia. I need to find out if some of my friends checked in. Their names are Gabrielle Harrison and Connor Faradene. Could you confirm that they have arrived?'

'Please wait a moment,' the receptionist said in his accented English. 'I am sorry, but these guests failed to show or cancel, and they will not be eligible for any refund on their booking,' he sounded defensive.

'Ngambui, are you positive that they did not arrive?'

'Yes, Mr Joe, I am certain, and as I said before, no refund. Could you please call back tomorrow morning, you know it is two o'clock in the morning here, sir.'

'No! I will not call back. I want to speak to the hotel manager right now, and I don't care what time of the night or day it is there. Something has happened to my friends, and I want the police called straight away.'

'Sir, it is a bad time of the night, please call back in the morning.'

'I have two friends who are missing and I need to get answers now,' Joe firmly told the employee.'

'Sir, I will have to contact the on-call manager.'

When the line clicked through to the hotel manager, Joe argued with him for several minutes until he hung up the phone in frustration. Despite Joe's urgency, the manager was adamant that it would take time to get the local authorities organised to investigate two missing foreigners.

'We need to make some phone calls to the families,' Joe gruffly told Ben.

The two dogs barked in agreement, then they despondently dropped their heads back onto their front paws.

'Ben, can you call Kathleen and her brothers first, then see if you can locate a number for Connor's parents?'

'No problem, I'll get straight onto it.'

Kathleen had only been home for two weeks when the phone rang twice and she picked it up. 'Hello.'

Ben could hear concern in Kathleen's voice and a terrible noise in the background. 'Kathleen, this is Ben. What's all that noise?'

'Ben, I'm sorry but the curlews started going crazy a short while ago. Now they're running all around the yard, screeching non-stop.'

Ben's heart sank with her words. He thought to himself that if the curlews and the dogs sensed trouble, then it was indeed true.

'Kathleen, it seems Gabby and Connor may have failed to arrive in Namibia yesterday, and I think the curlews up there and the Titans down here are trying to tell us that she's in danger.'

'No Ben, not Gabby. I can't cope with losing any more of my family,' Kathleen's voice rose over the phone.

'Hang in there, Kathleen. I'm going to talk to Connor's parents and between all of us we'll work something out.'

'Thank you, Ben.'

'I'll be back in touch as soon as we formulate a plan,' Ben reassured her before he hung up.

Ben found a business number for Faradene Enterprises and left a message. Joe was speaking with the hotel manager again on the phone, so Ben took the mobile and sat on the floor with the two dogs. They both moved closer to him to draw some comfort.

He couldn't think that Gabby was dead, such a thought was incomprehensible. He would have felt it if she was no longer in this universe. *We will find them*, he kept telling himself repeatedly.

Ben's phone began to buzz, and he answered it to the deep, resonant voice of Robert Faradene echoing across the connection. He explained that they were concerned about Connor and Gabby, and after some enquiries had discovered that they had failed to arrive at their destination.

'Has Connor been in touch since arriving in Africa?' he asked Robert.

'We received an email from him when they were staying at the hotel in Arusha, but we have not heard any news since then,' Robert responded to Ben's query. 'Leave it with me, Ben. I will give our foreign affairs department a call and see if there have been any reports of civil unrest. I'll call back once I have some information.'

Ben then called Kathleen back to keep her updated.

Joe got an assurance from the hotel manager that he would notify the local police, but there was nothing more he could do for the moment.

So they sat on the floor with the Titans to wait for the phone to ring. It rang forty-five minutes later, so Ben passed his phone to Joe.

'Joe speaking,' he said.

'Joe, it's Robert Faradene. The news is not encouraging, so I have insisted the local police start a ground and aerial search at first light.'

'Why didn't the hotel raise the alarm when they failed to check in? Joe asked.

'Apparently, in Africa not checking is quite normal, so they didn't think it strange.'

'Thanks, Robert. Will you keep us abreast of any developments?'

'Yes, of course, and thank you for calling us straight away. How did you find out there was a problem?'

'It may sound a little weird, but Gabby has a very close bond to her dogs and when they got upset, we suspected there was something wrong.'

'With anyone else I would believe that was impossible, but not with Gabrielle,' Robert agreed.

'We will stay in touch,' Joe said as he looked at the dogs.

Twenty-three

Across the world, far from Australia, another day was about to begin in New Delhi. As the sun peeked over the horizon, Abijah Sharma rose early to begin the morning feeds and baths.

As she dressed, she saw that Simran was still curled up tight in her covers. Squatting down beside her pallet, she gently shook her sister's shoulder to wake her from such deep slumber and was suddenly pushed backwards to land heavily on her backside.

'Who are you?' Simran's startled face was pushed up close to hers.

'I am your sister, silly girl. Did you have a bad dream?'

Simran sat up and slowly looked around at the room. Seeing the impoverished conditions, she began to wail like a banshee.

The orphanage mother came running and saw Simran crying and pounding her fists into the hard floor. 'What is wrong with your sister, Abijah? She looks like a demon has possessed her.' She came over to look more closely at the wailing girl.

'Go away, all of you, just get away from me,' she screamed at them, tears and snot combining to drip off her chin.

Shocked at the outburst, they retreated and stood in the corner whispering their concern about Simran's strange behaviour. 'Perhaps she is ill? I will take over her chores today and let her rest to get well again,' Abijah kindly offered.

The mother was the head of their small orphanage, and she just shook her head at both of them before bustling away.

Once all the babies had been fed and bathed, Abijah took Simran a small bowl of rice for her breakfast.

When it was placed before her, Simran scowled at her sister and picked up the bowl. Sniffing disdainfully at the rice, she screwed up her face and threw the food across the room. 'I refuse to eat such disgusting food. Bring me French toast and coffee,' she scornfully demanded.

Once Abijah had cleaned up the rice, she came back to look closely at her sister's face. 'Simran, where did you get those jewels? Did you steal them?'

Gina, who now inhabited Simran's body, reached up to feel the large diamond earrings. This gift from Dominic had been somehow overlooked when she was stripped of all of her belongings. 'No I did not steal them, they're mine. Now get out.'

Abijah just looked at her in bewilderment. This was not her beloved, kind-hearted sister. There was indeed some mad demon living in her body. Bursting into tears, Abijah spun around and left the room, unable to fathom what had become warped throughout the night. Her sister had been herself when retiring the night before yet now some monster had woken in her place.

Gina curled up and drew the covers over her head, wishing this was just some bad dream that she would awake from. The wailing of children drove her crazy with misery, and she kept whispering, *This, can't be real, this can't be real*, over and over again.

The hours passed by as she stayed huddled in those threadbare sheets until hunger and the need to go to the toilet drove her to explore these foreign surroundings. Dominic had been cruel to send her to such a place. It was so poor and smelled like baby urine. The ammonia tainted the air, and it hurt her nostrils to breathe.

How long would she be left here in this hovel, hell on earth for someone whose standard was a minimum of five stars? Finally stumbling into some kind of open bathroom, Gina realised that privacy here was an unaffordable luxury. She quickly squatted to pee and then washed her hands in a cracked sink.

Staring at her reflection in a broken mirror, she widened her large brown eyes, looking for any sign of green. Gina opened her mouth wide, examining the full lips that were so foreign to her own. Then she ran her hands over the long black hair, which hung past her waist in a thick plait, and then over her waist and hips. Curiously, she examined the shape and contours of this young woman's body and guessed her host was probably not even twenty years old.

The sparkling earrings in her lobes mocked her as they spoke of wealth and prestige, so Gina angrily pulled them out and shoved them deep into the pocket of her pyjamas.

Once her bladder was relieved, her stomach became the driving force, and it drove her to follow the smell of curry into a large kitchen. One equipped with the fundamentals to provide mass food and feed many hungry mouths.

Taking a cracked bowl, she ladled a large serve of curry and rice and sat at the wooden trestle table to gulp it down. Not long after the last grain of rice was scraped from the bowl, a scream broke the rare moment of solitude.

A tiny Indian woman appeared and grabbed a wooden spoon from the bench and began to whack Gina, all the time cursing her.

She could hardly believe she was getting a beating for eating food. Crossing her arms over her head, she fled from the bosom of nourishment.

The funny thing was that she could understand the language, which was rather fortunate as it would have been worse to be in this strange place and not know what they were saying.

Finding her pallet again, she lay down to consider her options. She could run away, but the thought of living on the streets of India gave her more shivers than her present humble abode.

There was no chance of escaping and contacting her family. Remembering her reflection in the cracked bathroom mirror, the dusky face of a young Indian woman staring back at her, she reached around to hold her plait and thoughtfully rubbed it against her lips.

Nobody would believe she was Gina Perry, not looking like this, and she wondered where the rightful owner of this body was. Dominic had not mentioned what happened to the host soul when hers had been unceremoniously dumped here.

Her only real option was to play the game and become this girl named Simran. If she did her best, it might convince the guild that she had learnt her lesson and deserved a second chance.

Life became a miserable merry-go-round of hard work, and Simran's back ached from carrying babies all day. Her fingers bled from scrubbing pots in the kitchen, and she constantly smelled like vomit and pee.

This was her version of hell on earth, and she knew that Dominic had chosen her destination for that exact reason. She plotted all kinds of revenge when she became more powerful than him, as Gina would never forget this insult.

Abijah still looked at her in bewilderment. Her sister Simran had never been one to complain about anything and yet now she complained about everything. The early rise out of bed, the lack of food, the babies that never stopped crying, the heat.

Helping the unfortunate no longer made her happy.

She tried to placate Simran and make her happy again but nothing seemed to work. Surely an evil spirit had taken residence in her body. All she could do was hope and pray that her true sister would come back and be her joyful self once again.

After a couple of weeks, Simran learned to keep her mouth shut, her muscles strengthened and her ability to cope slowly improved. It seemed that Abijah's prayers were being considered in another time and place

After a particularly long laborious day, Abijah gently rubbed the thin sponge over Simran's back as they stood knee deep in the bath. They had to use the same water as the children and by now it was cloudy and murky with old suds. Filling the cracked tumbler, she rinsed the soap out of Simran's long, silky black hair that fell below her buttocks.

The water flowed through the dark tresses and stuck them to her dusky skin like seaweed on a mermaid, and once she was finished, her sister did the same with her own long dark tresses.

'Oh, that feels so good. Even if it's not clean, it still soothes my tired muscles,' Simran said.

'The water is God's gift. Without it, the world would die of thirst,' Abijah reminded her.

'God has many gifts, like wine, for instance. Oh my God, I've forgotten the taste of wine!' Dramatically, Simran dropped into the pool of water, causing it to splash over the side of the tub.

'Simran, why are you so upset?'

'Because I'm beginning to forget my other life, my real life,' she sobbed into her water-wrinkled hands.

'Don't cry, little sister. It pains me when you cry. Don't you want to be here with me anymore?'

'I just want to go home.' Simran's nose was blocked from tears, and her red eyes pleaded for Abijah to understand.

'You are home. I am your home.'

To which Simran just cried louder.

Abijah gently helped her out of the bath and dried her glistening body. She dressed her like a child and led her unprotesting and sniffling to their bed pallets.

Laying in the soft candlelight Abijah held her sister tightly against her. 'Simran, you must find your peace. This anger will only make life worse,' Abijah spoke softly into the candlelit room.

'I'm trying.' Simran hiccupped from so much crying.

'I love you, sister.'

'I love you too, Abijah, and I want you to have these earrings as a token of my love.' Simran passed over the diamond earrings in the candlelight.

Abijah held the treasures up to the light to watch how the facets shimmered blues and greens. 'You never told me where you got these from.'

'They were given to me by a rich and powerful man,' her sister said.

'You never leave here, so how did you meet this man?'

'A lot can happen while you are sleeping, big sister.'

'You snuck out?'

'No, I snuck in. Oh, never mind. No matter how I try to explain, it would never be believed.'

'There is a man in here?' Abijah looked around as if the mystery man would suddenly appear.

'No, not here. Never mind, Abijah. It's all in the past now. That man is no longer interested in me.' She sighed with regret.

'What did you do for him to receive such a gift, Simran?'

'I sold him my soul.'

Abijah gasped in shock. 'Simran, you should never do such a thing! Your soul belongs only to God.'

'Well, sometimes God has to share. Anyway, he won't miss my little soul when he has all of these babies to look after.'

'Simran, you are acting so strangely. I am troubled to see you so miserable. How can I make it better?'

'Dear Abijah, I am stranger than you could possibly imagine.'

'Well, I refuse to stop loving you, no matter how strange you become.' Her beautiful, kind smile lit up the room. 'Thank you for the earrings. Would you be offended if I sold them and used the money for the babies?'

'Only you, Abijah, would put the needs of others before your own. You are a wonderful, caring girl who deserves your own happy ending.'

Abijah reached over to hug her tightly. It seemed her gentle Simran was finally coming back to her.

Have I changed enough Dominic? Have I been forgiven? How long will I be punished? This was her last thought as she drifted off to sleep.

But instead of falling into sleep, she began tumbling through the silent void.

Gina opened her eyes to find she was back on the altar with all the priests around her, like she had never left. Was this the same night they had performed the soul exchange ritual?

Disorientated and confused, she looked around the room. When she pushed herself up to a sitting position, she saw her hands looked worn and damaged from hard work, and her nails were cracked and broken. Her body was different too; it was leaner and harder. How long had she been in that other life? There were no memories, only a residue that she had been living in poverty and the work had been hard.

The priests moved back as Dominic stepped forward to gently pick her up. As soon as Gina felt his embrace she began to cry, the sobs coming from deep within her heart.

'Come with me. There is one more step in this journey,' he murmured into her hair as he strode away with her in his arms.

He carried her to a prayer temple and swept a robe over her nakedness, asking her to stay here until she was enlightened.

Gina lay on the floor of the temple, listening to her own breathing get slower and slower until her mind became trance-like. Slowly she became aware of another presence in the room. It was a tall man, who was wearing a silver mask over his face. One that shrouded his features but allowed movement and expression. A strange sight indeed.

'Come sit with me,' he invited her.

Gina swept the robe around her and moved to sit beside him on the steps in the darkness and waited for him to speak. She felt so tired, but it was more than her body. This weariness came from deep within her soul, like she had just climbed a high mountain and now she could rest.

'What have you learnt?' he asked quietly.

'I have learnt humility. I am now prepared to follow orders and accept any task commanded of me.'

He answered her with silence.

'What happens now?'

'That depends on you, doesn't it, Gina Perry?' He answered her question with a question.

'What do you mean?' she chewed on her lip nervously.

'With this maturity, a new life can begin.'

'Or?'

'I think you now understand that we cannot have a member of our organisation use spiritual powers for personal gratification. These skills must be used for the glorification of Lucifer's return to power. You know too much about us to go back to your old life, and we must decide tonight what your future is going to be.'

'I am not sure who you are, but I repent for my pride. I wasn't aware of the spiritual war raging around us. Actually, I still don't know that much, but now I want to. I want to be a part of something bigger than myself, so please don't end my life here tonight. Give me that second chance, and I promise you won't be sorry.'

After a poignant pause, he reached out with a small blade and slashed it across her palm.

Gina jumped from the sting of the blade and clenched her fist around the pooling blood, while she watched him do the same to his own hand.

Ceremoniously, he clenched the two bleeding hands as he made a pledge. 'Gina, this night you are reborn as part of The Omega Guild. Your new name of service is *Crimson Thorn*. If called upon, you will offer your life for this cause and the Morning Star. You must be ready when summoned by the darkness,' he said as he brushed her hair back from her brow, leaving a bloody smudge across her face.

When she lifted her face, he was gone. It was strange how these people could appear and disappear so easily, without a sound or ripple in time. Only the blood dripping from her hand was evidence of the encounter.

Twenty-four

Gabby slowly regained consciousness. Laying there stunned, she looked around at the bits of debris scattered across the cracked, dry ground. She couldn't remember the impact of the crash; her last memory was when the plane started tumbling crazily towards the ground.

There was no sign of Connor amongst the burned-out wreckage of the aircraft. A couple of snakes lay coiled on the ground around her, so Gabby carefully dragged herself away to avoid causing them any alarm.

'Connor, Connor where are you?'

She sat up and scanned the landscape, but Connor was nowhere in sight. When she turned her head, the pain shot through her temples. She reached up to feel the dried blood across her forehead. *Ouch, I must have really hit my head during my own crash landing.*

Maybe Connor was scouting further afield; however, it wasn't like him to leave her here alone. He was too protective for that, always wanting to see her safe.

Where had Connor gone? She staggered to her feet and giddily walked towards the tangled metal. The plane was just a burned shell, as the fire had consumed the interior and twisted the frame out of shape. It was a miracle to survive this crash. Had Connor been flung further away? Was he still alive?

Calling out and walking in ever-widening circles, there was only silence to discover. Coming across some fresh tyre marks in the sand, she could see where a heavy vehicle had driven away.

Maybe some help had arrived and Connor had gone with them, but that didn't make sense. He wouldn't just leave her there, so maybe he was forced to go. Something like this could happen in Africa.

The more she thought about that scenario, the more she became convinced that Connor did not leave of his own free will. Why did they leave her behind? Two hostages were better than one, especially if they were going to bargain their lives for a ransom?

Gabby had to get help to find him, and to do this she had to find a settlement.

She staggered forward, keeping the sun over her right shoulder as she moved into the cool interior of the thick forest. The monkeys screeched in the branches above as she made her way through the forest, each step forward was one less in the quest to find Connor.

Night fell quickly, and Gabby found shelter against a huge tree trunk, but her head still throbbed from the accident while her stomach churned with anxiety. Sleep came reluctantly, and it seemed that all the noises of the forest followed in her dreams. She dreamed of Africa and all the experiences she had enjoyed with Connor.

Jerking awake as a huge cat settled beside her, Gabby tentatively reached out to touch her wiry musky-scented coat. She sensed that the lion's intention was to protect and guard, so with a sigh she fell back into a deep sleep.

The morning presented a second surprise: Her feline guard had been joined by an enormous pachyderm. She stood there like a mountain of grey and gently flapped her gigantic ears to sweep a soft breeze over Gabby lying below.

Staggering to her feet again, she reached out to touch the dusty beast's wrinkled trunk. Gabby felt completely humbled by the contact between a wild animal and capricious human being. She named the lion 'Tau' and the elephant she named 'Udo', and she asked these new friends to help her find the settlement of her own kind.

In response, the grey mountain turned away to what appeared to be the east, but with her head pounding it was difficult to tell in which direction she stumbled behind them. The lion walked a little to her right and kept her pace to Gabby's slow shuffle, until she half-fell to her knees under a large acacia.

'I think we need to rest for a moment.'

The elephant's trunk reached up to the branches to pull off their greenery while she stood over Gabby. The lion disappeared to hunt and came back with a small rodent, which she dropped at Gabby's feet.

'No meat, Tau.' Gabby used her mind to show them pictures of the food she needed.

Without ceremony, the lion lay down and began to crack the small rodent bones and rip the flesh away. Gabby was thirsty more than hungry, and she would need water soon if she was to survive long enough to raise an alarm.

Udo did find water for her soon after as well as every day of their trek through the wilderness. Even when it seemed they would have to keep going without slaking their thirst, she would take them to a patch of sand where a river had once run.

There she would begin to dig the sand with her massive feet. Realising there was moisture under the sand, Gabby dived under her to dig as well until they reached the dirt-filled water. Sucking the gritty muddy liquid with her cracked, dry lips, she used her teeth to sieve out the bigger chunks of sand and small rocks. She told herself to always remember that this was 'the real taste of Africa'.

As they walked along, Gabby found little black berries growing on the bushes they were moving through. With little choice, she decided to take the risk and hope that they were good enough to eat. She popped one into her mouth and bit through the tough outer skin. The berry burst suddenly filled her mouth with a bitter stringent juice, and her taste buds responded by filling her mouth with saliva. The berries weren't sweet like a strawberry, more like a raspberry but nowhere near as nice.

It was better than nothing at least, and they provided her with some meagre nourishment. Udo would wrap her trunk around the highest branches and bring them down for Gabby to reach the fruit. Her stomach cramped but she didn't get diarrhoea or void the contents onto the dry grass.

Her needs were reduced to shelter, water and sustenance, and her world narrowed to taking the next step on what seemed a never-ending journey, moving one foot in front of the other. Her sparkling engagement ring would no longer stay on her thin finger, so she wore it on her thumb instead.

During the isolation of their journey, the trio formed a close bond. It wasn't a communication like human to human but there was a level of understanding and empathy for each other. They shared memories, and it was distressing to see that many of the animals' experiences with humans had been traumatic.

Udo planted images in Gabby's mind of how her mother had been killed and her tusks butchered in front of her when she was just a young calf. The tears wet the drought of dust covering her face as she remembered being tied to her dead mother's body to stop her getting away. The pain and loss had been overwhelming, and she had called out for her mother and aunts for weeks. She had stumbled along in a cloud of depression until she was herded in with many other orphaned elephants, but they were an unruly bunch without the role models from the old bulls and matriarchs.

Eventually Udo had broken out of the sanctuary to find her family, where she had raised her own calves in the freedom of the savannah.

Tau had grown up in her pride with very little human intervention, but in the last few years they had been hunted several times by poachers who wanted their hides as a prize, and she had seen many of her kind slaughtered for trophies.

Gabby mourned with them for their losses. It was heartbreaking to share such sad memories. To compensate a little, she showed them images of humans fighting to save the animals, and the conservationists around the world fighting to save endangered species.

She wanted them to know that some humans were dedicated to protect and preserve their lands. Her thoughts told them that not all of her kind acted so cruelly, that some did have compassion.

They settled into a routine, resting during the heat of the day and walking through the night. As they travelled, Gabby felt completely safe with these two companions.

The blue-marbled sky stretched over her like a party tarpaulin, and the stars twinkled like fairy lights at night. This vastness was only broken by patches of twisted acacia trees. Sometimes to get perspective, they climbed to the top of rocky kopjes and stood there gazing at the beauty of this other world.

Their silhouette of three, Udo so huge, Gabby standing in the middle with Tau on her other side as protector, there they stood with the setting sun in the background. Perhaps a symbol of the future, man and beast living in harmony side by side instead of against each other.

There was now time to wonder at the colour of the lion's eye, so yellow and intense, Tau's gaze could look right through her. There was time to wonder at the size and royal bearing of her elephant friend, and there was certainly time to reconnect with those who shared this land.

One day, they came to the edge of a fast-flowing river. As Gabby stood there looking across the muddy, troubled waters, she worried how they were going to traverse this obstacle. It looked like a perfect crocodile habitat.

Gabby walked to the wet edge and saw the water lap over the toes of her worn tracking boots. Udo lumbered beside her and raised her trunk to sniff at the air, which was cooler with the moisture lifting off

the water. Slowly she turned so that one of her tusks was resting under the back of Gabby's knees and gently lifted the weight off her
feet.

Gabby shouted with excitement when Udo offered to carry her
across the river and swung herself up to take hold of her head as she
was lifted high. Udo wrapped her trunk around Gabby's body to
hold her firm as they stepped into the swirling river.

Tau wasn't keen to enter the water, so she hesitated and paced up
and down the edge of the bank flicking her tail like an annoyed
household cat. Finally, she took the leap to plunge into the water and
swim up to Udo's massive grey shoulder, staying in that position as
they moved sideways across the flowing waters.

Gabby's cries of surprise and joy at such an experience filled the
quiet bush scene until they stepped out on the other bank, dripping
and exhilarated. Even Udo raised her trunk and trumpeted to the
blue sky while Tau grumbled and rumbled a small roar in response to
being unpleasantly wet. It was such a wonder to see the two animals
react so differently – an unforgettable moment and a happy interlude
in Gabby's tragic circumstances.

Twenty-five

Ben sat on the veranda with the Titans on either side of him and looked up at the stars that were shining into oblivion. So much was happening below, with people laughing, crying, loving and praying. Ben himself was praying tonight. Gabby and Connor had been missing for a couple of days now, and the plane wreckage had been located with no sign of either of them.

He and Joe were planning to fly across to Africa with Robert Faradene the next morning. Everyone wanted to be there on the ground when the news came through.

Where are you, Gabby? God, I pray that we find you soon.

At that moment Joe came out and sat beside him on the bench seat.

'Do you think she's still alive, Joe?' Ben took the plunge and spoke their fears aloud.

'My heart tells me she is alive, and it has been true before. I trust it to be so once again.' He grasped Ben's shoulder to reassure him.

'Joe, I hope you're right. I don't think I could go on without her.' Ben's voice trembled with emotion.

'I know, son, I know.'

Joe had never spoken to Ben like this before and it touched him to the core. He had never known his own father, and to have a giant of a man like Joe step into that role was the greatest of honours.

Connor woke and lay there with his eyes closed tightly as he listened to the sounds of the jungle, the screech of the monkeys as they moved through the upper branches and the unfamiliar bird calls filling the air.

Running his tongue around his dry mouth it tasted sour and unwashed, but before he could look for water, the door creaked open and he opened a bleary red eye to look at his visitor.

A man with a pack came through the small door. He stood still and looked Connor over before making any introductions. He was quite old and had a shock of grey hair with bushy grey eyebrows almost hiding faded green eyes. He must have been over six feet tall and had a slight stoop that comes from bending over too much.

'Well, young man. Who have they stumbled across in their adventures?' he asked in a crisp British accent.

Connor groaned as he lifted his head to have a better look at this foreigner. 'My name is Connor Faradene. I am an Australian citizen, and these criminals have killed my fiancé. They have injured and abducted me into this godforsaken place. Who are you?' Connor could have cried with anger and frustration.

The doctor's eyes showed compassion as he squatted beside Connor. 'My dear lad, my christened name is Edward James Howard, but here in this godforsaken place I am just 'the doctor' and that suits me fine.'

'Why do you live here with these madmen? You must be able to go home to your own country? Do they hold you as a prisoner too?'

'This has been my home for more years than London ever was. My wife and children are buried here, and many of my much-loved friends have lost their lives here. So, Connor, I am a prisoner too, but held by memories and bonds of love not by threats of death from the rebels.'

'I brought my beautiful, young fiancé here to get her away from grief and loss, and now I have suffered the greatest loss of all.'

'I can't heal your broken heart, Connor, but at least let me have a look at that leg of yours.'

The doctor squatted by Connor and felt the hot, swollen flesh where the bone had been snapped.

Connor screamed as the two ends of the broken bones grated against each other.

The doctor took scissors out of his medical bag and cut along the side of his trousers. He pressed some more around the swelling. Connor didn't make a sound this time, but when the doctor looked up, he saw the sweat dripping off his Connor's clenched jaw and stopped his prodding.

'Luckily it's not a compound fracture but it's still a bad break. I will have to get help to re-set your leg.'

'Just let me die,' he pleaded.

'I can't do that, Connor. I took a Hippocratic oath to do no harm.'

'Just do no help then,' Connor muttered as the doctor left him lying on the dirty hessian bag.

Not too long after his first visit, the doctor was back with a tall, slender African girl. Connor saw a young woman who carried herself with a calm serenity. Her shy smile bespoke kindness and dedication.

'Connor, let me introduce you to my daughter, Mosi Howard. Mosi, this is Connor.' Edward grunted as he bent to lift Connor to his feet, with Mosi assisting him.

'Connor, my father is a brilliant doctor. Please trust him to treat your injury,' she spoke with a musical tilt to her words, like she was singing rather than speaking.

Connor cried out in pain when the blood flowed into the in-flamed tissue, and he stood there breathing hard as he rode the waves of agony. The doctor and his daughter supported Connor's weight as they half carried him through the small door.

An armed guard was there waiting to escort them to the small infirmary set up in the middle of a cluster of rudimentary buildings.

The village had an arrangement of grass huts set out in a circle around an open meeting platform, which was raised on wooden posts and also had a thatched grass roof.

The doctor's building was a bit larger than the other basic establishments. It also had a grass thatched roof but in consideration of germs and the spread of illness, this building had a wooden floor. The surface assisted in keeping dirt off the equipment, and in spite of the simplicity, everything in it was spotlessly clean.

Connor was panting with exhaustion when they assisted him to lay down on the wooden examination table. The doctor gave him a piece of timber to place between his teeth.

'I'm sorry, Connor, but best be prepared, as this is going to hurt like hell.'

When Connor nodded, the doctor got Mosi to hold his upper body while he grasped his foot to pull the leg and align the bones again.

The scream was so agonising that even Mosi jumped in fright. She held onto Connor with all of her strength while the doctor didn't even glance up. He was concentrating on getting the broken leg as closely aligned to the other leg. Once satisfied, he got Mosi to come and hold the lower leg steady as he prodded around the break some more to see if he'd managed to pull the leg far enough.

'Connor, without an X-ray machine, there's a lot of guess work but I think I've got your leg lined up. Now, if we can just stabilise it and keep it in this position, we may get you back up on two feet again,' he said as he kept a firm grip on Connor's foot.

Turning to a small preparation table, he nodded for Mosi to get the plaster of Paris bandage and dip it in the bucket. Once it was soft, she carried it dripping across the floor.

Mosi held the leg in position as the doctor slapped the wet, sticky bandage around it, and then they both placed their hands for warmth and support while it dried and set.

The white cast covered Connor's whole leg from the ankle up to his thigh, and the doctor chatted with him until it was strong enough to hold his weight.

'Africa is like a young woman, unpretentious with no worldly weariness, and this country really gets into your blood. I came here over thirty years ago as a medico with the Red Cross for a fixed contract. Back then, I was a bitter, disillusioned man in my forties; however, once here, I fell in love with the place and the people. After some years of service, a beautiful local tribeswoman consented to be my wife.

'We were very happy when we had our Mosi, aptly named as our firstborn, and when she was two years old my wife was once again expecting. Heartbreakingly, Mosi and I lost all of them when the twin boys were born.

'So here we are, looking after each other and managing quite well.' He glanced across and smiled at his beloved daughter, who looked to be in her mid-twenties.

Edward continued. 'The rebels have stolen more than just chickens and goats – they have stolen the innocence of the local tribes. They have killed indiscriminately and changed the landscape that we had come to love. Since Nawvlee came here, death walks too closely beside life.'

So Mosi was half English and half African. It was an exotic combination as she was tall and long-limbed with lighter chocolate-coloured skin than her African cousins. Her eyes were almond-shaped but instead of dark brown like the other tribal women, Mosi's eyes were green like her father's.

Altogether, she was a fascinating mix of the two worlds. Connor watched her working quietly and efficiently alongside her father. She hadn't even looked up when he was explaining their family history.

Mosi said something to her father in the local dialect, to which the doctor smiled and nodded.

'What's funny?' Connor asked.

'Mosi calls you *blue eyes*. She thinks it suits you better than your real name.'

After the plaster was dry enough, they got two of the soldiers to carry him back to his hut. Another armed soldier stayed outside guarding his hut, but Connor wasn't sure how they thought he could escape into the jungle with one of his legs bound from toe to hip.

As he fell back onto the hessian bags, he felt close to hysteria. It was a combination of pain, exhaustion, dehydration and starvation from no real sustenance in several days. The doctor saw him sinking into shock, so he turned to the soldier and spoke in some local dialect, asking for food and drink. The soldier stalked off to another building and he could hear more talking in the same language inside.

Edward left Connor with Mosi and quickly walked into the same building as the soldier, where loud shouting could be heard as each party said their piece.

'What's he saying to them?' Connor asked.

'He is telling them that you won't be worth a penny if they kill you. He also says that you cannot run away with a broken leg.'

Connor was trembling uncontrollably when the Edward strode back to them with the soldiers following behind. They carried him to another hut with a high wooden fence around it. The gate wasn't locked, so they made their way inside to find a bed set up off the ground with a sheet and a dirty blanket thrown across it. The doctor and Mosi both helped Connor to slump down onto the bed, and then Mosi took off to get him some food and drink.

The food was just porridge gruel but it was hot, and he thankfully swallowed each mouthful. They also gave him some goat's milk, which tasted like a watery version of cow's milk as it slid down his throat.

'I've put a sedative powder into your milk to give you respite from the pain and some much-needed sleep. We'll come back later to give you a wash and some clean clothes, but for now, just rest.' The doctor gently assisted Connor to lay back on the bed as Mosi lifted his plastered leg into a more comfortable position.

Connor nodded dreamily as the sedatives began to take effect, and they waited a little longer to see him drift off to sleep.

The soldier made sure Mosi and the doctor left the small compound before he locked the gate behind them.

It was late afternoon when Connor woke from his sedated slumber. The pain was still there but its teeth weren't as sharp. It also felt better to have the leg supported by the plaster cast as it stopped the bones from grinding against each other.

Rising into a sitting position, he managed to swing both legs over the edge of the cot, and sat there taking stock on his new lodgings. *Surely this was just a dream?* Surely he would soon wake to find Gabby asleep beside him? He longed to look into her eyes once more.

The grief sat on his shoulder like a dark cloud that threatened to engulf him. This shadow was swallowing him whole, making him wish he'd died in the plane crash.

When the doctor and Mosi came back, they had two buckets of water and towels with clothing stacked on top.

'How was your sleep?' Edward asked.

'I wish I never woke up.'

'The pain will be unbearable for quite a while, Connor, and not just the physical.' He patted Connor on the shoulder before he sat down beside him. 'Let me have a look at your leg,' he said as he felt along the edges of the plaster and checked the capillary return on his toenails.

'We really need to keep it stable until the bones can grow again. It is such a bad break that you may need to have it re-broken and set with pins when you get back home. If it stays this way, it is quite possible you will be left with a permanent limp,' the doctor said as he laid out what they needed to bathe him.

'Now, I want you to stand as best you can while we cut those clothes off you and modify these to fit around your cast.'

243

Connor looked at Mosi quizzically and then at the doctor.

'Yes, my daughter will stay to wash you, but there is no need to get embarrassed. She is a fully trained and experienced nurse,' Edward smiled at him reassuringly.

Connor shrugged in resignation. He was hardly in a position to bargain or protest, especially when these good people were caring for him.

Mosi helped him undo this trouser button, and the doctor used scissors to cut the rest of them off his body. The shirt was ripped and bloody where Connor had rolled across the ground, so they rolled that up to be burned.

Edward placed one towel on the floor and had Connor precariously balance on it while Mosi sponged the warm soapy water over him. Initially, he was embarrassed at his nakedness and avoided eye contact as Mosi gently washed around his upper thighs and genitals. However, after a while, he realised he was just another patient to them, so he began to relax and enjoy the sensation of feeling clean again. Days of sweat, blood, dirt and tears were swept away by Mosi's sponge. If only heartache could be obliterated the same way.

When they were satisfied he was clean again, they towelled him dry and then the doctor dabbed a tincture on his grazes before dressing him in baggy clothes. A belt was drawn around the waist to hold up the trousers, and one of the legs had a slit cut along the seam to sit around his plastered leg.

They helped him back to sit on the side of the bed, and Mosi left with the buckets, old clothing and towels. Edward took out a battered wooden pipe and sat on a rickety old chair across from Connor, where he tapped the old tobacco out of the pipe and started packing it with new leaf.

'Why don't you tell me everything that happened, Connor?'

At first there was silence. Connor wasn't sure if he was ready to talk about the accident or Gabby; however, once he began, the words just tumbled out.

'It's my fault this happened. I wanted to take my girlfriend away for a holiday and propose to her.' Connor's eyes filled up with tears, which he dashed away with the back of his hand.

'I never knew that bringing her here would be a disaster.' He turned his face away in embarrassment as the tears would not stop.

'You could never have foreseen something like this, Connor.'

'You know, Gabby was special, not just your ordinary person,' Connor whispered.

'In what way?'

'Every way.'

'You can tell me anything. I'm a good listener.'

When Connor fell into silence, the doctor tried to get him talking about the accident. In spite of the discomfort, he knew it would be cathartic to release some of his bottled-up emotion. The heart and body couldn't heal until you confronted the pain and were allowed to grieve.

'Tell me about the plane crash?' Edward gently pushed for more information.

'It was sudden. One minute we were flying along and the next I was executing a crash landing. We were shot from the sky by these bastards, and I would give anything to get revenge for their careless concern of human life.'

'I can understand how you feel, Connor. I have lost my friends in this wave of violence too. Tell me more about the days before the plane went down.'

Connor looked at his wrinkled, kind face and was reminded of Old Joe, Gabby's friend and mentor. These two men had lived their lives for causes not based on greed or material gain and their auras were kind and good.

'We visited Arusha and spent most of the time there saving a baby gorilla that Gabby rescued from a poacher's tent. She loved animals so much, and uncannily enough, they loved her too.'

Connor spent the next two hours telling the doctor all about Gabby, her connection with animals, and how much her mare Bella adored her. How she dedicated her life to save the planet and animals. Thinking of all her goodness made him so angry – angry with God and with himself for the waste of losing her so young, for him and the whole world.

'Now it's my fault that she's dead. If only we'd stayed at home.'

After ranting over the unfairness of what happened, he broke down. Once he let the pain out, it was like lancing a boil, and the poison kept coming.

Edward got up to sit beside him on the old cot and placed his arm around Connor's shoulder, offering him comfort and understanding.

'It's alright, son, let it all out. It helps the body to heal.'

Eventually the crying stopped, Connor was slightly shamefaced to show so much emotion in front of a virtual stranger. When he sheepishly looked up, all he could see was empathy in those kind eyes.

The doctor knew the young man needed this outlet more than he realised, after allowing himself to openly mourn her death, he could then go on without carrying such a heavy burden of guilt.

'I feel so confused. My head tells me she's gone but my heart cries out that she is still alive. How can I accept this truth when everything inside of me tells me otherwise?'

'Connor, I overheard the soldiers talking about the wreckage of the plane and how they found your fiancé lying there, covered in spitting cobras. I'm sorry to say that she was in tragic and fatal circumstances.'

'Really, you say snakes were all over her? That's not unlike other situations I have seen Gabby in. You don't understand the bond that Gabby had with animals. It was uncanny and surreal to see how they responded whenever she was close. I can't imagine any animal, even a venomous snake, hurting her.'

'Connor, these are spitting cobras we are talking about.' Edward shook his head in disbelief.

'If it were anybody else, I would agree, but not Gabby.'

'The soldiers would not leave behind another potential hostage if there was any sign of life. I know these soldiers and their greed. It is better that you accept that she has passed, and for that I am sorry, my young friend.' He squeezed Connor's shoulder.

Mosi arrived with some chicken soup for dinner. Connor quickly wiped the tears off his face before he took the bowl from her. The soup was tasty with some root vegetables and shredded chicken floating in the broth.

'Thank you, Mosi.'

She offered him a piece of bread to make the meal go a little further. The soldiers had taken most of the local produce and didn't have any remorse in leaving the locals in a state of virtual starvation. There was no bartering when guns were involved, and you did as you were told or they shot you dead, which was the end of the negotiation.

After the meal, the doctor helped Connor get to the outside privy and then eased him back onto his cot. They stayed to keep him company until the sun went down, when soon after, the soldier came with his gun to lock Connor up for the night.

He lay back with his arms under his head and listened to the night sounds. He could hear owls hooting somewhere in the forest and there was a call that sounded like a large cat. He wasn't sure what kind of animals hunted in this part of Africa, so he used the time to try to identify them from the calls around him.

The temperature had dropped a little after the heat of the day. There didn't seem to be the extremes here as there were in other parts of Africa. The days were quite humid but the nights pleasantly cool.

His mind once again strayed to Gabby. Something wasn't quite right about what the soldiers saw at the crash scene. Had she died when the plane hit the ground? It didn't seem possible that any animal would ever harm her, and he just could not believe she had died from snake bites. Not even spitting cobras could bring themselves to do that to Gabby, so why did they cover her body? Was she dead or alive?

He would probably never know what really happened that day but there remained a nagging doubt, like a missing piece in a puzzle when something didn't add up to the truth. He couldn't get any satisfaction from this line of thought so he concentrated on the memories he had stored away so conscientiously. As the night waned, he lay there recalling every detail of her long, lustrous hair, the aroma that was so unique to her, her smile and most of all, her eyes.

He let his mind's eye remember the expression in her eyes when they made love. There had been so much love in her gaze that he wanted to drown in them forever.

There would never be a woman like her in the whole wide world, and it wasn't just her beauty. Gabby had been unique in ways he couldn't explain as there was something ethereal about her.

He felt humbled to think she had loved him, and out of all the people who'd admired her, she'd chosen him. But now they would never to get to share this life.

'Gabby, how can I go on without you? Please take me with you,' he called out into the empty African night.

The pain was physical. It made his heart ache and punctured his lungs until he couldn't even draw breath.

Twenty-six

The next morning the soldiers came and escorted him to meet the big chief of this revolution. His name was Nawvlee, which meant 'Big Devil'.

The doctor warned Connor not to antagonise or blame him for their accident. He told Connor he'd seen Nawvlee shoot other prisoners in the head just for disagreeing with him.

Once he hobbled into the room, Connor could see why he had got the top job as he was a huge brute of a man. With very dark skin and a massive cannonball head, he looked evil and menacing even when he smiled at Connor.

He pointed to Connor to sit at his desk. It was almost like a business meeting except they were dealing in life and death, most likely his death.

'We are part of the revolution to change the corrupt government and see the people rule the Congo. We are freedom fighters and live and die for this cause. My friend, you must understand that a campaign with such big ambitions is expensive to maintain, so we need funds to become strong enough to fight other factions and gain control of the capital.'

Connor could not stop his thoughts from mocking these protests of altruism and good intentions. Nawvlee was the one who wanted to rule. It was his personal ambition driving the so-called campaign.

He dragged his attention back to the giant black man as he started talking again.

'My white friend, you are now part of our cause. I am going to contact your family with a ransom so that we can see you safely back to your people.' He spoke to Connor with a heavy African accent.

'My people are in Australia, on the other side of the world, so how do mean to contact them from this remote part of Africa?' Connor asked him bluntly.

'I have friends who work at the consulate, and they will see that my message gets to your family. A little bribe to the right person can get whatever you desire: cheap women, guns and lots of ransom money.'

'How much is my freedom going to cost?' Connor was seething inside.

'I am going to ask your family for ten million American dollars.' He smirked at Connor.

'That's ridiculous. Even a wealthy father doesn't have access to that much money,' Connor snorted with derision.

The big man leaned close to Connor and hissed into his face. 'You dare to argue with Nawvlee! When I see you talk, I smell money. When I see you walk, I smell money. Everything about you Mr Connor, sings money, and your people will pay. Or you will die.'

The big man puffed himself up to appear even more intimidating, and when he saw that Connor refused to cower, he leaned back in his chair and crossed arms over his massive chest.

'I do not argue with the big chief, I only try to reason.' Connor made his tone less confronting.

'Well, we will see just how much your family wants you back, won't we, white brother?' His eyebrows lifted sardonically. 'If they don't pay me, then I will shoot you myself, no problem at all,' he promised casually as he lit a cigar and blew the smoke into Connor's face.

Connor shrugged his shoulders in resignation. The threat of death didn't trouble him anymore, not since he'd lost Gabby. Life seemed meaningless, so why should he run away when he could hear the grim reaper panting from behind. It was about to catch up and take him away from this misery, and he was glad.

'Take him back to the hut,' Nawvlee shouted to the guards standing at either side of the door.

When Connor slumped back onto his cot, it was good to get the weight off his broken leg. He lay there until he got a visitor.

Mosi put her head in the door and smiled at him. 'Can I come in, Connor? I need to give you medication to keep away the malaria.'

'Of course, Mosi, come in.' He struggled to sit up.

Mosi helped drag him upright and then passed him a quinine tablet and some water.

'This morning I survived my meeting with the big, scary Nawvlee. He has threatened to shoot me if my family don't send the money,' Connor ironically told her.

'He won't shoot you until he is sure you are not worth anything to him. He only keeps people alive if they are useful,' Mosi murmured as she sat down beside him.

'Is that why he let you and your father live?' he asked her.

'Yes, Connor, as he's shot so many already. He only spared us so that we could treat his army with our medical skills.'

'Do you hate them?'

'Yes, I hate them, but I am alive and still here to look after my father, so for that I am thankful.' Mosi spoke as one who had walked close to death and seen too much.

The doctor made a walking stick for Connor to take some weight off his injured leg. As the days went by, there wasn't as much pain, just instability and weakness.

Connor became anxious that Nawvlee had not mentioned his ransom again, so he asked the doctor if he should be alarmed.

'This is Africa, Connor. Nothing happens here in a hurry. I am sure we would know if he wasn't confident of getting his money, quite sure.'

The days blurred as a routine of sorts filled the time. Connor was slowly recovering from his injuries, even if his heart refused to heal. He spent a lot of time with Edward and Mosi, sharing stories of his life in Australia, of which Mosi was very curious. She asked lots of questions about kangaroos and koalas, as these two mammals seemed to be the most famous for his country.

A couple of weeks into his captivity, they were woken in the middle of the night, when darkness was at its blackest hour, by a flash of light that illuminated the whole village. This brilliance was followed by a massive explosion. Connor sat up in bed and looked around, thinking he was having a nightmare, until shouts and running feet alerted him that this was no dream.

Struggling into some clothes, he pushed his foot into a shoe and had his walking stick ready, hoping someone would remember to release him.

Gunfire was exchanged and angry shouts filled the enclosure, followed by cries of agony as many of the soldiers fell to the attack.

The lock rattled in the gate, and Connor was relieved to see Mosi and the doctor hurrying towards his hut.

'Quickly, Connor. We must escape before we are slaughtered with the rest of the rebels.' Edward rushed them both to the gate.

'Who's attacking us? Maybe this is a rescue mission for me?' Connor looked around hopefully.

'No, Connor. I heard Nawvlee shouting that they were being attacked by another rebel faction fighting for this territory. They will kill us just as quickly as his men. We must hurry to the marshes before they know we are here.'

They rushed across the packed dirt towards the edge of the village as the night was lit up with flashes of gunfire. The noise was deafening, and heat beat at them from fires burning through the grass thatch on the huts.

Just as they were about to leave the village behind, a whistle of bullets flew past their heads. Connor grabbed Mosi and roughly pulled her to the ground to lay flat and out of harm's way.

The doctor dropped down beside them, and they all lay still until the noise moved to another section.

'Quickly, Mosi, grab your father and let's get out of here,' Connor urged her to hurry.

'Come on, Father. We must hurry.' Mosi shook her father's shoulder to move off with them.

When he didn't respond, Mosi tried to turn him over but he was too heavy. 'Connor, help me. I think my father has been shot,' Mosi said frantically.

Connor kneeled beside the doctor and turned him onto his back. There was a huge, ragged hole where the bullet had exited through his chest. It was a kill shot, and he would have been dead before he hit the ground beside them.

'No, Father, not you too. Connor, we need to take him with us. Somehow I will make him better. Please help me get him up so that we can take him with us,' she begged in desperation.

Connor took Mosi by the shoulders and made her look into his eyes. 'Mosi, he's already gone, and there is nothing we can do now to save him. We must escape before it's too late. I won't let you die here too.'

Connor took her hand and dragged her screaming and protesting in the direction they had been running, stumbling along as fast as his injuries would allow.

As they entered the marshes, they heard shouts behind them. There were two soldiers following them into the swamps.

'Let me go in front, Connor. The swamps can be treacherous if you take the wrong way. Be careful to follow me closely and do not fall too far behind,' Mosi whimpered through her tears.

Connor's leg was trembling but he couldn't slow down. In the moonlight, he watched Mosi carefully, following her exact steps as best he could with a leg cast and walking stick.

The soldiers fell behind and not long after they heard shouts and splashes as they fell into the murky water.

'This path keeps us above the water, and we would never find it again if we fell in. In the waters, there are crocodiles lurking, waiting for their opportunity. The marshes don't give you any second chances,' Mosi huffed breathlessly ahead of him.

The air was stifling, burning their sinuses with rotting vegetation, and no ventilation could get into the enclosed humid environment. At morning light, they rested in the shade of some papyrus reeds and dozed to the serenade of mosquitoes, until Mosi shook him awake to continue their perilous trek.

The soggy ground oozed through their shoes and sometimes they walked knee deep in mud, yet Mosi stayed on course like a bloodhound following the scent. The foul, odorous habitat was infested with clouds of insects that shrouded them day and night.

They sucked on grass stems for moisture, and Mosi found some slugs and showed him how to dig the raw flesh out of the shell. It tasted like mud and slime, but as least it was protein. When he bit into the slippery Mollusca, a black slush filled his mouth, which he spat out in disgust. After that, Connor found it easier just to gulp them down whole.

The reeds became so thick that they had to walk backwards through the mass, with the deeper menacing water stalking both sides of the track. Connor kept imagining a hungry reptilian swimming alongside them as they trudged through this perilous march to safety.

His heart beat like a drum, and sweat blinded his eyes as they used their body weight to push through the impenetrable wall of weeds, until with a great sense of relief, they reached drier ground again.

His leg was burning so painfully now that he considered surrendering to the marsh, imagining crawling along with his cast dragging behind instead of staying upright on the tormented limb. Connor was so exhausted that he began to consider the benefits of giving up: no more mosquitoes, no more heat and no more pain.

Mosi drew further and further ahead until he could only see her head bobbing through the rushes in the distance. As his will ebbed, so did his speed. He tripped over an exposed root and fell flat on his face, and there he lay. Connor couldn't even find the strength to raise his face out of the mud, and the smelly, sticky consistency blew in and out of his nostrils with each gasping breath.

When Mosi looked behind, she couldn't see his head above the reeds, so she turned back to find him flat-faced in the mud.

'Come on, Connor, we are almost through. Don't give up on me so close to the end. Lean on me, and I will support your weight. It is for just another hour or two, I promise you.'

'Let me die, Mosi. Let it end here, please,' he begged.

'No, I won't let you die, blue eyes. You must fight to live or I'll kill you myself,' she shouted the contradiction at him, determined not to give up on her father's last patient.

He rolled over and lay there looking up at her.

Her hair was a halo of curls, and her skin was a network of red mosquito bites. But it was her eyes that caught his gaze: they were alive with fire. It was her burning gaze that propelled him to sit up to groan in agony.

Mosi pulled him upright onto his protesting leg, and tucking herself under his armpit like a crutch, she staggered along supporting his much larger frame.

They stumbled like this for what seemed like hours, and his mind had wandered into a zone of numbness. The pain was there but it felt distant now as his body was slipping into shock.

Finally, Connor heard human voices shouting in a local tongue and Mosi hoarsely responding. Strong arms lifted him away from Mosi's bent frame, and he caught a glance at her flushed, exhausted face. He humbly noted the great price she had paid to get him this far. This young hero had saved him once again.

After collapsing into the corner of a hut, he couldn't keep his eyes open. So still covered in grey mud and stinking like the swamp, he slept for a couple of hours until they roused him with fresh food and water. The floury bread and clean water were the best he had tasted, only to be outdone by a bath in an old-fashioned copper tub that the villagers had positioned behind a bamboo screen for privacy. Connor was grateful to lay awkwardly with his mud-stained plastered leg suspended over the side of the tub.

Looking back on their ordeal, he still couldn't believe they had gotten through that impenetrable maze alive.

Before dinner that night, Mosi sat in his hut and looked at him sadly. She too wore the scars of their ordeal, and she looked different. He saw the lines of sadness and grief on her face, saw that her arms and legs were scratched raw from the sharp reeds, marking her unblemished mocha skin.

'I just can't believe my father is gone. He has been with me every day of my whole life. Now the only family I have is my elderly grandfather. I feel so lost, Connor. Without my father, I don't know what to do.' She turned her face away to wipe her tears on the shoulder of her robe.

'Mosi, I will be your family now. When I leave here, you will come with me to my own country. I promise to be there for you and to look after you.'

She smiled at his declaration. 'So far, Connor, all I have done is look after you!'

'Yes, that is true, but one day you will see what a good brother I can be,' he reassured her.

'Connor, you are a good man. My father trusted you, and so will I. If you are sure that you want me to be in your life, then I will agree to be your sister from this day. Now you are my family.' She smiled with a small degree of happiness and kneeled beside him to press her forehead against his in a symbol of a union of spirits.

He reached up and pulled her down beside him.

As they lay together on the straw mat, he talked more about the unique animals she would see in Australia. Strange species, with the most unusual being the platypus.

He told her all about the cities, like Sydney and Melbourne, and the enormous proportions of Uluru in the red centre. Connor painted a picture of the country she would be adopting as part of his family, giving her hope that she could still have a full life after losing so much.

Mosi's grandfather Jelani called them to dinner as the sun was setting.

Sitting around the fire afterwards, Jelani told stories of his exploits from his youth. Interpreting, Mosi told Connor that her grandfather had been a great tracker in his day. He had worked with professional hunters who killed hundreds of elephants for their tusks.

Jelani meant mighty, and he was tremendously courageous in his youth during the days of thunder – the thunder of bullets that silenced the giants of Africa.

As Connor watched Jelani's wrinkled face and toothless smile, he was reminded once again of Old Joe back home. In the firelight, tears ran down his face as he thought of returning home without Gabby. How her death would break so many hearts: her family, Old Joe, her friends at the society, the whole world would cry when they knew she was no longer their symbol of hope.

Just as Mosi had to learn to live without her father, he would somehow have to go on without the love of his life. It would be a pale shadow of the future he had envisaged when he'd slid the sparkling diamond ring on her finger.

Connor wanted to take Mosi with him. They would find a way back home, but for now it was about healing and recovering his strength for the very different life ahead.

Twenty-seven

Gabby wasn't sure how long they had been travelling. She had tried to count the starry nights and thought it must be almost two weeks since the plane crash, but it had begun to blur into long treks and the continual search for food and water.

It was the late afternoon of possibly the fifteenth day that Udo's mind touched Gabby's and told her that her kind were close by now. Just over the next hill, she would come upon the huts of a village.

Tau confirmed that she could smell them.

You cannot come any further. I will not put your lives in danger after all that you have done to keep me safe. Gabby sobbed as she pressed her face into Tau's magnificent golden coat. From this moment on, she would never fall asleep without remembering her musky scent.

In response, Tau pressed into Gabby's embrace, actually making a growling purr.

I can never thank you enough my friend for protecting me. Gabby spoke to her mind as she placed both hands on either side of those mesmerising golden-yellow eyes.

Tau showed Gabby her own sadness, and to say goodbye, she flashed many images of their journey through Gabby's mind as they drew apart.

Udo dropped her head low and wrapped her soft, sensitive trunk around Gabby to hug her close, the tip gently tapping her on the back. This was a gesture of love that elephants reserved for their calves and beloved sisters.

'You are my true sister, Udo. You have cared for me, quenched my thirst, sated my hunger and provided shade from the sun. I will remember you forever.' Gabby cried her goodbye into the rough, wrinkled skin.

The massive elephant closed her eyes to seal away the sadness of farewell, but even this couldn't prevent the tears seeping out to wet a trail of moisture down her dusty face. Udo rubbed her trunk up and down Gabby's back to comfort her and say her own goodbye.

Gabby walked away from them without looking back. A second goodbye would be too much to endure. Suddenly the air filled with the mighty roar of a lion and trumpeting of a matriarch elephant. The tears rolled down her face as Gabby tucked this moment away in her heart, as these sounds were the true resonance of Africa.

Now it was Connor calling her forward. Like a compass, it had been the need to rescue him that kept her true to this course.

She had filled the nights dreaming of his embrace and the days storing away memories to share with him later. There was even a small chance he could be waiting for her over this hill, and by some miracle he may have made his way back to find her.

Either way, she felt this accident could finally be put behind them, and that their lives could return to normal once more.

A few more steps and she may be back in his arms.

Her shoes had succumbed to the hardships of the terrain days ago, so it was a few more steps on her cracked and broken feet.

Just as her animal guardians had promised, as she reached the top of the hill, she gazed down upon a traditional African village.

The red earth was scattered with brown grass huts, and there was smoke coming out of some of the chimneys. She could see children running amongst goats and chickens as they chased one another around their homes.

The children stopped running suddenly and stared at the apparition coming towards them.

Gabby realised they were frightened of her. She must look like a wild witchdoctor with her long blonde hair dreadlocked in knots. A half-starved banshee with her clothes hanging in shreds, and to their young eyes the overall affect must have been terrifying.

They ran screaming for their mothers, and the whole village came out to see her slowly walk into their midst.

She had no idea how to speak their dialect and motioned with her hands for food and water. They were Masai, tall, regal people with long red robes. The women nodded their understanding at her sign language and led her away, all the while chattering in their own tongue. The men stood around discussing how a white woman could have traversed the wilderness and survived.

Taking a long drink of fresh water from their well, Gabby relished liquid without the need to sift sand and grit through her teeth. After quenching her thirst, she was escorted into a woman's hut.

The women bade her sit on a grass mat and brought a bowl of vegetable stew. It was hot and delicious, and her stomach swelled at the novelty of food again.

They stripped off her destroyed clothes, and standing her in a dented tin tub of water, the women gently washed away the dirt and cares from the long trek. The scratches and bruises could not be instantly fixed as only time could heal and restore Gabby to her former self, but the bathing soothed her exhausted muscles.

The tall women with the high cheekbones dressed Gabby in a beautiful red robe and sat her down in the middle of them as they combed the tangles and knots out of her long hair. They giggled and shyly marvelled at the silky texture of such soft hair. Their own was thick and curly, strong like the land they belonged to.

After all this glorious attention, she fell into an exhausted sleep on a mat in the corner of their hut, missing the open air above her but too tired to stop slumber as it enveloped her in a contented, peaceful shroud.

Tomorrow she would begin the next step in reaching home, but for now, sleep was insistent on her submission.

The next morning, she woke to porridge gruel and a hot drink that looked like tea from some unknown origins. It was bitter but cleansed her mouth and left her feeling awake and refreshed.

The men were excited but had no way to explain to the white woman that they had sent a runner to a mission to bring a priest back here.

Gabby could not speak to these people in words, yet they managed to co-exist happily with sign language and pictures drawn in the dirt.

They drew a picture of the church and motioned it was coming here.

After a couple of days in their village, an old jeep bumped to a halt in front of the main hut. A young priest climbed out with the runner, who had enjoyed the much faster trip home.

The men told the women to bring Gabby to meet the priest, and soon she was ushered into open space between the huts.

The priest welcomed her in English with an Italian accent. 'My name is Giano. I was told you that stumbled in from the bush.' He reached his hand out in welcome.

'Good morning, Giano. My name is Gabrielle Harrison and I am very happy to see you.

I was in a plane crash with my fiancé, who has gone missing from the site. I really need to talk to the police about his disappearance as soon as possible.'

Over refreshments, Gabby gave Giano the full account of their accident and her fears for Connor.

'It could be renegades, but that would be unusual as the Serengeti is so busy with safari tours. But I'm not saying an abduction is out of the question, so tomorrow we'll head back to the mission and from there we can radio help for your fiancé,' Giano said.

'Thank you so much.' Gabby smiled with relief.

'I am very surprised you were able to travel so far in the Serengeti without getting killed or attacked by some wild beast. It is truly a miracle.' He spoke fast with a great deal of expression in his voice and hands.

'You are correct. It is indeed a miracle that I got here safely.' She smiled back at him, thinking of her two bodyguards.

Before climbing into the battered jeep, Gabby hugged the women close to her chest in thankful affection then she respectfully shook each of the men's hands.

At the catholic mission outside Mugumu, Giano helped her make radio contact with the police to report her whereabouts and confirm that Connor was still missing.

After speaking to Gabby, the police sergeant contacted the Mwanza police to report that Gabrielle Harrison had been found. To her overwhelming relief, they were told that Robert Faradene would soon collect her by helicopter from Giano's mission.

Gabby slipped her engagement ring into a buttoned pocket for safekeeping. She wanted Connor to be by her side before announcing their news. She raced into Robert's arms as soon as he came clear of the whirling propellers, and he held her close.

'Thank God, Gabby. We've been worried sick about you.'

'I am so very relieved to see you too. Have you found Connor?' She was desperate for news of him.

'Gabby, yes, we've found him. Now we just need to get you both safely back home.'

Gabby held him tight with tears on her cheeks.

'You poor woman. How on earth did you survive that long in the wilderness? You are almost skin and bones.' He hugged her gently, being concerned he would break something if he squeezed too hard.

'It's a long story, but for now I just want to see Connor again.'

'I promise you that I'll get him back, for you and his frantic mother.'

Before they flew back, he explained how the embassy had received Nawvlee's ransom request. 'Ten million American dollars to get him out of that hell hole.'

'Are you paying the ransom?' She held her breath.

'No, instead the police have arrested the corrupt official. He is now cooperating with them to identify where Connor is held hostage. But I have made a generous donation to the police force for them to act faster than normal.'

'How soon, Robert?' Gabby pressed for urgency.

'Soon. Once they have all the information, the police and army are planning an exercise to retrieve Connor from the Congo.'

'After the plane crash, I saw car tyres in the dirt and believed he had been taken against his will.'

'Your hunch was right, but it's a mystery why they didn't take you as well.'

'I have no idea either. I was unconscious after the crash, so I cannot say why they left me behind.'

Gabby looked across at Connor's father. Here was a man who was used to being in control, and this gave her confidence that Connor's rescue would be successful.

They flew straight back to Mwanza, a small Tanzanian city on the shores of Lake Victoria, where Ben and Joe were impatiently pacing the hanger.

Gabby rushed into their waiting arms, and they both wrapped her close and tight. Ben and Joe were both unashamedly crying tears of joy, forever thankful she was safe and returned to them.

After not finding her for so long, everyone was preparing themselves for the worst, but now a miracle had blessed them with the best news.

'I've missed you both so much.' Gabby smiled and hugged them just as fiercely.

'Oh my God, Gabby, we've been so worried. Worried sick that you were injured or hurt by some wild animal.'

'Ben, it was the wild animals that kept me safe,' Gabby reassured him.

'Of course it was,' Ben said with admiration.

'Now we just need to get Connor back and we can all go home,' Gabby reassured them.

They were staying at the Isamilo Lodge in the hills above the city. The rooms were basic and small but they were not there for a holiday: It was just a convenient base to plan their rescue of Connor. Gabby still felt emotionally and physically drained. She would begin fresh each morning, but after only a couple of hours, her strength waned and she would have to retire and rest for several hours again.

Gabby worried about Connor every waking moment, despite Robert's reassurance's that they would soon have him safely returned.

Keep safe my darling. Soon we will be reunited, and I promise that nothing will keep us apart again.

She could hardly wait to see him again and tell him all about Tau and Udo.

They planned to land a large group of soldiers in helicopters near the camp and then march in the middle of the night to launch a surprise attack.

The day dawned when 'Operation Connor' was launched. The family huddled together all day and night waiting for news of his rescue.

At dawn the following day, they were told the mission had returned. Gabby was tingling with excitement as they were driven to the Mwanza base. Connor must be in one of those white concrete buildings.

When they were ushered into the captain's office, their hearts sank at the expression on his face. He didn't have the look of a conqueror; instead, they saw someone with bad news.

'I am sorry to say that I have terrible news for you.' He sadly shook his head.

Robert Faradene had refused to sit. He stood tall and resolute behind the rest of the group.

Gabby's breath caught in her throat, and she held onto Joe's hand so tightly that its circulation began to suffer.

'Our soldiers were successful in their ruse to catch the rebels unaware, and we have captured most of them. The information we gathered is that this group had recently repossessed the base camp from the group that attacked your plane, Ms Harrison.

'We asked about the Australian prisoner and they told us that he was killed in crossfire when they invaded the predecessors. They showed his body to our soldiers, and they could see his white, bloated skin stretching over the decaying corpse. I am so sorry, so sorry.' He looked down into his lap in defeat.

Gabby couldn't even cry, unable to believe a word spoken. How could Connor be dead?

It seemed impossible that she wouldn't sense this. Her heart cried 'no' while her head was being told 'yes'.

'Are you sure, captain? Perhaps it was some other white man they murdered? Maybe a foreigner was living amongst the rebels, someone who was not known to authorities?' she asked him in desperation, still clutching at some small glimmer that this was instead an awful mistake.

'I am truly sorry, Ms Gabrielle. Our intelligence has confirmed that there was no other white man living in this vicinity. I have evidence that Mr Connor was amongst them from the ransom note. I have evidence that this Nawvlee was overrun, and I also have evidence of the corpse of a white man. It all adds up to this terrible truth. Once again, I am truly sorry, Ms Gabrielle and Mr Faradene.'

Gabby hung her head in defeat. What would her life be without Connor?

Robert Faradene stood frozen, as if made from stone, but his tear-filled eyes and trembling mouth spoke of his tragic loss.

Joe wrapped his old arms around her as Ben stood behind and gently placed his hand on her shoulder, stroking her bony frame through the thin fabric of her clothes. They led Gabby to the sofa where she sat forward with her head between her knees. The world was suddenly tilting, and she felt like the plane was crashing all over again. But this time it was her future and her dreams of happiness that were going up in flames.

Gabby had still not shed a tear. How strange that your whole world could implode and yet there was no outside sign of such a disaster. This was too great for tears. Nothing could adequately express how much her heart was aching.

Robert Faradene's face was drawn tight over his cheekbones as he shook the hand of the police captain and thanked him for everything he had done. He asked if they had brought the body back with them, but the army captain shook his head and told him that it was too badly decomposed to move.

'My men buried it deep in the Congo forest and left a cross with Connor's name roughly painted on it. I am sorry, Mr Faradene, but they felt this was the best way to show respect for your loss.'

Robert nodded as he could no longer contain the tears that were welling in his eyes. Joe came over to grasp his shoulder in compassion. Joe left Ben looking after Gabby and led the mute father outside where they could talk in private.

'Robert, I'm deeply sorry. Connor was a fine young man and this is a tragic loss for us all, but especially for you and Faye.' They sat on a stone ledge outside in the crisp morning light.

Robert just inclined his head as he brushed the tears away on the sleeve of his shirt. Listening to the sounds a new day, it seemed impossible that his son was no longer. 'How am I going to tell Faye?' he whispered in shock.

'Do you want me to call her for you,' Joe offered

'No, this is something we have to face together, no matter how much it hurts.'

He was wide awake in the middle of every parent's worst nightmare.

The flight home in Robert's private jet was spent in profound sadness. No one said much, but instead stared out of the window. The hostess was unable to tempt them with food, so she just served copious amounts of coffee and whiskey.

Robert kindly offered his Gulfstream Jet to Joe for the society to use in the future. 'Here is the pilot's contact card, and if he's available, then the plane is yours to use.'

'Thank you, Robert. This could be handy in an emergency.'

Small talk dwindled as they fell into silence.

Exhausted from so much internalisation, everyone sighed with sadness when they saw Faye waiting beside the car at the hanger. Her eyes were red from crying, and her shoulders seemed slumped with despair.

Gabby held her close as they shared the loss of love. Different for each, but for both it was heartbreaking.

'Faye, I am so sorry.' Gabby sobbed against her shoulder.

'Me too, Gabby. He was the light of our lives.'

'Mine too.'

'Please don't forget us. You are like a daughter, and we don't want to lose you as well.' She held her away to look into Gabby's tear-washed eyes.

'Of course you won't. You are my only link to Connor, and I love you both too,' Gabby reassured them.

Robert added his own invitation as he helped his shattered wife into the car. 'Please come to see us, and Bella. She misses you too. That poor little filly has almost starved herself to death since you went missing.'

'Of course. I will come down very soon. The homestead will always hold a special place in my heart, and I love Bella as much as she loves me.'

When she got home to the cottage, her whole family was waiting. Kathleen, Jacob and Thomas, and even Eddie had made the trip to Melbourne to rejoice in her safe return.

Gabby was grateful for their company but her heart longed to retreat and just live in her memories of Connor.

The next day, Eddie and Gabby took the Titans for a walk in the park.

'Eddie, you cannot imagine how many times I wished I could share this city with you, all its sights and flavours. I just wish you were here at a happier time. I am afraid my spirits are very low without Connor.'

'I'm so sorry, Gabbs. It's just too cruel that this happiness was stolen from you so soon.'

'Life can be cruel, especially for us, Eddie.'

'So true, but I think I'm stronger for the hardships.'

'Are you happy living in the gulf?'

'Yes, very happy. The 'Kowie Crusaders' are even winning a few football games.'

'If anyone can help these kids, it's you Eddie.'

'Thanks for your vote of confidence. What about you? What does your future now hold?'

'I still have my own crusade. The environment continues to spiral, so there is plenty to dedicate my life to, even without Connor at my side.'

'I'm sorry, Gabbs'.

'Me too.'

Eddie reached out to drape his arm across her shoulder, and it felt comforting to put her arm around his waist and hold him against her side.

Eddie would always be her rock, the one constant in her tumultuous life. From the very beginning, they had been there for each other, and nothing or no one could break a bond forged in the fires of adversity.

Twenty-eight

Adapting back to life in Melbourne was exhausting. Losing Connor was like losing a limb, especially so close after the loss of her father. Gabby made the necessary adjustments to survive this much grief, but it was never going to the same as before. First Father Gerry, then her father and now Connor, the love of her life, had all been taken from her far too soon. Death had seemed so much easier to bear from the spiritual realm; it was easier to accept when she wasn't so emotionally involved. The pain in this life was more than she could bear. Everything was unbalanced, out of kilter.

She couldn't even cry that much for Connor as her heart kept refusing to accept that he was no longer alive. No matter how many times she tried to tell it otherwise, it was a law unto itself and wouldn't listen to facts or reason.

Grief started to dislike time. It moved at a selfish pace and overwhelmed all of the senses: taste, sight and particularly smell. Living with such sorrow made sleep especially difficult. At night, her mind would replay the many times She and Connor had together. Loss seemed determined to crush her spirit and keep her under a fog of unhappiness. This underlying sadness caused Gabby to lose her appetite, and now to make it worse, she was getting dizzy spells every time she stood up.

Kathleen blamed the dizzy spells on Gabby's poor diet, but in spite of her mother's concern, just the thought of food most days twisted Gabby's stomach and dried out her mouth.

Joe kept a close eye on her as well, making tantalising snacks and encouraging Gabby to eat just a little. Even a few bites would suffice. He was worried the weight of this grief would spiral her back into a state of depression.

Gabby's condition continued to worsen until one day at work the room began to spin as a dark haze moved across her vision. She didn't remember falling when her legs crumbled, and she collapsed onto the office floor. For a split second, nobody moved, then suddenly everybody did. Ben rushed to her side and cradled her head, and her long blonde hair fell across his arm as he looked at her closed eyes and pale face.

Miranda kneeled on the other side of her. 'Gabby, can you hear me?' Leaning in close to Gabby's face, she looked for some reaction or response.

Elisabeth dialled 000 to get an ambulance and watched Michael and Paul as they hovered worriedly in the background. After what seemed an eternity but was probably only a few seconds, Gabby's eyelids fluttered open.

Ben and Miranda swam in those sea-green depths as Gabby slowly came back to the present.

'Why are you all around me, and why am I on the floor?' she tried to sit up until Miranda pushed her back down again.

'I have called for an ambulance, Gabby, so lie still and they should be here soon,' Elisabeth said as she kneeled beside her.

'Elisabeth, I'm fine. Please, they can't come all this way for a simple faint,' Gabby murmured wearily.

'No. I think after all you have been through, you should go in and have a really good check-up before you waste away to absolutely nothing,' Ben firmly reprimanded her.

'If you all say so.' Gabby smiled at them in resignation. She felt too tired to argue against such united advice.

The ambulance crew agreed that they should take her to the hospital and make sure there were not any serious reasons for passing out. Bundled off in the station wagon, she gave them all a bit of a dirty look as the doors closed and the van sped off into the traffic.

'Ben, you and Miranda go the hospital, and the three of us will stay here to keep everything running. But you have to promise to call us when Gabby has been examined.'

Ben smiled his relief at Elisabeth's efficiency.

'Thanks, Lissy. We promise to call you. Do you think we should let Kathleen know?' Ben asked.

'No, not until we know what to tell her. It may be nothing then she will be anxious for no good reason. She has only been home a week so I'll give her a call once we know more. God knows the poor woman has been through enough lately.'

'Yes, of course. Grab your coat, Miranda. It's always cold at the hospital,' Ben said as he rushed around getting his keys and wallet.

They got to the Alfred Hospital and found Gabby in a small cubicle waiting in the emergency department. A doctor had checked her blood pressure to find that it was a little low but not dangerous, so he did blood tests to see if she was anaemic. Apparently these were both common causes of fainting.

Gabby smiled wryly as her two friends rushed into the tiny space. 'Really guys, this is such a waste of hospital time and resources. Having me here taking up a bed that someone genuinely sick could really use.'

'We'll let the doctor be the judge of that,' Miranda firmly responded as she sat on the side of the bed.

They passed the time discussing work until a young physician in a white coat pulled back the curtain and entered the room. He smiled at Gabby almost mischievously, and she wondered what her conspiring friends had told him.

'Could I get you good folks to step outside while I speak to Gabrielle in private,' he politely asked Ben and Miranda.

They shared a look of concern but didn't argue and stepped out into the corridor to wait.

Gabby could hear them whispering worriedly while they huddled together.

'What results do you have that can't be discussed in front of my two friends?' she asked him a little anxiously.

'I wasn't sure if you had told anyone, but you did know that you're pregnant?'

'What did you say?' she whispered in shock.

'So you didn't know. Yes, Gabrielle, you are pregnant. I will need to examine you but at a guess I would estimate almost four months.' He smiled that smile again.

Connor, my darling, we're going to have a baby. This is so exciting.

Then suddenly a great surge of loss crushed her into the pillows, and her face crumpled with sorrow.

Connor would never see his child, never hold him high in the air as he giggled with laughter. Never smell the sweet innocence as he wrapped a towel around his child after a bath, never read him a bed time story, never hug, kiss or love him.

Then the tears began. All the pent-up hurt came pouring out of her. The news hit her like a freight train, and she started sobbing, howling in fact.

The poor doctor didn't know what to do. He had never expected such a dramatic reaction.

Ben and Miranda rushed back to her side and took one of Gabby's hands in each of theirs.

'What's wrong? What did you tell her?' Ben demanded angrily.

The doctor looked at Gabby and at Ben and decided that he had done enough damage for one day. 'I told Gabrielle that she is pregnant. I am sorry that this is such upsetting news, but there is always adoption if she doesn't want to keep the baby.'

This statement only made her cry harder. Of course she wanted Connor's baby. She wanted this child more than life itself, but it was just devastating that he would never know his father. That Connor never knew about his existence before he died. It just wasn't fair to any of them, especially this precious little one.

Miranda's eyes shone with tears. 'Gabby, that's wonderful news. Think of your future with this baby. You will have a little bit of Connor with you forever. He's given you a gift to keep for the rest of your life, and it really is wonderful news.'

She drew Gabby's body across her chest, careful not to touch her abdomen, and hugged her so fiercely that Gabby's sobs had to subside, maybe through suffocation, but at least they did stop.

Ben took the young doctor outside to explain her circumstances, and he nodded in understanding when he heard that the child's father had passed away just a short time ago.

'That's tragic. I'm so sorry that I dropped such a bombshell. Gabrielle can go home, but I would suggest a visit to her GP in the next week or so to discuss prenatal care.'

Ben nodded his assent.

'Are you women ready to go home?' Ben asked as he stuck his head around the curtains.

They both looked back at him with red eyes and tear-washed faces.

Ben didn't know how to react to the news yet. Deep down, he still held onto hope that one day Gabby would love him, even if it wasn't as much as she loved Connor.

Now there was a baby. Connor's baby.

That dream was fading before his eyes, now that she had a constant reminder of someone she loved more than anyone else. Call him selfish, but these were the thoughts running through his head as the two women got ready to leave the hospital.

Damn you, Connor. You even reach out from the grave to keep your hold on Gabby.

Ben was lost in a moment of self-pity.

Hugging Gabby to his side as they walked out, he whispered, 'Congratulations' into her ear. He felt destined to be tortured by un-requited love his whole life. First his mother hadn't loved him enough and now his heart belonged to a woman who didn't want it.

What is wrong with me? Am I that unlovable, he asked himself

'Ben, could you please drop me home first? I want to share this news with Joe before I tell my family and friends.'

'Of course, Gabbs. Anything you want.'

Ben and Miranda dropped her off at the cottage, and she stood at the gate waving them off.

Joe came out when he heard the front door click open. 'Gabby, you're home early. Is everything alright?'

'Joe, come and sit in the lounge. I need to tell you something.'

Once they were seated on the couch, she reached out to take both of his hands and squeezed them.

'Gabby, you're scaring me,' he whispered.

'Joe, I'm having a baby.'

'A baby? Connor's baby? I don't understand how this could happen,' he stuttered, finding it difficult to speak.

'I know, and this is why it is such incredible news. I don't think this has ever happened before. Only you know who or what I really am Joe, so it was you I had to tell first.'

'Do you think the child will form as it should?'

'I don't know all the answers, but I sense it's a little boy. A little boy for us to love.'

'Gabby, this is mind-blowing. So this child will be half human and half celestial, a rare little miracle, a bridge between earth and heaven?'

'Yes, that's a beautiful way to see it. This child may the one who heals the rift between the realms.'

'I'm so happy for you, Gabby, and your mother will be over the moon.'

'Shall I call her now?' Gabby asked with a twinkle in her eyes.

'Yes, let's make her smile again.'

Kathleen's world was about to change once more with the shrilling sound of the phone ringing.

'Mum, are you sitting down?' Gabby said after Kathleen picked up.

'Why? Is everything okay?'

'Mum, I'm pregnant. I just found out today.'

'No way, Gabby,' Kathleen stuttered excitedly.

'The baby was conceived during our African holiday. Now a tiny part of Connor will be in our lives forever.'

'I'm going to be a grandmother! I can't wait to tell your brothers and Ruth Saila. Can I share this good news?'

'Of course, Mum. I'm over the moon, so tell whoever you want.' Gabby couldn't stop the bubble of laughter that burst out of her.

That afternoon, when Gabby went back to the office, she told them her astonishing news. Elisabeth, Paul and Michael were dumbfounded, until they all began to talk at once. There were a lot of hugs and tears of joy, but some sadness that Connor was not here to share the excitement.

Gabby called Robert and Faye Faradene, and their voices conveyed their own surprise and anticipation to see the future continue with their grandchild.

After dinner that night, Gabby went to lay down on her bed, and for once she was not alone. Now it was her and the baby facing the world together. For the first time in months, she could consider the future without such bleakness in her soul.

She took the engagement ring from her bedside drawer and held it to the lamplight. The sparkles within the gemstone spoke of hope and love, both of which she would dedicate to this new life.

I will live a brave human life for my little one.

One day, he would become a man and a beacon of light in the night. From this very first moment, he gave her new purpose. Her angelic side was full of wonder that she could experience motherhood, and it was a miracle that no one could have predicted. How shocked and delighted Josiel would be when she heard that a child was coming to Fallon. This would re-write their history between the angelic and human worlds.

Gabby was overwhelmed with love and maternal protective instincts. She knew her cause to save threatened species and the environment was enough for a full and satisfying life, but after knowing true love there was an emptiness that no amount of work could fill. This child would be a constant reaffirmation of Connor's love. He had been created by that love, and she would tell him everything about his dad, every day.

Today's discovery had changed her future. It felt good to know that they would have each other, no matter what they faced.

Gabby took out her star pendant and closed her eyes. Meditating on the Blood Tree, she felt the hum that reverberated around the sprawling tree. In her mind's eye, she was standing before the wonder. She saw the red leaves flutter in a breeze, and in reverence, she reached out to place her hand upon the tree's gnarly bark.

'We have a baby,' she whispered to her icon of hope.

Just then, she felt the baby flutter in her abdomen. Clutching her middle, she opened her eyes in amazement. *Do you feel the Blood Tree too? Does its ancient wisdom stir your humanity? Will you be the bridge between the realms as Joe predicted?*

Please watch over this child and protect him from my enemies, Gabby begged the Blood Tree in the City of Angels, dedicating her child to the tree of knowledge, the tree that represented life itself.

Twenty-nine

There was a commotion in the Silver City. It rippled through the streets and temples like a pebble being tossed into a pond as soon as Josiel was escorted through the mighty gates.

The news whispered like a breeze from angel to angel. *Josiel is back!*

Without ceremony, she was led up the familiar stone stairs that led to the council chamber. Josiel looked around the same immense space she had stood in not so long ago, when she had been their esteemed spy and high-ranking scout.

How far she had fallen from grace.

Bowing before the three of the wisest of her kind, she tried not to dwell on the punishment that would be served out for her disobedience. How she would suffer for her loyalty to Fallon. Staying on bended knee, she was only welcomed with a stony silence. The council's anger was so palpable that the guards prudently retreated as far back as they could to avoid the coming wrath.

It was once again Remiel who showed the only sign of tolerance as he began to speak. 'Josiel, I am thankful that you have returned to us safely and that you are not suffering in the clutches of Lucifer and his misguided followers.'

Joisel kept her head down but raised her eyes a little to acknowledge his sombre greeting. She refused to beg as in her heart she still believed she had followed their creed, if not their direct orders.

Saraquel looked thunderous but said not a word. It was Zinnia who acted before speaking. The water in the fountain at the centre of the room slowly rose and began to move like a whirlpool above Josiel's head, spinning faster and faster while she was splashed by the spray.

Saraquel frowned at Zinnia's display of anger and swept his hand across her tumultuous force, moving it by wind back to its home in the fountain.

'How dare you!' she spat at his audacity as she rose from her seat.

Saraquel turned the energy of the wind and pushed her back into her seat. With it blowing a gale in her face, Zinnia sizzled with fury as she reached for her famous sword of fire.

Remiel also stood up and opened his hands, where a small flame hovered above each palm.

'Brethren, what is happening here? We cannot fight each other. Do not make me use the flame against you to stop this quarrelling.'

Saraquel and Zinnia both looked across at Remiel with reproach in their eyes, but before anyone else could act with recklessness, a shout boomed off the walls.

'Stop this insanity!'

Puriel stood before them with angelic company behind him.

His bold entrance seemed to break the escalation, and all three councillors inhaled a long breath to regain some sense of serenity.

'You are the best of us, and this is how you behave! I am shocked and disappointed in many things but such behaviour has never been seen before. I am not sure if Lucifer's wayward energy has infiltrated here enough to cause this bizarre disharmony or if your pride is the real enemy?'

Three sets of eyes looked back at him but no one said a word in their defence.

'When I heard Josiel had returned, I rushed here to implore you to act with compassion, unlike with your treatment of my beloved Gadriel. I never expected to find you fighting amongst yourselves.'

The three had the grace to look shamefaced.

'I am ashamed that I too had been previously hard-headed, but now we must work together. We must listen. Will you put aside your own sense of injustice and listen to what Josiel has seen and heard during her time in the world of mankind? I implore you to suspend judgement and listen to her!'

They all nodded without dissent, whereupon Josiel was invited to stand and give her account. It took quite a long time to explain that Fallon, in human form, was facing their enemies alone, without support and without her former powers. And the revelation that Lucifer was stealing the essence of life itself from innocents to recover his former glory made them gasp in horror.

Her story was so astonishing that all the other prejudices were forgotten, and a stunned hush settled amongst them.

Remiel reached out his hands in supplication as he apologised first with genuine sadness. 'My friends and allies, it is now obvious that this council has lost its way. We have failed to protect our own in the mortal and immortal world, and for this I am deeply sorry.'

'I too have been ambushed by my own pride and regret being more judgemental than compassionate.' Zinnia came before Josiel and reached for her hands.

'It is now obvious that I have been wrong in my judgement.' Saraquel also bowed his head to acknowledge the error of his behaviour.

'I don't need your apologies, wise ones. I need your action. Undo any disservice you have done to Gadriel and commence your battle plan to subjugate Lucifer and his minions. Also, see through fresh eyes that Fallon needs our support, not scorn.' Josiel's steady gaze held them to account.

Without delay, Raphael, Zadkiel and Anael were sent to bring Gadriel from his place of refuge to stand before them.

Josiel gasped in shock upon seeing the bolt holding Gadriel's wings tightly together. And Gadriel wept with joy when he saw Josiel standing unharmed before him. Once they had released each other, he stared warily between her and the council.

'There is no need to be afraid, Gadriel, as we have requested your presence to apologise. We should have never have punished you so harshly, and we beg your forgiveness for our pride and prejudice.' Remiel spoke on the behalf of the others.

'I will forgive you when you remove this abomination from my wings.' Gadriel glared at them with reproach.

'It shall be done without delay,' Zinnia promised.

Before too long Gadriel, Josiel, Puriel, Zadkiel, Anael, Uriel and Raphael all congregated under the Blood Tree. Puriel sincerely apologised to his best friend, hugging him fiercely against his chest. Gadriel's wings had been unbolted, but it would take time to regain his strength and be able use them without intense pain.

Here they all sat and told their stories, bonding over their shared experiences with the fallen angels and overseeing Fallon in her human form. The final consensus amongst the group was a sense of unity to protect their beloved City of Angels from Lucifer's uprising.

From now on, they were forged together as more than angels: they were a tight brotherhood of guardians, pledged to stand as one against the forces thundering towards them.

Gina was different these days, less arrogant and demanding. It seemed that living in poverty had improved her malleability.

As a reward, Dominic requested that she be invited into the dreamscape to meet Jinn.

The next night, he lay in his bed with Gina tucked up against his side. Closing his mind to the here and now, he let himself slip into the realm of dreams and nightmares.

'Gina, can you hear me?' he called softly. 'Stay asleep and let me come to you in your dreams,' he coached her.

'I see you, Dominic, but what's this about? Why do you enter my sleep when I am right beside you?'

'We have a visitor, but there is no need to be frightened as he is our friend.'

'Gina, now reborn as Crimson Thorn. Dominic speaks highly of you,' Jinn said as he materialised in front of her.

Gina stared at the apparition before her. This fallen angel, more of a demon now, was a fearsome sight. An angel once, but now a dark version of its previous glory.

'Dominic has not spoken of you at all.'

'A good and faithful servant should hold all secrets close to his heart.'

Gina stared at the fallen angel curiously. She noted the contorted features on his face, the rough skin that covered his body and there was a smell, a hint of decay or death, emanating from its being.

'Why am I here? Gina asked as she looked around at the background.

They were in a place with dark swirling clouds that were twisting and turning around between them. It was like standing in the skies, but on solid ground.

'I have news, startling intelligence,' Jinn whispered as if the clouds might hear his raspy voice.

Both Gina and Dominic remained quiet, waiting for the evil former angel to share his tidings.

'Gabrielle Harrison is pregnant.'

'That's impossible,' Dominic spat.

'Connor's baby,' Gina gasped enviously.

'Yes, this is not something any of us could have foreseen. But the Morning Star wants her child. It will be both human and angel, a rare treasure indeed. Dominic and Gina, you will be able to name your own reward if you aid me in retrieving the child and delivering it to Lucifer.'

The two looked at each other in anticipation. Dominic saw a lingering hint of greed in Gina's green eyes.

Maybe she hasn't changed as much as I believed, Dominic secretly fretted.

'When do we strike?' Gina asked in eagerness.

'We must wait until the child is fully formed and then as you said – we strike.' Jinn's twisted features contorted with glee.

Over the next couple of months, Ben watched Gabby flourish in her pregnancy. The nausea had passed and now her love of food was back.

There were still shadows of grief that passed over her countenance, but the baby had restored hope for the future. It was like Connor still shared a part of her life.

One night, Gabby got him to press his hand on her slightly rounded stomach.

'That's amazing! I felt it, Joe, his kick. It's unbelievable to think he's all tucked up in there.' Ben's grin was contagious.

Gabby delighted in the joy her son had already brought to the family – Kathleen, her brothers, friends at the society and most of all – Ben and Joe.

Ben was constantly worrying about Gabby, especially now with a baby. He felt she needed someone there to support her and to keep them both safe.

He had half a plan forming in his feverish mind.

The following week, he took her out to dinner and waited for the meal to be served. Once there was only the clink of cutlery, he voiced his idea, anxious he would lose his nerve if he waited any longer.

'Gabby, I want to ask you something, but don't answer until you think carefully about it. I want you to think about the baby's future. Will you marry me?' he asked breathlessly.

When the answer was silence, he risked a quick look at her face.

She couldn't respond straight away. Instead, she thought about sharing her life with Ben, as his wife. She knew he was trying to secure a stable home for her baby, especially now that Connor wasn't coming home.

It was such a virtuous offer that tears welled up in her eyes and tumbled down her cheeks. 'Ben, I can answer you now, but I think your heart already knows what I am going to say. I say 'no', but not for the reasons you think.

'It is because you deserve the whole love of your own special person. I love you so much, but it's agape love, the best friend love, a love that will last forever but is not the same as intimate, physical love. And I want this for you, my best friend, not only a half love, which is all I could give you.

'Please don't be sad, Ben. My heart is already about to burst.' She took his hand on the table and held it tightly to soften the pain of rejection.

His face tightened with suppressed emotion as he pulled his hand away and excused himself from the table.

Gabby watched him walk quickly out of the front door and into the darkened street. It was so cruel that she couldn't be what he wanted her to be.

Their meals sat unfinished as both were lost in a world of hurt.

Ben leaned against a light pole and took the ring box out of his pocket. He flipped the top open and saw the one solitaire diamond sparkle even in the dim light. He had seen it in the store window, and the deep shimmering light reminded him of Gabby and how she outshone all of them, no matter where she was.

What was I thinking, foolishly imagining some happy ever after for us? I'm a stupid and naïve clown. Without even a glimmer of encouragement, I still dared to hope that her feelings had changed. What an idiot to lay my heart on the line. He gave himself a good scolding as he watched a couple of smokers further up the street laughing and sharing a joke.

After a while, his equilibrium became more settled, and he reminded himself that the world did not revolve around Ben Giles. There were more important people to consider. Gabby and her child needed his love and support.

Shaking off his dark mood, he went back to reassure Gabby that he wasn't going to make a scene.

Gabby's green eyes were welling with tears when he sat back down. 'Ben, I am so sorry.'

He didn't say a word, but his deep blue eyes spoke of embarrassment and the pain of rejection.

Gabby had her own proposal and hoped he still had enough love in his heart to consider her plea.

'I have something to ask of you.' Her eyes begged for understanding.

'Ben, this baby has no father. I know that my mother and Joe will be there for him but they're both elderly, particularly Old Joe. I want you to be his guardian and take the role of his father if anything should happen to me.'

'Gabby, one of the reasons I proposed was to protect you and the baby. I would do this, as husband or friend,' Ben interrupted.

'No Ben, please listen. You know we have enemies, and who knows, something may even go wrong with the labour. If I don't make it, I choose you to raise this little boy into a man. I want you to guide and teach him how to be remarkable. Will you do this for us?' Gabby pressed her hand on the baby as it kicked.

'Gabby, call me stupid, but I will never entirely give up on the dream of us. For me, there is no one but you. It has been that way from the moment I met you and my devotion will remain true while I still draw breath.' He smiled sadly through his own unshed tears.

'In regard to your question, the answer is an absolute yes. I already love this child like my own and will be proud to call him my son.'

Ben reached across the table to gently frame her face with his large hands. 'This is my family, whether we do this as man and wife or best friends. Either way, I vow to love you both until the day I die.'

'Ben, this means the world to me, knowing he will always have you.' Gabby took his hands in hers.

Their meals were almost untouched, which upset the waiter when he collected the plates. Ben assured him there was nothing wrong with the food when he paid the bill.

The drive home was silent. Having both spoken their truth, there was nothing left to say.

High above the street in the exclusive suburb of Canterbury, Gina wandered through the dark moody decor of Dominic's apartment. It was a shame he couldn't appreciate the wonderful light streaming in from the floor-to-ceiling glass window that looked down on the street below.

Taking her brewed coffee back to bed, she placed it on the bedside table and slid back into the expensive sheets. Gina ignored Dominic, who slept on his side, with his nightmare mask out of sight. She caressed the large tattoo of a bloody thorn that covered the underside of her left arm, the symbol of her belonging to the guild.

Gina closed her eyes during sex when Dominic's disfigured face pressed down upon her. He was a skilled if not overly affectionate lover, using his mind and body to bring her to orgasm over and over again.

At the thought of sexual pleasures, Gina's hand crept into her panties as she excitedly imagined their victory over her adversary. The baby was almost due, and their plan would soon be complete. Everyone knew Gabby was dangerous, especially now that she had some of her former abilities, so they had to be thorough, with every detail examined for flaws.

Gina hated her even more now that Connor was dead. She mourned for the end of her ambitions to become his wife. The news had rocked Melbourne society, as it seemed impossible that someone with so much to live for had died so young.

It was her fault that Connor was buried in some unmarked grave in the wilds of Africa. If he had never met Gabrielle Harrison, then he would be married to her, Gina Perry.

She gasped in pleasure as the orgasm washed over her, and lay there feeling gratified that soon Connor would be avenged, that Dominic would be avenged and most important of all, soon Gina Perry would be avenged.

The next few months flew by faster than ever. Gabby's body changed shape and adapted to the life growing within, and she loved every minute of it.

The joy of those first flutters developed into definite rolls and kicks as her baby grew and filled every last inch of the space allotted to him. So strong and active, it was a little unsettling when he actually slept, as she became accustomed to his kicking most of the day and night.

The love she felt for this unborn child was so strong. He was a small piece of Connor from those last precious days together. As her pregnancy drew to the end, she really wanted to go home to San Remo, to have her mother close by at her due date. Her place of dreaming was calling Gabby back to where it all began. She wanted fall asleep again to the sound of waves rushing up the beach.

Gabby intended to spend the last few weeks at San Remo and have the baby at the Cairns Base Hospital.

Ben hugged her close when she flew out of Melbourne. Holding her away from him, he gave some last-minute instructions. 'Promise me you'll get enough rest, and eat well.'

'Of course I will. Joe and my mother will be hovering constantly.' Gabby smiled into his much-loved deep blue eyes.

'I'll be up there in two weeks and then you'll have the three of us 'hovering'. And once bub is born, the whole crowd from the society will be heading north to celebrate.'

'Joe's cottage and Mum's house will be overflowing.'

'I can't wait. We're really at the pointy end now, Gabbs,' Ben said as he placed his hand protectively on her cumbersome stomach.

'You mean the round end. If I get much bigger, this belly is going to pop.' She laughed at her distorted shape.

'Take care of my godson, and I'll see you shortly,' Ben called out as she boarded the Gulfstream Jet to Cairns.

The society was as busy as ever, and Miranda was working longer hours to cover Gabby's leave. On this particular evening, she felt especially exhausted and longed for an early night. The street lights had come on as she walked from the tram stop to her gran's little house. It no longer looked abandoned as her friends at work had helped her renovate the interior and paint the exterior, and the garden was now tended to, thanks to Ben. It now looked more respectable and not the eyesore of the street.

The key snapped the lock as Miranda pushed the door open enough to reach for the light switch.

She jumped in fright as a cold hand pulled her roughly into the dark house. Before Miranda could scream for help, someone forcibly covered her mouth and dragged her into the kitchen where she was pushed onto a kitchen chair.

Strong hands held her in place as Miranda tried to make out their features in the gloomy light. 'What do you want from me,' she whispered, terrified.

'We want your soul, Miranda. You made a blood promise long ago that must be paid tonight.' A voice filled the silence of the little house.

'No, I don't belong to him anymore. I no longer believe in him.' She tried to be brave but her voice betrayed the fear that was rising like bile in her throat.

Someone stepped closer and angrily squished her cheeks, grinding them into her teeth and making her mouth fill with blood.

'You think you can trifle with the dark one and just change your mind? It doesn't work like that, sister. You will sacrifice yourself just as Rowan did all those years ago, or have you forgotten him too?'

'Of course I haven't forgotten Rowan. You brainwashed and killed him for your wicked cause.' Miranda was outraged at their cruel accusation. 'You are all misguided fools, following some power-hungry monster.'

A soft, resigned voice silenced her dialogue. 'Whether you support us or not is of no consequence. We have brought the serpent.'

'No, please don't. Have mercy on me,' Miranda pleaded.

'This servant of Satan will keep you quiet until he is ready for you.' Fingers pried her mouth open so wide that the sides burned and her lips split, while another forced his fingers down her throat.

Miranda gagged and salivated as she tried to turn her head away from what they threatened to do. She never saw the black snake in the dark room. It was the texture and sensation as it filled her mouth and slid down her tight, protesting throat that made her mind and body retreat from the viciously executed terror.

She blessedly fainted and remained unconscious as they carried her limp form out of the darkened house. Unaware of the car ride to the airport and still laying silent throughout the chartered flight from Melbourne to Cairns, Miranda didn't even wake as the cultists sped towards her incarceration.

Miranda was 'as dead'. There was no sound, no movement, no fight as the serpent kept her in a world alone, without her friends to provide solace.

In her mind, she sat crouched in the corner of a dark room with the snake. She knew it was there as its beady eyes glowed red with menace. She was too terrified to move unless it was provoked to strike and ended the story that was her.

Thirty

The Titans had been so happy when they were collected from pet freight. They bounded into Joe's old car and pushed their heads out of the windows to get their first hint of the salty sea air.

Samson and Goliath had been up north for holidays before, and the beach was one of their favourite playgrounds. It was only the curlews who took offence that Gabby may need more than their protection.

Gabby was staying at Joe's cottage until the new paint fumes had dissipated from Kathleen's house. She planned to move in with her mother when Ben arrived.

It was her soul that sighed when the crashing sound of the waves lulled her to sleep that first night. It was that full circle of coming home that gave her this sense of wellbeing.

She'd had an emotional time catching up with Ruth, Billy and their daughters, but it was Eddie she couldn't wait to see. He'd promised to come home to see the baby when he was born. The next couple of weeks was going to be filled with love, and she felt blessed her baby would be born into the endless support of his own people.

Tonight they lounged on the old sofa, with the Titans laying at their feet. Gabby was reading a science journal, and Joe was lost in thought.

She absently rubbed her stomach and wondered what amazing qualities her offspring would possess. Half angel and half human, he would be a truly exceptional child.

Gabby was excited to meet the little person growing inside of her, even though it broke her heart that Connor wouldn't be here for the birth. The mobile buzzed on the table beside her and she looked at the number to see it was Ben.

'Hi Ben, you're up late tonight.'

'Yeah, sorry to call so late but I knew you would still be burning the candle at both ends.'

'You know me too well. What's the matter?'

'Well, I didn't want to worry you, but I am concerned about Miranda. She didn't come into work today or call to explain her whereabouts. There was no answer when I called and when I went over to her house, it was empty with the front door unlocked.'

'Ben, there is only one explanation for her disappearance. You cannot even call the police.' Gabby voiced the dread they were both feeling.

'I'm not sure where to start,' Ben fretted.

'I wish we still had Father Gerry. He would know what to do,' Gabby said as she thought of the consequences of Miranda's disappearance.

Joe sensed her concern and listened to their conversation with new interest.

Subconsciously she wrapped her arms around her protruded belly.

'I don't want to worry you, Gabby. Leave it with me, and I'll do some sleuthing to see if any of her neighbours saw something,' Ben tried to reassure her.

'Of course I'm worried. Miranda is family now.'

'Give me tomorrow and then I'll call you back.'

'Keep me informed, Ben. I have a really bad feeling about this.' Gabby looked across at Joe with dread all over her face.

'If I can't locate Miranda tomorrow, I'll come straight up north. I want to be on hand to look out for you both.'

'I would appreciate that. It worries me with the timing. Miranda goes missing just as the baby is almost due to be born.'

The next day, Gabby tried to call Miranda numerous times, but her phone just beeped out, and there wasn't even an option to leave a message. Pacing around the small cottage, with every horrible scenario going through her head, Gabby didn't know who to reach out to for help.

Instead of going for multiple swims in the ocean, the Titans sensed her alarm and stayed close all through the morning.

'I'm coming with you to the gynaecologist appointment today, Gabby. We can't take any chances with this latest development,' Joe insisted.

Gabby just nodded her consent. She could see his logic and didn't want to risk any harm to the baby.

'Remember to bring the pendant. Just in case,' Joe warned.

With the blood tree pendant secure in her handbag, she awkwardly climbed into the car for the drive into Cairns.

They parked underneath Flecker House, and Joe helped her to get out of the car. Everything felt clumsy now as she couldn't even see her feet below her protruding belly.

Once they checked in at reception, they waited for the doctor to call Gabby into his surgery rooms. They sat in silence, listening to the receptionist take calls for appointments.

When the doctor came to the door and invited Gabby in to see him, Joe waited outside rather than intrude on her privacy.

Once seated, Gabby smiled at Doctor Foster, the obstetrician.

After the examination, he seemed happy with the results. 'Everything seems to be in order, Gabrielle. Your blood pressure is perfect, the baby is engaged and I believe you could deliver anytime next week.'

'That long?' She looked down at the huge bulge sitting in her lap.

'Are you nervous or do you have any concerns about the delivery?'

'I think it's the unknown that makes me a little nervous and the fear that something might go wrong to hurt the baby. Even after all the antenatal classes I attended in Melbourne.'

'I don't think you have anything to fret or worry about. You are in perfect health, and all the signs point to normal birth and a safe delivery.'

'Thank you. I'll take your advice and try not to dwell on the possible dangers and instead anticipate meeting this little person. So, this is it, the next time I see you will be at the hospital?'

'Sure will be, probably in the middle of the night, like so many other babies before yours.' He smiled knowingly.

'We'll see you then.' Gabby smiled her thanks.

When they got back to their car, Joe turned to ask Gabby what the doctor had said. As he opened his mouth to talk, he suddenly put both of his hands over his head and began to groan in agony. To Gabby's dismay, he stopped and looked at her in terror, then sank to the concreted ground, where he curled his body into a foetal position to ward off the evil.

Gabby awkwardly kneeled down beside him. 'Joe', what's wrong!'

She grabbed his shoulder as she looked around the deserted car park. Not seeing any threat, she reached into her bag to find the pendant, just in case.

'It's my head, Gabby, someone is in my head. You need to run, get out of here right now,' he whispered between gasps of pain.

Before Gabby could even stand up or take hold of her pendant, she felt a sharp jab in the side of her neck. She spun around to find a black-suited man standing close behind her.

Where did he come from so suddenly?

When her legs refused to hold her up, it was her tear-filled eyes that condemned the stranger for the crime he was about to commit.

She couldn't cry out, she couldn't move. Instead, she fell helplessly onto the ground.

Like a living mannequin, she was carried off and placed in the back seat of a waiting black car.

One of the culprits crouched beside Joe's wiry frame. To all appearances he was just looking at him, but Gabby knew different.

The assailant moved the pain from Joe's head to his heart, where he squeezed the fearless muscles, making him clutch his chest instead. 'Old man, how does it feel to know your life is literally in my hands?'

'You can't kill me, no matter how hard you try. It is not yet my time. I'm still needed here,' Joe said between the spasms raking his body.

'So you foolishly believe,' his persecutor laughed. With a smile of pure evil, he let his mind's eye see Joe's heart. The organ filled his mind, and he grunted with pleasure as it fluttered within his grasp. Now all he had to do was finish him off.

With a final push, he closed his fist to stop it beating.

He pushed with his mind again and again. No matter how he hard he tried to make the killing blow, it would not work. A bright light held his power at bay and even when he threw his will against it, the shield would not yield.

'Come on, Nigel. We must go before someone sees us,' the other abductors called from the black car.

Nigel had encountered this force once before. He remembered the priest he'd tried to kill in the same way. Obviously, these men had a supernatural protection powerful enough to obstruct his mind control.

In frustration, he moved his concentration back to Joe's head and struck a blow that left him unconscious. Dragging him out of sight, he ran to the car that carried Gabby away.

Gabby was laying on her side, staring at the back of the front seats as they sped towards some unknown destination. *Josiel, Gadriel, how I wish you would come to save us. What have they done to you both in the Silver City? Are you in chains for helping me, or something even worse?*

Gabby could not understand why she had been abandoned by her angelic brother and sister. She feared they had been ostracised for supporting her in this unsanctioned human experience. Terrified this would end badly, her tears ran down her cheeks. She knew that what awaited her was a heinous act. It would be a battle of life and death, but now she fought not just for herself, but for her son, who meant more to her than anything else. It would be up to Gabby to get them out of this, as her pleas to her brothers and sisters in the Silver City had, just like before, fallen on deaf ears.

Josiel looked along the table that shone with an illumination from within, like it had a life of its own.

Taking a moment, she steepled her fingers and stared at them as she considered how to begin. Gathered around her were the few she had chosen to be a part of this assembly tasked to prepare for the coming confrontation with Lucifer and his demonic hosts.

'Brothers and sisters, thank you for heeding my call. I have asked you here because I trust you and know you are dedicated to serving the sons of man *and* protecting the Silver City.'

Staring around the group, she turned to Gadriel and asked, 'Where is Zadkiel?'

'He is delivering a soul, Josiel. He will join us upon his return,' Gadriel reassured her.

'I do want him to be alongside us when we are ready to proceed with our plan. Zinnia has commissioned me to muster a select group of warriors and establish where we'll need to be when our fallen brother makes his first move.'

'He being?' One of the assembled raised a delicate brow at the end of the table.

'Our brother and once-friend, Lucifer Morning Star. I have a story to tell you that will explain our presence here.'

Josiel told them everything about her visit to the cult headquarters in Rome. After gasps of shock and frowns of despair, she knew they were just as keen to see Lucifer's innocence-thieving stopped once and for all.

'Now you see that we have much to plan, as we must be ready for what is ahead.'

They began to lay out and discuss their weaknesses and how to reinforce their strengths. The first meeting ended with all feeling united in their cause.

As the room emptied, Josiel took Gadriel's hand and led him to an oak bench that ran along the great room. 'My dear friend, I yearn to go to Fallon. I must see what has transpired since I abandoned her to conceal myself Rome.

'I can feel how you miss her and how you always seem to be searching for those emerald eyes of hers.' Gadriel smiled as he remembered Fallon's startling green eyes.

'Soon we shall both go to visit our sister and tell her of all that has transpired. How we are no longer considered outcasts, but are now sought out for our counsel.' Josiel stood tall.

'I would welcome to opportunity to see her again too. But first we must gain traction with what we have started here today.' Gadriel held her hands tightly with affection.

Gabby was carried out of the car and through the side door of a wooden building, one that could have been a church or community hall. Her abductors moved her into the back of the large room where a couple of strong mesh cages had been constructed. All Gabby could do was move her eyes as she lay on the timber floor, as even her tongue was stuck to the roof of her dry mouth as she groggily looked around.

She gasped with shock when she saw another prisoner. In the mesh cage beside her lay a motionless Miranda.

Was she dead? Gabby watched her chest to see if it moved.

Gabby moved some moisture around her own mouth and found that a slight sensation was returning. 'Miranda, please wake up.' She fumbled over the words like a child learning to speak.

The former formidable angel wished her abilities would let her communicate with humans as well, and then they could converse without anyone knowing.

She felt the baby begin to move and reassured him with a promise. *It's alright, little one. I will protect you and keep you safe*

Gabby sent a message to the Titans and curlews to tell them she was in trouble, then in desperation, she called out to the animals all around them, to the birds overhead.

Help me!

She needed any chance of being discovered before it was too late.

Joe rolled over and groaned as he held his head in his hands. Blinking in the dim light, he saw the undercarriage and realised he was laying under his car. He checked the car park but could only find Gabby's handbag. It was beside the wheel of the car. He opened it up and saw the pendant was still inside.

If only she'd had time to use it! Joe's mind was in turmoil as he got back to his cottage, especially when he found all the guardians on high alert.

The hackles were standing up on Samson and Goliath's backs as they prowled the house with their lips pulled back over long, sharp fangs. Gabby's curlews had started calling out in distress as well.

Joe made the call. 'Ben, Gabby has been abducted.'

'Holy shit,' Ben gasped into the phone. It was their worst fear realised. 'We need to find her, Joe. The baby is almost due, and I couldn't live with myself if anything happened to either of them,' he almost moaned with desperation.

'I know, Ben. Do you think there is any point in calling the police?' Joe asked, trying not to scare Ben with his own sense of panic and approaching disaster.

'They won't do anything about it until she has been missing for more than twenty-four hours.'

'We don't have twenty-four hours.'

'I know.'

'Ben, call the pilot to see if we could use the Gulfstream to get everyone from Melbourne to Cairns as quickly as possible. The more we have here to mount our own rescue, the better.'

'On it, Joe,' Ben promised before ending the call.

They had to find Gabby fast, and most likely Miranda too.

Miranda lay so still, barely breathing, while Gabby did her best to stay calm. She watched the old abandoned church become a busy place, with black-robed priests moving in and out of the building.

They had carried in a heavy altar with a black marble slab laid on top. It was obviously a sacrificial site with a lip around the edge to contain blood. She tried not to look at it, or dwell on what was going to happen. The priests were painting the pentagon on the wooden floor and lighting candles all over the room.

If only Miranda would wake.

She could hear the cacophony of noise coming from the birds she'd called, and even the local curlews were crying their outrage.

Sometime later, three priests came to Miranda's cage, one holding a black cotton drawstring bag. Once they unlocked the door, two of them roughly took her limp form by the shoulders and lifted her head. The priest with the black bag began to chant a prayer, and to Gabby's horror, she saw Miranda's throat expand. Her mouth was pushed wide open as the head of a snake forced its way out. It kept coming and coming until the snake slid into the black bag held by the chanting priest.

Miranda fell lifelessly back to the ground. Gabby had trouble believing what she had just witnessed.

Glaring at Gabby from under their hooded cowls, they locked the cage and took their prize back to the group clustered around the sacrificial altar.

Gabby's attention was drawn back to Miranda, who was now lying across from her with open eyes. As she became aware of their predicament, she sat up unsteadily and began to cry in earnest.

Gabby concentrated on clearing the cloud of the sedation from her own mind and the dryness off her tongue.

Finally, she was able to whisper hoarsely. 'Miranda, I saw what they drew out of you, and it was horrible. I don't understand how that snake was inside you.'

'Gabby, they got you too! No! This can't be happening. They abducted and poisoned me with the serpent. Then in my mind, I was trapped in the dark with that snake. I couldn't move in case it attacked me. What are we going to do? The baby! I'm so worried about the baby, Gabby. These people are evil. We can't let them harm your baby,' Miranda reached her arms awkwardly through the wire to reach out for Gabby. She was frantic with worry for her best friend and the baby.

'Don't cry, Miranda. We must not lose hope. Joe will find a way to rescue us.' Gabby's voice wobbled a little with trepidation, in spite of her brave words.

A moment later she wrapped her arms around her hard, swollen stomach and felt her unborn child squirm with fear. *It's alright, little one. I will keep you safe, even if it's the last thing I do. What would I do if I were still Fallon? If only I had my angelic powers, then these people would*

302

flee from my rage at what they have done to me, to Miranda. If I can't fight my way out of this, I have to be smart and find another way.

'Miranda, we have to think of a way to stall them. We need to give Joe and the Titans more time to find us.'

'How can we do that? They're already preparing for the ceremony.' Miranda's shoulders shook with sobs as she apologised again. 'Gabby, if you had never met me, this would not be happening.'

'Miranda, you can't take responsibility for the evil that walks the earth. None of this is your fault. We can't lose hope, not yet. Just focus on the knowledge that Joe will be doing everything he can to save us. I know he won't rest until we are home safe and sound. He'll soon bring the police to stop their diabolical plan. I just hope you won't get hurt because of us.'

'Gabby, it's you I worry about. The priests are planning a sacrifice tonight.' Miranda clutched the wire between them in terror.

'Miranda, together we can fight this evil. They're not invincible. Remember that we stopped them before. Now we must have faith in Joe and our friends.'

Ben could barely sit still on the flight from Melbourne to Cairns. No one said much as they were all lost in their own versions of disaster. Rushing off the flight and straight into Joe's waiting car, they drove to the beach cottage to join Kathleen, Jacob and Thomas.

Everyone gathered around the table to examine what they knew. Miranda was missing along with Gabby, and both were in terrible danger.

Joe was impatient to act and wanted the discussion to turn to results. In his mind they were already running out of time.

'What if we ask the Titans to find them?' Ben asked.

'So, we unleash the dogs and see if they can take us to Gabby and Miranda. What if it's too far? Dogs can only run for so long.' Thomas was trying to remain calm to support his mother.

'Then what? There might be ten or twenty people involved in this abduction, and we would just add to the casualties if we went charging in there,' Paul said as he paced around the room.

'Do you think it could be some misguided protesters who don't agree with our work, or do you seriously believe it is something more sinister?' Michael asked tentatively.

Joe looked at Ben, and they were both thinking of what had happened to Father Gerry.

'We suspect something very sinister. These radicals have no respect for life, and the sooner we find them, the better.' Ben's face paled as he considered what could happen to Gabby and the baby.

Without further speculation, everyone focused on the best plan of action.

'We could wait at the police station and as soon as you have a location, we can arrange several police cars to surround the place. At least they're armed,' Jacob Harrison said as he looked at Thomas, who nodded his agreement.

'How are you going to convince the police to send cars when we don't even know what the threat is yet?' Paul tersely asked the brothers.

'I have a couple of friends who are coppers, and I'm pretty sure I can convince them to save my sister,' Jacob snapped back at Paul.

'Okay guys, just settle. We need to focus all our energy on saving our friends,' Ben reprimanded them.

Kathleen sat at the table, frozen with fear. Her daughter's and grandson's lives were on a knife's edge.

'I think we have a plan formulating now,' Joe encouraged the group.

'However, Thomas is right. What if the distance is too far for the Titans to run? They already have far too much lead time.' Ben pushed back his chair in despair.

'If the curlews flew ahead of us, they could sound the alarm when we got closer.' Elisabeth looked expectantly at the group.

'All I know is we need to hurry. My heart is saying we don't have much time.' Old Joe stood at the end of the table with tears in his eyes.

Kathleen started crying at Joe's distress as her emotions were at breaking point.

Her youngest son sat down to wrap his arms around her trembling body. 'Don't cry, Mum, we'll bring them both home safely,' Thomas murmured into her hair.

'Guys, don't forget Gabby is going to be sending a message to any animals close by. We should keep our eyes open for anything that doesn't look normal,' Michael did his best to reassure them.

'Yes, you're right Michael,' Ben said. 'Gabby will try to help us as much as she can as long as she remains conscious, at least.'

Ben felt bile rise in his throat when he thought of his godchild. He already loved that baby like his own. Miranda had become a close friend too, and he wanted to see her safe as well.

The action plan began to fall into place. Elisabeth would stay here to support Kathleen and act as a base contact. It was already late afternoon, so they needed to act quickly before it was too late.

Jacob and Thomas would go to the police and convince their cop friends to respond to the call for back up.

Ben and Joe would take Jacob's Ute back to Flecker House where they had abducted Gabby, and hope the Titans could track her from there.

Paul and Michael got the job of catching the curlews and securing them in Kathleen's car. The plan was to release the birds once they had a trace on the attackers.

It felt better to be doing something, and even Paul and Michael didn't mind the bites and scratches from three of the curlews. They carefully put them in a wooden crate Joe had found for the purpose of transporting them.

Only Kathleen and Elisabeth found the minutes ticking by far too slowly. They sat with the radio on and watched the television without seeing or hearing anything.

Thirty-one

The baby hadn't moved for hours. It seemed that he was picking up on her fear. Gabby tried to reassure him, but as the scene unfolded, this became more and more difficult. They had injected her again with more sedative to keep her from fighting back like the last time.

Groggily, Gabby sent a panicked distress call to any creatures in the vicinity. *Save us,* she cried out again to them.

The last cult member arrivals had to fight through a great host of animals congregated outside the fence as there were dogs, cats and birds everywhere.

The same sleek black car that had abducted Gabby had to drive slowly to get through to the back of the building, Dogs of all sizes were jumping all over the vehicle, barking and snarling at them, and cats leaped onto windscreens, screeching and hissing at them through the glass.

No matter how much the animals antagonised the priests, it didn't deter them from their mission. With Gabby and Miranda inside, the ritual could go ahead. Soon the cult master would arrive to sacrifice these gifts to the prince of darkness.

Lucifer would reward them for destroying the angel and her spawn, and consuming their blood would quench a long-awaited thirst.

As the sun dropped behind the mountains, Dominic arrived, ceremoniously donning his black robes to bring them together in prayer. The chanting got louder and increased in urgency as they called the Morning Star to come and join this sacrifice. There was a heavy presence in the air, until it felt hard to breathe. Gabby could sense a dark shadow drawing all the priests closer and closer together. It might be her imagination, but in the distance there was a beating of wings getting stronger and louder.

She knew her irredeemable fallen brother Lucifer was coming. He was now from a place where hope, faith and love had no home, but rather a place where cruelty, hate and despair ruled instead.

Miranda's and Gabby's hearts beat louder and louder, almost in rhythm to the chants filling the air, Miranda was cowering in her cage and shivering in fear as the hope of rescue became more and more desolate, while Gabby ground her teeth in frustration. If she wasn't so heavily sedated, she would use her power to force their way out of here. Why couldn't the council send a contingent of angels to come to her aid, and where was her sister Josiel?

Save me, Josiel, I beg you! she beseeched her sister.

Into this disaster, Gabby felt the first contractions of labour. She didn't have the heart to tell Miranda that they now had this to worry about as well.

When Joe and Ben arrived in the city, they released the Titans, hoping the dogs could pick up on Gabby's whereabouts. Taking off through the streets, the dogs turned south and raced like greyhounds, setting a fast pace. Running along the rough bitumen, it wasn't long before the pads on their feet began to bleed, but even this didn't deter them from finding Gabby. Ben and Joe followed behind them in the car.

The curlews were released once they reached the end of Mulgrave Road, as it was now obvious the abductors had taken Gabby south of Cairns.

Jacob and Thomas called to confirm they had convinced the police sergeant on duty to have patrol cars ready as soon as the location was identified.

Kathleen sat in the lounge in the dark, curled up in a tight ball. Knowing how distraught she was, Elisabeth left her alone to pray for her daughter and grandson.

Elisabeth sat by herself at the kitchen table listening to the local radio station when a caller said something that made her sit up straight. The announcer was asking her to say it again, and a young girlish voice wafted out of the radio.

'This afternoon, I was out riding my horse when I saw all these birds flying around an abandoned church. Out the front of the church there were heaps of dogs and cats, and when a car pulled up, they jumped all over it, acting really weird. There were dogs barking, cats attacking and birds flying all over the place. I've never seen anything like it before, and then my horse started going crazy, so I had to take him home. I just thought to check if anyone else has seen bizarre animal behaviour today?'

The radio announcer sounded slightly bored and cut the call short.

Elisabeth called the station immediately to demand the number of that last caller, explaining it was an emergency and a matter of life and death.

When she called the number, the same young girl answered.

Without giving too much away, Elisabeth managed to get the location of the building out of her and quickly called Ben and Joe.

Ben felt his mobile vibrating in his pocket and pulled it out to take the call.

Elisabeth was shouting into the phone, 'I have the address. Ben, I have the address.'

'Where? How?' Ben asked Lissy with a glimmer of hope.

'It was on the local radio station. A girl called in to say she saw heaps of animals going crazy and attacking people. It's an abandoned church in Edmonton, Ben, at the far end of the industrial estate. A secluded location.'

So, the dogs were taking them there. They had been heading in the right direction the whole time and were now approaching Edmonton.

'Call all the others, Lissy, and get the police there,' Ben instructed. 'We have the address, Joe. Let's get the dogs back in the car,' he shouted in exultation.

The Titans were gathered in the car, bleeding all over the seats and panting from their efforts to locate Gabby.

The curlews continued flying south, taking frequent breaks on the ground. Their wing span was not sufficient to keep them in the air for long periods of flight. But they knew their destination and were determined to do their part of the rescue.

Elisabeth quickly called Jacob and Thomas to explain the new information she had at hand, and everyone stepped into action.

Then she went into the lounge room and sat beside Kathleen to describe what had just happened. Kathleen sat up and hugged her, then she cried great heart-wrenching sobs against Elisabeth's shoulder.

'It's going to be alright, Kathleen. We've found them. I'm sure the boys will sort it all out and bring them home soon,' Lissy reassured her.

The old building had been re-invented into a temple of doom. There were candles flickering light throughout the large room, and the worshippers moved about in whispered reverence of what they were about to witness.

The robed figures gathered in a circle and prayed for the dark spirits to unite with them in their devotion. When they were satisfied they had the attention of the unearthly, the leader raised his sleeved arms and called out to the group, 'Bring me the scroll.'

Another supplicant moved to the altar and reached underneath to bring out a rolled parchment.

Once in Dominic's hands, he held it towards the heavens and shouted, 'I denounce this prophecy. By our actions today, we change the course of history. This ancient vision will never become a reality; instead, we shall be victorious. Praise be to the Morning Star.'

With that, he held the fragile scroll over a flame to see it crackle and become consumed, and to collapse in ash in his outstretched hands. With this ash, he placed a mark of the upside-down cross on the forehead of all those circled around him.

'You will be rewarded for your faithful service this day,' Dominic said, staring into Crimson Thorn's eager green eyes within the cowl

Once this ceremony was over, some of the priests moved with murderous intent towards Gabby and Miranda.

Opening Miranda's cage, they dragged her out screaming as she desperately held onto the door. Once clear of the cage, they plunged a sharp needle into her upper arm, even though she continued to push and kick against them. Not to be deterred, the priests held Miranda tightly until the drug could take effect.

'This will take the fight out of you and make it easier to surrender,' a high-pitched voice assured Miranda as he held her captive.

Miranda's head drooped down as she was half carried, half dragged across the wooden floor.

Stripped naked, she lay in the middle of the pentagon as they tied her into a spreadeagled position. Floating above her body, she could look down at her naked form and feel no alarm. There was just a calm acceptance of what was about to happen, and somewhere a thought arose in her, that this must have been how Rowan felt the night he was sacrificed. If so, at least he didn't suffer any fear or pain.

Gabby watched in horror when she saw Miranda prepared for the ritual, and then they came back across to get her. Gabby sent a scream across the consciousness of all around.

Help us now!

They entered the cage as a group and closed the door behind them. One priest caught Gabby's throat with his hand while another two took hold of her arms. While she was held tightly from behind, another plunged the syringe into her arm, not daring to take her out of the cage until she was compliant.

'We're doubling your dose, our enemy from the dawn of time.'

Once she was soft and yielding, Gabby was strong-armed into the centre of the gathering priests and priestesses. They stripped all of her clothing away and made her lay on the cold wooden floor with her hands and feet tied together, her swollen stomach clenching in protest as the labour kept drawing on.

When they pulled up outside the building, the Titans began howling as they rushed out of the car on their broken feet, whimpering their anguish.

Ben called Jacob again when he saw their distress. 'Jake, how far away are you? I think things are getting really desperate now.'

Jacob could hear the dogs and told Ben they were almost there. 'Can you see the church yet?'

'Yes, we're here, but we don't want to charge in without any backup,' Ben said.

'Hold tight, we'll be there in two minutes,' Jacob reassured him.

Joe was standing just out of sight of the building and holding on to the dog's collars. The curlews were here too, squawking with alarm.

Ben couldn't believe how strong Joe was. He had held the dogs at bay the whole time.

The chanting rose higher and higher as the priest raised the goblet up to the altar. In his rasping voice, he asked for consecration of the sacrifice that they were about to make. The robed figures surrounded the pentagon, clasping each other as they moved and swayed like one organism, their voices driving them into a state of frenzy.

Gabby watched with disbelieving eyes as a priest walked over to Miranda. He made several incantations over her body in Latin, and then without warning, he slashed his knife across her throat. The blood burst forth frothy and red as Miranda gurgled her last breaths from the jagged edges of her wound.

Gabby couldn't move as her whole world imploded. Her body was paralysed, so she could only moan and gasp with the pain of losing one of her best friends.

Her mind shouted at the council and the angels in the Silver City. *Why didn't you save us? You could have sent a patrol of angels to sweep this evil away. Instead, you turn your face away from the distasteful truth – even you, Josiel.*

Gabby tried to scream her betrayal, but only a strangled whimper emerged from her slack mouth. Desperately, her brain tried to tell her legs to run, but the message refused to transmit along the nerve pathways, so instead she lay there whimpering her anguish in vain. Only her eyes told the true story of the horror taking place, the pain of devastating loss.

The first priest had thrust a goblet under the fountain of blood and filled it with Miranda's life force, then he went around the circle to pass it to each priest and priestess to drink deeply.

Crimson Thorn was one of the participants, and she enjoyed the warm, salty taste of Miranda's blood as it slid down her throat smoothly and sat warm and heavy in her stomach. It was Gina's first taste of human blood, and in her present state of euphoria, she drank it with delight.

Gabby's whimpers became more and more agitated, and she thrashed her head back and forth in anger. It was impossible to believe that Miranda had just been murdered. She kept staring at her, so close, surrounded by a pool of her still-flowing blood and looking like a broken doll laying on the ground with no expression on her beautiful face.

When the goblet was placed on the altar, the coiled snake raised its head and began to sniff the air. Sinuously it moved to the goblet and wound its body around the stem and up the chalice until it was completely submerged in Miranda's blood.

The high priest wrote symbols of the goat and its master with the blood while the other priests untied Gabby. They then dragged her swollen, naked body over and laid her on the cold and bloody marble.

The chanting reached a crescendo, and when her eyes lifted, she could now see an intense dark shadow hovering above the priests. Gabby sensed that their Morning Star, her fallen brother Lucifer, had arrived to partake in this rare sacrifice of an angel and her child.

Knowing they were about to slay her, Gabby felt furious rather than scared. She wanted to fight back but the sedation wouldn't let the fire rise in her blood.

Why did evil have to win on this day? Goodness was the far greater force, and even though her life as a human was almost over, she still wanted to see the battle won for the people who held truth and light in their hearts.

If Christian could only survive, then I know he could be powerful enough to shift the balance.

She sent a message of love to him. *Christian, I love you, my baby, and no matter what happens now, I will always be with you, always be watching over you.*

The baby squirmed, and she felt another contraction. There was no pain now, just a tightening across her stomach. The approaching labour couldn't hold her attention for long when she was in fear for their very lives. Regardless of the circumstances, her stomach kept tightening over and over again as her body tried to deliver this baby.

The cult members laid her on the unholy surface, and the priest touched her stomach time and time again. He saw it tighten with contractions and realised that the time was now. The baby had to be sacrificed before her body could deliver it naturally. They had to tear it out of its place of nurture to satisfy their evil desires.

Gabby looked up and saw a face that was horribly burned and disfigured with eyes sealed shut and knew who he was: the cult master she had destroyed all those years ago.

Gabby reached out to the source of all life. *I beg you to save us from this evil,* she implored.

After suffering at her hand, he would have no mercy for her or Christian. If only she could access her power, she would destroy them all without hesitation, these people who were here to celebrate the death of her precious baby.

Unable to cringe away in terror, she could sense Dominic relishing his moment of revenge, and internally she cried out to prepare Christian for this unholy assault.

Raising the knife, Dominic shouted his prayer of dedication and then brought it down, slicing across Gabby's tight abdomen. The knife slid across her tight skin without resistance. The muscles parted, making a huge chasm in her stomach, which immediately began to pour forth an immense amount of blood.

No! Not my baby! Kill me, not my baby.

These fanatics destroyed her last shreds of belief that the virtuous would ultimately overcome the creep of darkness. Nothing in this brutal earth life could prepare her for this moment. To lose her own life was bad enough, but for Christian to be ripped away from her so cruelly, it was more than she could bear.

The paralysis drugs were not enough to stop the burning pain across her stomach and the tension release on her skin. Her maternal instinct was instant, and clumsily her hands fumbled down into the slippery, bloody mess to try to save her son before they could harm him too.

The moan that escaped her lips came from the depths of her soul. This heinous deed was the zenith of malevolence. To destroy her son's life was the final molestation of Gabrielle Harrison. Now her human measure was fading, and her immortal self was awakening and about to re-emerge.

Her heart was broken along with her mutilated body as she acceded defeat.

Thirty-two

The group of them held Joe back, telling him to wait for the police, until suddenly he collapsed heavily onto the ground and cried out in pain.

'Joe, are you hurt?' Ben crouched beside him.

'Ben, it's Gabby. I can feel her pain,' Joe cried, clutching at his own stomach.

'Something really bad has just happened, Ben. I think we're already too late,' he whimpered as he bent over in excruciating pain.

'Joe, we won't be too late. I won't lose her now, even if we have to do it alone.' Ben picked him up to throw him over his shoulder.

Gently placing Joe at the top of the steps, Michael and Paul crashed through the front doors with the Titans and curlews at their side, just as the police and Gabby's brothers pulled up outside.

When the double timber doors crashed open, the police came rushing in, shouting at the priests grouped around the grisly scene. 'It's the police. You're under arrest.' The robed figures ran in every direction, with screams and shouts filling the air. Some escaped out of the back of the building while others were caught and restrained with zip ties clenched tight around their wrists.

The Titans were lunging at the priests, tearing at their black robes and inflicting wounds upon their arms and legs. The curlews flew around the room, shrieking their fury at the cultists for injuring their beloved friend. Jacob and Thomas were grabbing hold of the priests trying to escape, roughly wrestling them to the ground so the police could restrain them.

In this cacophony, Gabby could feel a numbness settling over her body and knew that she was dying from blood loss. There wasn't much time to get Christian out before her heart stopped beating.

Ben and Joe had rushed to either side of her, tearing off their shirts to staunch the blood flowing out of her stomach. They stayed at her side, pressing their already sodden shirts into the wound.

'No Gabby, no,' Ben was sobbing hysterically.

It hurt so much to see his pain, but she couldn't say goodbye when the words refused to form on her tongue.

With only seconds left, she reached out to the light, the source of all life, remembering her power as a celestial and bathing in its glory and her service as a messenger. *I am your Fallon, your servant, and I will soon be back in the Silver City to answer for my actions, but until then, please help me. I beg you to sanction me to contact my human friend, mind to mind. If I can't speak to Joe, Christian will die, and I believe this child was created for your purpose. He is here for a reason. Please, there isn't much time!*

With a sudden burst of illumination, she was in Joe's mind, walking through his warehouse of memories. Gabby wondered how Old Joe really was with so much stored in his vaults of knowledge.

His mind was like the old whales and elephants, but with an even higher level of intelligence.

'Joe, it's me,' she spoke to him in his mind.

Old Joe leaned in close to look into her eyes. 'I hear you, Gabby. Please hold on. Don't leave us.'

'Joe, don't be sad. You know this life is not the end.' She gripped his hand tightly.

'No, Gabby, you belong to us, and we won't let you go.' He shook his head stubbornly.

'I have never belonged here, Joe. You know I was only meant to visit, never to stay.' Gabby smiled crookedly to take away the sting of loss, trying to comfort him.

'Please, Gabby.' His faded blue eyes begged her not to give up.

'Joe, this is not about me. I need you to take my baby - right now.'

'No, I won't. I can't. The ambulance will be here any minute now. You must hold on.' Joe looked wildly around, almost hoping a paramedic would materialise before him.

'There isn't time. If you don't take him now, then Christian will die too.'

'If I take the baby from you now, it will kill you, Gabby.'

'I am already dead to you Joe. Take my baby so that a part of me lives on in this life, I beg you.'

'I can't bear to hurt you, angel or not. I would never forgive myself.'

'Joe, if you love me, you will do this. As I said before, don't be sad for me. I am Fallon, an eternal angelic being. All I want is for Christian to live. I know you will be there for him, like you always were for me.'

She could hear Joe's doubts and fears playing over in his mind.

'Please Joe, for me,' she said as her body trembled with shock. 'You have to take him out now, before it is too late. I don't have much time,' she pleaded with the last of her strength as she retreated from his mind.

Beyond human awareness, there was another phenomenon taking place out of the sight and sound of all present.

Zadkiel was a life bearer, the most trusted of messengers with a sacred duty to all of mankind, being entrusted to deliver the spark of divinity promised to each soul born this side of the Eye of God. This mission would be as distressing as it was rewarding.

When he moved through the ceiling of the abandoned building with the life capsule held close to his heart, he never expected to be delivering the orb of light to Fallon's child.

In shock, he stopped mid-flight, his wings slowly beating to keep him airborne. Scanning the room, he saw that Fallon's mortal body was fatally wounded. A gaping gash ran the length of her stomach, and the flow of blood had bloomed red from underneath to form a circle of sorrow from above.

Zadkiel released the orb's contents into the soul of the infant, a gift the child would carry until he was returned to the source of this universal power. With great sorrow, he kneeled beside Fallon and placed his hand on her trembling heart, where a small glow spread out across her chest.

'Zadkiel, my brother. I beg you to have mercy on me. Do not abandon me.'

'Fallon, you are leaving this life. I feel the life force ebbing out of your body.'

'Yes, my time is done here, but you must give Joe the courage to take the baby. Do not let my child perish this day, Zadkiel. I know he is special and that we will have great need of him in our future.'

'I will stay, Fallon, until the end. Then I will accompany you home to your sister Josiel and the rest of your brethren.'

'Thank you, my brother.'

Exhausted, Fallon lay there feeling the small things for the last time: the hardness of the cold marble under her back, the warmth from the pool of blood oozing along the back of her legs, her heart slowing with each beat and matching the measured rising and falling of her chest until it didn't rise again, and all became still.

Ben saw a wondrous smile drift across Gabby's face as she seemed to reach out her hand to touch someone close by.

The Titans placed themselves on either side of her still body to howl their agony to the world. Ben lovingly cradled her head as his own head bent low, his tears bathing her silent, pale face, still unable to believe she was really gone.

Jacob and Thomas stood beside the dogs, tears pouring down their faces.

'No, not like this,' Jacob kept whispering over and over again.

Thomas had no words as there was no way to express the overwhelming loss of his precious younger sister. Reaching across to take his older brother's sobbing frame into his arms, he too couldn't breathe with the pain searing through his mind and body.

Joe gazed at the group around him. He saw the tears as everyone struggled to accept that this had really happened. But it seemed a force was asking him to put his own pain on hold, to do whatever it took to save his angelic friend's baby's life. Taking a deep breath to steady his nerves, Joe didn't falter in his resolve to listen to the mandate.

Fumbling in his jacket, he found the pocketknife and flicked open the sharp blade, all the while trying to remember how to take the baby out without causing harm. Hoping and praying that he wouldn't cut him, he put his hands into the gory mess to feel for the uterus wall. Once his fingers felt it, he cut and pushed deeper until a tiny hand brushed Joe's. He felt along the shoulder until he could scoop the infant's body out with one hand.

Gabby's body was still warm, even though her blood was getting glutinous and thick, when the blue baby was pulled from his dead mother. The tiny, frail body was covered in blood when Joe laid him face up on top of Gabby's motionless form, and the newborn was just as quiet and still. Hoping he wasn't too late, he had only moments to get him breathing.

Using his little finger, he prised open the tiny mouth, pushing over his blue gums and poking his finger down the throat to blow softly and clear the airways. No change. With his own mouth dry with fear, Joe began rubbing the baby's little chest to encourage a heartbeat.

Just at this moment, the ambulance officers rushed in, and without asking, one had scissors to swiftly cut the umbilical cord. He took the infant from Joe, while the other checked Gabby for any sign of life.

Ben gulped another sob when he heard the slice of the scissors cutting the cord, breaking the life force connection from Christian to his mother. This simple act broke Ben's heart, as it was one more sign that Gabby would never be his to love, nor would she be there to love her newborn son.

He looked around at the scene, hardly believing that Miranda was also gone. His beautiful, kind friend had been viciously and brutally murdered to satisfy the blood lust of these fanatical, depraved followers of Lucifer.

The loss of Gabby and Miranda pushed his shoulders down and anchored his heart at the bottom of a deep ocean of pain. How would he go on, how could he go on without them in his life, his to love and to hold? Ben was hurting from such overwhelming loss but at the same time he was acutely angry at the perpetrators, damning them all to hell in his heart of hearts.

One paramedic suctioned mucous from the baby's airways and then breathed small puffs of air into his lungs while the other tapped lightly on his chest to stimulate his heart. They refused to give up and kept trying the resuscitation while a couple of the police officers stood behind watching the resuscitation and secretly cheering the little fellow on.

Everybody held their breath until a mighty wail burst forth and took them all by surprise.

Christian howled outrage at his untimely entry into this world as all eyes turned to the infant that was changing from blue to pink before their eyes.

In the midst of so much tragedy, everyone sighed with relief that they hadn't lost the baby as well. Joe raised his eyes heavenward to where he hoped Gabby could see that her son had made it, the miracle of her last deed in this realm.

Behind the veil, Zadkiel had trouble drawing Fallon away from the tug of love that held her staring at Christian's tiny form. Eventually she understood her presence was required in the City of Angels, and she allowed herself to return to her former glory. A blinding white light filled the gloomy hall as she spread her gold-tipped wings to fill the space with their magnificence.

In that next stunned moment of silence, the snap of wings filled the space of this unholy place. Everyone jumped at the sudden explosion of air that rushed over their disbelieving faces.

'Holy shit, what was that?' Some of the police stopped to look up towards the ceiling, unable to understand the supernatural phenomenon.

Only those who knew her story understood that Gabby, now Fallon, was released from the confines of being mortal and was now returning to her celestial state.

Joe turned his eyes back to his beloved friend who lay still in Ben's embrace.

Seeing the pain on Joe's face, Ben moved aside for him to say his own goodbye.

Now that Christian was safely delivered, Joe felt the weight of loss. This young woman had come into his life and saved him from loneliness. It was her beauty and kindness that had breathed purpose into his empty existence, and until now, he hadn't known just how much.

For a moment, he just stared at her butchered body, unable to believe this could happen. Then he gently gathered her tightly to his chest and began to cry. Nobody had ever seen Joe cry, not like this. He had shed tears in empathy, and he had been rightfully outraged when Gabby had been raped, but never had he been this desolate, or bleak.

The tears flowed down the channels of wrinkles that networked his face and poured all over Gabby's face. Joe unashamedly howled that they had been too late, and he screamed at the audacity of evil to inflict this suffering on an innocent. Then he wept that Christian would never know his mother. Only when he could cry no more did he whisper, 'How can I keep going without you, Gabby?'

Joe's agony only added to the slump of Ben's already too-heavy shoulders. How were they going to ever be enough for this tiny infant of humanity? This baby boy with neither parent to care and love him, an orphan that was now his responsibility.

Looking at his godson in the paramedic's arms, Ben felt too scared, too inadequate to take him. Hesitating when the blanket-wrapped baby was passed to him, he silently breathed a prayer to Gabby, *Please let me be enough.*

Reaching out with his bloody hands, Ben took the whimpering baby to hold him close to his heart, hoping its beat would provide some comfort. Feeling the baby's warmth against his chest, he felt a rush of love burst out of his soul, and for the first time in his life, Ben felt complete.

Finally, he had someone who would be his to love unconditionally and who would love him in return.

It was almost like Christian understood, for just then he opened his eyes to gaze back, filling his world with Ben. At this moment, an unbreakable bond was formed between the two.

Ben gasped with delight to be staring once again into a set of heavenly green eyes, while his heart still yearned for Gabby. *Where are you now, Gabby? Can you still see us from another dimension or have you left us forever?*

When Fallon's feet touched the ground before the angelic statues and the mighty pearl gates, she cast her mind back at everything she had left behind. *Christian, my heart tells me we will be together again soon. I may not be your mother in the earthly sense but I know I will be there to love and guide you through the life ahead. But for now, I must make amends with my angelic family.*

With her wings folded against a straight back and her head held high, she walked through the gates with Zadkiel at her side.

No sooner had she entered the Silver City than Josiel ran towards her to embrace her close, heart to heart. 'My beloved sister, I was torn when I heard news of your homecoming. If you are here then darkness has terminated your human life, a life you sacrificed so much to uphold.'

'I too am torn, Josiel. My head tells me I'm needed here, but my heart yearns for another home.'

'Of course it does, and I want to hear every little detail. But, for now you must accompany me to stand before the council.'

'To be punished for my recklessness?' Fallon asked warily.

'Come and see,' Josiel tugged her arm along the path.

Fallon turned to thank Zadkiel before going with Josiel to the council chamber. 'Thank you, Zadkiel for guiding Joe. You saved Christian's life.'

'No, it was all Joe, I just gave him a small nudge,' he reassured her with a grin as he hugged Josiel close in greeting.

'Come both of you, there is much to talk about.'

Soon after, Josiel led her along the familiar paths and up the stone stairs where Gadriel stood in welcome at the top. Standing behind was Raphael, Uriel and Anael, all smiling with welcome.

Once inside the council chamber, Fallon bowed her head with respect as she stood alongside Josiel and Gadriel before the three most powerful angels of their kind, and she wisely said nothing in her own defence.

It was Zinnia who made the proclamation when she moved to stand before Fallon. Al three looked at the shiny black mantle that sparkled with energy as it draped over Zinnia's shoulders.

She looked at them almost sternly before speaking with a sense of ceremony. 'Fallon, we cannot condone your actions but nor can we condemn them. Rather than punish, we would like to incite you to join us. The scales have fallen off our eyes, and we understand the treaty with Lucifer and his minions has been broken. A war is upon us.'

'A war in which I believe Christian will play a vital part.' Fallon fiercely championed her child.

'Yes, you may be correct in this prophecy. For now, we agree a time of great tribulation is upon us, and it will take the strength of us all to force Lucifer and his demons into a prison from which there is no escape.'

Remiel and Saraquel came from behind the stone bench to stand at Zinnia's side. The three wise ones looked gravely at Fallon, Josiel, and the group of supporters,

Remiel spoke the call to duty. 'Sovereign angels, will you fight alongside us to defeat the darkness and save the sons of man?'

Fallon bent her knee first, soon joined by the rest of the angels as they pledged their allegiance to the battle for dominion that would soon be upon them.

The End

ACKNOWLEDGEMENTS

Thank you to my amazing editor and independent publisher, Dr Juliette Lachemeier at The Erudite Pen, who has made this second rough diamond into a bright star. To my book cover designer Judith San Nicolas for creating such an eye-catching, unique design for *Blood For Glory*. To my much-loved family, husband Fred Casella, my sons, Evan, Aaron and Ben, to their partners, Claudia, Makala and Loccy. To my sisters Gale Poyner and Leandra Watson for being my sounding board. Thank you to my beta readers, Mary Casella, Marcia Fry, Tairiau Bridgart, Nola Thorburn, Jenna D'Addona, Lucinda Drake, Janine Currie, Melanie Zappulla and Felise Johnston. You have all been invaluable in supporting my writing dream so that it could become a published reality.

ABOUT THE AUTHOR

Lyndell Casella grew up in Far North Queensland, Australia. She always remembers the thrill of learning to read. Words sparked her imagination and together they became a doorway into another world – an enchanted world. This infatuation with stories led to the desire to write her own story, her very own arrangement of words that would also transport readers into other worlds.

As a child, Lyndell's mind always thirsted for fanciful flights into exciting adventures. She was constantly reading and devouring every word her eyes could discover. As an adult, she became busy with life, and those imaginary flights of fancy took a back seat. However, her childhood wish to create and write her own adventures lay dormant like a seed buried deep beneath a winter snow. It only stirred and began to swell after a heartbreaking period in her life.

This heartbreak caused her to look closely at life and death. Was there still a consciousness when physical life ceased? This questioning ignited something deep within, and she 'saw' her own arrangement of words for this trilogy, strung out like a string of pearls, gleaming and beautiful to the eye. *The Blood Tree* is the first book in The Greater Good Trilogy, her gleaming string of pearl-words.

Enjoyed the book? You can follow the author at:

Email: lyndell.casella@gmail.com

Facebook: facebook.com/lyndellcasella.author

If you liked the book, please leave a review on Amazon, Goodreads or with the author directly. Reviews are invaluable in supporting an author's hard work and are greatly appreciated.